ECHOES
IN THE MIST

ALSO BY ANDREA KANE

HISTORICAL ROMANCES:

MY HEART'S DESIRE
DREAM CASTLE
MASQUE OF BETRAYAL
ECHOES IN THE MIST
SAMANTHA
THE LAST DUKE
EMERALD GARDEN
WISHES IN THE WIND
LEGACY OF THE DIAMOND
THE BLACK DIAMOND
THE MUSIC BOX
THE THEFT
THE GOLD COIN
THE SILVER COIN

FORENSIC INSTINCTS NOVELS:

THE GIRL WHO DISAPPEARED TWICE
THE LINE BETWEEN HERE AND GONE
THE STRANGER YOU KNOW
THE SILENCE THAT SPEAKS
THE MURDER THAT NEVER WAS
A FACE TO DIE FOR

OTHER SUSPENSE THRILLERS:

RUN FOR YOUR LIFE
NO WAY OUT
SCENT OF DANGER
I'LL BE WATCHING YOU
WRONG PLACE, WRONG TIME
DARK ROOM
TWISTED
DRAWN IN BLOOD

ECHOES
IN THE MIST

ANDREA
KANE

ISBN-13: 978-1-68232-015-0 (Trade Paperback)
  978-1-68232-016-7 (ePub)
  978-1-68232-017-4 (Kindle)

LCCN: 2018902766

ECHOES IN THE MIST

For questions and comments about the quality of this book, please contact us at CustomerService@bonniemeadowpublishing.com.

www.BonnieMeadowPublishing.com

Printed in USA

Publisher's Cataloging-in-Publication

Names: Kane, Andrea.
Title: Echoes in the mist / Andrea Kane.
Description: 25th anniversary edition. | Warren, NJ : Bonnie Meadow Publishing LLC, [2018] | Originally published: New York : Pocket Star Books, ©1994.
Identifiers: ISBN 9781682320150 (trade paperback) | ISBN 9781682320167 (ePub) | ISBN 9781682320174 (Kindle) | ISBN 9781682320181 (ePDF)
Subjects: LCSH: Nobility--England--Sussex--History--19th century--Fiction. | Man-woman relationships--England--Sussex--History--19th century--Fiction. | Sussex (England)--Social life and customs--19th century--Fiction. | Revenge--Fiction. | LCGFT: Historical fiction. | GSAFD: Romantic suspense fiction.
Classification: LCC PS3561.A463 E34 2018 (print) | LCC PS3561.A463 (ebook) | DDC 813/.54--dc23

Like Trenton, I am blessed to have a few special people in my life who never let me falter without purpose, who help me regain my balance when I do falter, who demand *almost* as much of me as I demand of myself … and who do it all with an abundance of love that is humbling. It is to these extraordinary people that I dedicate *Echoes in the Mist*. Brad, Wendi, Mom & Dad … you know what this particular book means to me. I hope you also know what you mean to me.

CHAPTER 1

Great white wings illuminated the sky. Piercing the heavens the owl soared, majesty of his domain, as regal in his splendor as a mountain peak splitting the night.

Ariana leaned, spellbound, against the balcony rail, taking in the grace of his motions, the abandoned freedom of his flight. Already this summer she'd sighted several owls in her savored explorations, but never in all her eighteen years had she found one this pure in color. His bold downy feathers, stark as a snow bank, were bathed in the soft golden glow cast by twin gas lamps heralding his path.

A burst of laughter from within the crowded ballroom pricked at Ariana's conscience, pressuring her to return to the betrothal party. She owed that much to Baxter. And she *had* been enjoying herself most thoroughly all evening. After all, seldom did she have the opportunity to attend so grand a ball, to chat with hundreds of equally grand people, to dance until her feet barely touched the floor. The experience was glorious.

But it paled in comparison to this awesome spectacle.

So when the owl's haunting call beckoned her, thoughts of all else had vanished.

Her breath caught in her throat as the magnificent bird alit in the walnut tree before her, close enough to touch. He leveled his fiery topaz stare in her direction, holding her captive with his probing intensity. Ariana gazed back, praying that the evening mist would delay its descent a few moments longer, delay concealing nature's priceless treasure from view.

For a time, the mist complied with her unspoken request, hovering just above the tree, and Ariana lingered, silently vowing to retrace her steps through the open French doors ... in just a minute.

At last the mist lost patience, settling over the vast estate like a milky blanket. The owl blinked once, then raised his great head, solemnly contemplating the heavens. With a resounding cry, he spread his wings and took flight.

"Wait!" Ariana called, grasping the air as if that action alone could summon him back. For an instant, she followed him with her eyes. Then she acted.

Gathering the full skirt of her mauve satin ball gown, she hastened down the winding steps that led to the gardens and raced off in pursuit.

The labyrinthine maze loomed ahead, stretching its wealth of manicured hedges as far as the eye could see. She reached the opening in time to see the flash of white soar inside.

She didn't hesitate.

She ran in after him.

Engulfed in fog, the owl disappeared in scant seconds, with only a reverberating call in his wake. Relentlessly, Ariana dodged through the winding paths, determined to find him.

A quarter hour later, two realizations occurred.

The owl was lost.

So was she.

Dark, forbidding, the man stared through the imposing iron gates toward the barely visible mansion, his eyes burning with hatred, his soul burning with anticipation.

Six years.

Six years of exile, of scorching hatred spawned by the crime of another. Six years to plan the perfect revenge. At last it was time. Within the hour, *his lordship,* Baxter Caldwell, the *eminent* Viscount Winsham, would solidify his fate. … But the outcome would not be the one the bastard expected.

Lifting the glowing cheroot to his lips, the man inhaled slowly, then blew out, watching the wisps of smoke swirl above him and vanish into the engulfing fog.

A sudden burst of cheers and applause split the hush of night, audible even from this great distance.

A toast, no doubt, the man deduced. *To the happy couple.*

He raised an imaginary glass in mock tribute. Yes, at this very moment the viscount was triumphantly celebrating, what was considered to be the match of the Season: his betrothal to the captivating Suzanne Covington. Caldwell was on the brink of realizing his most fervent dream: mating the old and respected Caldwell name with the widely sought-after Covington wealth.

A title for an empire. That heinous prospect would be untenable, were the marriage actually going to occur.

Idly rolling his cheroot, the man gave a malevolent smile, envisioning the mass pandemonium that would ensue when he issued his ultimatum and Covington made the only choice he possibly could. There were some motivators even more powerful than securing the *right* social position. Motivators such as blackmail.

So the betrothal's demise was a *fait accompli.*

After which, the viscount's demise—and his own revenge—were but scant moments away.

Inside the manor the music and dancing had resumed, and the French doors were once again thrown open to admit the fragrant July air. Strains of a lively Strauss waltz spilled forth, rolling across the grounds and through the iron gates.

The man went taut, the image of Baxter Caldwell instantly replaced by a more loathsome substitute. For the weak, unprincipled, lazy parasite of a viscount held not a candle to his deceitful bitch of a sister.

Vanessa.

Memories hurtled back in hard, stunning blows to his head.

Heaven alone knew how many rich men had been the recipients of that perfect smile … how many she had been willing to whore herself for in exchange for the promise of wealth.

With a quick, savage snap of the wrist, he sent the cheroot rolling to the grass, grinding it beneath his heel.

He slipped through the gates and moved toward his quarry.

The day of retribution had finally arrived.

Ariana wrung her hands in frustration. The mist had indeed grown thicker, plunging the maze into an opaque prison. Pangs of guilt intensified her worry. By now Baxter had discovered her absence and was undoubtedly furious. Not that she blamed him, given the cause of the night's celebration. She simply had to find her way.

The fog settled lower, shrouding the night's wonders in warm, hazy mists, eclipsing her earlier elation and clarifying the grim reality. When would she ever learn to listen to her head and not her heart?

Straining her ears, she listened for sounds of the ball, the music and laughter that had accompanied her on her walk. In reply, she heard only the chirp of an occasional cricket and the sweet call of a nightingale.

Lord only knew how far she'd wandered, Ariana conceded with a frown. The Covington estate was massive; the maze she walked within meandered endlessly. She quickened her step, stumbling on every unseen stone, hastening along the cold ground.

One hedge was the same as the next, leading nowhere but to another facet of the puzzle. Groping her way down each open path, Ariana carefully searched for the avenue that would guide her to safety. She found none. Nor did she hear even the faintest murmur to reassure her the manor was near.

Minutes ticked by.

Panic set in.

Breaking into a blind run, she cupped her hands over her mouth, hoping that, by calling out, she would alert someone to her plight.

The shout never emerged.

With a telltale tug, the full skirt of Ariana's gown lodged beneath her slipper, upsetting her balance and toppling her to the ground. Shards of pain shot through her right ankle as it bent awkwardly beneath her.

Biting back a cry, Ariana waited until the physical agony had subsided to a dull throb. Then, shakily, she gathered up her skirts and resolutely hoisted herself to a standing position—but collapsed just as quickly to the grass. Gingerly, she touched her ankle, wincing at its tenderness. It was badly sprained, at best. Walking was out of the question.

Gritting her teeth, Ariana silently admonished herself for hot having the good sense to tell someone of her destination. When it came to embracing nature's splendor, she seemed unable to retain a whit of judgment, continually succumbing to some foolhardy, whimsical inner voice that dominated her reason, urged her to relent. And inevitably got her into trouble.

She considered crawling, then dismissed the idea as ludicrous. How far would she get with copious layers of petticoats in her way? Trying once again to stand, she fell to the grass with a soft whimper of pain. It was no use.

She gazed around, acutely aware of the darkness, the seclusion that enveloped her. The ball would still be at its ebullient peak; how long would it be before anyone searched for her?

With a frightened shiver, she gave in to her earlier intent. Raising her face to the ominous hedges, she cried out, "Help!"

Only the sound of her own voice echoed through the mist.

He heard the scream.

Startled, he stopped in his tracks and scanned the milky darkness, trying to assess the direction from which the sound had emerged. He saw nothing. He had almost decided he'd imagined the cry, when he heard it again.

"Help!"

It was definitely real. The voice belonged to a woman, one who was obviously in distress.

Scowling, he cast a brief glance at the manor, contemplating his choices. He had waited this long. A few more minutes wouldn't matter.

That decided, he made his way through the fog.

Ariana brushed a damp auburn strand from her forehead, feeling the heavy tresses tumble free of their restraining pins to settle in a limp, disheveled mass on her back.

No one had responded to her call. That meant she was even farther away than she'd realized. Well, she couldn't just sit here forever, praying to be rescued. Perhaps if she managed to pull herself upright she could put all her weight on her uninjured foot and hop—but in what direction? She hadn't an inkling of her whereabouts. And she couldn't remain standing long enough to discover them. The throbbing in her ankle was intensifying, as was the swelling.

She bit her lip in frustration. Futile though it might be, she tried once again. "Help!"

Holding her breath, she waited. Silence. Surely she couldn't be the *only* one who had ventured from the party to stroll the grounds. But apparently she was. She dropped her head wearily.

A twig snapped, and Ariana's head came up in a flash. "Help! Please help me!" she cried out, flooded with relief when the soft but distinct plod of footsteps reached her ears.

"Keep talking," a deep, resonant voice instructed. "I'll follow the sound."

"I'm inside the maze," Ariana called, desperately wishing the mist would lift. She had no idea who her rescuer was; his voice was unfamiliar but disturbingly close. Uneasily, she wondered why he was walking alone in this particularly isolated section of the estate. On the heels of that thought came the reality of its absurdity: She, who had gone in avid pursuit of an elusive owl and was now hopelessly lost in a forest of trees, was concerned about a stranger's motives for strolling the Covington grounds?

"Can you hear me?" the stranger called, closer this time.

"Yes!" Ariana sat up straighten "Yes, I can hear you!"

A moment later the hedges parted and a towering figure emerged. "And now?" a deep-timbered baritone boomed into the night.

Ariana swallowed. "I can hear you. I can also see you. I'm sitting about ten paces to the left of where you stand."

The dark silhouette paused, then moved toward her with long, panther-like strides. He stopped, so close to her that the powerful muscles of his thighs were practically touching her face. Involuntarily, she shifted, the movement causing a shaft of pain to shoot through her ankle. She grimaced, fear mingling with physical anguish as, abruptly, she became aware of how precarious her situation was. She was alone, injured, unable to protect herself, in a secluded, private maze with a massive and forbidding stranger. What in God's name had she gotten herself into this time?

Hindered by the fog, Ariana was unable to see anything above the solid columns of her rescuer's thighs. Nonetheless, she could feel the intimidating force of his scrutiny. Instinctively, she tucked her skirts around her, wishing he would identify himself or declare his intentions. She felt totally vulnerable, defenseless. And bewildered. Surely he had stared long enough. Why didn't he say something?

"Thank you for answering my plea," she managed in a deceptively calm voice.

The thigh muscles rippled, then flexed, and the next thing Ariana knew she was gazing into burning cobalt eyes and the hardest, most starkly handsome face she had ever seen.

"Are you hurt?"

Mutely, she nodded.

"What happened?"

Ariana licked her lips nervously. Squatting so close beside her, his expression and tone rock-hard, her rescuer seemed more formidable than ever.

"I saw the most breathtaking owl," she began. "He had white feathers as pure as snowflakes and moved as gracefully as a Thoroughbred." Warming to her subject, Ariana's eyes sparkled with exhilaration. "Then he called out to me. Naturally, I had no choice but to follow. He led me into this maze. I became lost. I fell. My ankle …" Abruptly she stopped, realizing she'd been rambling. Staring up through the veiled layers of night, she studied the man's unreadable features.

For a long moment he was silent, his eyes boring into her. "Don't you know how unsafe it is for a beautiful woman to go for a midnight stroll, alone, on so expansive an estate as this?" he questioned at last. "Why, the mist could swallow up so ethereal a creature as you. … And never set you free."

Ariana felt gooseflesh break out on her arms.

He said nothing more, but his brazen stare consumed her from head to toe, as if memorizing every inch of her. Then, without warning, he reached for the hem of her gown, tugging it upward.

Ariana froze, recoiling automatically, crying out at the resulting pain she caused herself.

His hand paused in its purpose, his pensive gaze returning to hers. "Don't be frightened, misty angel," he murmured. "I have no intention of harming you." He glanced down at her injury. "But your ankle is badly sprained and needs to be tended to."

Ariana nodded, feeling foolish. This was what she had wanted, was it not? To be found, given assistance?

He bent his dark head over her leg, his brow furrowed in concentration. "Tell me if I hurt you."

Ariana nodded again, candidly surveying him as he examined the swelling. He was striking, yet frighteningly feral; tall and broad-shouldered, with black hair that framed a hard and arrogant face. His features were severely masculine, his nose straight, his jaw square, his lips chiseled and full. His brows and lashes were thick and dark, highlighting the blazing blue of his eyes. It was the harsh lines around his eyes, Ariana guessed, that made him appear dangerous, as if he were capable of extreme cruelty if threatened.

Ariana shivered.

"Are you in pain?" His tone was gruff, but his touch was gentle.

"No," she whispered, stunned that she'd forgotten her injury entirely—despite the fact that he had been probing it for the past few minutes. "I'm not in pain."

A slow, knowing smile curved his lips and Ariana was shocked by the transformation it made. When he smiled, he was magnificent.

"What's the matter, misty angel?" he queried, reaching out to lift her chin. "Are you still afraid of me?" Ever so lightly, he trailed his thumb along the pulse in her neck.

Ariana shivered, shook her head. "No. I'm not afraid of you."

"Then you are the first."

She recoiled from the severity of his tone, a harshness that was totally refuted by the gentleness of his touch. Added to that was her own confusing, quivering awareness of his blatantly sensual caress, a caress that left tingles of pleasure in its path. But in the end, it was the tenderness, as unintentional as it was palpable, that struck a chord within her, gave her the courage to continue. "If others are afraid, it could only be because you haven't gifted them with your smile," she blurted out.

He looked startled.

"Are we far from the manor?" she asked anxiously, remembering, in the unsettling silence, how long she'd been missing and how angry Baxter would be.

The ruthlessness returned, hardening the man's expression. "Yes. You've wandered quite a distance. It will take some time to get back."

"I don't think I can walk."

"You won't even attempt it." It was a command, not a suggestion.

"Then how ..."

She never finished her question. In one motion he slid his hands beneath her and stood, lifting Ariana effortlessly in his arms.

She gasped, clutching his shoulders for support, feeling the hard wall of his chest against her body. Once again she was face-to-face with those incredible, penetrating cobalt eyes ... eyes that reached to the very depths of her being.

"Still not afraid?" he taunted softly, his breath warm on her skin.

Slowly, Ariana relaxed her hands, flattening her palms upon his shoulders. "I'm still not afraid," she replied, stunned to realize it was true. For some inherent reason, she knew this man would not use his enormous strength against her.

He blinked, drinking in the flawless features so close to his: the pert, upturned nose and glowing alabaster skin, the soft sensual mouth, the huge, innocent eyes as turquoise as Osborne Bay at the height of summer. She trusted him. That was a mistake. But in this case it was irrelevant. For she was not the reason he had returned tonight, so no harm would befall her.

The harm he intended was for Baxter Caldwell.

Ariana felt the imperceptible tightening of his hold mere seconds before he turned on his heel and stalked off into the fog, clasping her to his chest.

"I don't know you," she burst out after a few moments had passed, desperate to relieve the hard knot of tension that coiled tighter inside her with each step. Nothing had prepared her for a predicament such as this ... she, who had never even been alone in a man's company, much less in his arms.

A hint of a smile was Ariana's only indication that her rescuer was aware of her discomfort ... and its cause. "No, you don't know me," he agreed.

"Do you live in Sussex?"

"Not anymore." His reply was terse, his jaw tightening so fractionally she would never have noticed were she not inches away.

"But you once did?"

"Yes. A long time ago." He wound his way around a line of hedges, his piercing gaze flicking briefly over her uptilted face. "I suspect you were little more than a child when I left."

She inclined her head. "Are you so old then?"

Dark memories flashed through his eyes. "Ancient."

"Funny," Ariana murmured, half to herself. "I would have thought you to be no more than thirty."

"Two years more," he corrected. "And a lifetime."

It suddenly occurred to her that he was only a year older than Baxter. Could he be an old friend, one she'd never met? "You are here for the betrothal? To take part in the celebration?"

A harsh laugh. "Yes, indeed." He emerged from the maze, heading toward the manor with long, purposeful strides.

Ariana blinked as the front door was thrown open, the bright lights of the hallway assaulting her eyes after long hours in the murky darkness.

"My lady … are you all right?" The old, haggard Covington butler looked anxiously from Ariana to the formidable man who held her.

"I'm fine," Ariana assured the servant, waiting for her rescuer to place her on the nearest chair. "Thanks to …" Flushing crimson, she realized she had never asked the man his name. Preparing to rectify her oversight, she turned her face back to his, abruptly recognizing by his steely expression that he had no intention of putting her down. Rather, he was continuing to move, carrying her decisively into the crowded ballroom. "What are you doing?" she demanded, struggling to free herself from his grasp.

"I am returning you to the party, my lady," he answered, his eyes gleaming with an emotion so dark that Ariana shuddered. "Since I, too, am ready to make an appearance."

"You cannot just carry me in as blithely as if—"

A sharp cry pierced the air and Ariana found herself accosted by a ballroom of pale, gaping faces.

"Good Lord …" James Covington gasped, echoing his wife's shriek of a moment before.

A shocked murmur began, grew, and vibrated through the crowd.

Ariana closed her eyes, wishing the floor would swallow her up.

Her rescuer seemed more amused than bothered. "Where is your family, misty angel?" he murmured, still holding her fast. "I'll deliver you into their hands."

Ariana ignored him, opening her eyes and addressing Mr. and Mrs. Covington with as much dignity as she could muster. "Forgive me," she began shakily. "I had no intention of making a scene. But I injured my ankle and this kind gentleman …"

A roar of anger exploded through the room as Baxter Caldwell stormed from the rear, blood lust in his eyes.

"Kingsley, you miserable son of a bitch! Put my sister down!"

CHAPTER 2

Kingsley?

Ariana's head snapped around, all the color draining from her face as she met her rescuer's chilling stare. Kingsley? *Trenton* Kingsley? It could not be: Trenton Kingsley had disappeared six years before, just after …

Ariana's lips trembled. No. He didn't dare return—not after the vile and monstrous act that had shattered her family, forever changed their lives. A cold-blooded animal, a murderer. And she had allowed him to touch her. To hold her so intimately.

Horrified, Ariana began to struggle for freedom, shoving at Trenton's granite chest and straining against his punishing grip.

Trenton's whole body went rigid, shock waves vibrating down to his very soul. Reflexively, his grasp tightened, his fingers biting more deeply into the woman's soft skin, crushing the fine satin of her gown. His pupils dilated, his piercing blue gaze sweeping her features, confirming the truth of Baxter's words.

How could he not have seen it? Only a fool would have missed the resemblance! It was evident in the fine arch of her brows, in the delicate, high cheekbones, in the unusual, startlingly vivid coloring. Yes, she was every inch a Caldwell. Just like Vanessa.

Fury suddenly replaced shock, etched into every line of his face. "Sister?" he hissed.

His lethal whisper sent cold waves of apprehension down Ariana's spine.

"Yes, you bloody scoundrel, *sister!*" Baxter snatched Ariana from Trenton's arms as if she were a mere parcel, letting her legs drop unceremoniously to the floor.

Ariana whimpered in pain, her ankle giving out beneath her.

"Ariana? My God, what did you *do* to her?" Baxter caught Ariana's elbows mere seconds before she crumbled to the floor. "Wasn't *one* sister enough for you?"

Black fire smoldered in Trenton's eyes. "I did nothing to her, Caldwell. She fell ... I carried her back. Had I known she was a Caldwell I would have reconsidered."

Taking in Ariana's anguished expression and disheveled appearance, Baxter's mind worked rapidly, acutely aware that a small crowd had gathered around them. "I have no idea why you've chosen tonight to reappear, but you're trespassing, Kingsley," he proclaimed loudly, twinges of long-forgotten fear awakening inside him. After six years in exile, why the hell had the contemptible bastard chosen now to return?

Ignoring the frantic pounding in his temples, Baxter wrapped one arm tightly about Ariana's waist, holding her to him with brotherly protectiveness. With his free hand he gestured grandly, summoning a burly footman who stood nearby.

"Yes, my lord?"

"Show the marquis ... oh, pardon me, *the duke,*" Baxter corrected bitterly, "out." He turned to Trenton with hatred in his eyes. "You'll forgive me, *Your Grace.* The last time we saw each other you had not yet acquired the exalted title of the Duke of Broddington."

Trenton shook off the servant's hand. "I am not going anywhere." His jaw clenched with purpose, he turned to James Covington. "Let me suggest that you allow me to have my say, James. Your bank holds too much of my money to risk arousing my wrath."

After a slight hesitation, Covington nodded, and the footman moved off. "This is my daughter's betrothal party, Broddington," Covington said tersely. "So speak your mind and then, please leave."

"That is precisely what I intended," the duke replied, ignoring the appalled whispers around him. "I assure you that I loathe being here more than you loathe having me. But you see"—his eyes narrowed—"I cannot allow this mockery of a celebration to continue."

Icy fingers gripped Baxter's heart.

"Call off the betrothal, Covington." Trenton's voice was an unyielding command, emotionless in its tone, lethal in its determination.

"What?" Covington started.

"You heard me." Trenton's quiet order was heard only by those for whom it was meant: the Covingtons... and Caldwell. Both Caldwells, Trenton amended silently, not permitting himself even a brief glance at the pale, tousled beauty who leaned against her brother for support, staring at Trenton with a frightened intensity he could actually feel but refused to acknowledge. Nothing and no one was going to alter his plan.

"Tell everyone in this room that your daughter cannot marry Baxter Caldwell," he repeated.

"You don't have to stand here and take this, James," Baxter choked out. "I'll have him thrown out."

"And I'll have every bloody pound of my money withdrawn from your bank and deposited in your competitor's," Trenton threatened softly, his gaze locked with Covington's. "I've already spoken to Willinger... He is most eager to receive my millions."

Covington ran his tongue over cold, dry lips. "But why? Why?" he asked, bewildered. He'd held the Kingsley fortune for decades now, since the late duke had been alive. Richard Kingsley had been not only a business associate but a trusted personal friend. Why, the duke had designed this very manor—a rare honor indeed, and a tribute to their friendship, since Richard rarely applied his unique architectural talent to anything save his beloved Broddington.

James mopped his brow, fervently wishing Richard were alive and vital, still in control of the Kingsley funds.

But he wasn't.

And while both his sons had inherited their father's wealth and flair for design, it was his elder, Trenton, who'd acquired Richard's keen business mind as well as his architectural genius. During Richard's declining years, Trenton masterfully designed numerous acclaimed churches and homes, while at the same time he assumed the running of Broddington from his aging father, tripling the enormous family fortune in the last years of Richard's life.

And every pound of that fortune had been deposited in the Covington bank. Where it had remained—until now.

James met Trenton's unwavering stare, ugly questions crowding his mind. "Why do you want the betrothal severed?" he repeated weakly.

"You know why."

Covington closed his eyes, remembering the horrid sequence of events that had preceded Trenton's self-imposed exile to Spraystone, his Isle of Wight retreat. "It's been six years, Trenton."

"Yes. And I've suffered every one of them for just this moment." Trenton refused to look at Baxter, knowing if he did he would kill him. "I mean you no harm, James. You are merely a vehicle needed to ensure the viscount's downfall. In fact, I'm doing you a favor. This parasite doesn't want your daughter, he wants your money. Believe me or disbelieve me; it makes no difference. Just call off the wedding. Or my solicitor will contact you tomorrow regarding the withdrawal of my funds. Every last penny. Now, is acquiring a title for Suzanne really worth total financial ruin?"

"Why you miserable ..." Baxter lunged forward, releasing Ariana, who fell against Covington, clutching his arm for support.

In one lightning move, Trenton caught Baxter by the collar, dragging him up by the throat until his own knuckles turned white. "I wouldn't suggest it, Caldwell," he got out between clenched teeth, hearing the appalled gasps around him. "I'd like nothing better than to tear you limb from limb."

"Then do it, you bastard," Baxter spat back. "At least this time we'd have evidence of your crime."

For a moment, Ariana was certain that her brother had breathed his last. Then, slowly, Trenton relaxed his hold, shoving Baxter away as if he were a hideous viper. "I wouldn't give you the satisfaction," he hissed. He jerked around to face Covington, who cowered beneath Trent's, brutal stare. "Your answer?"

James swallowed, feeling an unnatural silence permeate the room. Despite their attempts to remain discreet, the three of them had put on quite a show for his curious guests. Whatever he did now would be witnessed by a roomful of influential people. He weighed his decision carefully, trying not to hear the quiet, heart-wrenching sobs of his precious Suzanne, who was openly weeping in her mother's arms. For while her happiness meant the world to him, there were other things to consider: his own position in society, his standard of living, his entire future. In the end, there was no choice to be made.

"All right, Kingsley, I'll do as you ask. But only out of respect to your father's memory," he hastened to add, feeling hundreds of censuring eyes bore into him. "You have your answer. Now get out before I have you thrown out."

Trenton nodded. "Done." He cast a scathing look at Baxter, who had turned chalk white, his expression dazed. "I suggest you tend to your sister, Caldwell." For the first time he allowed his gaze to shift to Ariana, taking in her ruined gown, tear-streaked cheeks, and contorted stance. "Her ankle is badly sprained."

"Get out," Ariana whispered. "Just … get out."

Trenton gave her a mock salute, his features grim. "I shan't trouble you again, my lady." He turned on his heels and was gone.

Ariana watched him leave, feeling a sharp pain that had nothing to do with her ankle. Was this truly the compassionate stranger who had so gently examined her injury? How could she have been so wrong about someone?

"James … you can't really mean to—" Baxter was saying.

"You'd best take your leave as well, Baxter," Covington interrupted him. "I'll see to the guests."

Ariana acted, seizing her brother's taut, trembling forearm. "Please, Baxter. We've provided enough gossip for one night. Please… let's go home."

Baxter stared down at her with unseeing eyes. Then he turned abruptly and stalked from the room.

Ariana blinked after him, wondering what she should do. Her brother's reaction didn't particularly surprise her, for it was typically Baxter. No, her dilemma was not born of emotional distress but of simple pragmatism: She didn't think she could make her way to the front door unassisted.

Easing forward gingerly, she attempted to hobble, then whimpered at the pressure it exerted on her ankle.

"I'll accompany you to your carriage, my dear," James Covington offered. "Come."

Ariana had no choice but to accept his assistance, though she was not at all certain she forgave his severing Baxter's betrothal. Silently, she leaned against him, allowing him to escort her to the Caldwell carriage, where Baxter sat slumped and brooding.

"Oh … Ariana … did I leave you there?" he muttered, affording her a mere cursory glance.

"It doesn't matter," she replied, sliding onto the seat and nodding her thanks to Covington.

With a helpless shrug, the older man moved aside and gestured for their driver to commence.

The ride home was agonizingly quiet.

"Baxter …." Ariana tried at last.

"What do you want, Ariana?"

"Why would he return after all these years?"

"To ruin me; why else? He killed Vanessa, nearly destroyed our family, and now he intends to complete the task." Baxter leaned back, throwing his arm across his eyes.

Ariana winced. Since the age of twelve she'd listened to the sinister recounting of how Trenton Kingsley had charmed her older sister Vanessa: courting her with gifts and promises, leading her to believe they had a wondrous future together, compelling her to fall deeply in love with him.

And then … terrifying her with his bizarre possessiveness and violent threats, stripping her of joy and laughter and finally her will to live.

Forcing her to take her own life.

Or taking it himself.

The accusations were never proven and no charges were brought. But Baxter still believed, despite the passage of time, that Trenton Kingsley was, unequivocally, a murderer.

Ariana clenched the folds of her rumpled gown, wishing for the hundredth time that she could recall more details of the months prior to Vanessa's death. Perhaps then she could separate actual facts from exaggerations born of rage and grief. But as a mere child of twelve, she had hardly been her older sister's confidante. In truth, they rarely even saw each other. For while Ariana had been engrossed in learning the names of all the flowers that filled Winsham's gardens, Vanessa had been perpetually out, swept up in a storm of fervent suitors, each vying for her elusive hand.

And who could blame them? At two and twenty years of age, Vanessa had been extraordinarily beautiful, in love with life, eager to experience it all. With scores of avid escorts, settling down seemed the farthest thing from her mind. And with both parents succumbing to a fever in 1858, Vanessa had savored her freedom, answering only to Baxter, who was three years her senior and ever indulgent of his charming sister.

So despite Ariana's deep love and admiration for Vanessa, her memories were dim and few: quick good-night pecks on her cheek amid a flurry of dressing and the lingering scent of roses. And a vague but endless flow of handsome, earnest gentlemen callers.

Until Trenton Kingsley.

Vanessa had whispered his name to Ariana, implied that he was different, special. She would slip out mysteriously each night, staying away until dawn. Ariana could remember overhearing arguments between Vanessa and Baxter … the first they'd ever had. From what Ariana had understood, Baxter vehemently objected to Vanessa's new suitor, and Vanessa deeply resented Baxter's interference.

Ariana could recall nothing more, other than the shock and grief of that final nightmarish day and the lethal accusations that had followed in its wake.

But while she wasn't quite certain what had occurred the night Vanessa died, of one thing she was certain: She had never seen Trenton Kingsley before this night. For the turbulent Duke of Broddington, with his steely blue eyes and disturbing, feral sensuality, was a man she would never have forgotten.

With a shiver, Ariana recalled the penetrating intensity of his stare—as hypnotic as her white owl's—and the hatred that had blazed within when he learned she was a Caldwell.

Why in God's name did *he* hate *them*? If anything, it should be *they* who hated …

Baxter's groan interrupted her troubled thoughts, yanked her from her musings.

"The bloody madman has achieved his goal. I'm ruined."

Ariana frowned at her brother's melodramatic words. She knew his distress was not rooted in head-over-heels love for Suzanne Covington. Baxter's capacity for feeling was simply not that great. Then ... what?

"How will severing your betrothal ruin you?" she asked.

"Because without Suzanne's money I am practically destitute," he snapped. "And Kingsley obviously knew that."

"Destitute?" Ariana sat up straighten "But what about your inheritance, all the money Mother and Father left you?"

Baxter leaned forward and stared moodily out the window. "That's been gone for some time now."

Ariana started. She knew Baxter had always been extravagant with money and that lately he'd been gambling more than usual. Still, their parents had left Baxter a sizable sum when they died. How could he have squandered it all away?

Irate words crowded Ariana's mind, rushed to her lips. And just as quickly were silenced. Watching the quiver in her brother's taut jawline, she felt her anger waver and a surge of sympathy tighten her chest.

Life hadn't been easy for Baxter, she of all people knew that. From age sixteen, he had been forced to manage the Caldwell estate and simultaneously act as guardian for his two younger sisters. In truth, Ariana could scarcely remember her mother and father. Other than Theresa, her treasured lady's maid, Baxter and Vanessa were the only parents she had ever really known. And despite their impatience and occasional disinterest, Ariana truly believed that her brother and sister had done their best.

With that sentimental thought in mind she made a decision. "If your inheritance is gone, we can use mine," she declared with an encouraging smile.

If gratitude and elation were the reactions she'd expected, she was severely disappointed.

"I already have," Baxter muttered, without meeting his sister's gaze. "Most of that is gone as well."

A stunned silence filled the carriage.

"You spent the money Mother and Father left me? ... Without asking, without even mentioning it?"

Baxter tossed her a dark look. "How else was I to run the estate?"

"Perhaps with the funds you squandered at the James Street gambling houses."

Baxter scowled at Ariana's uncharacteristic display of defiance. "I didn't gamble away your funds. I gambled in an attempt to recover them."

Ariana opened her mouth, then just as quickly shut it. Baxter's matter-of-fact tone told her he actually believed his actions had been justified. Further confrontation would serve no purpose. "How will we live?" she asked instead.

Baxter's fists clenched in his lap. "My marriage to Suzanne would have solved all our problems. But Kingsley deliberately obliterated that prospect." He fell silent, apparently deeply engrossed in the pattern of his trousers. At length, he lifted his head, giving Ariana a measured look. "Now our only hope is you."

"I?" Ariana gasped, still reeling with the staggering reality of their impoverished state.

"Yes ... you," he repeated more decisively. "You're eighteen now. It's time that you marry ... that I select a proper husband for you."

Ariana stiffened, regarding Baxter with grim understanding. "What you're saying is, you plan to snare the first affluent gentleman you can find and then whisk me down the aisle with him."

"Nothing so coldblooded as that, sprite." His expression softened. "But, after all, you're not exactly a child any longer. In fact ..." He studied her with deliberate impartiality, inspecting her from the top of her tousled auburn tresses to the hem of her soiled evening gown, a surprised, satisfied smile curving his lips. Where had he been these past years? Obviously, and right before his unseeing eyes, his little sister had grown to be a ravishing beauty, something that not even her current disheveled state could disguise.

"Well, well," he murmured, shaking his head. "My tiny caterpillar has become a butterfly. You are truly magnificent, Ariana."

"Don't stoop to false flattery, Baxter," Ariana retorted, unmoved by his words. "I am fully aware that, at best, I am no more than average." Her tone was frank and completely devoid of malice. "Vanessa was beautiful. Perhaps I resemble her in my coloring. But 'magnificent'? Hardly." She set her small jaw, folded her hands in her lap. "You'll have to try another method to win my cooperation."

Baxter chuckled. "You really don't see it, do you? Very well, then; you are merely passable in your looks. However, you are both loving and biddable. On most occasions," he added pointedly. "Other than when you are lost among your precious flowers or off chasing birds. Still, your customary adaptability should provide the proper incentive for, as you put it, *snaring* a suitable mate."

"Suitable for whom?"

"Suitable for both of us. And for the bridegroom as well." He paused, choosing his method of persuasion carefully. "You know I would never force you to wed someone who repels you, sprite. But surely we can find someone who fits both our needs and can also restore some dignity to our family name?"

"Oh, Baxter." Ariana shook her head in confusion. Despite her decision to remain unyielding, she was affected by her brother's plea, his obvious desperation. Yet ... marriage? Not only hadn't marriage factored into her immediate plans, she could not even envision herself permanently tied to any of the gentlemen with whom she was presently acquainted. When she did wed, she dreamed of a union born of love, not the culmination of some business arrangement. No ... she couldn't agree to what Baxter wanted of her, but, then again, how could she refuse? He'd relinquished his youthful dreams for her, did she not owe him some of her own in return?

Ariana massaged her temples, trapped in a vortex of conflicting emotions: duty, guilt, remorse, resentment... resignation. "All right, Baxter," she said in a wooden voice. "I'll *consider* your suggestion."

Baxter beamed. "Good girl." He tapped his leg thoughtfully. "Our main problem is that the London Season is nearly past. Had I known our situation would be thus, I would have officially brought you out, introduced you to all the right people." He shrugged. "We'll just have to take advantage of the fall house parties."

Ariana leaned her head against the carriage's soft cushion, closing her eyes.

"Don't look so troubled, sprite. All will be well." Actually, Baxter felt like whistling, now that he'd convinced Ariana to do his bidding.

"I'm not troubled," Ariana denied faintly. "It's only that my ankle is throbbing painfully."

Baxter glanced down at the discolored, swollen bruise, experiencing a pang of guilt as he realized he'd all but forgotten her injury. "We're nearly home. Theresa will tend to it as soon as we arrive."

Ariana's lashes lifted. "Do you think he will be back?"

"Who?"

"Trenton Kingsley."

Abruptly, Baxter's good humor vanished. "Not if he values his life, he won't."

Fear gripped Ariana's heart. "Please don't talk like that."

Baxter inhaled sharply, bringing himself under control with great difficulty. "No, I don't believe we'll be seeing *His Grace* again. He accomplished what he set out to do and has probably already retreated to his refuge on the Isle of Wight." Baxter's brows drew together in a question. "He didn't hurt you, did he?"

Ariana shook her head. "No. He merely carried me to the house."

"But he frightened you?"

A prolonged pause. Then Ariana turned her head away, her eyes sliding shut once more. "No," she whispered. "He didn't frighten me."

She left the remaining truth unspoken, although she was painfully, shamefully aware of its existence.

Trenton Kingsley had unnerved her dreadfully. But what she had felt in his arms was neither fear nor pain.

What she'd felt was unforgivable.

"It looks worse than it is. Many things do. Except those that look better." Theresa placed another cool compress on Ariana's ugly bruise, then tucked a wisp of gray hair back into her own uncooperative bun. "Your ankle will soon be healed, fret not."

Ariana settled herself on the pillows, the pain in her leg already having subsided to a dull throb. "I'm not fretting, Theresa," she murmured, staring at the ceiling.

"Your mind aches more than your injury."

Theresa's curious observation elicited no response, nor was Ariana taken aback by its accuracy. She'd known Theresa all her life, for the tiny, eccentric old woman with the sharp black eyes, beaklike nose and abrupt movements of a sparrow had raised both Ariana and Vanessa from birth. Many called her daft, but Ariana knew better. Theresa possessed the wisdom of a scholar and a unique prophetic insight that few others were wise enough to perceive, much less understand.

"Yes, my mind aches," Ariana concurred softly, after a lengthy silence. "A great deal happened tonight, and I am dreadfully confused."

"Confused … or distressed?"

"Both."

Theresa adjusted her apron pocket, which bulged with a volume written by the seventeenth-century essayist Sir Francis Bacon, and sat on the edge of the bed. "Confusion can lead to distress … or distress can lead to confusion. Which is it, in this case?"

Ariana thought for a moment. "Partially, the former. And partially, the latter."

"Which is more severe, the confusion or the distress?"

"The confusion."

"Then let us discuss the latter first, and dismiss it quickly so we can get to the former."

"All right."

"Yes, I know. I've placed the compress there."

"Pardon me?"

"Your right ankle. I've placed the compress there," Theresa repeated, checking the swelling.

"No, Theresa," Ariana explained with customary patience. "I meant it's all right to begin with the latter."

"The latter?"

"My distress," Ariana reminded her.

"Yes, I'm waiting for you to speak of it."

Ariana laced her fingers together and rested them on the quilt. "I'm distressed because Baxter's betrothal was severed tonight."

"I cannot feel sadness over a union that did not include your brother's heart."

Ariana sighed. "I agree. No, my distress is caused, not by the fact that Baxter will remain unmarried, but by the consequences of his parting with Suzanne ... or, rather, the Covingtons. Which, by the way, is integrally related to the real reason why Baxter wanted this marriage to begin with."

Rather than appearing flustered by Ariana's muddled explanation, Theresa nodded sagely. "To gain access to the Covington wealth."

Now Ariana *was* surprised. She raised up on her elbows, staring at Theresa's impassive expression. "You knew?"

Theresa shrugged. "There are some things one does not need to be told in order to know. Your brother is as he is. 'It is in life as it is in ways,'" she said soberly, quoting Bacon, "'the shortest way is commonly the foulest, and surely the fairer way is not much about.'"

"He is a good man, Theresa," Ariana defended instantly.

"Goodness wears many faces. Who is to say which of them are real?"

"He is afraid. So am I. From what he says, our financial circumstances are quite bleak."

"It will take the viscount much time to find another wealthy young woman around whom to weave his charming web."

"He does not intend to find another woman. He intends to find a man ... for me."

Theresa blinked. "He wishes you to marry?"

"Yes."

"That could be for the best." Again, Theresa patiently tucked away a stray wisp of hair, immediately dislodging three additional strands, which fell in disarray to her nape.

Ariana sat up straighten "There is no one I care to marry, Theresa. No one I love."

"Do you know so many gentlemen then?"

"Of course not. It's just that I've never met a single one for whom I could feel anything. ..." She broke off, appalled at herself when an image of Trenton Kingsley sprang unbidden to her mind.

"You were saying ..." Theresa prompted.

"I don't remember."

"That is because you're confused. Wasn't that what we were discussing?"

"I don't know what we were discussing."

"The former."

"What?"

"The former. Your confusion. It is time to confront it."

"Yes." It was a whisper.

"You are confused over your brother's reasons for wishing you wed?"

"Of course not. Baxter wants me to marry a wealthy man, someone with enough money and generosity to satisfy all my brother's debts and restore his respectability."

Theresa nodded. "Well said. Then what is the cause of your confusion? Has it something to do with your fall?"

"No ... yes ..." Ariana buried her face in her hands. "I don't know."

"The precise definition of confusion."

Ariana raised her head. "Trenton Kingsley is the man who found me in the maze and brought me back to the party."

"The duke has returned to Sussex?" Theresa inquired.

"To sever Baxter's betrothal."

"I see."

"That doesn't stun you?"

"Whether or not it stuns me is not the question. Why his presence confuses you is."

"My instincts have never failed me so miserably."

"I have never known your instincts to fail you at all."

"Then this time is the first."

Theresa did not answer at once; she only studied Ariana with sharp, unreadable, dark eyes. "The allure must have been overpowering," she stated at last.

Ariana's stomach lurched with guilt. "The allure?" she managed.

"The night. The mist. The song of the birds and the scent of the flowers. All that normally beckons you. It must have been overpowering to cause you to wander from your brother's betrothal party."

"Oh ... yes. It was."

"It?"

"The allure," Ariana reiterated.

"The allure."

"Yes ... isn't that what we were discussing?"

"Were we?" Theresa's gaze was steady.

Ariana had the sinking feeling that the night's magic had little to do with this conversation. "I suppose we were not," she murmured.

"Tell me about him."

Instantly, Ariana's heart began to pound. "I should despise him … *I do* despise him."

"You were attracted to him?"

Ariana's hands curled into tight fists of denial. "I can't be."

"Yet you are."

"He was so gentle, Theresa, so caring." Small curls of warmth unfurled inside Ariana's chest. "He made his way through the maze until he found me and then carried me all the way back to the manor." She swallowed. "I could sense his anger, yet somehow I knew it wasn't directed at me. Or at least it wasn't, until he learned I was a Caldwell."

"I imagine that information didn't please him," Theresa agreed. "Nor you. But why are you confused?"

"He killed Vanessa!" Ariana exclaimed, tears filling her eyes. "Or at the very least he was responsible for her suicide!"

"It did appear that way."

"Then how can you ask why I'm confused?"

"Your instincts are at war with your principles."

"My instincts are wrong."

"Perhaps. Then again, perhaps not. Your emotions are intruding, preventing you from drawing an objective conclusion," Theresa reasoned.

"I cannot be objective about the man who murdered my sister!" Ariana said brokenly, accosted by the vivid memory of Vanessa's blood-stained gown the day it washed up on the Sussex shore, her body submerged forever in its watery grave.

"No, I would think not," Theresa agreed. She removed the compress from Ariana's ankle and checked the swelling carefully. Satisfied that the ankle was healing properly, she tucked it beneath the quilt. "Appearance is a fascinating thing," she commented. "It changes depending upon one's perspective and is often not as one believes it to be."

"I never want to see him again."

Theresa rose, smiling, and eased Ariana against the pillows, smoothing the quilt about her shoulders. "We've talked enough. I want you to rest, my lady."

Ariana complied, feeling abruptly and unbearably weary. "My head aches," she whispered, closing her eyes.

"Far more than your injury," Theresa agreed, drawing the curtains closed. "Yet sleep will come, for your heart is at peace."

Ariana didn't hear Theresa's last words, for she was already drifting into slumber.

Tenderly, Theresa stroked her lovely, troubled mistress's hair. "Your mind will know peace as well, my lady. But it has quite a distance to travel before that can occur."

Gazing at Ariana's serene features, Theresa saw far beyond, with an inborn ability believers called "intuition," skeptics termed "witchery." As it sometimes happened, an image appeared clear and unmistakable, a strong, revealing glimpse of what was to be. Rarely, however, was her vision as absolute as this. The last time had been six years before.

She'd been certain then. She was certain now.

Ariana's destiny had found her.

CHAPTER 3

His triumph and elation vanished by dawn.

Never breaking stride, Trenton leaned over and scooped up a handful of wet sand, crushing it in his palm until his skin burned from the abrasive contact.

He barely felt the sting, so great was the turmoil raging inside him.

Merely a day after the Covington ball and, rather than a pervading sense of euphoria from the outcome of his grand exhibition, all he knew was inexplicable fury and gnawing restlessness.

Damn Caldwell to hell.

Violently, Trenton hurled his arm out, casting the molded mass of sand toward the brilliant waters of Osborne Bay. He stalked onward, driven by demons, kicking a line of stones from his path. The action aggravated his already taut, aching leg muscles, reminding him of the great distance he'd traveled.

He'd been walking for hours. Bembridge, the small village that adjoined his beloved Spraystone, was nestled in the Isle of Wight's spectacular Chalk Cliffs over ten miles south of the Queen's Osborne House. Yet he'd hardly noticed the change in terrain, nor the passage of time. He'd simply walked, seeking a semblance of peace customarily offered him by the breathtaking Solent Sea, the narrow channel that separated Wight from the English coast.

He slowed his step, idly watching the graceful yachts as they glided past the island's shore, heading for the Royal Yacht Club in West Cowes. The vast number of billowing sails approaching at once came as no surprise, for the wind had picked up a bit this hour, and the waves, in turn, were slapping their foam on the sand with escalating intensity. One of Wight's exotic summer storms was brewing, promising its turbulent arrival by dusk.

Trenton wasn't worried, for he knew he had hours before the storm struck. Wiping spray from his forehead, he gazed expectantly out over the bay, awaiting that wondrous sense of tranquility to pervade his soul.

It never came.

What the hell was wrong with him?

Trenton walked toward the water's edge, brutally analyzing his dark humor. The night before his plan had come to fruition and the obsession that consumed him these long years had been fulfilled. At last, Baxter Caldwell was destitute.

If Trenton's painstakingly acquired research hadn't convinced him of the viscount's dire straits, the look on Caldwell's face when Covington conceded to Trenton's demand most assuredly did. Without Suzanne's dowry, Caldwell was penniless. And, to a coldhearted bastard like Caldwell, poverty was a more heinous condition to endure than the most lethal of diseases.

So where was the exalted sense of vindication Trenton had expected to feel?

Lowering himself to the ground, Trenton braced his weight on his hands, disregarding the icy tide that washed up around him, soaking his trousers and boots. He stared, unseeing, toward England's distant shore, instantly conjuring up an image of the one surprise last night had spawned.

His vague sense of familiarity had been immediate; he'd just been unable to place it. Although God only knew how he could have overlooked it, given that his arrival, his purpose, the very essence of his vengeful thoughts sprang from the Caldwells. And the resemblance *was* striking.

Still, he'd never met her, for six years before she'd been a child and he'd been consumed by her sister. That being the case, he'd simply forgotten her existence.

Squinting, he recalled the delicate features and waves of coppery hair, the turquoise eyes regarding him so solemnly as he approached her in the contorted maze. No, it was not so surprising that he'd missed the likeness, at that. The small, artlessly beautiful fairy-tale creature he'd rescued last night was but a subtle replica of her dazzling older sister. For he, better than anyone, knew that no one could equal Vanessa.

Fiery, turbulent Vanessa, with a flaming mane of red-gold hair that flowed down her back like a raging sunset, and the hypnotic scent of roses clinging to her skin. Lush, seductive, bold, deliberate … No, there had been nothing subtle about Vanessa Caldwell. And no man was immune to the hypnotic effects of her tantalizing spell.

Lord, how he despised her.

Trenton's face set in a fierce expression, hard waves slapping against his saturated clothing. *God help me*, he thought silently, *but I cannot feel regret for what I did. Perhaps at one time I could have. But that time is long gone, buried beneath the unalterable consequences wrought by Caldwell hate.*

He dug his fingers into the sand, the irony of the situation striking home yet again. He had caused Vanessa's death, but she had prevailed nonetheless, and the ultimate victory was hers. For the punishment she'd extracted was far crueler than death could ever be. So despite their pain and grief, the Caldwells had won.

And last night's triumph paled in comparison.

The constriction in his chest told Trenton he had just unearthed the root of his foul humor and utter discontent. He had still not taken all he must from Baxter Caldwell.

But what more could he take from a man who loved nothing but money and no one but himself? Aside, of course, from Vanessa.

Trenton could still recall how totally shattered and agonized Baxter had been when he discovered that his precious sister was forever lost. Could he truly have cared so deeply for that heartless bitch? Obviously, the answer was yes. For nothing short of bottomless grief and rage would compel a man to commit so conscienceless an act as the one Baxter had committed.

Could Baxter feel that same blind adoration for his baby sister too?

Trenton's thought materialized from nowhere, descending like the heavy blanket of mist that cloaked the maze where he'd found her. Did Baxter revere ... her name eluded him for a moment, then rustled through his senses like a warm, gentle breeze.

Ariana.

Such gentleness and faith had shone in her extraordinary eyes before she'd learned who her rescuer was. And such fire had replaced them when she discovered the truth.

Did Baxter dote on Ariana the way he had on Vanessa? He'd certainly exhibited a fine show of brotherly protectiveness at the Covingtons' ball: all righteous indignation, clutching Ariana to his side as if she were his most priceless possession. And indeed, could she be?

She wasn't cold and cruel like Vanessa, nor weak and shallow like Baxter. Her naïveté was too genuine, her responses too natural.

But respond she had.

The sensual pull between them had been immediate and undeniable. He hadn't imagined the insistent ache in his loins, nor the bewildered yet unmistakable awakening in her eyes as he'd carried her from the maze.

Still she was a Caldwell.

A sudden possibility struck Trenton, and a slow, sardonic smile curled his lips.

He could use their attraction to his advantage.

Mulling over that pleasurable prospect, he shifted his weight, stretching his legs in front of him, oblivious to the cresting waves now drenching him to the waist.

Ariana. A breathtaking angel, ready to be guided into the heavenly realm of passion. True, she would resist him at first, entrenched as she was in her brother's enmity. Still, Trenton had every confidence that she would eventually succumb to his calculated seduction. Quite simply, she wasn't sophisticated enough to combat his expertise or to fight the attraction that drove her to him.

Then there was the matter of her virginity.

As a rule, Trenton didn't prefer virgins. However, he found this one strangely alluring in her innocence. Yes, he would certainly savor every moment of his combined victory: sexually initiating Ariana and, in the process, bringing Baxter to his knees, ruining his baby sister and thereby fulfilling one contemptuous accusation that, until now, had been false.

At the memory, Trenton's jaw clenched. Ruin Vanessa? Hardly.

And yet she'd made that claim—repeatedly, as he recalled—on that final night ... the last night of her life.

Trenton could envision it as if it were yesterday, rather than six years before: the secluded shadows beneath the cliffs, the dark waters of the River Arun mingling with the rough waves of the Channel, the foam slapping at their feet

The rage that loomed in his heart as he'd faced her.

Her eyes were strangely lit, not only by the lantern's haunting glow but with a depth of despair that might have been pitiful enough to move him, had it been anyone but Vanessa.

His fists knotted at his sides in an attempt to restrain himself.

But to no avail.

And when she began to taunt him, his fury was uncontainable, condemnation and hatred blazing in his eyes.

He could still remember her plaintive cries as she begged him not to do this to her.

Please ... don't ... Trenton ... don't ...

Her pleas fell on deaf ears.

He was out of control and he knew it. What was more, Vanessa knew it too.

No ... no ... don't ... no ...

He didn't flinch nor look back. He simply walked away, leaving behind him only a sudden silence and an extinguished lantern.

Taking with him only an odd sense of relief ...

"Help me! Help!"

Trenton's eyes flew open, as it struck him that the scream he was hearing was no haunting voice of the past but a very real and fearful cry from somewhere in Osborne Bay.

He leapt to his feet, scanning the choppy waters, which had grown significantly rougher during the hour he'd been lost in thought. The yachts had long since disappeared from view, and the sky looked menacing, the clouds low.

"Help!"

He heard it again, and this time his keen gaze located its source. Far out in the bay was a small rowboat, bobbing idly on the waves, devoid of occupants. Splashing frantically near the boat, yet not close enough to grab on, was a woman, whose head appeared intermittently, then sank beneath the water.

Trenton wasted not a second. Simultaneously he kicked off his boots and tore off his shirt, flinging them to the sand. In three long strides he was deep enough to dive, then took hard, powerful strokes that carried him swiftly to the speck of color he recognized as the drowning woman.

His arm locked about her waist, dragging her head above water along with his own. Ignoring the boat entirely, he swam forcefully for shore, uncertain of the woman's state of consciousness, decidedly uneasy about her lack of coughing or movement.

Her face was ashen when he lay her on the sand, blood trickling from an ugly gash on her forehead. Trenton paled as he recognized her.

Not allowing himself to dwell on the devastating possibilities should his efforts fail, he proceeded to force the water from her lungs until her first shallow breaths evolved into a fit of gasping coughs.

"Your Highness!" Hurried footsteps accompanied the shrill voice. "Oh, Lord!" The maid watched helplessly as Trenton soothed the young woman's coughs, assisting her until her breathing was erratic but normal.

"The Princess will be fine," he assured the shaking servant, using his discarded shirt to wipe the blood from the princess's forehead. "None the worse for her ambitious adventure."

"I must summon Her Majesty at once." The slight, knock-kneed girl turned, then stopped. "Oh, thank you, Your Grace," she breathed, well aware that Trenton was a frequent guest of the Queen's. "Thank you ever so much."

Trenton glanced down at Princess Beatrice, who was now calming her gasps, shivering uncontrollably while attempting to still her nerves.

"Do not alarm the Queen," Trenton cautioned the servant. "I shall assist Princess Beatrice to the house. Then Her Majesty can see for herself that all is well."

"Yes, of course, Your Grace." The grateful maid wrung her hands, simultaneously bobbing her head up and down.

"Can you walk, Your Highness?" Trenton asked Beatrice gently.

Slowly, the Princess nodded, allowing Trenton to draw her to her feet. "I never imagined the weather would turn so dreadfully," she rasped. "Nor so quickly. When I went out rowing ..." she inhaled sharply, shakily, "the sky was light, the day lovely. I assumed I had hours before the storm hit. ... I'm normally a strong swimmer. But when I struck my head on the boat ..." She choked in more air, touching the gash on her forehead. "You saved my life, Your Grace. I don't know how to thank you."

"You can thank me by saving your strength. You can also thank me by walking into that house on your own two legs and assuring your poor mother that you are well." He offered her his arm.

Beatrice smiled faintly. "Done."

Queen Victoria abandoned her watercolor sketch of the upcoming storm the instant she saw Beatrice and Trenton approach Osborne House's lower terrace. She rushed forward, the color draining from her face as her child hobbled in unsteadily on Trenton's arm.

"What has happened?" the Queen demanded.

Trenton helped Beatrice into a chair beside the fountain, then moved forward, leaning over to brush the Queen's hand with his lips. "Everything is fine, Your Majesty," he soothed.

Victoria waved him off, bending over to anxiously inspect her daughter's condition.

"The Princess merely fell in the bay," Trenton assured her.

Satisfied that Beatrice would recover, Victoria turned to address Trenton. "Don't take me for a fool, Kingsley," she shot back, as regal in carriage at fifty-four as she'd been as a girl. "I've lived through far too much for you to patronize me. Beatrice did not merely fall in the bay. She is bleeding, not to mention totally saturated and white as a sheet!"

"The duke saved the Princess's life, Your Majesty," the maid piped up, scurrying onto the terrace. Quickly and respectfully, she relayed the incident to the Queen. "I saw the whole thing," she concluded, nodding vigorously for emphasis.

Victoria turned to Trenton, her lips quivering with emotion. "You've given me back my child, Trenton. For that, I am forever in your debt. Anything you ask of me is yours."

A corner of Trenton's mouth rose in amusement. "I am in need of nothing, I assure you, Your Majesty."

"That's preposterous!" she snapped. "Everyone is in need of something!"

"I beg to differ with you, Your Majesty. I've acquired all I can possibly take … at least for now." Trenton thrust aside the dark reflection, flashing Victoria one of his rare, infectious smiles. He had to restore the Queen's humor, so she would forget this nonsense of fulfilling some nonexistent need of his. "As a matter of fact," he continued, "it is *I* who have been needed these past few days ... twice, in fact. Both times I was called upon to rescue damsels in distress."

Victoria responded with a cold stare, unmoved by either his dazzling charm or honorable proclamation. "Dispense with this idle chatter, Broddington. I am aware that you require no monetary compensation. However, surely there is something you wish." Her features softened and she clutched the pillar beside her, as if for support. "Please do not deny me the chance to repay what you have restored to me this day. I could not have withstood another loss." Her voice trembled.

Trenton inclined his head in understanding. The Queen had suffered greatly over the past score, both personally and as a sovereign. First came the bloodshed of the Crimean War. That finally behind her, personal tragedy had struck. The Queen's mother, the Duchess of Kent, passed away in March of 1861. And then, a scant nine months later, Victoria was forced to survive the ultimate blow, the death of her beloved Prince Consort just before Christmas.

At this supreme tragedy, Victoria's mourning was boundless, for she adored Albert and relied upon him heavily. And it was no secret that, without her husband, the mercurial Queen felt lost and incomplete. Only Beatrice, the family baby and Victoria's constant companion, managed to offer her mother the solace she needed to go on living. No, Trenton knew that to lose her sixteen-year-old daughter would be devastating to Victoria.

"I greatly appreciate your kind and generous offer, Your Majesty," Trenton answered with quiet perception. "However, you know me well and we are both aware that my specific wishes, unfortunately, are not tangible things to be granted. Even by one with power as vast as yours."

A pause. "Perhaps, in your situation, that is true," Victoria conceded thoughtfully. She raised her chin, her gaze meaningful. "Vengeance is not for us to render. That is something only the Lord can do."

Trenton's expression hardened. "That being the case, I have no wish to be granted."

"I do not accept your reply." Victoria waited determinedly.

Trenton wondered what he could say to appease her. They had agreed he needed nothing material, yet he knew the Queen well enough to know she would not be deterred from her demand. And since she could not offer him peace of mind, what the hell was he to ask for?

Retribution.

How he wished there was a way to claim it. Yesterday he believed it had been his, but now he knew that he'd been a fool, for his victory was a hollow one. Mere poverty would never be adequate punishment for the viscount's despicable crime.

No, after viciously destroying Trenton's life and the lives of his family, Caldwell had twisted a lethal knife in Trenton's heart, taken something from him that could never be restored. So the only true retribution would be one that was equally irrevocable, one that would annihilate Baxter's heart in return.

A virtual impossibility, since the bastard had no heart, cared for no one, save …

Trenton's head shot up, his answer illuminating his mind in a sudden flash of genius, anticipation coursing through his veins in wide rivers of promise. Something irrevocable. Why hadn't he thought of it before?

An eye for an eye.

A sister for a father.

Seduction be damned.

"Very well, Your Majesty. I do have one request." Trenton's smile was caustic, his eyes gleaming with triumph.

"And that is …"

"A royal decree commanding Ariana Caldwell to become my wife."

CHAPTER 4

"Why?" The queen wasn't mincing any words.

"Why what?" Trenton repeated innocently.

"Do not toy with me, Trenton," Victoria warned. "For a man who draws women to him like bees to honey, you would hardly require a sovereign's power to procure a bride." She broke off, her gaze cold. "Unless there is a reason this particular woman would be opposed to marrying you?"

Trenton's brows rose in mock amusement. "I understood that you wanted to grant me my fondest wish, Your Majesty. I wasn't aware that an explanation was required for my choice."

Undeterred by Trenton's pointed sarcasm, Victoria raised her regal chin, brittlely assessing him from beneath her white widow's cap. "You and I both know how much you loathe Baxter Caldwell."

Trenton stiffened. "With good reason."

Victoria frowned. "I've never made a secret of the fact that I have little use for the man myself, nor of the fact that I believe you innocent in the sordid matter of Vanessa Caldwell's sudden and questionable death."

"No, you haven't," Trenton replied in a gentler tone. "And for that I thank you."

Victoria dismissed his uncustomary acknowledgment with a brusque wave of her hand. "You also know how highly I regarded your father. He was a fine and honorable man, a dear friend to both Albert and me. That, however, does not mean that I condone what you've become since his death. You've become a moody, bitter, vengeful recluse." She cleared her throat. "I assume by her surname that the young lady you feel suddenly compelled to marry is related to Baxter Caldwell."

"His sister," Trenton supplied.

"His sister?" The Queen looked startled. "But Vanessa ..."

"Not *that* sister."

"Ah, the child," Victoria murmured, remembering back six years to the tragic drowning that had rocked the *ton* ... and the family whose lives it had altered. "Ariana, I believe her name was. I'd nearly forgotten. ... She was such a shy little girl, so very much in Vanessa's shadow."

The Queen stared off thoughtfully, her memory conjuring up the image of a diminutive, copper-haired child with huge, turquoise eyes and a wistful, faraway expression. "But she wasn't even in her teens when Vanessa died!" Consternation registered on Victoria's face. She cast a quick glance at Beatrice, who was now being helped into the house by two fussing maids. Satisfied with the renewed color in her daughter's cheeks, the Queen turned back to Trenton, lowering her voice so as not to be overheard. "Why, Ariana Caldwell cannot be more than a year or two older than Beatrice!"

Trenton's lips twitched. "And were you so advanced in years when you wed the Prince Consort?"

Victoria was in no mood to be dissuaded from her course. "Precisely how old is she?"

Trenton shrugged. "Significantly younger than Vanessa; probably by a decade or so. I would judge Ariana to be seventeen or eighteen."

"You don't even know her age?" Victoria burst out, appalled. "How long have the two of you been acquainted?"

"We met last night." A glint of humor flickered in his eyes. "In fact, she was the other damsel in distress I rescued."

The Queen drew herself up angrily. "Just how far are you willing to carry your hatred, Trenton? In the name of heaven, she is but an innocent—"

"As was my father," Trenton said grimly, all traces of amusement having vanished.

"That changes nothing. I will not allow you to vent your hostility on a blameless young girl."

"You did give me your word, Your Majesty," Trenton reminded her. "Any request I made you would honor."

"Not at a guileless child's expense."

"She is no longer a child," he countered, recalling Ariana's vivid beauty, her soft and very feminine body against his as he carried her back to the party. "And I have no intention of harming her."

Victoria ingested this declaration silently, a meditative look on her face. "Tell me," she said at last. "Is there more driving you to the altar than mere vengeance?"

Trenton went rigid. "Ariana is a very beautiful woman. I assure you, she will not find marriage to me distasteful."

A faint smile touched the Queen's lips. "Very well, Trenton. You shall have your royal edict … and your wife. Lady Ariana Caldwell will soon be the Duchess of Broddington."

Trenton's eyes narrowed on Victoria's suddenly composed face, scrutinizing it for clues to explain her abrupt reversal. He found none. "And the stipulations?" he asked suspiciously.

"None." She shook her head, silently urging her instincts to be reliable in their direction. "You saved my daughter's life. This is the least I can do to express my immeasurable gratitude." She walked over to the fountain, gripping the back of the chair where Beatrice had sat. "I shall issue the decree at once." A private light glinted in the Queen's eyes. "Congratulations, Trenton, on your forthcoming marriage. May it yield all you truly crave."

"How is your ankle faring, my lady?"

Blinking, Ariana lowered her novel, reluctantly leaving *Alice's Adventures in Wonderland* to return to the more mundane reality of her own morning room. Putting the irrepressible caterpillar on hold, she smiled at Theresa.

"My ankle is much better. Practically all healed." She lifted her right leg from the sofa and wiggled her foot in an exaggerated motion. "See? A mere three days of your ministrations and my ankle is as good as new."

"Not quite, but nearly," Theresa agreed, propping up the slightly swollen foot on a feather pillow. Gently, she traced the circles beneath Ariana's eyes. "Yet your mind remains troubled."

"Baxter tells me we are practically penniless."

Theresa shook her bead. "Your unrest is caused by more than that."

Ariana leaned her head back, rays of summer sunlight trickling through the bay window to warm her face. "I have no other reason to be troubled; yet I am," she admitted in a small voice. "I have a nagging feeling that something else remains amiss. ..." Restlessly, she shifted the drapery, gazing out over Winsham's southeast garden, seeking serenity ... finding none.

"Amiss ... perhaps," Theresa murmured without conviction. "More likely, unsettled."

Ariana's head snapped around. "You know what it is," she accused.

"As do you."

"No. I don't."

A profound smile creased Theresa's wrinkled face. "You *choose* not to know. But the point is a moot one. Soon the choice will no longer be yours." Abruptly, her smile vanished. "Your blue silk day dress! I haven't freshened it!"

"My day dress? What has that to do with my dilemma?"

Theresa shot her an exasperated look. "Well, you can hardly wear it unless it is properly pressed, can you?"

Ariana sat up, totally at sea. "I have no urgent need to wear my blue dress, Theresa."

"Ah, but you have." Theresa stood, glancing quickly at the imposing grandfather clock that stood in the far corner of the room. She exclaimed at the lateness of the hour, then scurried toward the door with a look of total consternation on her face, vividly reminding Ariana of Lewis Carroll's errant white rabbit. "Fear not, my lady," she called over her shoulder, jabbing a loose lock of hair behind her ear. "I shall have it ready for you in a quarter hour. That will give us just enough time ..." Her final words were lost in the hallway, cut off by the click of the door as it shut.

Ariana shook her head, sliding down to return to her reading. "And Alice thought the caterpillar was daft?" she muttered to herself.

She had just begun to enjoy the mad hatter's tea party when Theresa exploded back in.

"Come now, my lady," she urged, tugging Ariana to her feet.

Ariana dropped her novel to the couch. "Where?"

Theresa supported Ariana's right side and eased her forward. "To don your gown, of course."

"But I am already dressed, Theresa." Ariana indicated her beige morning dress. "Why must I change clothes?"

Theresa was concentrating on leading her mistress into the hallway, then up the stairs. "Because the blue gown suits you better, of course."

"Better for what?"

"For your eyes, my lady." She maneuvered Ariana gently to the second-floor landing. "The pale blue of the gown makes them shine like the ocean."

"Thank you. But I didn't mean why the blue gown. What I meant was—"

"Here it is!" Theresa exclaimed triumphantly, running into the bedroom and waving the full, ruffled skirt in Ariana's direction. "I've added a darker ribbon at each sleeve. Every shade of blue will be reflected in your glorious turquoise eyes."

Ariana made an exasperated sound. "Theresa, I am not taking another step until you tell me *why* I am donning that gown." She waited just inside the doorway.

"Didn't I tell you?" Theresa looked surprised.

"Tell me what?"

"Really, my lady, if your head weren't so steeped in fanciful books, you would have heard me." Theresa shut the door purposefully behind Ariana.

"But you never …"

"Our guests will be here any moment."

"Guests?" That got Ariana's attention. Rarely did Winsham attract visitors—at least since Vanessa had died. Baxter customarily went out; gambling, Ariana suspected. Which left only herself and the servants. "What guests?"

"Now how would I know that, my lady?" Theresa was already unbuttoning Ariana's gown, whisking it off her. "I am, after all, only a maid and hardly provided with the afternoon guest list."

"But then, how did you know …"

"I just told you I don't." She smoothed Ariana's petticoats, then slid the blue silk gown over her head. "Now hurry, or I won't have time to arrange your hair."

"Is Baxter home?"

"He's in his study."

A sudden unpleasant thought occurred to Ariana. "Theresa, did Baxter ask you to ready me for something—or, rather, for *someone?*" she demanded.

Theresa smoothed the swirling folds to the floor, her brow furrowed in concentration. "Your brother shall not be deciding your fate," she replied.

"But …"

"My lady," Theresa took her hands, "the answer to your question is no. The viscount asked nothing of me, nor would it change what is destined to occur."

Ariana's fingers tightened around her faithful companion's. She wanted no more riddles; only the benefit of Theresa's far-seeing eyes. "Please … tell me. Who is coming to Winsham?"

"A spokesman for the Queen."

"The Queen!" Ariana gasped. Hurriedly, she pulled the pins from her hair, shaking out the loose waves. "Perhaps Baxter has done something commendable at last and all our worries are over!" She limped over to the dressing table, sitting obediently and awaiting Theresa's help. "Maybe this will be the answer to all we seek."

"I am certain it will be, my lady."

Ariana met Theresa's gaze in the gilded mirror. "You're not going to elaborate, are you?"

In response, Theresa reached for the silver-handled brush and proceeded to arrange Ariana's tresses.

Ariana let out a deep sigh. "I was afraid of that. Very well, Theresa. I won't press any farther."

"I pressed it perfectly, my lady," Theresa defended instantly, smoothing the fine silk of Ariana's sleeve. "There is not a crease to be found."

Ariana's lips twitched. "No, you are most thorough. I wonder if any of us *truly* recognizes your full capabilities."

Theresa laced a blue velvet ribbon through Ariana's hair. "I believe a carriage has just arrived. We'd best prepare to greet our guests." She turned Ariana gently to face her, placing aged but steady hands on her mistress's narrow shoulders. "I shall subdue your brother. You need only subdue your temper."

"Subdue Baxter? Why?" Ariana's brow furrowed. "And why on earth would I lose my temper?"

"Most of all," Theresa continued as if Ariana hadn't spoken, "remember to follow your instincts. They will not fail you."

"Instincts about what?" Ariana rose to her feet. "You're frightening me, Theresa. What news could the Queen's messenger possibly be bringing that would involve my instincts?"

"Fear will not be an issue, nor does it need to be. But then, you already know that. Your instincts have confirmed it. Now come, my lady." Theresa took her arm. "Your walk is still a trifle unsteady. That should grant us just enough time before we are needed."

A door slammed downstairs, and angry male voices reached Ariana's ears.

Theresa shook her head at the stricken look on her mistress's face. "Do not be distressed. It is time." With that, she led Ariana to meet her fate.

"I cannot allow you just to barge in unannounced! What are your names? Why do you wish to see the viscount?"

Coolidge, the portly Caldwell butler, made another unsuccessful attempt to block Trenton's entrance to the house.

"Your loyalty, my good man, is admirable, though misplaced." Trenton gestured for his crisply efficient solicitor, Lawrence Crofton, to follow him into the hallway. "Now, where can we find the viscount?"

"He is in his study, sir." Coolidge bristled. "Now, who shall I say is calling?"

Trenton stopped in his tracks. "Tell him the Duke of Broddington is here to see him."

Coolidge blanched. "The Duke of …"

"Dammit, Coolidge, what is going on out here?" Baxter slammed open the door to his study, glowering in the direction of the ruckus. His gaze locked with Trenton's, and hot color flooded his face. "You! What the hell are you doing here?"

Trenton held up a silencing hand. "Spare me the theatrics, Caldwell. I'll be brief." He gestured toward Crofton. "My solicitor … should his verification be needed."

Baxter's flush deepened. "Your solicitor? I have no debt to pay you, Kingsley."

Trenton's temples pounded with rage, and it took every shred of control he possessed not to kill Caldwell where he stood. "I beg to differ with you," he bit out. "What you *owe* me can never be repaid." He drew his breath in slowly. "But I'm here to collect nonetheless."

"Get out!" Baxter crossed the hall, prepared to bodily evict Trenton.

Trenton stopped him in his tracks, grabbing him roughly by the arm, wishing it were the viscount's treacherous neck in his grasp. "Read the edict, Lawrence," he commanded, never dragging his smoldering gaze from Baxter's.

Nervously, the solicitor adjusted his spectacles, rustling the official-looking document and clearing his throat. Trenton had warned him this would be unpleasant, and he, of all people, knew the history behind Trenton's hatred. Still, his hands trembled a bit, the bitter tension a palpable entity in the quiet entranceway.

"This is a royal edict from Her Majesty, Queen Victoria," he began.

Baxter looked stunned. "A royal edict?"

"Yes, my lord," Crofton confirmed. "Now, if I may continue …"

"Read it, Lawrence." Trenton's tone was lethal, his heart pounding with triumph as, beneath his rigid grasp, he felt Baxter's blood pump faster, his pulse beat accelerate.

"Very well." Crofton stood up straighter. "Her Majesty, Queen Victoria, by the Grace of God, of the United Kingdom of Great Britain and Ireland, Queen, Defender of the Faith, Empress of India, wills and commands Lady Ariana Caldwell be joined in wedlock to His Grace, Trenton Nicholas Kingsley, the seventh Duke of Broddington, on the 5th day of August, 1873, the ceremony to take place without fail at the appointed hour of—'"

"*No!*"

The protest was torn from Ariana's chest, a horrified cry uttered midway down the staircase where she stood, frozen with shock and outrage. Clutching the banister, she shook off Theresa's supporting hand and fought for composure, staring into the sea of faces below.

For a minute, no one moved or spoke, incredulity pitted against fury and determination.

Trenton reacted first, walking purposefully to the foot of the stairs, addressing Ariana with businesslike composure. "Obviously, you heard the Queen's edict. That saves me the trouble of repeating it."

"I … won't … do … it." Ariana choked out each word, descending until she was but three steps from the bottom, eye to eye with her enemy.

Trenton appraised her with slow deliberation, his probing blue eyes missing nothing. Then, maddeningly, he smiled. "It?"

"Marry you!" she clarified in a frigid hiss.

"Ah, but you will, misty angel," he corrected, seizing her elbow and tugging her the remaining distance to him. Holding her captive with his gaze, he extended his hand toward Crofton. "Give me the edict."

His solicitor complied, walking over and hastily placing the official paper in Trenton's outstretched hand.

Unblinking, Trenton offered the page to Ariana. "Read it yourself."

Ariana snatched it, scanning the contents, her cheeks growing flushed. "Why?" she demanded, thrusting the paper back at Trenton.

"My reasons are my own. But the signature belongs to our Queen. Will you disobey her order?"

"Baxter is right … you are a bastard," Ariana breathed, her voice breaking.

Trenton's jaw tightened. "Then on August 5th you will become a bastard's wife."

"Please … don't do this." She tried one last time to beseech him.

Something flashed in his eyes, something sympathetic and vulnerable … then it was gone. "Until August 5th, misty angel," he repeated, backing away. "After that you belong to me."

"Baxter?" Ariana averted her head, gazing pleadingly in her brother's direction, wondering why he remained so deadly silent.

Baxter's mind was still reeling. Ariana ... marry Kingsley? Was this the scoundrel's final revenge? To rob Baxter of his only remaining sister and force her to become *Mrs.* Trenton Kingsley?

Baxter closed his eyes. The idea was abhorrent, intolerable. If he honored the Queen's command, Ariana would belong to his most despised enemy, the bastard who had taken all he had, the anathema of his existence.

The most affluent man in Sussexshire.

That realization brought Baxter's conjecturing to a dead halt, as greed reared its ugly head. Pride intervened, warring with greed, determined to prevail. But need pride be sacrificed? If he and Ariana found a way to outwit the blackhearted snake, couldn't Baxter retain his pride *and* usurp Kingsley's fortune? Wouldn't that be the ultimate form of vengeance?

A twinge of guilt pricked Baxter's conscience. This was Ariana's life he was toying with. Wasn't she entitled to more than an empty life with a husband who despised her?

No, he corrected himself. It wasn't Ariana who Kingsley despised; it was *he*. And Baxter knew Trenton well enough to know that, no matter what else he was capable of, he wouldn't abuse an innocent girl.

As for Ariana, well, she would prevail. Despite her diminutive size, his sister was a survivor. She could withstand a life with Trenton Kingsley ... especially if it meant partaking in his vast fortune.

And sharing the wealth with her brother.

"Let me see the edict," Baxter heard himself say.

Stiffly, Trenton extended his arm, clearly unwilling to take even one compromising step in Baxter's direction.

Ignoring the blatant insult, Baxter strode over and seized the paper, wondering how Trenton had managed to gain Her Majesty's cooperation. Despite her fondness for the Kingsley family, Victoria had never interfered on their behalf. At least until now.

Suspiciously, Baxter studied the mandate to make certain it was what Kingsley claimed it to be. But the decree was genuine, the Queen's signature authentic.

Baxter raised compassionate eyes to Ariana. "I'm sorry, sprite." He winced at her agonized expression. "There's nothing I can do." He ignored the triumph on Trenton's face, reminding himself that it was temporary.

Ariana's eyes filled with tears. "This is barbaric!"

"My lady." Undetected, Theresa had descended the stairs. Now she took Ariana's arm gently. "You are overwrought. Come. I'll take you to your room."

"It's settled, then," Trenton concluded, satisfaction gleaming in his eyes. "The wedding will take place on August 5th. The reception will be held at Broddington. Hundreds of guests will attend to see the Viscount Winsham's little sister become the Duchess of Broddington."

Ariana stared at him, numb with increasing rage and shock. "I hate you," she said in a fierce whisper.

His lips twisted into a cynical smile. "Do you, misty angel? Well, I look forward to seeing how much."

CHAPTER 5

Ariana was drained.

Pushing herself into a sitting position, she blinked at the small walnut clock on her nightstand. Three o'clock ... more than two hours since she'd fled to the sanctuary of her four-poster bed. Her tears had long since dried, her resistance dwindled to despair. She *had* to face her dilemma ... alone.

For the first time in her life Ariana had refused both Theresa's comfort and company, dismissing her the instant they reached the bedroom door. Overcome with emotion, she'd then flung herself across the bed, sobbing violently into her pillow. Shock, outrage, hurt, humiliation: all the emotions she had anticipated and held at bay poured out in a rush. She wept for the act of vengeance that had decided her fate, for her helplessness to alter the outcome, for Baxter's indifference to her plight. She wept for every reason she had expected to weep.

Harder still for the one she *hadn't* expected.

She could deny it no longer: She was drawn to Trenton Kingsley.

Pondering the silent admission, Ariana's hands balled into fists of self-loathing, pressing heavily into the soft feather pillow. How could she? cried her conscience, immediately providing her with every heinous act the man had committed.

But she was.

She could label it curiosity, fascination, bewilderment; but whatever name she gave it, the pull was there. She felt it. Worse still, so did he.

Her traitorous heart thudded as she recalled the explicit, knowing look in the duke's probing eyes. She might be a total innocent when it came to men, but her body understood his message nonetheless—and responded with a will of its own, caring nothing for the dictates of her conscience.

Coupled with her disturbing physical reaction was the small but insistent voice of some deeply submerged instinct, which refused to be silenced, negating all the evidence her reason presented, reminding her instead of the glimpses of compassion she'd seen beyond the duke's iron mask, both today and when he'd rescued her from the Covington maze.

And yet the final emotion she'd seen gleaming in his eyes just before she'd fled was vengeance and triumph, telling her that she was no more than a pawn in some sick attempt at retribution.

Or was it resurrection?

Was it Vanessa the duke saw when he scrutinized Ariana so thoroughly? Did he wish it were Vanessa he was punishing, breaking …

Possessing as his wife?

If all the stories Baxter had told Ariana were true, it was irrational jealousy over Vanessa that had driven Trenton Kingsley to madness, to torment … to murder.

Ariana shuddered at the thought.

For two hours her conflicting impulses warred, tearing her apart. Numbness was her body's method of self-protection, her message that she could no longer sustain this heightened level of emotional turmoil. Besides, the issue was a moot one. No matter which emerged victorious—be it her reason, her conscience, her instincts, or her attraction—the end result was the same. The Queen had issued a decree. So, like it or not, on the 5th of August, Ariana would become Mrs. Trenton Kingsley.

The bedroom door eased open, and then closed just as quietly. "You're ready for me now, my lady." It was a statement, rather than a question, and Theresa crossed the room to sit beside Ariana on the bed.

Ariana turned slowly to face her. "You knew."

"Yes." Theresa smoothed tousled wisps of coppery hair from Ariana's flushed cheeks. "You've been alone long enough. I knew you were ready to share your thoughts with me."

"That's not what I meant." This time Ariana was giving her friend no quarter. "You knew about the Queen's edict."

Theresa paused. "No."

"But you knew Trenton Kingsley was her messenger?"

"I knew he was your future."

Ariana gripped Theresa's hands. "But you told me yourself he was a murderer!"

"No," Theresa countered again. "I only said that it *appeared* that way. And that appearances—"

"Are often wrong," Ariana finished for her. "He didn't kill Vanessa?"

"I wasn't there that night, my lady." Theresa's fingers tightened around Ariana's. "What do you think?"

Their eyes met.

"I *think* and *feel* too many things to recount," Ariana whispered. "Anger, betrayal, hurt, humiliation ..." A small pause.

"Attraction?"

"Yes."

"And fear?"

Ariana blinked. Trenton had asked that very question of her in the maze, and her answer had surprised them both. Regardless, it had been true then; it was true now. She looked Theresa squarely in the eye. "Fear? No. The duke has made no move to hurt me."

"One could argue that marriage to a murderer would incite fear," Theresa pointed out. "And yet you feel none. Does that not tell you something?"

"That I am a fool?"

"That you doubt the duke's guilt."

"I don't know if I doubt his guilt. ... I simply see another side of him."

"There are many sides to a man, just as there are many sides to a story. Each of them is part truth and part illusion. It is up to us to discern the difference."

Ariana absorbed Theresa's words quietly. "You're talking about more than Trenton Kingsley's character now. You're talking about his involvement in Vanessa's death."

"Am I?"

"But I've heard the story a thousand times, Theresa. From Baxter, yes, but also from hushed conversations among the servants, an occasional slip from Baxter's colleagues—"

"And from the duke?" Theresa interrupted.

Ariana's brows rose. "Of course not."

"Hmmm," Theresa murmured thoughtfully. "Since Trenton Kingsley is directly involved in these 'details' you've heard, isn't it sensible that he should be allowed his say?"

"He chose not to say anything. Instead, he made his guilt clear by running away."

"Did he?" Theresa asked wisely. "Was that guilt that compelled him to go? Or was it injustice?"

"I don't know." New tears sprang to Ariana's eyes and trickled down her cheeks. "I'm so confused. Just as I have been ever since the night I met Trenton Kingsley. Please, Theresa, help me."

Theresa gathered Ariana close, stroking her hair with a gentle hand. "As Sir Francis said, 'If a man will begin with certainties, he shall end in doubts; but if he will be content to begin with doubts, he shall end in certainties.' Some things must be left to fate, my lady. And fate presents many questions before she supplies the answers. Your course, as I see it, is clear. You cannot disobey Queen Victoria's mandate, so you must marry Trenton Kingsley. After that, time will clarify your future."

Ariana rested her cheek against Theresa's narrow, capable shoulder, another nagging thought intruding in the wake of conflict and resignation. "The duke said the wedding would be held at Broddington. Yet from what Baxter has told me, Broddington has been deserted since ... *then*."

Theresa nodded. "It has. Other than an occasional visit from the Marquis of Tyreham, the estate has been unoccupied for six years."

Ariana sat up. "The Marquis of Tyreham?"

"Dustin Kingsley. Your *betrothed's* ..."—Theresa used the term gently, yet with enough emphasis to accustom Ariana to the notion—"younger brother."

"I've heard no mention of the marquis." Ariana ignored Theresa's pointed reference, her interest captured by this new and unexpected development.

"Your brother is not in the habit of discussing the Kingsley family, pet," Theresa reminded her. "The marquis is two years his brother's junior, a kind and personable gentleman. You will enjoy his company immensely ... as he will yours."

Ariana opened her mouth to ask Theresa how she knew this, then closed it with a snap. If Theresa stated something as fact, then fact it was.

"What makes the duke believe that hundreds of guests will attend this wedding?" she asked instead. "He is despised by many, feared by most, and shunned by all. Why would anyone wish to appear at this mockery of a ceremony?"

"Many reasons, my lady." Theresa's shrug was matter-of-fact. "Curiosity. Gossip. Human nature is astounding; the idea of resurrecting an old scandal is an enticement few can resist. And then, of course, there are those who will attend for the *right* reasons. Respect for the Kingsley name. Regard for the late duke. Faith in the present one."

Theresa's implication sank deeply into Ariana's mind. "*You* believe in him," she said slowly, studying her maid's unreadable expression.

"In this case, what I believe doesn't matter." Theresa lifted a corner of her apron to wipe tears from Ariana's cheeks. "It is what *you* believe that counts. And only time ... and your future husband ... can provide you with the truth. Not I."

Ariana stiffened abruptly. "You'll come with me," she pleaded, desperation in her voice. "You won't leave me."

Theresa's wrinkled face creased into a smile. "Have I ever left you, my lady?"

Ariana shook her head. "But what if the duke refuses to allow it?"

"He has already agreed to my accompanying you to Broddington. My things will be sent along with yours."

Ariana stared. "You've spoken with him about this?"

"Of course I have!" Theresa's reply was brisk. "Just after I took you to your room. How else could I make my plans?"

"What did he say?"

"He said yes."

"No, I mean what *else* did he say?" Ariana pressed.

Theresa folded her hands primly in her lap. "He was pleased I would be accompanying you. He said that it would make your new role less painful to accept."

"Painful?" Ariana's face drained of color. "Theresa, I retract my earlier statement: I *am* afraid."

Now Theresa did look surprised. "He will never raise a hand to you, my lady."

Ariana licked her lips, shaking her head emphatically. "I know that. That's not what I meant. It just occurred to me ... that is, I only just realized ..."

"Ah, your wedding night."

"My wedding night." Ariana repeated the words slowly, stunned by the ambivalent feelings they aroused. She did have *some* idea of what to expect. Along with Winsham's brightly colored gardens, her favorite refuge was the stables. And, having spent half her waking hours among dogs, horses, and chickens, she'd certainly seen animals mate. "Do people follow the same procedure as animals?" she blurted out, then blushed at her own outrageous question.

Theresa didn't flinch. "More or less. With one addition: If they choose, people can mate with their hearts as well as their bodies."

Ariana tried to imagine that sort of intimacy and her flush deepened. Could she actually do *that* with *him?*

Calmly, as if they were discussing the weather, Theresa continued, counting off on her fingers. "We've established the fact that the duke appeals to you. Physically, that is. We've also concluded that he does not intend to hurt you. So what is it you fear?"

"I'm not sure. It's just that I don't know how to ... I've never ..."

"He does and he has."

"I don't doubt it." Ariana shifted uncomfortably. "I really should be repelled by the idea or, at the very least, opposed to it," she reasoned aloud. "Which I am, of course," she was quick to add.

"Of course."

Ariana was too caught up in her worry to pick up on the hint of amusement in Theresa's tone. "But, if I am to be totally honest, I have to admit that I also feel ... well, curious."

"And that surprises you?" Theresa's eyes twinkled. "The duke is a very handsome, compelling man. He is obviously drawn to you as you are to him. The rest will come naturally."

"You make it sound so simple." Ariana sighed. "But what if he really is dangerous?"

"As I've said before, I've never known your instincts to betray you. Heed them well, my lady."

Ariana squeezed her eyes shut, picturing the bitter, enigmatic man who would soon be her husband. "God help me if my instincts are wrong," she whispered.

Baxter tossed off the last of his drink and lowered the empty glass to his desk with a triumphant thud. So Kingsley thought he had won, did he? He would soon learn otherwise.

Reflecting on the countless times in the last fourteen years Trenton Kingsley had bested him, Baxter's mouth twisted sardonically. Their long and disagreeable history had started in 1859, when they were both still in their teens. Baxter's parents had just died, leaving him guardian of his sisters and overseer of Winsham, while Richard Kingsley's deteriorating health had forced Trenton to assume the running of the Kingsley estates and numerous family businesses.

They met in London through a mutual business associate and, though never friends, they had, at first, felt a grudging respect for each other.

The respect had rapidly dissipated.

Their first business clash should have served as an omen to Baxter of what lay ahead, the defeats he would suffer at Kingsley's hands. Outbidding Baxter for a minor ownership stake in Bryant's and May's small manufacturing firm in Tooley Street, Trenton saw his investment multiply tenfold in value when the company, utilizing Kingsley funds, developed an award-winning line of revolutionary safety matches.

Trenton prospered and Baxter seethed.

After that, it seemed their paths crossed constantly; every venture Baxter pursued found Trenton one step ahead, every bloody wager they placed Trenton won, every woman Baxter coveted preferred Trenton's bed.

The bastard's luck never seemed to run out.

Even with Vanessa.

Baxter lowered his head, determined to submerge memories long since buried away. What was done was done. Vanessa was gone, and no amount of vengeance could bring her back. All thanks to Trenton Kingsley. He'd robbed Baxter of everything: his dignity, his money, his sister.

All but Ariana.

And now he thought to strip Baxter of her as well, to emerge the victor once again?

Not this time.

Baxter pressed his clenched fists to the desk, evaluating the implications of the day's startling event. A royal edict commanding Ariana to become the Duchess of Broddington. He still couldn't get over that interesting twist of fate. He had planned to use Ariana's beauty to attract a husband, one whose wealth would be sufficient to recoup his losses. At the same time, he had yearned to punish Kingsley for his final ruinous act: severing Baxter's betrothal to Suzanne Covington and leaving the Caldwells destitute. And here fate had presented Baxter with the perfect opportunity to combine both his fondest wishes into one ultimate revenge.

Ariana might become Trenton's by law, but, ceremony or not, she would always be a Caldwell. Baxter could count on that. Yes, he would have his money ... and Trenton Kingsley would be the one to restore it to him.

A fitting finale for a vehement enmity.

Baxter's thoughts were interrupted by a quiet knock.

"Yes?"

Ariana opened the door and entered. "Baxter ... we need to talk."

A slice of guilt cut through him at the sight of her wet, spiky lashes and flushed cheeks. He forced the feeling away. "Of course, sprite. Come in."

Ariana crossed the room and stood before her brother, raising her chin to see his face, mincing no words. "Tell me again about Vanessa's death."

A dark cloud crossed Baxter's face and, abruptly, he turned away.

"Please, Baxter … I need to know."

"You already know everything," he replied, his head down. "I've recounted that hateful day dozens of times. There is nothing left to say on the subject."

"I'm being forced to marry the man you believe killed our sister!" Ariana burst out. "Of course there is more to say!"

Baxter kept his back to her. "There was no proof of Kingsley's guilt," he said evenly, staring intently at the oriental rug. "Besides, Vanessa's … accident happened six years ago. It has nothing to do with your marriage. You're quite safe, sprite, believe me."

Ariana crushed the folds of her gown between trembling fingers. "Is there truly nothing you can do to prevent this marriage? Or merely nothing you *wish* to do?"

Baxter swerved to face her, his brows arched in surprise. "You've changed, little one. You never used to be so outspoken."

"My future was never at stake."

He nodded. "All right, then. Both. There is truly nothing I can do and also nothing I wish to do. The Queen has always been partial to the Kingsley family. Lord alone knows why."

Ariana drew in a sharp breath. "Her edict is binding. But so is marriage, Baxter. So why is there nothing you wish to do?"

Reaching out, he fingered one of her tousled curls. "You will have everything you could ever want, sprite. Everything I can no longer give you." He saw the look in her eyes and hastily added, "Aside from your romantic notion of love, that is. And as much as you believe otherwise, I hold not a shred of hope that true love actually exists. Therefore, this marriage affords you more than any other I could have arranged."

"And what exactly does it *afford me?*" she demanded in a choked voice. "Our family's most loathsome enemy, possibly a murderer, as my husband?"

Baxter's jaw set. "He won't lay a hand on you. I guarantee it. He wouldn't dare … not after what happened with Vanessa. Remember,

Ariana, all of England knew the questionable circumstances surrounding our sister's death. Rampant whispers circulated throughout the *ton* labeling Kingsley a murderer. A scandal of that magnitude may lie dormant, but it is never truly forgotten. Should Kingsley do *anything* to further defame his character, it would totally decimate his beloved family name… something he would rather die than risk."

Ariana searched his face. "You really believe that, don't you?"

"Yes," he answered without hesitation.

She nodded, resigned and, in some small way, relieved. "Thank you for that. At least I know you would only compromise my happiness for money. Not my life."

"Good Lord, Ariana!" Baxter's fingers bit into her arms, willing her to understand. "What kind of an ogre do you think I am?"

She smiled faintly. "I don't think you're an ogre, Baxter. In fact, perhaps I understand you better than you understand yourself." She extricated herself from his grasp, walking slowly away. "I shall begin plans for my wedding." Closing the door behind her, Ariana leaned back against the wall, loneliness clogging her throat. With a wave of intuition, she wondered where she mattered less: here, or at Broddington.

"A wife? Christ, Trenton, when did this happen?"

Dustin Kingsley bolted to his feet, gaping at his older brother who lounged casually in one of Tyreham's deeply tufted library chairs, a library the two brothers had designed.

Trenton shrugged. "Today."

"Today," Dustin repeated inanely. In a customary gesture of agitation, he smoothed his thumb and forefinger over the tapered curve of his mustache, all the while studying Trenton's face. "All right, Brother. Now tell me the rest of the story."

"The rest of the story?" Trenton's expression was the picture of innocence.

Dustin's midnight-blue eyes narrowed suspiciously. "This is *me* you're talking to, Trent. *No one* knows you better than I. You've stayed away from Sussex for six years. Suddenly, during my last visit to Spraystone, you announced that you would be returning for the sole purpose of severing Baxter Caldwell's betrothal. Which you did. You never mentioned a betrothal of your own. Now, like a bolt from the blue, you're to be wed? Who is she, and why are you marrying her?"

Trenton chuckled, crossing one impeccably tailored leg over the other. "So much for subtlety, I see. Very well." He leaned back, deceptively nonchalant. "Her name is Ariana, and I'm marrying her because she's Baxter Caldwell's little sister."

Dustin's jaw dropped. "Have you lost your bloody mind?"

"Years ago."

"Trent, what the hell are you doing?" Dustin demanded.

"Satisfying a debt to our father."

"By marrying Caldwell's sister? Didn't you learn *anything* from what happened with Vanessa?"

Fury deepened the lines around Trenton's eyes, lines that hadn't been there before Vanessa. "Too much, Dustin. Far too much."

"And yet you're still going through with this." Dustin began to pace, shaking his head. "What makes you think the Caldwells will abide by your plan?"

"Oh, they'll abide by it, all right. Queen Victoria has seen to that."

Dustin came to an abrupt halt. "You'd better explain."

Succinctly and without pause, Trenton relayed the events of the past few days to his brother.

"So you're forcing this young girl to marry you."

"She'll be amply compensated." Hostility glinted in Trenton's eyes. "She'll have everything Vanessa coveted and never managed to acquire: wealth, position, even an exalted title. Remember, I was a mere marquis when Father was alive."

"Are you so certain your future bride craves the same things Vanessa did?"

Trenton's expression softened. "To the contrary. I'm certain Ariana craves far different things than Vanessa did. But she's quite young and has obviously lived a very sheltered life. She has yet to be exposed to the wonders money can buy. She'll change."

Dustin regarded him thoughtfully. "Tell me about her."

"Ariana?" Trenton's mouth curved into a slow smile. "She's a tantalizing little bundle of contradictions: innocent, trusting, idealistic, an inquisitive child, a breathtaking woman." His smile faded. "Loyal to her brother and her family."

"She sounds enchanting," Dustin replied, missing not one iota of his brother's inadvertent response.

"She's a Caldwell."

"Not for long, apparently."

Trenton stood, walking rigidly to gaze out the window. "Her name will change; her blood will not."

"And so you will punish her?" Dustin fished.

"I'm not going to harm her, if that's what you mean."

"Not intentionally, perhaps," Dustin returned slowly, assessing the extent of his brother's feelings. "But your anger is sure to be conveyed to her nonetheless." He came up to lay a hand on Trenton's taut shoulder. "Are you sure this is what you want, Trent?"

"I'm sure it's what I must do."

Dustin fell silent, weighing his next words carefully. "Is this duty alone we're discussing?"

"Duty, yes. And retribution."

"Nothing more?"

Trenton's jaw tightened fractionally. "If you're asking me if I want her, if I'm burning to feel her under me, the answer is yes. Even *I* am not so noble as to marry a woman I didn't crave in my bed."

The passion behind Trenton's admission brought a new concern to Dustin's mind. "Trent ... if she's *that* young ..." He cleared his throat. "How does she feel about this union?"

A wry smile. "The union? Or me?"

"Both."

"She despises the idea of a forced marriage. And me? She loathes me. She's bewildered by me." Something flickered in Trenton's eyes. "She wants me."

Dustin swooped down on his brothers final words. "Are you sure?"

"That she wants me?" Trenton's expression was a picture of smug certainty. "Very sure. Surer even than Ariana herself."

"By any chance ..." Dustin paused, knowing he had to ask. "Does Ariana resemble Vanessa?"

Trenton swung around, his mouth drawn in a tight line of fury. "That has *nothing* to do with my decision."

"You've just given me my answer."

"Leave it, Dustin." Trenton stalked the length of the room to pour himself a brandy. "I'm marrying Ariana. Period." He tossed off his drink, slamming the glass to the table.

"All right," Dustin agreed, astutely recognizing that his remaining questions would have to wait. "What can I do to help?"

Trenton turned his head, his expression softening. "You can make the church arrangements. Then you can help me open up Broddington and ready it for guests."

"And for living quarters?"

Trenton stared thoughtfully at the carpet. "Yes," he said at length. "There's nothing at Spraystone for a young woman. Ariana will want to experience parties, theatre—all the finery of her new role as a duchess." He nodded, decisive and resigned all at once. "Yes, Dustin, for the time being, my bride and I will be staying at Broddington."

"Very well." Dustin hid his surprise, remembering the Trenton who had vowed never to return to Sussex. "I'll begin making arrangements at once."

"And Dustin?" Trenton regarded his brother solemnly. "I have one other favor to ask of you: Will you stand up for me as my groomsman?"

Dustin grinned. "Need you ask?" Growing serious, he clasped Trenton's shoulders in his hands, looking him squarely in the eye, reinforcing the gravity of the unalterable step Trenton was about to take. "Don't sacrifice any more than has already been lost, Trent," he advised quietly. "The past cannot be undone. And marriage is forever."

"No, Dustin." Haunted memories cloaked Trenton's eyes, twisted his features into a mask of remembered pain and hatred. "What is forever is death."

CHAPTER 6

The Church was nearly invisible, lost on the busy Sussex street amid throngs of people and a line of traveling chariots.

Ariana stared out the carriage window in stunned disbelief. Apparently Theresa had been right: The Duke of Broddington's black reputation had done nothing to prevent a record number of guests from attending today's ceremony.

Ariana's stomach lurched.

Nervously, she sat back against the cushions, praying for God to grant her the courage to proceed with the wedding.

"Are you all right, sprite?" Baxter leaned forward to squeeze Ariana's hand.

"I'm terrified," she confessed in a whisper. "Good Lord, Baxter, there must be five hundred people in that church."

"And that surprises you?" he asked dryly, glancing out the window. "This is, after all, quite an event. Did you truly think anyone would turn down the opportunity to see you wed the infamous Duke of Broddington?"

Something in her brother's tone made Ariana bristle, and, unconsciously, she tugged her hand free of his. Theresa's words sprang swiftly to mind, taking on new meaning in light of the enormous crowd.

Human nature is astounding; the idea of resurrecting an old scandal is an enticement few can resist.

"Are all these guests here to enjoy the ceremony? Or to ogle the woman who is marrying a potential murderer?" Ariana's own cynicism surprised her.

Apparently it didn't surprise Baxter, for he shrugged carelessly. "Either way, enjoy the attention, little one. You can be a heart-stopping spectacle and a martyr all at once."

Fortunately, their carriage came to a halt at that moment, sparing Ariana the indignity of a retort. But, as an attentive footman swung open the carriage door to assist the bride to the street, Ariana came to a profound, crystal-clear realization.

Perhaps she was walking headlong into a raging, unknown tempest, but she had no reason to feel tied to her life at Winsham. In fact, other than her romantic dreams, she was sacrificing nothing at all.

It was time to leave her childhood behind.

Taking a deep breath, she stepped down, raising her head to face the magnificent columns of the church, following the proud spires to their peaks. With forced deliberation, she looked around her, seeking the tranquilizing effect nature always offered her. She drank in the unfailing beauty of velvet green trees and brightly colored flowers, filling her lungs with the fragrant August air, infusing her senses with joy and her soul with faith.

"Are you ready, sprite?" Baxter alit, taking her arm.

Ariana opened her mouth to reply when, from her peripheral vision, she spied a sudden flash of white winging through the air. Searching intently, she found her mark, sucking in her breath at the instantly recognized, magnificent spectacle. Snowy feathers descended, graceful wings fanned slowly shut, until the glorious owl lit on a thick tree branch and was still.

His penetrating topaz gaze swept the street until it captured hers.

For an endless minute time remained suspended, the heart-shaped face staring solemnly, unblinking, into Ariana's eyes, emanating power and strength and certainty.

Conveying all to her.

This done, instinct propelled him onward. He raised his head, emitted a loud cry, and, spreading his great white wings, disappeared into the morning sky.

"Ariana?" Baxter's concerned voice seemed to come from far away. "You're not going to swoon on me, are you?"

"What?" Ariana turned blankly in her brother's direction, still seeing the splendid owl. She didn't doubt for a moment that he was just what he seemed to be: her wondrous symbol of hope.

"You're white as a sheet." Baxter gripped her wrists. "Are you going to faint?"

"No ... of course not." Ariana shook her head, returning to the reality of the moment. With a hand that trembled slightly, she smoothed the silk taffeta of her flowing ivory gown, shaking out the lace tiers that draped to her feet. She glanced briefly into the now-deserted skies, then raised her face to Baxter's. "I'm ready."

He smiled, reaching down to drape the veil over her face, careful not to disturb the garland of white roses and orange blossoms that adorned Ariana's upswept auburn tresses. "You look beautiful, sprite. You make me very proud."

She smiled faintly. "Let's make our entrance before Lady Pendlington's neck snaps off from too much craning," she suggested lightly, noting the expectant faces turned in their direction.

Baxter looked thoroughly relieved. "As the bride wishes." He offered her his arm.

The strains of Mendelssohn's *Wedding March* grew louder as the bride and her brother climbed the church steps. Almost in unison, the rows of guests moved forward in their seats to watch the drama of the decade unfold: to witness Ariana Caldwell wed the man who reputedly caused the death of her majestic and treasured sister, Vanessa.

Walking slowly through the doors and down the aisle, Ariana could feel their scrutiny, read their expressions. And the fact that a roomful of people thrived on cruelty and gossip both appalled and sickened her.

Fixing her gaze on the altar, she found she wasn't alone m her sentiments.

Trenton Kingsley's gaze locked with hers, delved deep inside her. On some level, Ariana was aware of the total effect wrought by his massive, intimidating presence: the way his dark frock coat hugged his broad shoulders, how his doeskin trousers outlined the powerful muscles of his thighs.

But all she could think about, focus on, was the potency of his fiery cobalt stare, which burned with a cynical force that defied her to turn away, dared anyone to question his motives, mocked the insipid shallowness of their guests.

There it was again. Ariana blinked as she caught a glimmer of that same emotion she'd seen in his eyes twice before: be it gentleness or vulnerability or compassion. She hadn't imagined it; it was real. She watched him shift a bit, glance briefly about the room, then look back at her, the feral ruthlessness back in place.

He was expecting her hostility.

The perception struck Ariana with the same intensity as her earlier realization about her life at Winsham. Trenton Kingsley knew what everyone believed him to be and was waiting for Ariana to reinforce their conviction by being every bit the reluctant, terrified bride society anticipated.

There are many sides to a man. Theresa's voice sounded in Ariana's memory. *Each of them is part truth and part illusion. It is up to us to discern the difference.*

Straightening her shoulders, Ariana swallowed her trepidation and let instinct guide her past illusion to truth. Gracefully she glided toward the man Theresa had called her future, looking every bit the radiant bride.

Seeing the unwilling relief on Trenton's face as he recognized the subtle change in her manner, as well as its significance, Ariana felt a wave of compassion sweep through her. He had endured total ostracism these past years. Despite his rebellious behavior and impenetrable veneer, he had been affected by the indignity of public rejection. For a proud man like Trenton, the flagrant scorn of his bride on their wedding day would be the supreme humiliation.

Accordingly, Ariana tilted her head back, held her chin high, and vowed to let the guests—and the world—think what they would. She would provide no fuel for their vicious fire.

"Your bride is breathtaking," Dustin Kingsley murmured beside his brother's ear.

Trenton nodded slowly, his throat clogged with some intangible emotion. "Yes. She is." He dragged his eyes from Ariana, strangely moved and equally unwilling to display it. His gaze settled instead on Baxter, and all tenderness fled. Without hesitation, Trenton walked forward, ready to claim his bride. Much to the disappointment of the crowd, Baxter offered no resistance, relinquishing Ariana's arm and stepping away.

Profoundly aware of Trenton's presence beside her, Ariana's insides clenched with nerves. Battling for control, she stared straight ahead and was greeted with a broad, understanding grin. Shyly, she smiled back, knowing immediately that this must be Trenton's brother, Dustin. The two men were of the identical height and build, possessing the same hard good looks and dark coloring. Only the marquis's near-black midnight eyes and dashing mustache set him apart—that and the genuine warmth on his face as he acknowledged his brother's soon-to-be wife.

She felt Trenton's hand close around her arm and she turned to face him, willing a drop of the gentle warmth she'd spied earlier back into his blazing eyes. She saw none.

The room grew hushed as the ceremony began. Ariana remained poised, repeating the customary phrases without hesitation ... until the bishop turned to her and spoke the words *until death do you part.* A suffocating stillness ensued, followed by a tingle of apprehension that swelled to fill the room. A pulse beat later Ariana continued, reciting the words dutifully, meeting Trenton's gaze squarely and without fear.

With a congratulatory lift of his brows Trenton acknowledged Ariana's spunk, his eyes holding her captive as he repeated the identical pledge. Seconds later, he slid the heavy gold wedding band on her finger. Then, raising her veil, he brushed her cold lips lightly with his firm, warm mouth, sealing their joining in the eyes of God and man.

The trip to Broddington was a blur.

A strained silence accompanied them in the coach, Trenton scowling moodily off into space, Ariana anxiously twisting the new, foreign-feeling ring on her finger.

The iron gates were flung open, admitting the bridal procession to some of the most exquisite grounds Ariana had ever seen.

"How lovely!" she exclaimed, the ponderous tension pervading the carriage instantly forgotten as she leaned forward to drink in the vast, rolling hills.

"We have hundreds of acres on the front lawns alone," Trenton supplied, unsurprised that Ariana, like every woman, was impressed with Broddington. He studied his wife's face, taking in the turquoise splendor of her eyes when they were alight with pleasure. Without warning, he found himself wondering if those same eyes would darken with passion in his bed.

Unexpected lust surged through his blood.

Oblivious to the direction Trenton's thoughts had taken, Ariana was half out of her seat, staring delightedly out the carriage window. "Do you have stables?"

Trenton blinked at the naïveté of the question. "What?"

Ariana cast an apologetic look in his direction. "I'm sorry. If you haven't any stables, I'll find animals in the woods."

"Of course we have stables!" he blurted out, totally stupefied. "Years ago Broddington housed dozens of Thoroughbreds for racing. But that was before …" He broke off, his expression closed.

Ariana heard him, but she chose to ignore the implication of his words. It was enough that they were finally managing a civil conversation—an unexpected experience that would surely be shattered were they to discuss the events leading up to Trenton's exile.

"Are all the horses gone, then?" she asked instead.

"Do you ride?"

"Since I could walk."

He studied her glowing face. "I'll arrange to have proper horses delivered immediately."

She smiled, touched by his generosity. "Thank you." Her forefinger traced the outline of one of her gown's lace panels. "And while I'm expressing my gratitude, thank you for allowing Theresa to accompany me to Broddington. She raised me from birth and is more like a family member than a servant."

"I'm not a monster, Ariana." He spoke her name for the first time, and the deep-timbred syllables sounded strangely exhilarating to her ears. "You're my wife. Anything you ask for … anything within reason … is yours." He leaned forward, his hands gripping his knees. "And while we're exchanging thank yous, I owe you one as well. I appreciate your composure during the wedding ceremony. It prevented an unthinkable amount of ugly gossip from spreading."

Ariana nodded slowly. A thousand questions bubbled up inside her, but she doggedly fought the impulse to blurt them out. She would know when the time was right to ask each one.

The carriage rolled onward until the enormous Broddington manor came into view.

Again, Trenton watched Ariana's face, curious about her reaction to the formidable dwelling. He saw her eyes widen with surprise just before she began plucking at the satin edging of her gown.

"Will there be many people living here?" she asked in an odd tone.

Trenton frowned. "No. At least not once the reception has ended. There will be a small staff of servants, most of whom I've borrowed from my other estates, your Theresa, and us. Why?" He was annoyed at this unplanned development. He hadn't anticipated that Ariana would want a houseful of servants to direct. Perhaps he should have, though. Given her isolation at Winsham, she had doubtlessly envisioned her life as a duchess to include the running of a huge staff.

Ariana sagged with relief, shrugging her slim shoulders in apology. "It's just that I'm dreadfully unprepared to answer to anyone, let alone have dozens of people answer to me. At Winsham it was only Baxter, Theresa, myself, and a few other servants. Baxter was rarely home and I spent most of my time in the stables or the gardens. I'm much more accustomed to a simple life … one I can hardly expect to continue living as your duchess."

"I see." For the life of him, Trenton couldn't think of another thing to say to her astonishing admission.

"I will try to adapt," she continued, taking his silence to mean displeasure. "But remember, this marriage was your choice, not mine."

Trenton's lips twitched. "I remember."

The conversation was cut short as the carriage pulled up to the entranceway door and halted.

Unorthodox to the last, Trenton waved away the footman and descended first, extending a hand to help his wife alight.

Ariana placed her fingers in his.

Even the fine material of her glove could not deflect the spark of electricity that passed between them, blazing through his blood to hers like wildfire. Stunned, Ariana froze in place, staring at their joined hands. Slowly, she turned her face to his.

Trenton gave her a slow, dark smile. "Ah, misty angel, I'm beginning to share your preference for an uncluttered household. Already I'm eager for the privacy you were just describing." He brought her gloved hand to his lips, turning it over to kiss her trembling palm. "There are some aspects to this marriage that I promise you will find infinitely more pleasurable than you expect." He kissed her fingertips, one by one. "Infinitely."

He released her hand and caught her by the waist, lining her from the carriage and lowering her to the ground. For the briefest of instants he pressed her against him, his eyes twinkling wickedly at the soft flush that inadvertently stained her cheeks. "Your innocence is bewitching," he murmured. *"You* are bewitching."

"The guests are arriving," she whispered inanely.

He chuckled. "Very well. We'll act the dutiful bride and groom. But later, when I have you to myself, we are going to stoke the flames of this fire that rages between us." He brushed her chin with his thumb. "Tonight, misty angel."

Totally dazed by the exchange and drowning in a deluge of unfamiliar sensations, it took Ariana a few minutes to realize that Trenton was guiding her, not into the house as she had expected, but along the path that led around Broddington's magnificent manor.

"Where are we going?" she asked faintly.

"To receive our guests."

Ariana gave him a quizzical look. "But …" Her question ended in a soft gasp as she beheld the magical picture that unfolded before her. The conservatory doors were flung open, and countless servants were scurrying about, carrying trays of everything from cold lobster salad, roast duck, and meat pies to wine jelly, lemon cake, and coffee cream, and placing them on dozens of miniature tables scattered across the grounds as far as Ariana could see.

"Does it please you?" Trenton asked brusquely.

Ariana turned enchanted eyes to his. "It's beautiful! How did you ever manage to do all this?"

He fought the pleasure her joy evoked. "I didn't. Dustin arranged it all, and the servants did the rest."

She gave him a radiant smile. "Thank you."

Another unwilling tug at his heart. "You're welcome."

"Broddington is massive!" Ariana peeked into the conservatory. "Oh ... how lovely! Geraniums, heliotrope, violets, poppies, honeysuckle ..." She paused to catch her breath. "Goldenrod, heather, bluebells ..."

"You know the names of all those flowers?" Trenton asked in amazement.

"Of course! I told you, I've spent most of my time in Winsham's gardens and stables. I adore the blossoms that thrive in summer, and the animals that emerge from their winter's sleep. And—"

"White owls?" Trenton teased.

Ariana flushed. "You remember."

"I remember." He grinned as she flitted around, pausing to sniff a bud here and there. "Your ankle appears to have fully recovered."

Ariana laughed. "It has." Curiously, she peaked through the inner conservatory door. "Where does this lead?"

"Into the drawing room. It's designed so you can look out into the conservatory and enjoy its beauty, winter or summer. Beyond the drawing room is the library, and beyond that, the chapel."

"Why wasn't our wedding ceremony held in the Broddington chapel, then?"

"We designed it to seat two hundred people. There were over six hundred guests at the church today."

"*We?*" She latched onto that reference at once, her eyes widening with interest. "Did *you* assist the architect in designing this house?"

Trenton glanced about him, assessing the room with great pride. He'd forgotten just how magnificent Broddington was. "I am the architect," he responded simply. "Or, rather, one of them. My father is primarily responsible for the manor's exquisite detail. Dustin and I merely assisted him."

"You're an architect." She looked both amazed and impressed. "But I thought you were a duke."

A rumble of laughter exploded from Trenton's chest. "I am both, misty angel. Believe it or not, a man can be many things."

"You're superbly talented."

"My father was a genius." The words were out before Trenton realized he'd spoken them.

Ariana reacted to the raw emotion in his voice. "I'm sure he was," she said carefully. Again, the urge to continue, to ask him all about his father, was nearly overpowering. She knew only that Richard Kingsley had died shortly after Vanessa, presumably from the shock of his son's reprehensible behavior. And Trenton's strangled tone and pained expression certainly concurred.

Ariana's instincts did not.

"Our guests will doubtlessly wonder where we are," she said, touching his arm.

Instantly, Trenton's mask was back in place. "Doubtlessly," he agreed. As if on cue, the strings began to play, calling for the dancing to commence. Trenton offered Ariana his arm. "Come. I believe the first dance customarily belongs to the bride and groom."

Ariana slid her fingers through his arm.

"Brides are supposedly too nervous to eat."

Dustin's teasing voice interrupted Ariana's last bite of lemon cake.

She laughed. "You're right. And I'll certainly pay with a terribly upset stomach. But you see"—she leaned conspiratorially forward—"when I get nervous, I eat huge quantities of sweets."

Dustin caught her elbow as she weaved a bit on her feet. "I see. And do you also drink huge quantities?"

"What?"

"How much punch have you had?"

She considered the question. "I'm not certain. Perhaps four or five glasses. It's really quite tasty for fruit juice."

Dustin looked utterly incredulous. "Fruit juice? Sweetheart, there are countless pints of French brandy and white wine in that 'fruit juice.'"

"There are?" Ariana frowned. "Does this mean I'm foxed?"

"Hopelessly."

She laughed. "And *you're* the duke's brother."

"That I am." He gave a formal bow. "And *you're* the duke's wife," he said with a twinkle.

Ariana chewed her lip, glancing around to make certain they were alone. "Can you keep a secret?" she whispered at last.

"I think so."

She leaned closer. "I have no idea how to be a wife."

Dustin couldn't help himself; he burst out laughing. "Ariana, I think you are going to be a very quick learner." He took her elbow. "Are you up for a dance?"

She nodded, her face flushed from wine and excitement. "But only if you lead … Dustin. May I call you Dustin?"

"Since we are now effectively brother and sister, I believe it is mandatory," he replied, leading her into a waltz.

"I've never drunk wine or brandy before, but I do enjoy them," she confessed.

"I can tell." Dustin studied her delicate features objectively. The coloring, the inherent feminine charm: Yes, he could see Vanessa. But there was so much more here, not only beauty, but depth and character.

And passion.

Dustin felt a twinge of envy for the treasures Trenton had yet to discover.

"May I borrow my bride, Dustin?" Trenton tapped his brother on the shoulder.

Dustin blinked, surprised at the anger in Trenton's tone. The last time he had seen his brother he was dancing with the Dowager Duchess of Cantington, in seemingly high spirits. "Of course." Dustin stepped away, feeling the presence of the dark emotion that drove Trenton relentlessly, was always buried just beneath the surface. It emanated now like an ominous thunderstorm.

Ariana felt it too, and was suddenly and entirely sober. "Will you be staying at Broddington?" she asked Dustin, anxiety clouding her lovely face.

He was about to say no, when he met the pleading look in her eyes. He glanced back at Trenton, saw the antagonism, and knew he couldn't leave Ariana alone. Not with his brother in this foul, unpredictable humor.

"For a day or two," he compromised, feeling Trenton bristle. "Then I must get back to Tyreham."

Relief swept Ariana's fragile features. "Wonderful! Then we'll have a chance to get to know each other."

"Tomorrow," Trenton interrupted. He took Ariana's arm. "It's time for us to take our leave."

All the color drained from her face. "But the guests are still here."

"The guests will be here for hours. It's perfectly acceptable for us to retire." He drew her to his side. "Come. Let's say our good-byes."

Ariana cast a final glance at Dustin. She felt like a small lamb being led to slaughter, while being torn from an old friend rather than a new acquaintance.

Dustin interceded to kiss Ariana's cheek. "I'll see you at breakfast," he promised. Turning to his brother, he extended his hand. "Congratulations, Trent. Be happy." He leaned closer, murmuring, "And for God's sake, be gentle."

The tightening of Trenton's jaw indicated that he had heard.

Whether he would comply was another thing entirely.

CHAPTER 7

"Theresa, I think I'd like to try wearing my hair in a different style."

The silver-handled brush paused for a moment, then continued its downward journey through Ariana's glowing auburn waves. "If you wish, my lady." Theresa regarded Ariana calmly in the dressing-room mirror. "We'll experiment tomorrow."

Ariana whirled around, gazing up at Theresa with frightened eyes. "No. Why don't we begin tonight?"

Theresa patted her cheek gently. "I don't suppose your new husband would appreciate being kept waiting for hours while we dress your hair."

Ariana swallowed. "I suppose not."

Laying down the brush, Theresa took Ariana's hands and eased her to her feet, inspecting her like a mother hen would its chick. She smiled at the youthful picture her mistress made. In her pristine white cotton nightdress with the frilly trimmings down the front and at the neck and sleeves, with her turquoise eyes wide as saucers, she looked more like a child about to be tucked into bed than a bride awaiting her husband on their wedding night.

Ariana ran her tongue over dry lips. "Will I do?" she whispered.

Theresa clasped Ariana's cold fingers in hers. "To quote Sir Francis, 'Virtue is like a rich stone, best plain set.' You are beautiful, both inside and out. You are also nervous, which is perfectly natural. But all will be well; I promise you." She gave Ariana a slow, infinitely knowing nod. "Yes, all will be as it should."

Ariana let the reassuring prediction soak in like warm honey. Then, hesitantly, she peeked around to the bedchamber beyond. "He was so angry," she murmured, remembering Trenton's earlier behavior.

"Anger is easier to admit than many of the emotions it conceals."

"There is more to him than he allows the world to see," Ariana concurred instantly. Her expression unclouded, her small chin set. "I just *know* it."

"Then follow your instincts, pet. And leave any foolish notions behind."

Ariana pondered the advice, and slowly her anxiety began to wane. "You're right." Impulsively, she hugged Theresa. "Thank you, my dear, dear friend."

"Go," Theresa ordered, her voice choked. She kissed Ariana's brow and shooed her off. "The duke is on his way."

With a determined expression, Ariana stood tall and marched through the connecting door.

She had unpacked her things earlier that night, so it was not the first time she'd been in her new bedroom. Nevertheless, its enormous size and austere presence still unnerved her. Aside from a low wooden table and two straight-backed chairs clustered around the far wall housing the marble fireplace, the room was barren, almost completely devoid of furniture. The polished wooden floors stretched endlessly beneath a towering domed ceiling, with nothing below save a china basin and pitcher, a tiny nightstand …

And, in the dead center of the room, a massive four-poster bed.

Tentatively, Ariana walked over, brushing her fingers across the soft coverlet and cool linen. She noted that the bed had been turned down in preparation for sleep … or whatever preceded sleep.

Ariana tried to imagine lying here with Trenton Kingsley. Her stomach lurched, and turning away, she wrapped her arms about herself for reassurance. It was probably best to keep her mind occupied with other things. She strolled about the room, noting its magnificent elegance and symmetry. The great sash windows were wide and multipaned to allow the maximum amount of daylight in; the walls were intricately tiled … yet oddly and utterly bare of paintings or personal touches of any kind.

Contemplating that unusual fact, Ariana's eyes drifted to the great gilded lighting fixture suspended from the ceiling, illuminating … the bed.

She gulped and looked away. Was it just her nerves creating an illusion or had the bed really been designed as the focal point of the room?

The click of the door latch shattered her thoughts, and she whirled about, her heart thudding in her chest.

Trenton lounged formidably against the closed door, watching her with predatory intensity. In his black dressing robe he loomed, an ominous shadow in the dimly lit room, his shoulders massive, his features set in harsh, unfathomable lines.

Ariana felt a chill go up her spine as his cobalt stare bore through her, then raked her slowly from head to toe. He spoke not a word but began moving purposefully toward her.

"Would you care for a drink, Your Grace?" Totally unprepared for the impact of having a man … especially *this* man … in her bedchamber, Ariana blurted out the first thing that came to mind. Immediately, she wanted to kick herself for sounding such a ninny.

Trenton came to an abrupt halt, his brows drawing together in a scowl that displayed neither mockery nor amusement but annoyance. "I'm not thirsty. And my name is not 'Your Grace.'"

Ariana curled her fingers tightly into her palms to stop their trembling. "I'm sorry," she faltered. "I thought 'Your Grace' was the proper form of address for a duke."

"It is." His enigmatic gaze flickered briefly to her clenched fists. Then, wordlessly, he closed the distance to where she stood, lifting her chin with a strangely gentle forefinger. His scowl had vanished, in its place a look of tender understanding. "You're shaking."

"I'm cold."

"Broddington is well heated. Seldom in August do we need a fire for additional warmth." He glanced toward the unkindled marble fireplace. "Would you like me to light one?"

"No," she whispered, willing her knees to stop knocking. "I just …"

"Frightened, misty angel?" It was no taunt, but a question, uttered with the same sensitive insight he'd shown in the maze.

And suddenly her answer was the same one she had given him then.

"No." Ariana shook her head slowly from side to side.

"Good. Because there is nothing here for you to fear. Nothing." Trenton stroked her cheek, slid his warm, strong hand beneath her heavy auburn mane to caress her nape.

Ariana's breath came a bit faster, and she stared up at him, wide-eyed.

"You're beautiful," he murmured, running the knuckles of his other hand along the slender column of her neck, down to the lacy yoke of her gown. His eyes followed the path his hand had taken, lingering on the spot where the curve of her breasts disappeared beneath the thin cotton material. "God, I can hardly wait to see how beautiful."

Ariana knew what was going to happen the instant she felt his hand tighten around her nape, drawing her forward. She was astonished to find herself leaning toward him, raising up on her toes and lifting her face to meet his descending mouth.

"That's it, sweetheart," he muttered thickly. "Let the fire that burns between us take over."

Ariana's eyes slid shut, her emotions suspended, waiting, her intuition alerting her to the fact that this moment would forever divide her life into before and after.

Their lips touched, brushed, touched again. And then Trenton's mouth opened over hers in a soul-shattering kiss that dragged the breath from her lungs … and gave it back again, consuming her and pervading her all at once.

How wonderful, her dazed mind proclaimed. *How incredibly wonderful.*

With a soft, dreamy sigh Ariana gave herself up to the rapturous swirling feelings. She moved closer to her husband, gliding her hands up the elegant silk of his robe, resting them lightly over his rapidly escalating heartbeat.

Trenton responded instantly, leading Ariana into a marvelous new world of sensual bliss dictated by the magic of his kiss. He molded her lips possessively beneath his, fitting and shaping them as perfectly as two interlocking pieces of a puzzle, his fists clenching in her hair.

Hopelessly immersed in the kiss, Ariana was floating away on a silver-tipped cloud, oblivious to everything but sensation. She jerked back to reality, tensing with surprise when Trenton's tongue glided across her lips, seeking entry.

"Y-Your Grace …" she began.

"Shhh …" As if sensing her shock Trenton paused, soothing her with lazy brushes of his fingertips up and down her back, waiting until she relaxed in his arms once more. Then, with an almost imperceptible motion, he eased her closer, bringing her up against the hard wall of his chest.

Ariana gasped aloud. Even through the thin fabric of her night-dress, the contact was electrifying, wildly erotic, shaking her down to her toes. She gripped the open edges of his robe, her breath unraveling on a soft exclamation of physical awakening.

Trenton captured the sound, tangling his hands in her hair and easing his tongue into the warm, honeyed recesses of her mouth.

Ariana's knees nearly gave way beneath her. Never had she imag-ined a man penetrating a woman in this manner … nor that it could feel so incredibly good. For a time she remained passive, letting him teach her how it was done, glorying in each sensual caress, opening her mouth eagerly to receive the suggestive invasion of his tongue.

Then, with artless curiosity and grace, she touched her tongue to his, fencing lightly as he had with her.

Trenton made a harsh sound deep in his throat, his body jolting with shock and desire. He tore his mouth from hers, his breath coming in harsh pants, and stared down in amazement.

"Did I do something wrong?" Ariana whispered, seeing his intense expression.

"No, my little innocent, you did nothing wrong." Trenton sounded as if he'd been running a great distance. "I just never expected such passion … not from you, or myself."

A hint of a blush stained Ariana's cheeks, and she attempted to free herself from his grasp. "I don't know what you expected, but apparently I've disappointed you."

Trenton's arms tightened like steel bands. "To the contrary, my extraordinary bride, you've exceeded my wildest fantasies." His lips curved slightly. "And believe me, I've had many about this night."

Ariana ceased her struggles. "Oh." She gave him a quizzical look. "That's good then, isn't it?"

He chuckled. "Very good." He bent to press his lips to the pulse beating erratically at her neck. "You smell like flowers."

"Which ones?" she answered weakly, her head reeling. "There are hundreds of different varieties of—"

"Sweet ones," he interjected, taking light, nipping sips of her skin until he reached the delicate curve of her jawbone. "Ones that are new, untouched." He grazed the soft skin of her cheek. "With buds just waiting to be picked." He kissed her chin, her nose, the corners of her mouth. "Flowers that are ready to open to the sun, to be bathed in its fire, to drown in its heat." He buried his lips in hers, and she relented in a rush, melting into a boneless puddle of sensation. She clutched his arms for support, drowning in the inferno of their kiss.

"Put your arms around me," he commanded against her mouth, urging her hands higher. "Hold me."

Ariana obeyed without question, reveling in Trenton's low groan of pleasure.

He molded her body to his, hungry and insistent, forcing her to know her effect on him, every hardened contour, every throbbing inch. And while moments before it would have frightened her, Ariana felt an answering leap inside her, an inner voice that, despite her innocence, knew just what to do.

She pressed closer, moving experimentally against her husband, and was rewarded by the violent shudder that wracked his massive frame.

Trenton lifted her from the floor and crushed her in his arms. "Say my name," he ordered.

Ariana barely heard him.

"Say it, Ariana." He tore his mouth from hers. "My *given* name. Not 'Your Grace' … or any other form of ducal address. I want to hear my name from your lips."

She opened her eyes and stared into his, feeling lost and yet somehow not lost at all, knowing what Trenton needed … even knowing why.

"Trenton," she whispered.

"Again."

"Trenton."

Something profound and beautiful flashed in his eyes at her response. "Come to bed with me," he said hoarsely.

Whether it was a request or a command, Ariana didn't care. The answer was the same: "Yes."

He swept her into his arms, reaching the bed in two strides and lowering them both to the soft mattress.

"Misty angel," he rasped, his voice harsh with need, strained with the discipline of holding back, "I want you … God, how I want you." He buried his face in Ariana's hair, his hands slowly exploring the soft contours of her body through the thin nightdress.

Explosions of pure sensation seized her ... raw, dazzling, galvanized sensation: the exquisite softness of the bed beneath her, Trenton's warm mouth and hands burning through her skin, his words of desire reverberating in her ears. No one had ever needed her like this, not ever. The reality was exhilarating.

But it wasn't enough.

Ariana squirmed, her body desperate for more, but of what, she had no idea.

Trenton did.

Slowly, gently, he reached up to unbutton her gown, lingering over each button as if to give her time to adjust to the inevitability of what was to be. Ariana lay quiet, her eyes wide open now and glued to his.

"I won't hurt you," he promised, smoothing his thumb over the bare skin of her collarbone. "Don't be afraid."

"I'm not," she breathed back, her chest rising and falling with anticipation and ... yes, anxiety. "Well, maybe a bit," she clarified, her voice barely audible.

He smiled at her admission, bending to brush his lips across her naked flesh. "Fear is not what I want you to feel," he said huskily, easing the cotton edges of her nightdress farther apart. "What I want you to feel is pleasure." He bent his head to the inner slopes of her breasts, exposed now to his seeking mouth and hands. "Flowers," he murmured, inhaling deeply. "Intoxicating flowers."

"Trenton." Ariana said his name on a sigh, her trembling fingers sliding into his hair, unconsciously holding him to her. Her slivers of fear fragmented, splintered more completely with each brush of his lips, each tug of her gown, until she was nearly frantic to be naked to the total possession of his mouth. "Please ..." she whispered.

He didn't need to ask for what she was so desperately pleading. With one purposeful yank, the gown was down at her waist, trapping her arms within it and baring her breasts to his will. He didn't wait but drew one taut, aching nipple into his mouth, laving it with his tongue, scraping it lightly with his teeth.

Ariana heard herself cry out, but she couldn't have silenced herself if she'd tried. She arched, needing more of Trenton's magnificent caresses, needing them now.

Trenton obliged her by deepening the contact, sliding his arm beneath her back, lifting her to him and enveloping her nipple with a suction so powerful she had to bite her lips to keep from crying out again.

"Am I hurting you?" he demanded hoarsely.

She shook her head wildly. "Don't stop."

"Never, misty angel. Never." He bent to claim her other breast, taking it with the same force as he had the first, evoking the same reaction from his bride. "Do you have any idea what you're doing to me?" he rasped, unwilling, unable to tear his mouth from her sweet, sweet flesh.

"What *I'm* doing to *you?*" she responded weakly. "What about what *you're* doing to *me?*"

Despite his raging, devouring passion, he couldn't help but smile. "What am I doing to you, Ariana? Tell me." He licked teasing circles around one damp, swollen nipple.

"I'm drowning," she moaned softly. "And I don't know how to make it stop."

"I'll make it stop. I promise you: I'll make it stop." He dragged the nightdress down her legs, crumpling it into a discarded ball at the foot of the bed.

Ariana opened her eyes in time to see Trenton's ravenous gaze rake her nakedness, lingering hungrily on the auburn curls between her thighs. Instinctively, she reached down to cover herself.

"Don't." He caught her hand in his, a look of stark longing on his face. "You're exquisite. Don't ever, ever hide yourself from me."

Ariana's protest dissipated, not at his command, but at the genuine emotion on his face, in his voice. She relaxed, silently giving her husband free reign of her body.

Trenton brought her hand to his lips, kissed her fingers. "Close your eyes," he instructed softly. "Close your eyes and feel."

Ariana's eyes drifted shut.

She felt his breath tease her sensitized skin as his warm mouth descended, and her stomach contracted with pleasure.

"Do you like this?" he murmured, pressing hot kisses across her abdomen, cupping her hips and massaging her soft bottom with the tips of his fingers.

"Yes ... oh, yes ..."

"Good. And this?" He knelt between her legs, lifting her foot to his mouth, kissing the smooth arch, the dainty sole, wetting her tingling skin with his tongue, biting lightly to intensify the sensation. Ariana moaned. "Good," he whispered, moving to the curve of her ankle, her calf, the delicate slope of her knee. Ariana shivered uncontrollably, whimpered for him to stop, then sighed with disappointment when he complied.

"Don't ..." she protested in a breathy whisper.

"I won't."

Ariana's body leapt with pleasure as Trenton turned his attentions to her other leg.

"And this? Do you like this, misty angel?" He shifted a bit higher on the bed, his open mouth caressing her warm inner thigh.

The ecstasy was so acute she couldn't answer.

"Good," he replied as if she'd spoken. He eased her legs apart, settled himself between them. Open-mouthed, he teased first one thigh, then the other, moving higher and higher, tasting every satin inch of skin until he'd reached the exquisite joining that defined her womanhood. "And most especially, this," he breathed, burying his mouth in her sweetness.

Suspended on the dazzling threshold of passion, Ariana never uttered the token protest that formed in her mind, for it dispelled into nothing before ever reaching her lips. The rapture erupted inside her in a blaze, every nerve ending screaming with pleasure so acute it was like pain. She tossed her head on the pillow, taut with a need she had never imagined and an urgency she didn't understand. All she knew was that something inside her coiled so tightly, clawed so powerfully, that if it didn't ease she would die. She called out to Trenton, begged him to help her, greedily arching into each wildly erotic plunge of his tongue.

Abruptly, he stopped, and Ariana sobbed a protest, beyond coherent thought, beyond any thought at all.

He loomed over her, his body shuddering more powerfully than hers. "I'm too selfish," he ground out. "I want you with me, not alone." He vaulted from the bed, leaving Ariana dying.

"Trenton … please …" she pleaded, pride insignificant beside the unendurable ache he'd created inside her. "I can't … bear it."

"You don't have to." He tore off his robe, lowering his sweat-drenched body over hers, providing Ariana with her shocking first glimpse of a naked man. "Open to me," he commanded, his face, his tone, harsh with need. "Let me in … deep, deep inside you. Filling all of you with all of me." He lifted her legs, placed them around his waist, leaving her totally open to his penetration. He paused. "Ariana, look at me."

Ariana tore her gaze from his huge, rigid erection, looking up at him with stunned eyes.

"My bewitching misty angel," he murmured, stroking her cheek with a shaking hand. "So dazed, so passionate." He inhaled sharply. "Are you frightened?"

Ariana's body screamed for relief. "Will it hurt?"

He fought the reflexive motion of his hips, already urging him into her. "At first… yes."

Ariana closed her eyes, totally, maddeningly on fire. She felt her husband lock his arms on either side of her head, battling for a control he no longer possessed. And all because he didn't want to cause her pain.

Slowly, Ariana's eyes opened, gazing directly into Trenton's tortured stare. With quivering fingers and innate perception, she reached down and guided him into her, feeling his body jolt with urgency, his life pulse beneath her fingertips. "I'm not frightened," she whispered.

"Ariana …" he choked out, his features contorting with passion. He pressed deeper into her, stretching her delicate flesh with his powerful invasion, filling her so totally she gasped.

Instantly, he stopped. "Does it hurt?"

"Not really," she answered in breathless wonder.

He eased deeper, deeper still, until he reached the thin veil of her maidenhood. His chest heaved with each breath, his hips circled spontaneously, readying her for his possession. Slowly, gently, he slid his hand between them, finding and caressing the delicate, swollen bud of her passion, gliding his thumb over her dewy wetness, repeating the caress again and again until Ariana cried out, arched her back for more.

"Yes, misty angel … like that, yes." He thrust into her, taking her from girlhood to womanhood in one famished, irrevocable stroke.

Slices of pain cut through the cresting pleasure, and Ariana bit back her anguished cry, digging her nails into the sheets and squeezing her eyes shut. She felt torn in two, filled to bursting, raw and aching.

Trenton held himself completely still, balancing his weight on his elbows and staring down into his wife's pale face. Two tears slid out from beneath her long lashes and trickled down her cheeks.

"Don't cry, sweetheart," she heard him murmur. "I won't have to hurt you anymore. I promise." He slid his fingers between them once more, stroking ever so lightly, bending his head to her breast, drawing the still-hard nipple into his mouth and bathing it with his tongue.

Ariana felt the impact of his ardent seduction, her body responding on cue, coming back to life beneath his expert touch. But it was the tender concern in his voice she reveled in, opened her eyes to, gave herself to.

Moving sensuously, eagerly beneath him, she curled her arms around her husband's neck, showing him she wanted him with every fiber of her being.

Trenton gritted his teeth. "Is the pain gone?"

"Nearly." Ariana shifted restlessly into Trenton's caressing hand, the movement driving him deeper inside her, increasing the exquisite friction where his rigid shaft stretched her moist, sensitive softness. Ariana whimpered with pleasure, and Trenton threw back his head, emitting a low sound of pure animal need.

"Damn it, Ariana," he growled, his eyes darkening to nearly black. "I'm not a saint." He was already moving, unable to hold back any longer.

"That feels so good," she whispered, awed and totally oblivious to Trenton's warning.

With a husky laugh, he bent his head, covering her mouth with his, gliding his hands beneath her silky bottom to lift her into his thrusts. "Ah, misty angel, my beautiful, innocent seductress," he murmured, drawing back only to press deep within her once more. "You burn me down to my soul." He bit lightly at her lower lip. "Tell me what you want, sweetheart."

"*You*. I want *you*, Trenton." The frantic feeling had returned, her body wild for release.

He stared down at her for an endless moment, taking in her rosy cheeks and flushed breasts, her shallow breathing, the helpless arching of her body beneath his. A look of raw, naked emotion crossed his face just before he took her mouth purposefully, ready to give her what she so desperately craved.

Penetrating her mouth with his tongue, Trenton drew Ariana's hips up to meet the powerful surge of his. Again and again he repeated the dual motion, possessing her so totally she couldn't breathe, nor did she want to.

The tidal wave of sensation roared to life inside her once more, drowning her in its wake, and Ariana struggled recklessly for that elusive relief that hovered just out of her reach.

"Don't fight, love," Trenton panted into her open mouth. "Let me take you there. Trust me."

Ariana stopped struggling at once.

She felt Trenton's hands tighten on her hips, his thrusts become deeper, more powerful, faster. Ariana's nails scored his back, her cries mounted with each plunging thrust. Fervently, her body tightened around his, beneath his. And all the while he breathed hot, explicit instructions in her ear, guided her from one shimmering plateau to another, until they teetered on the highest precipice, plummeted over its magnificent edge.

The tidal wave burst, sending waves and waves of sheer, dazzling euphoria exploding inside her, cresting and falling with each spasm of her body. She cried out his name, heard his exultant shout of release, and then there was only the wondrous feeling of being crushed in his arms, the very essence of him pouring into her body, melding her climax with his own.

And at last there was peace.

CHAPTER 8

Timeless, languorous minutes elapsed.

Ariana sank into the mattress, blanketed beneath Trenton's solid weight, dimly aware that his sweat-drenched body was still shuddering with powerful aftershocks. Reality held at bay, she drifted, her limbs weak as water, her mind floating on clouds of contentment. So this was the glorious aftermath of passion, this feeling of incomparable oneness. She closed her eyes. *Please,* she prayed silently, *never let it end.*

Long moments later, Trenton raised his head, gazing wearily down at his wife through sober, sated eyes.

Feeling his scrutiny, Ariana forced her lids to open, and what she saw on Trenton's face made her heart leap with happiness. His expression was unguarded, devoid of its customary anger and arrogance, filled with awe ... and a touch of remorse.

Instinctively, Ariana reached up, erasing the lines of concern from his forehead with gentle strokes of her fingertips, gliding her hand through the damp, silky texture of his hair.

Trenton bent to kiss her soft, bruised lips. "Are you all right?"

She nodded, giving him a shy smile. "Yes. A bit crushed, but fine."

Instantly he eased off her, frowning when she flinched at his withdrawal. "You're in pain."

"No," she quickly denied, unwilling to relinquish this wonderful new intimacy that flowed between them. Never having imagined such closeness existed, she longed to preserve the wondrous bond they had just forged with their bodies. "I'm not in pain. Just discomfort."

She wanted to sob out a protest when Trenton rolled to his feet and left her, crossing the room to fill the china basin with cool water. Alone in the massive bed, bereft and unsure, Ariana felt abandoned, insignificant and utterly alone. For the briefest of instants, she seriously considered begging him to come back and hold her, then dismissed the notion as nonsensical. Trenton would think she had lost her mind.

Perhaps she had.

Raising her head, Ariana studied him candidly. He was bronzed, magnificent and as totally oblivious to his own nakedness as he was to the loneliness settling heavily on her heart. She sat up straighter, the sheet falling to her waist, making her abruptly aware of her own nudity.

Hastily, she covered herself, wondering what Trenton expected of her now. She could hardly excuse herself and leave, as this was her bedroom. Should she rise and don her nightgown? Act nonchalant and pretend nothing was changed? Impossible.

She watched him pour water on a clean cloth, chewing her lip nervously and wishing she had thought to ask Theresa questions about what happened *afterward.* Would he speak of what had transpired between them and expect her to do the same? Would he sleep in her bed or retire to his own room now that their marriage had been consummated?

With total candor, Ariana admitted to herself that she longed to have him spend the night beside her. Was that improper? Her lips twitched at the thought. *Everything* she'd felt and done tonight had been improper. Improper and absolutely wonderful.

Hesitantly, she searched for the right words to say, words that would convince him to stay without sounding foolish and pathetic.

Perhaps he read her thoughts, for, to her joyous surprise, he turned and walked back, pausing beside the bed with the cloth in his hand.

Seeing her uncertain expression, Trenton smiled. "Let me ease this ache as well." He sat beside her and peeled away the sheet, gently sliding her thighs apart to cleanse her.

Ariana tensed, instinctively closing her legs and catching his arm. "What are you doing?"

"I told you. I'm alleviating your soreness." He smoothed the rumpled tendrils from her cheeks, giving her a look of pure male satisfaction. "Your modesty is a bit belated, wouldn't you say?" He brought her fingers to his lips, unable to disguise the husky possessiveness in his voice. "Considering that I've just caressed and tasted every inch of you?"

Ariana blushed scarlet and lowered her eyes.

"I won't hurt you," he murmured solemnly. "Let me."

Ariana felt herself responding to Trenton's sensual command with the same innate trust he always seemed to elicit from her. Silently, she relaxed her legs, watching him wash the insides of her thighs ever so gently with the soothing cloth. Her eyes widened at the sight of blood.

"I'll never have to hurt you again," he promised quietly, answering her unspoken question.

She nodded, following the motions of his hands as they came to rest at the junction of her thighs. She sighed with pleasure at the exquisite relief of the cool compress on her raw, sensitive flesh … relief followed by a tingle of pleasure.

"Feel good?"

She started. How could he know?

"Yes." He answered for her, his voice deep, rich.

"Yes," she breathed, blushing anew as she remembered what he had been doing when he had last asked that question of her.

Trenton chuckled, stroking softly. "Such a wonderful embodiment of contradictions, misty angel. So passionate, so very shy."

"As are you."

His dark brows rose in amusement. "Passionate? Or shy?"

"Neither. I mean … well, yes, but what I meant was an embodiment of contradictions."

He continued the sensuous circling of the cloth. "To the contrary, my breathtaking bride, at this moment I am singularly driven in my intent."

"I'm not sure I understand your intent," she whispered, hot pleasure radiating out from his caressing hand.

He stared down at her, his eyes hooded, dark with reawakened passion. Slowly, he tossed the cloth aside, replacing it with his fingers.

Ariana shivered. "Trenton …" The rekindled sensations escalated rapidly inside her, obliterating whatever inhibitions she might have had. Urgently, she reached for her husband, needing to share the exhilaration.

Trenton's gaze followed the path of her slender fingers as they feathered across his shoulders, the muscles of his arms. His features tightened, and a hard tremor shook his body.

"You're unbelievable," he muttered, catching her hand and guiding it to his chest. Slowly, he drew her palm down his torso, gliding her fingers through the pelt of dark hair, along his rib cage, rubbing her palm over his nipples, groaning as they tightened instantly at her touch. "Feel my heartbeat," he rasped, placing her hand flat over the drumming in his chest. "Feel what you do to me."

Ariana was lost in the wonder of his body. The rough textures, the powerful muscles … so this was what made a man different from a woman. Not so different, she amended, feeling his nipples stiffen against her hand.

Warming to her sensual explorations, Ariana squirmed free and came to her knees, her other hand joining its mate. She felt the thundering of Trenton's heart, heard his breath expel in a hiss, just before he seized her hand again and dragged it down to his painfully rigid erection.

"Touch me," he commanded. His grip tightened at her hesitation. "Ariana ... I need to feel your hands on me."

Ariana did as he asked, gliding her fingers over his smooth, throbbing shaft, learning his size, his incredible heat. His chest heaved with the exertion of restraint, his eyes burned cobalt blue. But he made no attempt to move, submitting totally to her innocent exploration.

Ariana stroked her fingers lightly along his length, gliding up to the satin tip. She looked down in stunned wonder when her fingers grew damp, repeating the caress as if to verify his reaction.

"I ... can't ... hold ... back ..." he got out through clenched teeth. "Your hands ..." He shook his head in disbelief.

"I don't want you to hold back," she answered, transfixed by the miracle of life he contained. "*I* didn't."

That did it.

With a growl of severed control, Trenton caught her in his arms and toppled them both to the bed, pressing her thighs apart even as he shook his head in denial. "It's ... too ... soon. Your body ..."

"Wants yours," she confessed breathlessly.

"You're sore ..." He crowded slowly into her, dragging air into his lungs with great, shaky gulps.

"Yes," she agreed, wincing a bit, yet opening herself fully, eagerly, for his possession. "But I don't care."

"God ..." he choked out, burying himself inside her hot, tight wetness.

Ariana wrapped her arms around his neck, lifting her legs to hug his flanks as he had taught her. There was some pain, yes, but it was eclipsed by an almost unbearable surge of passion that seized her, obliterated all else from her mind.

"Tell me if I hurt you," Trenton grated, easing himself from her velvet heat, only to push deeper, farther inside her. Part apology, part command, his words swirled through her mind, impalpably lulling as a soft summer breeze. Entrenched in sensation, Ariana barely managed to nod, silently giving Trenton his answer.

This time was stunningly brief, unchecked and unimaginable. Trenton waited only until he felt his wife dissolve around him in rhythmic spasms of completion, her cries echoing inside his head, before he lunged forward, pouring himself into her in a great pulsing release.

Still trembling with reaction, Ariana knew the moment Trenton's anger returned, a viable entity that crept between their tightly joined bodies. His hands balled into fists, digging into the damp sheets, and he swallowed audibly, fighting some inner demon, struggling to bring himself under control. In one taut, fluid motion, he rolled away from her, lying rigidly on the far side of the bed.

The narrow space dividing their bodies was as vast as an unbridgeable chasm. Ariana closed her eyes, tears burning behind them. This was not what she'd visualized for the aftermath of their passion. This was ... beyond bearing.

She turned onto her side, her back to her husband, seized by a bleakness that was worse than any she'd endured in the past. Until today she'd been a child: alone, perhaps, and insignificant. But tonight she'd shared herself wholly with this stormy, enigmatic man who was now her husband, taken him into her bed and her body.

And, in the process, into her heart.

Had it meant nothing to him? Could he so easily relinquish that miraculous sense of completion, replace it with the frigid distance that now loomed between them?

Ariana felt the bed give as Trenton swung his legs to the floor, preparing to arise.

"Trenton?" Her voice was tentative, her eyes filled with bewildered questions.

Trenton paused, his breathing uneven, his hair and forehead slick with perspiration. He stared down at her, his mouth set in grim lines. "What?"

"You're angry. Why?"

His expression softened at the uncluttered candor of the question, the baffled distress it contained. "I'm not angry, misty angel. At least not at you. Perhaps at myself." Almost against his will, his self-deprecating gaze swept her fragile nakedness. "I should never have allowed this to happen. I lost control."

Ariana knew he referred to far more than their physical union. For some reason, he was angry at himself for the intensity of his own response. And she suspected that his reason involved Vanessa.

An icy chill blanketed her heart. "You have no reason to be angry at yourself," she countered, her tone wooden. Slowly, she raised up on one elbow. "You didn't hurt me. … Nor did you force me."

Trenton made a move toward her, then rapidly checked himself. Rigidly, he turned away and reached for his robe.

"Don't." The word was out before Ariana could call it back.

His head jerked around. "Pardon me?"

The flush on Ariana's cheeks deepened, but she took the plunge nonetheless. "Please don't leave."

"It's late, Ariana. I'm going to my room so you can sleep."

"I know where you're going." She fought the urge to retreat. With forced bravado, she raised her chin a notch. "And I'm asking you to stay."

"Stay." He repeated the word slowly, as if it were foreign to him.

"Yes, stay." She drew a sharp breath. "With me."

Trenton's jaw clenched, and for a moment she thought he meant to relent. He seemed to battle some fierce inner conflict, one that had no answer.

For a long while he said nothing, only stared at her, taking in her innocent sensuality and honest allure. Suddenly he came to his feet. "No." He shook his head emphatically, refusing not only Ariana's request, but all that went with it. Snatching up his robe, he shrugged into it, keeping his gaze averted. "Good night, Ariana."

The door closed behind him.

Ariana stared into the darkness, aching as much for Trenton's sake as she did for her own. Filled with unanswered questions and unexpected emotion, and too drained to cope with either, Ariana wrapped herself in the blankets and, with a weary sigh, surrendered to the relentless pull of slumber.

"Are you awake, my lady?"

Theresa's voice, followed by the sound of running water, coaxed Ariana out of a fitful doze. Blinking, she sat up, momentarily disoriented. One glance at the tangled sheets was enough to remind her where she was.

Nearly bolting from the bed, she collided with Theresa in the center of the room.

"Good, you're awake," Theresa said brightly, adjusting her wilting bun and looking not the least bit ruffled over her mistress's stark, disheveled nudity. She gestured toward a small door. "I've run your bath."

Ariana blushed, glancing discreetly about, wondering where, amid the heap of bedcovers, her nightgown was buried.

"Your gown was soiled. I've taken it to be laundered." On the heels of answering Ariana's unspoken question, Theresa paused. "Are you in discomfort, my lady?"

Ariana averted her eyes. "A bit." She dragged her gaze back to Theresa's. "That *is* normal, isn't it?" she asked anxiously.

"Normal and unavoidable. Hence the bath I've run." She took Ariana's hand. "Come. You'll feel refreshed and renewed in no time."

The luxurious bathroom was grander, more elegant, than any Ariana had ever seen, its marble tub polished and gleaming with alabaster hues identical to those lining the room's exquisitely paneled walls. Sinking gratefully into the scented water, Ariana had to admit that Theresa was right: The bath did indeed feel glorious. She closed her eyes and let the hot water work its magic, seeping into her throbbing muscles and soothing her in places that had never before ached.

Her mind drifted to last night … and the cause of her discomfort. Trenton.

Just thinking about him made her body quicken and her heart skip a beat. Her wedding night had been a turning point in her life, an introduction to physical pleasure and an awakening to her own dormant passion. She was still awed by the power of her husband's lovemaking, the oneness of their union.

And yet, despite the intimacy they'd shared, Ariana was no closer to understanding Trenton than she'd been yesterday … no nearer to discovering the true cause of his anger.

Soaping her hair, she again wondered how she could feel so totally safe with a man who harbored a rage that erupted like lightning, a man with a secret that threatened to destroy all in its path. Recalling Trenton's tenderness, his anguished expression when he'd breached her maidenhead, his gentle ministrations, his tortured ambivalence when he'd left her bed … recalling all that, Ariana had her answer. She might not understand her husband, but, deep inside her, she knew him. Better, perhaps, than he knew himself.

What she didn't know was what he wanted of her. Not in bed, but in fact. Why had he married her? What had happened between him and Vanessa all those years ago? Did he hope to assuage the agony of losing Vanessa by wedding her sister?

Filled with questions, Ariana ducked beneath the water, rinsing the soap from her hair, wishing she could just as easily wash the insecurities from her mind.

"Would you like some help, my lady?" Theresa leaned over to wipe Ariana's eyes with a thick towel.

Ariana smiled at the irony of the question, knowing Theresa too well to assume she'd merely meant help with the bath. "I'm more than a little muddled. Yes, I'd say I need some assistance."

Theresa perched on the side of the tub. "You're feeling better, my lady?" She broke off, her eyes twinkling. "Pardon me ... *Your Grace*," she corrected herself. "Now *that* is going to take some getting used to!"

"For both of us," Ariana agreed quietly.

With a knowing lift of her brows, Theresa continued: "Shall we begin by confronting your questions about last night?"

"You were right," Ariana blurted out. "He didn't hurt me.

"I never believed he would. Nor did you."

Ariana nodded, her gaze fixed on the gentle ripples of the water. "What happened between us ... was so wrenching," she whispered, half to herself.

With gentle understanding, Theresa smoothed a wet strand of hair behind Ariana's ear. "I would imagine so. Your husband is a very intense man."

"Intense. Yes. He is that." Ariana hesitated. "Theresa, do you think he sees Vanessa when he looks at me? Do you think he imagined it was she he was holding last night?"

Theresa stared silently into the soapy tub. "The duke doesn't want you because of Vanessa, pet," she said at last. "He wants you in spite of her."

"What do you mean?" Ariana jumped on the statement at once, sitting bolt upright in the bath. "Why would he want me *in spite* of Vanessa? Is her memory still so very clear and painful? Did he love her so deeply, then? Or is it only the consequences of her death that have haunted him all these years and made him so bitter?" Urgently, she gripped Theresa's arms. "Please, Theresa. I must know."

"You're no longer asking if he killed Vanessa," Theresa noted.

Ariana conceded that point without hesitation. "I don't believe he did. Still, Vanessa *is* dead. And Trenton *was* involved with her when she died. The question is, was it love that drove her to kill herself? Or was it fear?"

Theresa's mouth set in a grim line. "I don't believe love was ever the issue."

"How can you be so sure?"

"You recall your sister. How can you *not* be?"

Ariana fell silent, unable to refute Theresa's candid, dispassionate observation. Yes, she recalled her sister. Vibrantly beautiful, filled with life, captivating and charming. But sensitive, prone to deep and lasting emotion? No. Vanessa had never been that. Still, when she'd met Trenton ...

"Even I remember the way Vanessa spoke of Trenton." Ariana voiced her thoughts aloud. "The things she said ..."

"And what did she say?"

Ariana wet her lips, snatches of memories coming to mind. "How handsome he was, how powerful, how intriguing. What a respected family he came from. How different he was from her other suitors ..."

"And those revelations led you to believe she was in love with him?" Theresa asked dryly.

"Not love, perhaps," Ariana conceded, trying to reconcile her childhood memories of Vanessa with an adult realization of what her flamboyant sister had truly been. Suitors had swarmed to Vanessa. ... and been treated with careless indifference. All but Trenton. "Whether it was love or fascination, she cared for him," Ariana concluded.

"At best."

Something about Theresa's tone gave her pause. "You think she was toying with him?"

"Oh no. Vanessa took the duke quite seriously."

"And he?"

"He took her seriously as well." Theresa caught Ariana's chin, lifting it in time to see the hurt in her eyes. "That disturbs you."

Ariana's lips trembled. "I'd be lying if I said otherwise. However, it does clarify many things."

"Such as?"

"Such as the passion that drives Trenton to me and then away. Such as the war he is constantly battling within himself, the scars he carries and is unable to shed. Such as the real reason he went to such lengths to make me his wife." A tear slid down Ariana's cheek. "I can't be Vanessa," she whispered.

Slowly, Theresa shook her head, her eyes filling with undiscernible emotion. "No, you cannot be. Nor should you try."

Ariana was about to respond when suddenly another possibility struck her. "Theresa," she said, paling a bit as she searched the older woman's face, "you said that love was never an issue. Does that mean that Vanessa feared Trenton?"

Theresa took both of Ariana's hands firmly in her own. "Listen to me, pet ... and hear me well. Fear had as little to do with the events of the past as did love." She inhaled slowly, seeking the words that would ease Ariana's anguish. "I was not your sister's confidante, nor was I with her the night she died. All I know is what I remember ... and what my insight reveals. I can't give you the answers you seek, for they're not mine to give. But they are within your grasp, if you have the courage and faith to reach for them."

Before Ariana had digested her words, Theresa came to her feet, fetching a thick towel and holding it out to her mistress. "It's late. Your husband has been up and about for hours. Let's ready you for breakfast."

Theresa's announcement conjured up another thought, and, wistfully, Ariana stepped from the tub, wondering why Trenton had been so eager to leave her bed. She would have enjoyed sleeping beside him, awakening in his arms, beginning the new day with the same wondrous sensations he had taught her last night....

She blushed, appalled at her own wanton thoughts.

"... so I assumed this morning you'd prefer the lemon." Theresa paused, hands on hips. "My lady?"

"Pardon me?" Ariana started.

With an impatient lift of her brows, Theresa repeated, "I said, I assumed this morning you'd prefer the lemon."

"The lemon?"

"Yes … rather than the cream. The cream is too heavy for such a hot summer day. I thought the lemon would be more to your liking."

"Oh … of course." Ariana wrapped the towel around her and smiled brightly. "I'll have the lemon, of course, but not here. In the dining room."

"You plan to dress in the dining room?" Theresa inquired.

Ariana stopped in her tracks. *"Dress?* I thought we were discussing my tea!"

"No, pet. I was speaking of your gown." Theresa swept past Ariana, clucking under her breath. "And they call *me* daft!"

Laughing, Ariana followed Theresa into the bedroom and gave her a warm hug. *"I've* never called you daft, my dear friend. To the contrary, I find your wisdom staggering. As for the rest of the world …" She shrugged, slipping into her underclothes and lemon-colored morning dress. "Let them think what they will."

Theresa gave a disdainful sniff and patted the volume of Bacon's essays that lay snug in her apron pocket. "They are ill discoverers that think there is no land, when they can see nothing but sea."

"I concur wholeheartedly … with you *and* Sir Francis," Ariana replied. Impatiently, she assisted Theresa in fastening the long row of buttons that spanned the front of her dress. "Do you think Trenton is still in the dining room?"

"I think you should let me arrange your hair so you can find out," Theresa returned briskly.

Ariana was eager to do just that.

But when, a scant twenty minutes later, she hastened down the stairs, she found only Dustin at the table, finishing his coffee.

"Well"—he came to his feet at once—"good morning! I was wondering if you *ever* planned to rise!"

"Good morning, Dustin." Ariana's gaze quickly swept the room, simultaneously noting that the grandfather clock registered three quarters after ten and that she and Dustin were indeed the sole occupants of the vast mahogany dining room. Disappointment clouding her lovely face, she turned to Trenton's handsome, smiling brother. "It's good to see you."

Dustin's grin widened. "You don't do much for a gentleman's ego, sweetheart," he teased, raising her hand to his lips. "You look positively crestfallen."

"I apologize," she said at once, blushing. She gazed appealingly up at him, mortified that she had offended such an important person in Trenton's life, a man she had hoped to call a friend. "I didn't mean ..."

He waved away her objection. "I understood what you meant." He raised her chin with a gentle forefinger. "Are you all right?"

Her blush deepened, but Ariana didn't pretend to misunderstand. "Yes."

His astute midnight gaze studied her intently. Then he nodded. "My brother is a very lucky man."

"Is he at home?" Ariana burst out eagerly.

"No, Ariana, he's not." Dustin glanced tactfully away from her disappointed expression. Adjusting the collar of his morning shirt with exaggerated dignity, he pulled back a chair and, in a grand, teasing gesture, motioned for Ariana to sit. As she complied, he admonished gently, "The day is half over, sweet. You must be ravenous." With authoritative ease, Dustin signaled to a waiting footman. "Breakfast for Her Grace," he ordered.

"Thank you, Dustin." Ariana smiled, determined not to show how disappointed she was to learn that Trenton was away. She composed herself, counting to ten as she traced the lace pattern of the tablecloth. Then, unable to resist, she casually inquired, "Will Trenton be gone long?"

"He left for Spraystone just after dawn." Dustin eased himself into his chair, folding his arms across his chest and studying Ariana with perceptive compassion. "He didn't mention when he planned to return."

"Spraystone?"

"Trent's estate on the Isle of Wight," Dustin supplied, reminded, yet again, how very little his brother and Ariana actually knew of each other.

"I see."

Dustin wondered if she did. Even *he* had been astounded this morning by the severity of Trenton's foul humor, which was darker and more forbidding than usual. Up before the sun and ornery as a wounded bear, Trenton had slammed downstairs, nearly knocking Dustin over on the staircase. He hadn't spoken two dozen words, but gulped three cups of black coffee, then announced his decision to leave for Spraystone. Given the circumstances, Dustin hadn't argued. Inwardly, however, he was worried. Not for himself, for he had braved Trenton's fury more times than he cared to recall. But for Ariana, who, with or without her consent, had doubtlessly become Trenton's wife last night … in fact as well as name. Dustin only prayed that Trenton had retained enough common sense not to hurt his innocent new duchess. Still, Dustin intended to be there when Ariana arose, to see for himself that she was unharmed.

Studying her now, he could see that his concerns were unfounded. Obviously, Trenton had kept himself in check and initiated his bride gently. A small smile curved Dustin's lips. In truth, if he considered Trenton's wretched mood together with Ariana's artless eagerness, he could almost believe that something significant had happened last night … something that involved far more than a physical consummation. An interesting possibility indeed.

"Spraystone must be lovely," Ariana was saying, frowning at the plate of poached eggs and buttered toast that was placed before her by a dutiful footman.

"It is." Before Dustin could ask why Ariana was displeased with her breakfast, she had pushed away her plate and instead helped herself to a dish of caramel pudding. "All of the Isle of Wight is picturesque," Dustin continued, watching Ariana lick the last creamy drop from her spoon, then enthusiastically bite into a jam tart. "But Spraystone is especially beautiful. It not only overlooks a breathtaking section of the Solent but also provides a clear view of the entire coast of Hampshire. ... Sweetheart, you're going to make yourself ill," he put in, as Ariana began nibbling at her second tart.

She paused, licking the jam from her lip. "Pardon me?"

"In the last five minutes you've eaten a huge bowl of custard and two tarts. Granted, you could stand a few additional pounds, but wouldn't you like some substantial food?"

Ariana blinked, her stomach lurching as it registered the arrival of its unusually sweet breakfast. "Oh ... I didn't realize ... That is ..."

Seeing her face take on a greenish cast, Dustin came to his feet, snatching a piece of toast and holding it up to Ariana's mouth. "Eat this," he ordered. While she chewed, he poured a cup of tea and thrust it at her. "Now drink."

It took only a few seconds for her stomach to settle. Then she sagged in her chair, giving Dustin a mortified look. "I don't know what to say ..." she began.

Dustin's lips twitched. "You did tell me that you eat an extraordinary amount of sweets when you're nervous."

Despite her embarrassment, Ariana found herself smiling back. "I do."

"Therefore I must sadly conclude that, since you've ... overindulged on both occasions I've been in your company, I evidently make you nervous."

"Oh, no!" she burst out, unconsciously reaching for his hand. "To the contrary, Dustin, you make me feel very much at home and remarkably relaxed." Her brows knit and her mind began racing, desperately seeking the words to make Dustin realize how crucial his companionship was to the overwhelming adjustment that now confronted her, how extraordinary she found their instant rapport. "Why, yesterday I was beside myself with jitters and you knew just how to calm me. And this morning you're here to make my first official meal at Broddington so much more pleasant. If only Trenton ..." She broke off, horrified by what she had implied.

"I understand, Ariana." Dustin covered her small hand with his large one. "And it's all right. My brother is not an easy man to know ... to understand," he corrected his choice of words, seeing Ariana blush. For some reason she inspired powerful feelings in him: protective, tender feelings. The last thing he wanted was her discomfort. "I tell you what," he said on impulse, rising to his feet. "Since Trent is away, why don't I take you on a tour of Broddington? After all, this is your new home, and I'm sure you're curious to see it."

Ariana tried, unsuccessfully, to disguise her excitement. "I don't want to keep you from anything. ..."

He waved her protest away. "Nonsense. I left all my work at Tyreham. And since I plan to stay at Broddington for several days"—he bowed deeply—"I am at your disposal."

"Oh, Dustin, can we begin now?" Ariana nearly toppled the chair in her zealous attempt to rise.

"Immediately." He gave her a lopsided grin. "That is, of course, if you've had enough to eat."

Ariana smiled. "I believe I've had my fill, thank you."

"Good. Then let's begin our tour."

"Given the size of Broddington, 'excursion' would be a better choice of words," she pointed out as they strolled into the marble-columned billiard room.

"True." Dustin gestured toward the carved billiards table. "Do you play?"

"Me?" Ariana gave him a wan smile. "Hardly."

"You probably prefer badminton," he rectified, mistaking her adamant response for a display of offended female sensibilities. "Now *that* sport is certainly catching on rapidly and is, undoubtedly, more appealing to a lady."

Ariana shook her head in apology. "I'm afraid my knowledge of sports is sadly lacking. I've played tennis once or twice and, of course, I ride, but ..." She shrugged with casual acquiescence. "I'm alone a great deal and there was never anyone to properly instruct me. However, I'm never lonely: I have my flowers and my animals."

"I'll instruct you."

She blinked. "You will?"

"Name your preference," he confirmed, grinning at her amazement. "Let's see ..." He began counting off on his fingers: "There's badminton, billiards, tennis, sailing ..." He leaned forward conspiratorially. "Poker ..."

"Poker?" Now she did look shocked.

"Queen Victoria plays," he tempted.

A spark appeared in her eyes. "Does she, now? Well then, so shall I!"

"Done," Dustin concluded with a snap of his fingers.

His infectious enthusiasm made Ariana bold. "And Dustin?"

"Hmmm?"

"The game I've always wanted to learn is croquet."

"Then our tour will lead us to the front lawn, where your training will commence."

"Today?"

"What better time than the present?"

Ariana felt gratitude well up inside her. "Thank you," she said in a small, choked voice.

Dustin smoothed his mustache, suddenly furious at his brother for abandoning this exceptional young woman. Didn't Trenton *see* what a treasure he'd been granted?

With great difficulty Dustin bit down on his anger, knowing full well that Trenton saw nothing, for he was blinded by his bloody vengeance. For the time being, Ariana's happiness was in Dustin's hands.

Resigned to his delightfully appealing task, he cupped Ariana's elbow and winked. "Instructing you in croquet will be my pleasure. Now, shall we move on to the drawing room?"

Ariana followed Dustin down the endless tiled hall to the drawing room. Pausing in the doorway, she caught her breath. "How elegant!"

Stained-glass windows lined the walls, admitting just enough light to emphasize the domed ceilings, green velvet sofas, and magnificent marble fireplace. Huge trefoiled mirrors hung between the windows, making the room seem even grander and more enormous.

Awed, Ariana strolled about, running her hand over a priceless statue, terrified that it might shatter at the merest touch. She traced the gilded trim along the room's marble columns with one tentative fingertip, marveling at the talent it had taken to design such a palace.

"Winsham's drawing room is half this size," she murmured, half to herself. She gazed off, a faraway look in her eyes. "We celebrated Christmas there when Mama and Papa were alive. I was so small … it seemed to me that the tree filled the whole room. I recall thinking what a miracle it was, the transformation from drawing room to winter garden." Self-consciously, she glanced up. "I'm sorry, Dustin … I'm babbling." On the heels of the apology she dimpled. "Babbling is something I do, not only when I'm nervous, but all the time."

Dustin chuckled. "Actually, your memories are charming."

"They're few and far between," she replied with a sad shrug. "My parents died when I was three. I scarcely remember them." She turned back to the painstakingly crafted columns. "In any case, Winsham isn't, nor was it ever, as grand as this."

Squinting, Dustin tried to view the room, the entire estate, through Ariana's untrained eyes. "My father adored Broddington," he said, his tone rich with his own memories. "This particular estate was not only his home but his greatest achievement."

Ariana looked up. "Trenton told me your father designed Broddington … assisted by his two sons."

A half-smile played about Dustin's lips. "Trent told you that, did he? Well, despite my brothers foul temper, he is far too modest. He and my father did the actual designs. I merely provided an occasional suggestion."

"Trenton also said your father was a genius."

"And he was."

"I can see that." She hesitated. "Will you tell me about him?"

A gamut of emotions played over Dustin's face. "Father was a proud and brilliant man. But despite his incredible talent he was, by nature, a traditionalist, devoted to his family and his home." Dustin stared at the floor. "The Kingsley name meant the world to him."

"You're very fortunate," Ariana replied softly, leaning against the sturdy column. She studied Dustin's bowed head, her heart swelling with a compassion that surmounted the questions crowding her mind. "I suppose, being a young child, I was spared the full wrenching impact of losing my parents. While in your case, you were a grown man when your father died. How his loss must have hurt you."

"Yes, it hurt me." Dustin's voice was raw. "But it nearly killed Trenton." Everything inside Ariana turned cold. "Dustin ..."

"Come." Dustin turned away, his firm tone telling her that, for now, the subject was closed. "Let's go on to the music room."

Their tour of the music room, library, and morning room were conducted in near silence, punctuated only by Dustin's clipped descriptions and the plodding sound of their footsteps sinking into the plush Axminster carpets.

On the stairway, Ariana halted, turning abruptly and seizing Dustin's arm. "Please, Dustin. I apologize for asking questions that were none of my business. I only wanted to understand you better ... to understand Trenton better," she added honestly. "I never meant to pry. Forgive me."

Dustin's troubled expression cleared and he kissed Ariana's cold fingers. "It is I who should be asking your forgiveness. You did nothing wrong. It's very natural for you to ask questions about your husband's family. The only excuse I have for my behavior is that our talk made me remember things I haven't allowed myself to think about for many years." He hesitated. "As you know, the entire Kingsley family disintegrated when my father died. Nothing's been the same since." His voice dropped to a whisper. "Sometimes I wonder if it ever will be."

"It will." Ariana had no idea whose strong, determined voice that was, but it appeared to be coming from her mouth. "I'll make certain it is."

Dustin started, then a slow smile curved his lips. "I'm counting on that, sweetheart," he told her, squeezing her hand. "If ever there was hope for us, you're it."

"'If a man look sharply, and attentively, he shall see Fortune; for though she be blind, yet she is not invisible,'" Theresa announced, marching by them on her way to the kitchen. "I'll have tea served on the front lawn this afternoon. You'll need refreshment after your croquet lesson." She disappeared around the corner of the first-floor landing.

Dustin gaped. "Who the ... what the ... how did she ..."

"Theresa," Ariana supplied helpfully. "My lady's maid. She was quoting Sir Francis Bacon for you; he's her favorite. The only one of your questions I cannot answer is 'how she.' I assume you are asking how she knew we would be playing croquet. I assure you she did not eavesdrop. My only explanation is that Theresa knows many things that we don't. I suggest you not ponder it too deeply; just accept it, for it is the truth." Ariana grinned. "You can close your mouth now, Dustin."

He snapped it shut. "I see."

"No, you don't. But she does." Ariana continued up the stairs. "Can we visit the second level now?"

Dustin nodded, still totally at sea, and proceeded to the second-floor landing.

The bedrooms were lavishly decorated and as impressive as the rest of the house. Still, Ariana experienced the same vague sense of inconsistency she had in her own bedroom the night before. For despite the magnificent craftsmanship and detail, the walls were devoid of paintings, the desks barren, the rooms sparsely furnished and cold, austere—a complete contrast to what she would have expected from the late duke.

Upon entering Trenton's private sitting room and finding nothing more than a bare desk and an untouched armchair, Ariana could no longer contain her puzzlement.

"Why is this floor so impersonal and stark?" She gestured toward the empty walls. "I know Broddington has been deserted since ... for six years," she amended, unwilling to bring the late duke's name back into the conversation and risk upsetting Dustin, "but the ground level seems so rich, so ... lovingly crafted. Why are the living quarters so drastically different?"

Dustin folded his arms across his chest, staring into space as if seeing into the past. "This sitting room belonged to my father ... His favorite room in the house. Not aesthetically, but spiritually. He spent long hours alone here, thinking and dreaming. The entire second floor was designed like that, for living as well as sleeping. It looked very different than it does now, filled with all my father's personal things, paintings of my mother, rare sculptures he'd acquired in his travels, sketches of Broddington long before it was built." Dustin sighed, leaving the past behind. "Trenton had everything removed when Father died. It ceased to be a home. It hasn't been one since then."

"Where are your father's things?" Ariana asked, her eyes damp. "Trenton didn't ... They weren't destroyed, were they?"

Dustin shook his head. "No. I stored them at Tyreham. All but the paintings of Mother, which are hanging in Broddington's gallery."

"May I see them?"

He smiled gently. "Of course. We'll stop there on our way to the chapel."

"When did she die?"

"When Trent and I were boys. Mother was very beautiful, but very delicate. During most of my childhood, she was confined to bed. She died of scarlet fever when I was ten."

"Your father obviously loved her a great deal."

Again, Dustin smiled. "Unfashionably so. He missed her dreadfully; that I do recall. His work, remaining productive, meant more to him than ever after her death."

Ariana inched forward and touched Dustin's arm. "I've done it again, haven't I? Upset you with my questions?"

"No, of course not," he returned warmly. "All this happened a long time ago. I'm quite recovered, honestly." With a reassuring look, Dustin led her into the hall. "Let's visit the gallery and the chapel, then move on to what will doubtlessly be your favorite spots." Seeing Ariana's perplexed expression, he supplied: "The stables and the gardens."

Ariana's eyes lit up. "And can we go to the conservatory again? I saw it briefly yesterday, but it was so breathtaking. ... Do you mind if we stop there for a moment?"

Dustin chuckled. "How can I resist so lovely a plea? Very well, we shall stop at the conservatory on our way to the gardens. And *then*"—his eyes twinkled—"you shall learn the proper handling of a croquet mallet."

"I can hardly wait!"

"Those wickets have no openings. It is all an illusion," Ariana complained two hours later. Sprawled on a lawn chair, sipping her tea, she had all but given up ever learning the proper way to strike the ball so that it went *through* the wicket rather than crashing *into* it.

Dustin threw back his head and laughed. "Trust me, sweetheart, the wickets do indeed have openings. You just have to learn how to find them."

Ariana made a face and brushed a loose strand of hair from her damp forehead. "I don't hold out much hope," she muttered. "I don't know why I ever wanted to learn that silly game anyway."

"It was only your first lesson," Dustin pointed out, finishing his third scone and settling comfortably back in his chair. "You'll improve."

She laughed in spite of herself. "I suppose my pride is wounded. I'd assumed I would master the sport on my first attempt and hear nothing but praise from you."

"I had no idea praise was required."

Trenton's deep baritone startled them both, and, simultaneously, they jumped in their seats, watching as he strode toward them.

"Trent, I didn't know you'd returned ..." Dustin began, shading his eyes, praying that his brother's early appearance meant his anger had dissipated, that he was ready to spend time with his bride.

Dustin's hopes were instantly dashed.

"Obviously you weren't expecting me." Trenton's tone was frigid, his jaw rigidly clenched. "But I'm pleased to know my bride has been properly entertained during my absence. As far as her mastering a sport on the first attempt ..." He turned to Ariana, ruthlessly scrutinizing her relaxed, tousled appearance. "Let me be the first to offer you the praise you so fervently requested." He gave her a mock bow. "I commend you highly. If you take to all amusements as quickly and proficiently as you did to the one you learned last night, you will garner nothing but compliments and pleas for more."

Dustin was on his feet even before Ariana's shocked gasp reached his ears. "For God's sake, Trent, are you insane?" he demanded.

Trenton tore his gaze from Ariana's white face. Swerving to meet his brother's fierce stare, he gave a harsh laugh. "Indeed I am! But I thought that was established years ago by the Caldwells."

"Don't, Trent," Dustin warned, his tone tight, controlled. "You're obviously drunk. And you don't know what you're saying."

"I'm as sober as you are," Trenton contradicted icily. "And I know precisely what I am saying."

Shakily, Ariana rose, her lips quivering with embarrassment and hurt. "You're not insane," she whispered. "Nor are you drunk. But you *are* terribly cruel. I don't know why you feel such anger toward me, but I *do* know it is directly linked with Vanessa."

Trenton's inadvertent flinch at the mention of Vanessa's name confirmed Ariana's suspicions. With as much dignity as she could muster, she gathered up her skirts and smoothed her hair back into place. "When you're ready to treat me civilly, I shall manage to do the same. Not because I'm afraid of you," she added candidly, raising her chin a notch, "but because, despite your abominable behavior, I know there is goodness inside you." Tears glistened on her lashes, but she blinked them away, holding her head high. "However, I won't be the recipient of your hatred any longer. Remember that … or don't address me again."

With a regal turn, Ariana marched off toward the house.

Astonishment and respect welled up inside Dustin, and he had to forcibly restrain himself from going after her.

"I see you've taught my bride to forgo reticence in favor of an acidic tongue. … And that, in the process, you've become her guardian."

Trenton's caustic comment made Dustin seethe. "Someone has to protect Ariana."

"From whom? Me?"

"Yes, you bloody lunatic. From you." Dustin faced his brother squarely, fury racing through his veins. "She's not Vanessa, you damned, stupid fool," he stated flatly. "When are you going to see that?"

Trenton's fists clenched. "Leave it alone, Dustin."

"Then leave Ariana alone," Dustin shot back. "She deserves better than your brutal treatment." He shook his head, longing to shake some sense into his brother, to make him see the obvious.

Ariana was not Trenton's enemy but his salvation.

Half tempted to blurt out that Trenton needed Ariana to make him whole again, that Ariana was already half in love with her unworthy husband, Dustin fought the urge, painfully aware that it was a realization they would have to arrive at themselves. Frustrated and livid, he threw up his hands. "Open your eyes, you bloody blind man," he bit out. "Before it's too late."

He turned on his heel and stalked off.

Dustin's uncharacteristic assault triggered the familiar battle that raged inside Trenton, and his features contorted with the strain of internal conflict. He could deal with it. He knew he could. He could deal with all of it: the vengeance that ate at his soul, the painful falling out with Dustin, the scars that time refused to heal.

All but the pain he'd seen on Ariana's face when she'd walked away from him.

And the knowledge that he was its cause.

CHAPTER 9

Trenton was caught in a tangled web of his own creation.

Shifting his weight in the chair, he stared moodily through the shadowed room to the bed where Ariana slept peacefully, unaware of his scrutiny ... and of the fact that he'd been watching her for hours.

Rolling the brandy glass between his palms, Trenton idly studied the swirling amber liquid as he reflected upon the complications the past few days had wrought. His decision to marry Ariana Caldwell had been spontaneous, yet purposeful: a brilliant solution to the vengeance that swelled inside him, a remedy for his unremitting torment.

Revenge was close at hand; he had only to be patient to achieve it.

After all, it had been just over a day since the wedding, giving Baxter a scant thirty hours to agonize over his sister's fate, and only one sleepless night to ponder the best way to acquire the Kingsley fortune.

With a sardonic smile, Trenton took a deep swallow of his brandy. Evidently, Caldwell took him for a fool. Did the bastard honestly believe Trenton wasn't aware why he had so easily relinquished his precious little sister into the Duke of Broddington's murderous hands? That Trenton didn't know that what the viscount hoped to gain from his sister's advantageous union was a sizable portion of the Kingsley fortune?

Trenton drained his glass. He'd always recognized Caldwell's intentions. So when Baxter summoned Ariana to Winsham to devise the best plan by which to avail himself of the Kingsley funds, Trenton would be ready. Baxter would never see a bloody penny.

Briefly, Trenton wondered how Ariana would react to whatever conniving plan Baxter had conjured up, and if she would agree to help him. True, she was a Caldwell, but she was the only Caldwell who seemed to possess some sense of honor. Would she stoop to theft and deceit, even for her brother? And, if she refused, would she be strong enough to resist the pressure Baxter would doubtlessly exert? She was far too innocent to suspect what her brother was capable of … or to what extremes Trenton would go to ensure that Baxter failed.

Inevitably, Ariana would be caught in the crossfire.

Which brought Trenton back to his unanticipated quandary.

Unwillingly, his gaze slid to the slumbering angel lying before him. Caldwell or not, she was breathtaking when she slept, more so when she was awake.

And so incredibly passionate.

His body still burned with the memories of last night, memories he'd been unable to squelch all day, memories that had driven him from her bed at dawn … and brought him back hours earlier than he'd intended. For despite his vehement struggles to the contrary, Ariana unfurled something raw and warm inside him, tested his control in ways he'd never guessed, bared emotions he'd long since forsaken.

He remembered the way her eyes had blazed sparks of outrage when she'd stood up to him today, the tears she'd refused to shed. She was a brave little thing, his bride, brave and innocent and principled.

So unlike Vanessa.

Bringing his glass to the nightstand with a thud, Trenton forced himself to face the truth. He could no longer use the Caldwell name to justify his irrational behavior toward Ariana, no longer punish her by pretending she was an exact replica of her despicable older sister.

In truth, Ariana was the antithesis of Vanessa. And, having already taken away his untainted wife's childhood, stripped her of her former life and home, why did he still want to strike out at her, to hurt her as he had that afternoon?

With mounting ambivalence, Trenton contemplated the humiliating cruelty of his verbal assault. What the hell had possessed him to say such a degrading thing? He gritted his teeth. Just because he'd returned to find his bride rumpled and laughing on the front lawn with his brother, chatting as if they were old friends, looking so incredibly *happy* ...

Unconsciously, Trenton slammed his fist to his knee. He'd never been a jealous man before. Certainly not of Dustin, the one person he *knew* would never betray him. Yet that's exactly what he was: jealous, vulnerable ... and livid about both.

The cold truth was, Trenton hated the pull that drew him back to Broddington and his bride, detested the fact that she had barely noticed his absence and gotten along fine without him, loathed the idea that Dustin could make her smile in a way he knew he couldn't. Damn it to hell! Why did this one woman inspire such emotional upheaval inside him?

Savagely, Trenton gripped his thighs. He wanted to hate her incessantly.

He hated to want her incessantly.

And he couldn't muster the former, nor master the latter.

So marriage to Ariana would reap him his vengeance, but it would do nothing to appease his relentless anguish. In fact, it would worsen it, for he'd be trading one type of agony for another.

"Trenton?"

Trenton started, blinking dazedly at the bed. Ariana was sitting up, waves of coppery hair tumbling about her slender shoulders. She reached for her robe and slipped it on, climbing from beneath the bedcovers. "Why are you here?"

He didn't answer at first, watching her walk toward him, the soft folds of her nightgown outlining every luscious curve of her body.

How could someone so exquisitely beautiful represent everything in his life that was so very ugly?

"Why are you in my bedroom?" Ariana repeated, stopping in front of him. She glanced at the glass on the nightstand. "Drinking?" she added.

"I've had only one drink," Trenton replied. "And I was watching you. And thinking."

She drew a shaky breath and purposefully straightened her shoulders. "About the apology you were going to extend to me?"

Despite his black humor, Trenton's lips twitched at her dignity and courage. "In part."

Her expression shifted from startled to relieved to curious. "I see."

"Wouldn't you like to hear what else I was thinking?" he inquired.

Her small jaw set. "First I'd like the apology."

Trenton drank her in, head to toe. "I was reflecting on how intoxicatingly lovely you are." He leaned his head back, his voice deep and rich, his gaze seductive, as hot and explicit as an intimate caress.

For a moment, Ariana's face registered indecision. Then she shook her head adamantly. "No!" she burst out, refusing him ... and herself. "You treated me inexcusably! You humiliated me in front of your brother and made me feel like a harlot!" She turned her back, unable to bear seeing the derisive censure in his eyes. "Last night ... well, you led me to believe my responses were acceptable, even enjoyable." Her voice grew small. "Why didn't you tell me that my wanton behavior angered you?"

Trenton's jaw dropped. "You thought I was angry because—"

"Let's not play games, Trenton," she returned, whirling about to face him, twin spots of red staining her cheeks. "I cannot be like Vanessa. It just isn't possible. But I *did* try to please you. So if I was too bold ... too vocal ... why didn't you tell me? Not in public, but when we were alone?" Despite her shame, she pushed on, candid and direct. "After all, I don't *know* how a wife should behave. I have no means of comparison. The only way I—"

"Come here."

Trenton's husky command cut into her tirade.

"What?"

"I said, come here." He extended his hand, caught her fingers in his and drew her closer until the fabric of her nightgown brushed his knees. Releasing her fingers, he cupped her hips and, in one gesture, tugged her down until she was straddling his lap.

"Trenton …" She sounded more puzzled and breathless than angry, and Trenton smiled.

"What?" He glided his fingers up the contours of her torso, then framed her face with his hands. "I'm driven by demons, misty angel," he murmured, caressing her cheek with his thumb, giving her the repentance she deserved. "Demons I cannot control. I allowed them to strike out at you, and for that I profoundly apologize." He brought her mouth down to his. "Do you forgive me?"

She nodded, unable to speak.

"As for last night," he muttered thickly, molding her lips to his and tangling his hands in her hair to keep her from pulling away, "you didn't just please me. You set me on fire, burned me to ashes, re-ignited the embers." He kissed her deeply, thoroughly. "You aroused me in a way I thought was impossible, seduced me with every innocent touch of your hands, your breath, your mouth."

Catching her tiny whimper, he pulled her closer still. "Do you have any idea how exciting I found your responses? What your soft moans, your breathless pleas for more did to my control?" He rotated his hips slowly, letting her feel the full force of his arousal. "Can you possibly imagine how much I want to be inside you?" he rasped, pressing insistently into the cradle of her thighs, the heat of his body burning through her. "Can you, misty angel?" He didn't wait for an answer but slid his hands beneath the pristine cotton of her nightgown, up along the silky softness of her legs.

"Oh … Trenton …" She sagged against him, shivering uncontrollably at his words, his touch.

"You make me tremble too," he whispered against her parted lips, gliding his shaking hands higher along her inner thighs, dragging the flimsy gown up with them.

With graceful abandon, Ariana arched her back, instinctively inviting him to take more of her.

Trenton's expert fingers found the warm haven they sought, delving hungrily into the glorious wetness that told him of her avid response.

And suddenly, everything converged inside him at once, splintering his control into fragments of nothingness.

"Ariana …" he choked out frantically, urgent in a way he could explain no more than he could understand. "I've got to have you … now." He raised her up, simultaneously reaching for the buttons of his trousers.

Ariana clutched at Trenton's arms, trembling violently. Confused and overwhelmed, she stared down at him, shocked by his frenzy … and her own. Immobilized, she watched her husband work desperately to free himself so they could be one.

"I have to fill you," he panted, pausing only to ease a finger inside her, gently testing her readiness. "I have to."

With a whimper of longing, Ariana tugged free, ready to bolt the short distance to the bed.

"No." Trenton's hands closed on her hips in a vicelike grip, and he shook his head wildly.

"But I want to—"

"So do I."

"But the bed—"

"I can't wait that long. Here. Now."

Before Ariana could reply, he'd freed his rigid erection and, in one deliberate motion, lowered Ariana onto his full length. "Take me, misty angel," he breathed into her hair. "Let me lose myself inside your softness." He heard her gasp, then eased her away so he could see her face. "Am I too deep?"

Wordlessly, she shook her head, reaching for him even as he dragged her back, impaling her with his turgid flesh.

"Don't stop," she whispered, pressing her flanks tightly to his. When he didn't reply, she raised up to see his face. "Trenton?" she managed.

"What?" His teeth were tightly gritted against the rapture that was escalating too hard, too soon.

"Please ..." she repeated, looking lost and bewildered and so damned beautiful that he longed to merge their very souls into one.

"Move," he told her instead. "Like this." He seized her hips, raising and lowering her, teaching her the rhythm ... and driving himself insane in the process.

He felt it the moment she took over. Her small hands gripped his shoulders, her slender legs hugged his thighs. And her tight, velvety wet passage absorbed him, enveloped him, stroked him with fingers of fire.

Trenton groaned, letting Ariana set the pace, greedily arching into every downward shift of her hips. With each thrust he penetrated deeper, withdrew, farther, reveling in his wife's glorious, abandoned response, her limbs tightening around him, possessing him as totally as he was possessing her.

Waiting was never an option. Trenton was peaking too fast, the pleasure too acute to repress. With a guttural shout, he lunged upward, lifting her with the force of the motion, clamping his hands on her hips and forcing her down to meet him until he heard her softly cry out ... in pain or pleasure he wasn't sure. And then he was plummeting over the edge of white-hot sensation, calling out to her, over and over, spilling himself in an endless, unbearable, shattering release that drained his strength and renewed his soul.

He was still moving as he opened his eyes, and the look on Ariana's face made him shudder anew. She was watching his expression intently, her own registering both awe and joy.

"You're magnificent," she whispered.

Trenton's gaze dropped to the hard points of her nipples, so clearly defined through the fine cotton of her gown, and he felt a stab of guilt and regret. "I gave you no pleasure."

"But you did," she protested, profoundly aware of him still hard and pulsing inside her.

Slowly, he shook his head. "No, my little innocent, not the kind I intended." Before she could protest, he brought her mouth down to his and, with their bodies still joined, slid his fingers between them. Slowly, erotically, he touched her, caressed her, moving his body and his hand in the ways he knew would maximize her pleasure.

Ariana melted around him, her body so feverishly aroused that it took mere seconds to push her beyond herself. Her eyes widened with shock as she realized how frantic she was for release.

Trenton smiled darkly, unsurprised by the magnitude of her response. "Now, Ariana," he said, nipping lightly at her lower lip, "now you'll feel it." He arched into her, never breaking the motion of his fingers. "Come apart in my arms," he ordered softly. His thumb circled her achingly sensitive flesh. "Now, misty angel," he demanded, pushing that extra inch inside her. "Now … give yourself up to it. … Give yourself to me."

The pleasure exploded into rainbows of shimmering sensation, so powerful that Ariana cried out again, clinging to Trenton and sobbing his name. Succumbing to the wrenching spasms, she buried her face in her husband's shoulder until the tremors had subsided. Then, with a weak, sated sigh, she collapsed against his chest.

She was floating, limp and dazed in his arms, when he gently carried her to the bed.

He lay her down, tugging off her robe and nightgown, and quickly stripped off his own clothes. Then he lowered himself beside her and began to pay slow homage to her body, relishing the silky texture of her skin in a way his urgency hadn't permitted mere moments before.

"All night, Ariana," he promised huskily, "I'm going to make love to you all night." Lightly, he outlined the shell of her ear with his tongue, breathing explicit vows in a rough, deep voice, describing all the different things he planned to do to her … all the exciting things they would do to each other.

And then he showed her.

"Trenton …"she whispered at one point during the night, placing a restraining hand against his shoulder, her eyes, her voice filled with the shadowed questions that lay between them.

"Later," he replied, easing over her, kissing her hand and bringing it around to his nape. "Much later." He parted her thighs and penetrated her wet warmth inch by glorious inch until her eyes slid closed and she said his name again, this time not in question. "Ah, my beautiful, exhilarating, misty angel," he murmured, guiding her legs around his waist, "… much, much later."

Dawn's first rays were flickering through the narrow opening in the drapes when Trenton finally eased away from his exhausted wife.

Feeling the cool air strike her body, Ariana came instantly awake, a wave of panic sweeping through her. *Will he want to leave again?* she wondered silently. *Like he did the other night?*

She closed her eyes and waited. Would the magic vaporize along with the darkness?

The minutes ticked by, the tension in the room intensified. And suddenly Ariana could take no more.

She curled away from Trenton, determined to keep her agony her own, fighting back the tears even as they trickled down her cheeks. Her shoulders jerked subtly with sobs, their movement the only overt sign of her anguish.

Silently, Trenton closed the distance between them, wrapping his arms around Ariana with possessive tenderness, enfolding her against his solid warmth. "Have I done this to you, misty angel?" he murmured into her hair, feathering kisses into the tangled tresses. "Forgive me; I never meant to cause you pain. Please ... don't cry."

Without a word, Ariana turned to him, burying her face in his powerful chest, accepting the comfort he was offering with childlike trust and gratitude.

"Don't allow my hatred to taint your spirit, Ariana," Trenton whispered fervently. "This war is not between us. Don't let me hurt you."

Ariana raised her head, searching her husband's face with damp, questioning eyes.

"Go to sleep," Trenton replied, kissing the teardrops from her wet, spiky lashes. Brushing her lips with his, he tucked her head beneath his chin. "Rest ... it's nearly day."

"Will you leave me then?" she blurted out, twisting around to look up at him.

His expression hardened. "Do you want me to?"

"No, oh no!" she burst out. "I mean ..." She blushed. "I had hoped we could sleep together ... awaken together. ..." Her voice trailed off, and she paused, hopeful and vulnerable and embarrassed.

Trenton's eyes flickered that same strange light she'd seen in them several times before—and he drew her back to his broad, muscular chest. "Then we shall," he replied in an odd tone. Without further explanation, he curled her body into his, kissing her damp forehead. "Now go to sleep."

Ariana dutifully closed her eyes, physical exhaustion commanding that she comply with Trenton's bidding. But the dictates of her mind refused to be silenced, whispering their speculations about the enigma that was her husband.

She forced herself to think rationally.

The indisputable facts were that Trenton's anger and thirst for revenge, justified or not, stemmed from her family. And, like the ocean, they ebbed and flowed along with the dark recollections so tightly locked in his complex mind. The terrifying questions plaguing Ariana were two: What memories could be agonizing enough to breed Trenton's overwhelming bitterness and inspire his implacable decision to wed her? And exactly what part had Vanessa played in creating those memories?

Silently, Ariana vowed to uncover the truth, to learn precisely what had occurred six years before. Because only by understanding the details of Trenton's past could she perceive what was hers to combat.

Time passed, the slow, even rise and fall of Trenton's chest telling Ariana he had fallen asleep. Quietly, she slipped out of bed, donning her discarded robe and walking soundlessly over to the window. She moved the drapes aside, gazing into the faintly lit skies and silently addressing the heavens, praying for the strength to endure the ordeal she knew lay ahead, the wisdom to discern her path, the insight to distinguish truth from deception and the courage to face the outcome.

But face it she must. For despite Trenton's biting animosity, Ariana had been drawn to him from the moment they'd met, trusted him when reason and caution warned her away, sensed on some fundamental level that he needed her.

And that she needed him as well.

Inherently, she'd always known that what she was feeling ran far deeper than the mere physical. She'd known it in the Covington maze when logic told her to fear him but instinct refused to obey; known it throughout the weeks preceding the wedding when all she could think of, dream of, was Trenton; known it in the chapel when she'd seen the flashes of vulnerability in her new husband's eyes. And now that they were truly man and wife, it wasn't attraction alone that compelled her response; for the angry torment in his eyes called out to her as profoundly as did the passion in his arms. Nor was it attraction that caused her to weep for Broddington's emptiness, which was a mirror reflection of the emptiness that pervaded Trenton's heart.

It was more.

Ariana squeezed her eyes shut against the glaring knowledge, willing back the resentment, the ambivalence, even the sliver of fear. But to no avail; they were gone forever, replaced by an emotion far more frightening.

God help her, she was falling in love with her husband.

A man who was unapproachable, unreachable, untouchable … and unwilling, if not unable, to accept her love and to give her his in return.

Ariana bowed her head. *Please,* she beseeched the ubiquitous powers above, *show me my course. Please.*

The fluttering sound broke the silence, faint, but audible and persistent nonetheless. Ariana's chin came up and her eyes flew open, scanning the brightening skies of the new day … skies that, moments before, had been deserted.

The owl traversed the heavens, flying directly toward her, his snowy wings cloaking the dawn. As he approached, his piercing stare captured Ariana's, bathing her in a momentary glow, his expression solemn, his message sage. Then he veered abruptly skyward, disappearing over the spires of Broddington, leaving behind a shrill cry, a silent sky. …

And hope.

CHAPTER 10

"Have I kept you waiting?"

Ariana rounded the hall to the second-floor landing, hastening her step at the sight of her husband's restless pacing.

Trenton's head snapped around. "No," he replied with stiff formality. "I've only been here a moment longer than you."

His gaze flickered briefly over his wife's titian-haired beauty, her huge turquoise eyes and slender shape accentuated by the blue-gray taffeta gown that fit closely to her hips, then draped delicately behind her.

"Is there something wrong?" Ariana managed, shifting beneath his scrutiny.

Trenton tore his gaze from her. "Not a thing."

"Good." She forced a smile. "Then, shall we dine?"

"Yes." Without proffering his arm, Trenton gripped the banister and started down the staircase, maintaining a considerable distance between himself and his wife.

Painfully aware of Trenton's unspoken message, Ariana swallowed her pride and followed silently beside him, making no move to catch up. Her head was spinning from lack of sleep and from the pain of her husband's pointed rejection.

His complete behavioral turnabout had occurred the instant they'd awakened. Despite his tenderness during the night, he'd opened his eyes and stared at Ariana as if she were a stranger, rolling away from her with the same icy withdrawal that repeatedly accompanied their physical separations, donning his robe and heading for the door without glancing back.

"I'll wait for you on the second-floor landing," he'd instructed, his tone as impersonal as if he were speaking to a business associate. And then she was alone, with only the damp sheets and the savored warmth of his body as lingering memories of the long hours when he'd belonged to her.

I can, I WILL, obliterate the invisible wall between us, Ariana vowed to herself now, watching her husband's rigid descent. Deliberately, she summoned strength by recalling the flight of her rare and magnificent white owl. His appearance at dawn's first light had been no accident, but a sign that what she was seeking could be hers. He seemed to materialize whenever her faith was raw and needed renewal—specifically, at the brink of each emotional precipice with Trenton. First there was the night they'd met, then the day she'd become his wife, and now this morning, when she'd accepted the reality of her love for him. Like a true miracle, her owl had become a symbol of inspiration and a promise of the future.

A sense of lightness and inevitability replaced Ariana's melancholy. Somehow, some way, she would reach into Trenton's heart, extract his pain, and procure his love. She needed that … and so did he.

Resolutely, she racked her brain for a safe topic of conversation, intending to rectify the fact that, despite their physical intimacy, she and her husband scarcely knew each other. Their time together had thus far been dominated by either anger or passion, leaving little room for verbal discourse.

"Broddington is an extraordinary home," she offered cautiously.

Trenton acknowledged her words with a curt nod. "So you've told me."

"Yes, but at the time I had seen only the conservatory."

"And that's changed?" Surprised by his wife's implication, Trenton swung his head around to look at her.

Vigorously, Ariana nodded. "Yesterday Dustin gave me a tour … or at least a partial one," she amended, warming to the memory. "The music room, the drawing room, the billiard room, the gallery … he showed me all of them." She paused to catch her breath. "They're every bit as impressive as the conservatory."

Throughout Ariana's enthusiastic recounting, Trenton's scowl had intensified. "I'm pleased you feel that way," he returned in a clipped tone. "You and Dustin were apparently even more productive during my absence than I'd originally realized."

Ariana started. *NOW why is he angry?* she wondered. *Is it the fact that I invaded his domain? Or is it the memories this conversation evokes … memories he'd rather forget?*

Whatever his reasons, Ariana was determined to learn all she could. "I saw the paintings of your mother in the gallery," she began, racing on before trepidation compelled her to reconsider. "She was an incredibly beautiful woman. I see only a slight resemblance between the two of you. … She looks so ethereal, so small and delicate. Dustin has her midnight-blue eyes, don't you think?"

A glimmer of humor softened the rigid lines of Trenton's face. "Yes, my mother was beautiful; no, I don't resemble her much; and yes, Dustin does have her unusual color eyes. Anything else?"

Ariana flushed, recognizing how absurd her inane babbling must sound. Still, as a first step in isolating Trenton's suppressed ire, it had served its purpose. His unruffled reaction told her he wasn't bothered by her visit to the gallery or by her viewing of his mother's portraits. In fact, he seemed totally unaffected by Ariana's intrusion into that aspect of his past. Further, his own reference to his mother was made with relative ease, indicating that she was excluded from the bitterness that ate at his heart.

Which left, as she'd suspected, his father.

And the Caldwells.

Trenton had reached the foot of the stairs. Leaning against the wall, he studied the engrossed expression on his wife's face as she made her way toward him. "Evidently you were greatly impressed by your tour," he commented dryly.

Ariana blinked, snapping out of her reverie. "Your talent is visible in every one of Broddington's rooms." She tilted her head back to watch Trenton's reaction. "As well as Dustin's talent …" She paused. "And, of course, your father's."

A dark cloud settled over Trenton's face.

"As I told you, my father was a genius." He straightened, purposefully tugging each of his coat sleeves to the wrist. "As for your observations of Broddington's assets … they will have to wait." Clearing his throat roughly, Trenton headed for the dining room, putting an end to any discussion of Richard Kingsley. "I have a great deal to accomplish today. I believe we came downstairs to eat?"

Ariana followed slowly. "Yes, we did."

"Then suppose we do that. You can entertain me with tales of your excursion through the manor later today."

"But you won't be here later today." Ariana was stunned by her own boldness.

Trenton stopped in his tracks. "Meaning?"

"Meaning that I expect you'll be off to Spraystone immediately after our meal."

Silence.

Nervously fingering the folds of her gown, Ariana walked around in front of her husband, facing him squarely even as she prayed she was not overstepping her bounds. "Unless, of course, you'd planned to remain at Broddington today. Had you?"

Trenton stared down at her for a timeless time, his eyes hooded. Ariana's heart slammed in her chest as she awaited his reply, fervently wishing she could read his thoughts. What she wouldn't give for an iota of Theresa's foresight right now!

"I would enjoy seeing the rest of the manor," she went on, lightly touching Trenton's sleeve. "And I would rather *you* showed it to me. That is"—she swallowed, carefully treading on unsure ground—"if you wouldn't mind."

Trenton glanced at the small hand on his arm. "I could remain at Broddington today," he conceded at last. "If you'd prefer it."

Ariana's whole face lit up. "Oh, yes, I'd prefer it!"

"Fine." He resumed walking. "I'll take you through whatever rooms you have yet to see." Pausing in the doorway of the dining room, he turned to add, *"After we eat."*

Ariana wanted to jump up and sing with triumph. With the greatest of efforts she controlled herself. "That would be wonderful," she replied instead, smiling beatifically.

She was instantly and unexpectedly ravenous.

"Who studied in this lovely schoolroom?" Ariana asked, drinking in the open feeling of the high ceilings and wall-to-wall windows.

"Both Dustin and I took our lessons here." Trenton stood rigidly, arms folded across his chest, in the doorway. During the past hour he'd taken Ariana through Broddington's library, kitchen, and guest wing, describing each section of the manor with the brilliant detail of an architect and the removed indifference of a cynic. Despite the insight provided by the former, the latter spoke volumes more.

"I don't understand," Ariana said in a puzzled tone. "How could you have studied here if Broddington was not yet built?"

"The original manor was standing long before I was born. Dustin and I helped my father redesign the entire estate when we were in our teens. The schoolroom, however, is mostly unchanged. The double doors are of a thicker construction, and a washroom was added just on the other side of that wall." He pointed.

"What a miraculous haven for learning!" Recalling her own dismal hours in the dreary Winsham schoolroom, Ariana was entranced. She ran her hand over one of the two low wooden stools, trying to picture a dark-haired little boy laboring over his lessons. "You must have been an exemplary student."

"I don't remember much of my early schooling."

Wincing at the brusqueness of his tone, Ariana pushed on, determined to reach inside the stony man standing before her and extract the sensitivity she glimpsed only in their bed. "You must have had favorite subjects," she prodded.

He shrugged. "I suppose. I've always had an aptitude for business, a flair for detailed types of sketching, and a fascination with the way buildings are designed."

"Is sketching a building that much different from sketching any other subject?"

"Identical in some ways, worlds apart in others."

"How so?"

Trenton rubbed his palms together thoughtfully. "Obviously, all drawings require discipline and imagination," he explained. "But planning a building is not merely an aesthetic process. It's a pragmatic one." His brow furrowed in concentration. "In designing a home the architect must combine the owner's personal tastes with his lifestyle." Warming to his subject, he crossed the room to stand beside Ariana, displaying the room with a wide sweep of his hand. "For example, Broddington's schoolroom adjoins the governess's quarters, yet is far removed from the living quarters ... and the distractions they pose." He indicated the long line of windows on the far wall. "However, the room is also well lit and directly over the gardens, hopefully making it more conducive to learning." Pride shone in his eyes as he surveyed the entirety of his family's creation. "Each room is strategically placed and carefully constructed ... a thriving entity unto itself and a harmonious segment of the whole."

"I'm terribly impressed," Ariana admitted. "I had no idea so much was involved in being an architect. In fact"—she looked sheepish—"my own sketches are so atrocious that Theresa hid my sketchpad in the hopes that I would abandon painting."

Trenton's lips twitched. "And did you?"

"Yes. In truth, I was dreadfully relieved."

"What *did* you enjoy doing?" he asked curiousiy.

"I kept a detailed journal of every animal, bird, and plant at Winsham. But most of my day was spent on French lessons."

"Ah, so you enjoyed French."

"I loathed it."

Trenton's brows drew together in question. "Then why …"

"Because Mademoiselle Leblanc commanded it."

"Who on earth is Mademoiselle Leblanc?"

"My governess," Ariana supplied. "She thought all other studies but French to be frivolous." So saying, she marched behind the straight-backed chair and slapped her palm on the walnut desk, pinching her nose with the other hand. "You *will* learn your French, *enfant* … or there will be no breakfast today!" Ariana recited in a nasal monotone. "We cannot waste time on idle daydreams, nor can we learn what is most important by scribbling rubbish on paper."

Wagging a finger in Trenton's direction, Ariana scowled in mock disapproval. "Someday you will marry a wealthy, titled gentleman and travel abroad; you *must* be thoroughly familiar with *français … la langue de beauté*. Oh, you spout terms such as *le moineau* and *le rouge-gorge* flawlessly, as well as *le jasmin, le chèvrefeuille,* and every other bird and flower in Winsham's garden. But I assure you, *un noble* will be unimpressed by hearing you translate 'sparrow,' 'robin,' 'jasmine,' and 'honeysuckle'! No, *enfant,* he will *not* be at all pleased with a wife whose only French consists of the names of *les oiseaux et les fleurs!*"

Involuntary laughter erupted from Trenton's chest. "She sounds monstrous! How did you ever tolerate her?"

Ariana lowered her arms and dimpled. "It was quite simple really. You see, Mademoiselle was completely blind without her spectacles.

So twice a week I merely *misplaced* them for her, and while she was in the midst of a long-winded soliloquy on the beauty of the French language, I climbed out the window. She never noticed. And fortunately for me, Winsham's schoolroom leads directly to the stables. So my mornings were heavenly."

"And here I thought you were the most docile and obedient of children." Trenton chuckled.

Ariana leaned forward, pressing a conspiratorial finger to her lips. "Everyone thought so. And I was ... *most* of the time."

"I'll remember that."

"And *I'll* remember to be docile and obedient."

"*Most* of the time," he clarified. "There are places where submissive behavior is most undesirable."

Their eyes met ... and all the amusement suddenly vanished.

Ariana drew a slow breathy her heart accelerating to a rapid thud. Trenton's gaze darkened and fell to her mouth, and Ariana could actually feel his inadvertent movement toward her.

Then, abruptly, he turned away.

Tension crackled in the air, suffocating the beauty of the past moments. Desperate to preserve, if not the fervor of their longing, then the easiness of their banter, Ariana blurted out the first thing that came into her head.

"Did Dustin follow in your footsteps?"

Trenton swung his head around to look at her. "Pardon me?"

"In his academic preferences. Did Dustin follow in your footsteps?"

Visibly, he relaxed. "Dustin preferred initiating his own footsteps." A faint smile touched Trenton's lips. "From early on, his interest in women far exceeded his interest in learning. Fortunately, his talents are innate. Otherwise, I shudder to think how he'd be spending his time now."

"Talents?" Ariana's questioning emphasis was on the plural.

Trenton nodded. "Architectural design is merely a hobby of Dustin's. And conventional business opportunities were never his forte. No, Dustin's true aptitudes lie in an area that will please you greatly. He buys and breeds some of the most magnificent racehorses I've ever seen."

"At Tyreham?"

Yes. His contenders have placed in the Derby, the Two Thousand Guineas ... I could go on and on. He has a unique flair for selecting prime horseflesh and, through inbreeding, creating extraordinary offspring. His prize mare, Sorceress, nearly took the Goodwood Cup last month, and I believe he's grooming one of his colts to run at Newmarket's Rowley Mile course this fall."

"I had no idea!" Ariana said in amazement.

"Dustin is modest about his achievements."

"He said the same of you."

"Did he? Well, my redeeming qualities are questionable. Dustin's are not."

"You're very proud of him," Ariana commented, uncertain of how to respond to Trenton's self-deprecating statement.

"Yes, I am. He's a remarkable man whose brotherly allegiance is, to say the least, exceptional."

"Did you both attend Oxford?"

Trenton clasped his hands behind his back. "For a time, yes. But my father's health had already begun to fail, and running Broddington was all he could manage. I left Oxford to take over the remaining estates and the family businesses."

Ariana started at the humility Trenton was displaying while recounting an utterly unselfish act—one her own brother had bemoaned for years after her parents died. "What a massive undertaking that must have been!" she exclaimed. "And how difficult ... Why, you were still in your teens!"

Trenton shrugged offhandedly. "I only did what was necessary for my family."

"And succeeded beyond their wildest dreams, I expect. Your father must have been very proud!"

A muscle worked at Trenton's throat. "I suppose. We didn't discuss it; I merely did what I had to do. I never questioned nor resented my responsibilities."

"I can see that." Unconsciously, Ariana walked forward, admiration shining in her eyes. "And yet you doubt your worthiness as a human being?" She reached up, laying her hand against his jaw. "The way I see it, you are more than worthy."

His expression turned grim. "You don't know me, Ariana."

"I think I do."

"You're a romantic child, misty angel."

"Romantic, perhaps, but not a child." She raised her chin a notch. "Not anymore."

The underlying significance of Ariana's words sank in, and Trenton frowned, catching her wrist and pushing her hand away. "Don't delude yourself, Ariana. What happens between us in bed has nothing to do with romance."

She flinched. "Perhaps not in your case."

Trenton stared down at her, a flash of pain crossing his face. Then he shook his head ... hard. "Don't make the mistake of allowing your heart into this marriage."

"It's too late," she stated simply.

"You're selling your soul to the devil," he warned.

Ariana shrugged. "I'll take that chance."

Before he could respond, she moved away. "May I see the rest of the manor now?" She paused in the doorway.

Trenton nodded mutely, his eyes darkening with some unfathomable emotion. Then he led her into the hall.

"I've seen most of the bedrooms," she commented, gazing down the corridor. "But I'd like to see your sitting room again."

Trenton stiffened. "Why?"

"Because I spent very little time there." She was already walking in that direction.

"As did I," he said, his voice laced with irony. Reluctantly, he followed her path, opening the door to the Spartan room within.

"Why is that?" Ariana strolled about the barren floor, reinforcing her earlier impression: that this room was virtually unoccupied.

"As you know, I haven't been at Broddington for years. "And when I was ..." Trenton shoved his hands in his pockets, averting his face. "Let's say I have no affinity for this room. I associate it with pain and loss."

"I understand," Ariana answered softly. Lines of stress were etched on every plane of her husband's handsome face, and his bitterness was a palpable entity.

He stared off, his expression tormented. "I wonder if you do."

The urge to go to Trenton at that moment was almost beyond bearing, but Ariana fought it, reminding herself that he would not welcome her comfort nor her compassion. For now, all he would accept from her was her body.

She surveyed the room, imagining how it must have looked years ago, alive with memories, vibrant with Richard Kingsley's personal touches; paintings, sketches, intricately designed furnishings and rugs. She could visualize it all: a fire burning merrily in the fireplace, fresh flowers—violets and marigolds and hawthorn, perhaps—decorating the room, permeating it with their sweet perfume. There would be a sweeping mahogany desk at the window, sunlight illuminating its polished surface; and at the desk, Trenton, his dark brow furrowed as he contemplated the series of designs he was developing. The image was so real, it was almost as if ...

The idea exploded in her head like crashing thunder, so vivid that Ariana had to keep herself from shouting in exaltation. She might not be able to wipe out Trenton's past, but she could alleviate its pain by offering him a present, something to build on other than dark memories.

She smiled, a secret smile, anticipating how she would begin. Within these very bare, unlived-in walls, she would create the actual room she had just imagined, present Trenton with a private refuge that was all his, one that would offer him the solace he sought at Spraystone, yet be far more meaningful, for it would encompass a glowing tribute to Richard Kingsley within a glorious domain that was Trenton's alone.

And it would be a giant step in Ariana's plan to make Broddington a home.

"P-p-pardon me, Your Grace." Jennings, the Broddington butler, hovered in the doorway. Smoothing a hand over his cap of red hair, he peered nervously at Trenton over a long, needlelike nose, requiring only a tree trunk beside him to complete Ariana's vivid image of a tiny, terrified woodpecker.

"What is it, Jennings?" Trenton snapped.

Jennings quaked at the duke's sharp, impatient tone. "I have a message for the duchess." He inclined his head in Ariana's direction. "It appears to be important, so I thought ..."

"I'll take it." Trenton strode forward and snatched the note from Jennings's bony fingers. "That will be all for now."

"Y-y-yes, Your Grace."

No woodpecker had ever taken flight that rapidly.

"He's petrified of you," Ariana said, chewing her lip in distress.

Trenton scowled. "He is new and totally unsure of himself. I had no choice but to hire him; none of my other estates could part with their butlers, and I didn't have adequate time to interview properly."

"What about Spraystone?"

"Spraystone has no butler, there is no need for one. There is only myself, my manservant, and his wife. Gilbert assists me on the estate and Clara helps with the meals and the cleaning. The majority of the work is mine." Trenton awaited his wife's inevitable distaste and surprise at her first hint of Spraystone's unpampered lifestyle.

All he encountered was the surprise. "Truly?" Ariana had heard enough about Spraystone from Dustin to know that the estate was not of diminutive size. "That must be a staggering responsibility!"

"Not really ... I've had an inordinate amount of free time these past years," Trenton responded dryly. "And physical labor keeps many ghosts at bay. So I've learned to be tireless."

"But not overly kind."

His appraisal was cool. "What does that mean?"

"Give Jennings a chance, Trenton," Ariana urged him. "You're a very forbidding man. Don't intimidate him. He means well."

Trenton shook his head in amazement. Always they came back to the same thing: feelings. His new bride was governed by them, he was incapable of them, "You're hopelessly tender-hearted, misty angel."

"Yes I am ... hopelessly," she admitted with a shy shrug.

A jolt of desire shot through him: desire mixed with a curious swell of protectiveness. "How did you ever survive eighteen years without losing such unheard-of innocence?" Trenton asked in husky disbelief.

"I thought you preferred my innocence?" Ariana baited softly, giving him an engaging smile.

"I did." His eyes darkened, consuming her with their intensity. "I also preferred being its recipient."

"I'm glad," she said simply, wetting her lips with the tip of her tongue.

With a muffled curse, Trenton moved toward her, reaching forward to drag her against him.

The message crackled its reminder in his palm.

"Your note." Trenton halted, staring blankly at the paper as if recalling its presence, then extending it to his wife.

Reluctantly, Ariana took the page, forcing herself to concentrate when all she wanted was to be in Trenton's arms. She unfolded the note mechanically, her brows drawing together in puzzlement. "Who could have sent it?"

"Your brother." Trenton spat out the words as he would a profanity.

A cold premonition of dread cloaked Ariana's heart as she smoothed out the tersely worded page. *Sprite,* it read, *It is vital that I see you. Come to Winsham as soon as possible. B.*

Ariana raised her head to find Trenton's gaze upon her, his expression that of a vicious predator. A shiver of apprehension tingled up her spine. "Baxter wants to see me immediately," she said, pushing her words past the constriction in her throat.

"Of course he does," Trenton returned with mocking bitterness. His mouth tightened into a grim line, his eyes glittering contemptuously, raking deep inside her. Turning on his heel, he stalked to the door and crashed it wide open, gesturing grandly into the empty hall. "Then by all means, *Mrs. Kingsley* ... go."

CHAPTER 11

Winsham was the same … and yet it was so very different. Had it changed overnight? Or had she?

Ariana rested her chin on her hand as she leaned out the carriage window, watching her old home loom closer. Certainly Winsham was modest-sized compared to Broddington, but size was not the cause of Ariana's odd feeling of unfamiliarity. It was as if, after only two days, she didn't belong here anymore, that it was a part of her previous life … a life that was no more. Stranger still, that realization evoked no sadness, only a peaceful acceptance.

For despite his grim complexity, Trenton was her husband, and her home was with him now.

The carriage stilled with a jolt, and Ariana swiftly gathered her skirts, her mind turning to Baxter and the cryptic note he'd sent her. Was something amiss? she wondered uneasily. Could Baxter be in some kind of trouble?

Alighting, she ascended the stairs, just as Coolidge opened the front door and bowed deeply. "My lady … pardon me … Your Grace," he hastily corrected, "the viscount is expecting you."

"Thank you, Coolidge." Ariana followed him down the hall to Baxter's study, amused at the solemn formality of the greeting. Just last week she'd resided here, floated in and out of the house at will, with no grand proclamations trumpeting her arrival. Was it her newly acquired title or her husband's black past that elicited such awe?

Coolidge rapped purposefully on the study door.

"Yes … come in," Baxter called.

"The Duchess of Broddington, sir."

Shuddering with distaste at the mere mention of the Broddington name, Baxter rose, folding the letter he had just completed and gifting Ariana with his most charming smile. "Hello, sprite." He extended his arms, coming forward and embracing her affectionately.

Ariana drew back. "Is everything all right?" she demanded.

Baxter blinked. "Of course." From the corner of his eye he noted that the butler was about to take his leave. "Oh … Coolidge," he called, making his way back to the door.

"Sir?"

"See that this message is sent at once," Baxter said quietly, pressing the note into Coolidge's palm. "By telegraph. It's urgent."

"Of course, sir."

Baxter nodded tersely. "And please arrange to have tea served in my study," he said in a pointed return to his normal tone.

"Certainly, my lord." With the note clutched tightly to his side, Coolidge made his exit.

For a moment Baxter stared idly after him, lost in faraway thoughts. Then, abruptly, he recalled Ariana's presence and, drawing a sharp breath, he turned, his smile restored. He had to tread carefully, seize this opportunity to elicit Ariana's help. For without her cooperation he hadn't a prayer of securing Kingsley's vast fortune.

"So, how is my beautiful little sister?" Baxter asked with a wink. "I've missed having you underfoot. Let me look at you. … You are quite a vision."

"I've only been gone two days, Baxter," Ariana said wryly, wondering if the reason for his flattery had anything to do with the urgency of his summons. "I don't think I've changed *that* much."

He chuckled. "Still convinced you are the ordinary mouse, I see."

"Baxter, in all due respect, you hardly sent for me in order to discuss my physical attributes, did you?"

A shadow crossed his face. "Do I now need a reason to see my sister?"

A pang of conscience tugged at Ariana's heart. "Of course not. I only wondered why you delivered so formal and insistent a message."

Baxter gave a mirthless laugh. "Well, *I* could hardly visit *you*, now could I? Stroll into Broddington and announce myself ... I who am your brother and the head of the Caldwell family? I think not."

Ariana dropped her gaze sadly. "I see your point."

"I rather thought you would." Catching her chin, Baxter lifted her face for his inspection. "Are you all right?"

"I'm fine."

"Kingsley hasn't hurt you, has he?"

Ariana averted her head.

"*Has* he?"

"No!" She felt her cheeks burn. On a cognizant level, she was aware that Baxter's question pertained only to her physical well-being, bearing no resemblance to the wanton thoughts it immediately evoked. Still, the images of her sensual intimacy with Trenton sprang vividly to mind: the intensity, the fervor, the indescribable pleasure he induced. But hurt her? "No, of course he hasn't," she denied hotly.

Baxter studied her another moment, then nodded. "Very well." He crossed the room and poured himself a drink. "Would you like one?"

"No." Ariana sank into a chair. "I'll wait for the tea."

"Suit yourself." He took a deep swallow. "So, you've survived two days of marriage to Trenton Kingsley."

"Survival was never an issue." Her fingers tightened on the folds of her gown, bracing her for an unpleasant exchange.

Baxter tossed off the rest of his drink. "In other words he's returned to the Isle of Wight, as I suspected, and you haven't been burdened with his presence."

"He's at Broddington."

"What?" Baxter looked stunned.

"For the most part," she clarified. "He did visit Spraystone, but not for long. Predominantly, he's stayed with us at Broddington."

"*Us?*"

"Dustin's been there since the wedding. He'll be returning to Tyreham in a few days."

"Ah ... the marquis." Baxter refilled his glass.

"He's a wonderful man," Ariana said defensively.

"I don't doubt it." Inclining his head, Baxter gave her a curious look. "You're enjoying his company, then?"

"Who?"

"Your husband's brother ... wasn't that who we were discussing?"

"Oh, yes." Ariana felt unusually flustered. "Yes, Dustin is great fun. He's teaching me to play croquet. Or at least he's trying to," she added ruefully.

Baxter traced the rim of his glass. "Well, that certainly explains your rapid adjustment." He raised his probing gaze to Ariana's, weighing her reaction. "So you've had very little time alone with Kingsley, then."

Twin spots of red reappeared on her cheeks.

Baxter's glass slammed to the desk as comprehension struck, the true cause of Ariana's embarrassment finally registering its full impact. "Did he force himself on you?" When Ariana only blinked in total stupefaction, Baxter stalked across the room and yanked her to her feet. "Did that bloody bastard force you into his bed?"

Ariana snapped out of her stunned silence. "*Force* me? For God's sake, the man is my husband! Surely you knew what that meant when you agreed to the marriage!"

"I didn't *agree* to it," Baxter shot back. "The blackguard had a royal edict from the Queen! My hands were tied."

"You certainly didn't try very hard to untie them."

Baxter winced at his sister's cutting accusation. "What could I have done?" he beseeched, his grip tightening in frustration. "Kingsley is a close personal friend of Victoria's. From the day Vanessa died, the Queen made it clear she believed unconditionally in his innocence. Given that fact, what grounds did I have to prevent her decree that you wed him?"

Ariana twisted free of Baxter's grasp and turned away. "There's nothing to be gained by this argument. The point is a moot one. ... My marriage is *a fait accompli* and cannot be undone."

The finality of Ariana's proclamation descended upon Baxter like a heavy boulder, crushing him—but at the same time making him supremely aware of how ludicrously he was behaving. Yes, the marriage was a *fait accompli*—perhaps not with his blessing, but without his vehement objection. Ariana was Kingsley's wife now ... and that meant in body as well as name.

Baxter stared at Ariana's tense back, assailed by a sense of melancholy that his baby sister was a child no longer. The looming reality was that Kingsley's entire purpose in forcing Ariana to the altar had been to steal her innocence and possess her as his own, thus seizing the ultimate opportunity to destroy the Caldwells. And despite Ariana's obliviousness to her own desirability, she was indeed a rare beauty, one any man would want in his bed.

Baxter fought back his anger and regret, reminding himself that the Caldwell reward was still to come.

Clearing his throat roughly, he placed gentle hands on Ariana's shoulders. "I'm sorry, sprite. I had no right to rant at you like that. It's just ..." His voice faltered. "You're all I have left and I worry about you."

Ariana twisted slowly to face him. "I know," she said softly, covering his hand with her own. "But there's no need. Trenton would never hurt me."

A blaze of fury re-ignited Baxter's eyes. *"Trenton ..."* he repeated, more horrified by her use of Kingsley's given name than by the knowledge that they'd lain together. The latter was a necessary evil, the former an unwelcome warning.

"You still hate him so," Ariana murmured, studying the enmity in her brother's eyes.

"Have you forgotten that he was responsible for Vanessa's death?"

"Was he?" she responded swiftly, her body going rigid. "Tell me how."

Baxter's expression grew savage.

"I want to hear the details of Vanessa's death," Ariana repeated. "All these years I've been told only the barest of facts ... plus endless speculations. I understand I was merely a child at the time and you wanted to protect me. But I'm not a child any longer ... and I need to know."

"No, dammit!" Baxter jerked away and walked to the window. "I have no intention of reliving that day."

Ariana's palm struck the desk. "I am *wed* to the man, Baxter. Exactly how did he factor into Vanessa's death?"

Baxter lurched around. "Vanessa loved that bastard. She planned to marry him. She gave him everything ... her heart, her love ... *everything*. And he abused her."

"Physically?" Ariana interrupted, her heart screaming an instant denial.

"He brought her to the very depths of despair." Baxter jabbed his hands in his pockets, either oblivious to Ariana's question or unwilling to answer it. "He taught her the meaning of jealousy, fear, and cruelty. Until she had nothing left inside her. Nothing."

Ariana forced herself to consider Baxter's implication objectively, striving to reconcile her memories of their stunning, vibrant older sister with Baxter's description of the despondent, lethargic woman who had lost all will to live. Had Vanessa truly been *that* devastated? Over a man?

Ariana pressed her lips together, contemplating the Trenton she knew: his anger and vengeance, his potential for ruthless brutality. Then, with an adamancy she never knew she possessed, she shook her head in definitive repudiation. "No. It makes no sense." Ignoring Baxter's stricken expression, she pressed on, purposefully avoiding any mention of Trenton. "Vanessa was an independent, self-assured woman."

"Perhaps she appeared that way to a twelve-year-old."

For a second, Ariana faltered. *Could* her memories of her sister be merely the misconceptions of youth, clouded further by the passage of time?

As Ariana hesitated, Theresa's words crystallized in her mind, unbidden yet strangely enlightening. *I don't believe love was ever the issue… You recall your sister—how can you not be sure of that?*

"No, Baxter." With renewed strength, Ariana stood her ground. "One man's rejection would not be enough to incite Vanessa to take her own life."

"Then he took it for her."

Ariana inhaled sharply. It wasn't the first time Baxter had uttered those words aloud, but it was the first time they had cut through her like a knife. "Why would he?"

"He's a vicious animal … that's why."

"That's an opinion, not a reason," Ariana refuted, trying to still her body's involuntary trembling. "What proof do you have?"

"Proof?" Now Baxter's anger was directed at Ariana. "If I had actual proof, the bloody madman would be in Newgate!" He advanced toward her, his eyes narrowing on her face. "What's happened to you, Ariana? You never questioned my word before. You're a Caldwell, dammit! And we're talking about our *sister!*"

"I know we are!" Tears stung Ariana's eyes. "But why are you so certain that her death was either murder or suicide? Why couldn't it have been a horrible accident?"

"Because it wasn't." Baxter clamped his fists together. "Why? Has your *husband*"—he spat out the word—"managed to convince you of that fact?"

"Trenton and I haven't discussed Vanessa."

"Of course not! If you'd discussed Vanessa, then *Trenton* would be forced to tell you of her journal!"

An onerous silence descended, heavy as a fatal blow.

"Journal?" Ariana managed at last. "What journal?"

Baxter's mouth snapped shut, as if by doing so it could recall his hastily blurted words.

"What journal, Baxter?" Ariana prodded.

"The one she kept during the months preceding her death," he answered reluctantly.

"Why wasn't I ever told of this?"

Baxter snatched up his glass and refilled it, desperately in need of fortification. "You said it yourself, Ariana. You were barely twelve years old. You were told as much as you needed to know."

"What was in Vanessa's journal and how did you get it?" Ariana asked, her stomach knotted with dread.

"You don't really want to hear this," Baxter warned.

"Let me be the judge of that."

He sighed ... heavily. "I found the journal beneath Vanessa's pillow the day after she died. It was almost as if she'd left it there because she *wanted* me to find it." He rubbed his temples. "If the journal had been there prior to that day, Theresa would have stumbled upon it when she straightened up. So I can only assume that Vanessa placed it there ... *that* night."

"Go on." Ariana leaned against the side of the desk, struggling for composure.

"It contained recountings of Vanessa's courtship with Kingsley. The madman coveted her like some cherished possession ... one *he* controlled. As long as she was by his side he was content. But when she wasn't, he became irrational. He hired men to follow her, to see where she was going, whom she was meeting. His twisted jealousy evolved into a hideous, insane obsession. As the months went by, he became more and more unbalanced, totally convincing himself that Vanessa was being unfaithful to him … repeatedly, wantonly … like some common street trollop."

"And was she?"

"Never." Baxter bit out the words. "But that didn't deter Kingsley. If a gentleman so much as tipped his hat in Vanessa's direction, he suspected the worst and threatened to kill the man on the spot. When Vanessa eventually rebelled, he threatened to kill her too. She was paralyzed with fear."

"You witnessed all this?" Ariana whispered.

"I didn't need to!" Baxter snapped. "I knew Kingsley was unstable; I'd seen enough evidence of that. And I knew he had some kind of unique hold over Vanessa. … Initially, I assumed it was merely because of how much she loved him. But as time passed, I watched her change before my very eyes. She became depressed, jumpy, withdrawn. She rarely left the house except when Kingsley summoned her. Then she sped to his side, as if she were terrified of keeping him waiting. That's when I intervened, begging her to sever their relationship. She refused, insisting that she loved him with her whole heart. Had I known all her journal later revealed, I would have murdered the bastard in cold blood. Instead, I learned the truth too late." Baxter's voice broke. "He'd already killed Vanessa."

"The journal couldn't possibly have stated that," Ariana gasped, paling.

"The implication is there," Baxter spat out, exuding raw hatred. "Whether it was suicide or murder, the end result remains unchanged: Trenton Kingsley killed our sister."

"Dear Lord." Ariana covered her face with trembling hands.

"So … at last you believe me?"

She raised her chin, ignoring Baxter's question in lieu of her own. "Despite these monstrous possibilities, you allowed me to marry him?"

Baxter didn't flinch. "Yes."

"How could you?" Her voice shook.

"As I've said before, I knew you'd be safe."

"You knew I'd be safe? How in the name of heaven could you know that?"

Guilt flashed briefly in Baxter's eyes, ugly memories rearing their heads. "I gave you that answer the day Kingsley brandished his royal decree at Winsham. No one has forgotten the unresolved tragedy of Vanessa's death ... and suspicion has resurfaced along with Kingsley's re-emergence from the Isle of Wight. All eyes are upon him, and he knows it. No, Ariana, Kingsley wouldn't dare harm you."

Ariana dashed bitter tears from her cheeks. "I want to see the journal," she demanded, needing something more tangible than Baxter's accusations to strip away her last filaments of intuition and faith.

"I don't have it."

"Who does?"

"Kingsley."

Weakly, she sank into a chair, her eyes widening with shock. "You'd better explain."

With a defeated sigh, Baxter nodded. "At this point I might as well tell you everything." He clasped his hands behind his back, studying Ariana's face to monitor her mental state. "As I said, I discovered the journal beneath Vanessa's pillow. On her nightstand was a letter she'd written to me the day before she died. It was heartbreaking, filled with torment. ... And its message was painfully clear." He paused to compose himself. "Our sister was saying good-bye."

Ariana dug her fingers into the arms of the chair. "A suicide note?"

"Seemingly so ... yes."

Baxter's dubious tone found its mark. "You still believe she was murdered ... why?"

"Because Vanessa's final journal entry, penned the same day as her letter, revealed far more than her note." Baxter shuddered, remembering. "I had gone out that evening. Apparently, sometime during my absence, Kingsley delivered a message commanding Vanessa to meet him at once. Whatever his words, the tone was obviously far beyond reason or sanity. Vanessa's terrified state of mind was chillingly evident in her writing. Her references to Kingsley were sinister, ominous. She was obviously petrified about what Kingsley planned to do to her." Baxter's jaw clenched. "I'll never forgive myself for being away when Vanessa needed me."

"What did you do once you'd read the letter and the journal?" Ariana prompted, a hairsbreadth away from collapse.

"Do?" He leveled his gaze on hers. "Right after Vanessa's mutilated gown was found washed up on shore, I ordered Kingsley to Winsham. I confronted him with both documents."

"What was his reaction?"

"He coerced me into giving him the journal."

Ariana shot up like an arrow. "*Coerced* you? How did he coerce you?"

Bitterness twisted Baxter's features into a mask of hatred. "He threatened me, swore he'd strip me of everything I had left if I didn't turn the journal over to him. I knew by the burning lunacy in his eyes that he was capable of anything ... even murder. I had you to consider, sprite. You were my responsibility ... and all I had left. He'd already robbed me of Vanessa. So I gave him the journal."

"But if you'd delivered it to the authorities—"

"They'd say it was the unstable ramblings of a suicidal woman," Baxter cut in. "The journal was rife with implications, Ariana, but no concrete proof."

"Yet Trenton insisted on having it."

"Of course he did! There wasn't enough evidence to convict the bastard, but there was certainly enough to destroy his name and ruin his family. Society is not nearly so discerning as the courts: They would condemn him on Vanessa's words alone."

Ariana nodded numbly. "So you gave him the journal."

"Yes. All I wanted was to expel Trenton Kingsley from our lives forever."

The irony of the situation was almost too much for Ariana to bear. The man Baxter had sought to banish from their lives was now her husband.

"I never expected him to return, Ariana," Baxter said softly, reading her mind. "Even though no one ever saw the journal, news of Vanessa's probable suicide quickly spread … along with speculation about its cause. The combination of Kingsley's own guilt and public pressure was too much for him. He fled to Wight six years ago and hasn't returned … until now."

Baxter's words triggered a thought in Ariana's mind. "Where is Vanessa's suicide note?"

Baxter kneaded his taut neck muscles. "I have it."

"Please show it to me."

"Sprite …" Baxter began gently, bending to reach for her hands, "I don't think that's a good—"

"I want to see it, Baxter." Ariana snatched her fingers away, defying her brother for the first time in her young life.

"Very well," Baxter agreed, his brow knit with concern. "I'll get it."

Ariana sank back into the chair the moment she was alone, trying to absorb the shock she'd suffered—and the one she had yet to bear. Her sister's suicide note. What would it say? And what of the journal Baxter had relinquished? Had it described Trenton as a madman, a murderer? Ariana closed her eyes, lowering her head to ward off the bleak despair. It wasn't true. It couldn't be true. How could she have been so totally wrong about her husband?

Violent, groundless jealousy. The memory of Trenton's unwarranted tirade yesterday stirred to life, in Ariana's mind, refusing to be stifled. Had *jealousy* been its cause? Jealousy, incited by discovering her with Dustin? *Irrational … groundless.* Yes … both. *Violent.* Lord, yes … Trenton had been capable of almost anything. But … murder?

As if from a great distance Ariana heard Coolidge's voice asking if Her Grace were feeling well, and her own automatic reply, assuring him that she was perfectly fine. Gratefully, she accepted a cup of tea, then dismissed him, sitting back to await her brother's return.

Baxter reached the study just as Coolidge emerged.

"The telegraph?" Baxter asked at once.

"Everything has been arranged, my lord. The telegraph will be sent immediately."

"Good." Baxter glanced past him into the study. "Is my sister all right?"

"I'm not sure. She's terribly pale. I poured her a cup of tea."

"Thank you, Coolidge." Baxter removed the folded sheet from his pocket and stared down at it. How long had it been since he'd read Vanessa's final words? "I'll take care of things from here," he vowed quietly.

"Of course, sir." Coolidge held the door ajar for Baxter to enter, then closed it securely.

"Ariana?" Baxter frowned at her bent head and glazed expression.

Ariana stood at once, placing her teacup on the table and advancing toward her brother, hand extended. "Let me see the letter."

Wordlessly, Baxter gave it to her, standing protectively by her side while she read.

Ariana's hands shook as she smoothed out the page, instantly recognizing Vanessa's bold, flowing hand.

Dear Baxter:

I never meant for it to come to this, but my choices have all been seized. Each day I prayed for it to end, for the sun to shine again, yet my prayers went unanswered. The pain that possesses me becomes more than I can bear, and even you, dear brother, can do nothing to stop its perpetual assault. All I crave is peace, and there appears to be but one way to attain it. Do not be angry, with me or yourself, for numbness will mean blessed relief and I am too much a coward to refuse it.

Know always that I love you and that you were right about Trenton. Had I only listened, we could all have been spared these months of sorrow.

My course is set. Prosper and grieve not.

Vanessa

Ariana raised her head, tears trickling down her cheeks. Wordlessly, she thrust the letter back at Baxter, internally numb, outwardly limp and unresisting as he gathered her against him.

"I'm sorry, sprite," he murmured, stroking her hair. "I tried to warn you."

"And you're saying that the journal is even worse than this?" she asked in a small, strangled voice.

Baxter swallowed audibly. "Yes. This letter implies suicide ... the journal alludes to something much worse."

Ariana pulled away. "I have to leave now." She drew a quivering breath and headed for the door.

"Where are you going?"

She turned, every trace of the innocent child gone from her eyes. "Back to Broddington. There are ghosts to uncover and put to rest. And I intend to do just that."

Instinctively, Baxter took a step forward, then checked himself, halting in his tracks. Perhaps it was better this way. She was angry now, all fragments of her earlier softening having vanished. If she returned to Broddington now and confronted Kingsley, it could only serve to broaden the chasm between husband and wife, unraveling the fragile relationship that had apparently been forged.

Massaging his throbbing forehead, Baxter silently cursed Kingsley for all he had taken, all he was still taking.

But it was far from over. Ariana was a Caldwell: She would return to Winsham. Next time, Baxter would tell her of his plan.

Reflexively, he gripped Vanessa's letter tightly in his hand.

At long last, he and Ariana would bring Trenton Kingsley to his knees.

CHAPTER 12

She had to face Trenton.

Ariana stood in the sheltering warmth of the conservatory, her instinctive haven at Broddington. Lulled by the warmth of the summer sun, she drank in the solace of the fragrant flowers and velvet greenery that surrounded her.

But in this case, nature alone was not enough to comfort her. In truth, nothing could truly alleviate the turmoil wreaking havoc in her heart and mind.

What would she say to him? How should she behave?

Vanessa's letter had been the writing of a desperate woman. And Trenton was the cause of her desperation: Of that there was no doubt. The questions remaining were several: How far had Trenton allowed his rage to carry him? And how much of Vanessa's ramblings had been actual truth, how much distorted perceptions of it?

Most important of all, did Ariana dare continue to trust her own instincts when it came to Trenton? Could she permit herself to care for a man who was a cruel and possessive blackguard—or worse? Would *she* be his next victim?

Ariana rubbed her closed eyelids with her fingertips, praying she could somehow, some way, separate fact from fiction, delve into the past so the present was clear, the future fathomable.

"Well, my wayward bride returns."

Ariana whirled about, her startled gaze finding her husband where he lounged in the open conservatory doorway, watching her with scorching intensity.

"Trenton ..." She could hear the hollow, phobic quality of that one uttered sound as it reverberated through the vaulted room.

Trenton heard it too. He dropped his lit cheroot to the grass, crushing it beneath his heel, and stalked menacingly toward his wife.

Trenton Kingsley killed our sister. Baxter's earlier accusations crashed down in torrents, the litany a harsh, stinging blow to Ariana's composure. *The madman coveted her like some cherished possession. ... His twisted jealousy evolved into a hideous, insane obsession. ... Kingsley was unstable. ... He killed our sister.*

Ariana visibly recoiled.

"I commend your brother," Trenton commented bitterly, halting only when he loomed directly over her. "He's done his job well."

"W-what do you mean?" Ariana groped behind her, clutching the thick stalk of a potted fern for balance.

"An ineffective weapon, at best."

"Pardon me?"

Trenton gestured behind her. "The fern. Surely you can find a more compelling object than that with which to fend me off. I hardly expect to be felled by a plant."

Ariana released the stem at once. "Do I need to fend you off?"

"What do you think?"

His voice was low, chilling, his body ominously still, emanating the controlled power and turbulence of a coiled viper ready to strike.

Torn between the urge to run for her life and the equally pressing urge to beseech her husband to deny all she had just uncovered, Ariana did neither, merely staring at him in bewildered silence.

"Poor misty angel," Trenton droned, his husky tone alluding to something that could have been either tenderness or derision, "you look like a terrified doe." Ignoring the inadvertent stiffening of Ariana's body, he slid his hand around her nape, stroking softly, running his fingers through the thick waves of her hair. "Frightened at last?" he taunted.

"I don't know," she whispered. "Should I be?"

His grip tightened. "What did Caldwell tell you?"

She paled. "Tell me?"

"Ah, what an atrocious liar you are," Trenton mocked, drawing her nearer. "As I said, your brother has done his job well."

"Please, Trenton ..." She flattened her palms against his chest, staving him off.

"Please ... what?" The question was a tantalizing caress, completely belied by the furious sparks flaring in his eyes.

Apprehension constricted Ariana's chest. "Let go of me," she commanded, softly at first, then insistently, struggling to free herself. "Let me go!" She jerked loose of his grasp, retreating backward a dozen paces.

Trenton made no move to follow but held his arms rigidly at his sides, fury radiating from his massive frame. "How much do you want?"

"What?" Ariana was lost ... lost and afraid.

"How much did he tell you to ask for, dammit!" Trenton sliced the air with his open palm, knocking over an entire line of geraniums, sending ruined flowers scattering at Ariana's feet.

"I don't know what you're talking about!" she cried.

"Your brother..." Trenton ground out between clenched teeth. "He wants money ... as always. How much did he tell you to bleed me for?"

Ariana straightened, her own eyes smoldering as comprehension dawned. "Money? Baxter and I never discussed money!"

Trenton threw back his head and laughed: an eerie, disbelieving laugh. "Never? I find that dubious, at best. Jewels, then? Or valuable paintings? Or perhaps every bloody treasure Broddington has to offer?"

"Baxter and I want nothing from you!" she shot back, the emotional impact of the day converging to explode inside her. "You got what you wanted when you coerced me to marry you! Now all I want is for you to leave me alone!"

"Leave you alone?" Trenton's laughter faded, replaced by a forbidding stillness that was far more frightening. "Funny, that's not the plea I recall hearing in our bed last night. Or was that coercion too, my indignant wife? Did I *coerce* you to give me your beautiful body, not once but countless times? Did I take you against your will, command you to lie with me? Did I, Ariana?"

Ariana's lips trembled, but she didn't flinch. "No," she said in a tiny voice, admission and sadness reflected in her magnificent turquoise eyes, "that I did on my own." With heart-wrenching candor, she added, "And I don't regret a single moment of it."

A muscle flexed in Trenton's jaw and he dragged his gaze from the honest emotion in hers. "If you and your brother didn't discuss wresting my sizable fortune, what did you discuss?"

"Vanessa."

A deafening silence.

"I read her suicide note." Ariana raised her chin, valiantly confronting Trenton with the truth. "I never knew it existed."

Shutters descended over Trenton's eyes, and his lips curled sardonically. "Well, well. Caldwell was even busier than I anticipated."

"You and I have to discuss—"

"No."

Ariana's chin came up. "Let me clarify my statement. We *must* discuss Vanessa's death; there is no longer any alternative."

"I *will not* speak of your sister," Trenton growled. "Not now ... or ever. Listen to me, Ariana, and heed me well. Do *not* pursue this matter. You don't know what you're talking about ... or what the consequences could be."

Prickles of fear ran up Ariana's spine as she studied the biting hatred on her husband's face. Fox. a fleeting instant she saw Trenton as Vanessa must have: as a man who was, beyond the shadow of a doubt, capable of murder.

Trenton correctly interpreted his wife's apprehensive expression, and the realization that she so profoundly feared him splintered the last of his control. Striding forward, he grabbed her elbow, jerking her roughly against him. "You're my wife, Ariana! Loathe it or not, you belong to me. And no evils of the past can alter that."

The color drained from Ariana's cheeks and she voiced a token protest, shaking her head haltingly from side to side. With a muffled curse, Trenton brought his mouth down on hers, bruising her lips with the violence of his kiss. "Damn her to hell," he muttered, ravaging Ariana's mouth with his own. "Damn each and every bloody Caldwell to hell."

He crushed Ariana to his chest, forcing her to accept his brand of total possession. His tongue thoroughly plundered her mouth, his arms held her captive with a grip of iron. Fiercely, he used his brutal kiss to proclaim her as his until at last, unable to conquer the assault, Ariana went limp and unresisting in his arms.

Feeling his wife's struggles cease, Trenton tore his mouth away, dragging air into his lungs, desperately trying to still the red haze of fury that had accosted him. Panting, he stared down into Ariana's ashen face, scrutinizing her to see if her terror of him remained.

Tears glistened in her eyes, on her cheeks. "Are you finished?" she asked quietly. "Or do you plan to hurt me too?"

Abruptly, he shoved her away from him. "Get out of here," he ordered, veering away. He crossed the room, slamming his fists against a marble pillar. "Just get out of my sight—now!"

Ariana needed no further invitation. Gathering her skirts, she raced from the conservatory, never looking back.

Trenton listened to the sound of his wife's heels echoing down the hall until they faded and finally disappeared altogether. Slowly, he averted his head, staring at the empty doorway, the tormented fires of hell raging in his soul. It had been years since he'd lost control like that: striking out at a woman without thought or sanity. The last time had been six years ago—and the consequences had been fatal.

But his motivation this time was drastically different.

And that difference sent warning bells clanging through every nerve cell in his body.

Trenton raked his fingers through his hair, the sweetness of his wife's reluctant mouth still lingering on his tongue, her anguished tears still etched in his mind. He wanted to choke Baxter Caldwell with his bare hands for showing Ariana that letter.

And the letter was only the beginning: merely one layer of the monstrous past for Caldwell to peel away.

"Why am I not surprised to find you here?" Dustin teased, leaning against the stable wall.

Ariana looked up from where she sat, amid a tall pile of hay on the stall floor. Tenderly, she stroked the soft head of a small yellow chick that sat contentedly cradled in her hands. "Were you looking for me?"

Dustin frowned, taking in Ariana's tear-streaked face and wide, haunted eyes. "What's happened, sweetheart?"

She lowered her head. "Nothing I want to discuss."

Dustin crossed the stall and lowered himself beside her, lifting her chin and forcing her to meet his gaze. "Is it Trent?"

Ariana gave a hollow laugh. "Isn't it always?"

"No, not always," he countered softly. "There are times when he makes you look positively radiant."

Pink-cheeked, she turned away. "That's because I'm a romantic fool."

"Romantic yes. A fool, never."

"You're wrong, Dustin. I'm the very worst of fools. In letting my instincts guide me, I'm afraid I've allowed myself to fall victim to a heinous lie."

Dustin was silent for a moment, sifting a handful of hay through his fingers. "Trenton's feelings are no lie, Ariana. He cares for you … a great deal. Probably more than he knows, definitely more than he cares to admit."

"To the contrary, Dustin, the only feeling your brother has for me is contempt. He loathes me for being a Caldwell, and married me out of some obsessive need for vengeance." She buried her face in the chick's downy feathers. "Although why in heaven's name *he* should seek retribution, when it was *my* sister who died, is beyond me."

Dustin's jaw set. "You've been at Winsham?"

Ariana's head came up, her brows arched in surprise at Dustin's icy tone. "Yes … today, as a matter of fact."

"Then that explains whatever stormy encounter you had with Trent."

"Why?" she asked incredulously. "Surely Trenton didn't expect me to break off all ties with my brother simply because I married a man who despises him. Why would my visit to Winsham enrage him so?"

Uneasily, Dustin smoothed his mustache, measuring his reply. "Trent has his reasons," he said at last.

"What are they?"

"I'm not the one you should be asking, Ariana."

"But I *am* asking you," she pleaded, clutching his arm. "Please, Dustin … You're the only friend I have at Broddington. Won't you give me *some* insight into the past?"

Dustin stared at the small hand gripping his arm, torn between loyalty and compassion. When reason interceded on the side of compassion, reminding him that Trenton's future happiness hinged on the eradication of his past, he made his decision. "Baxter and Trent go back many years," he explained cautiously. "Since they were in their late teens."

"Before Vanessa and Trenton were …"

"Yes."

Ariana blinked in surprise. "I didn't know that. How did they meet?"

"They were both competitors for an investment in a small manufacturing firm. The details don't matter anymore. Suffice it to say, they had different methods of attaining their goals. Their antipathy was rapid and mutual."

Ariana scooted the chick off her lap and drew her knees up, resting her chin thoughtfully atop them. "Was Baxter unethical?"

Silence.

"Dustin, I know my brother ... quite well, in fact. I have no false illusions about his character." Seeing Dustin's startled expression, she hastened on, qualifying her statement. "Baxter loves me; I know he does ... in his way. But he will go to great lengths to retain his material comforts or, as is too often the case, to regain them. So if he stooped to somewhat shady methods to achieve his ends, it wouldn't surprise me."

"*You* surprise *me*," Dustin replied, shaking his head.

"Why? Because I'm objective about those I love?" Ariana shrugged. "To me, love means recognizing someone's flaws and caring in spite of them." Tilting her head, she gave Dustin a searching look. "Isn't that what you do?"

His lips curved slightly. "I suppose I do. My, my ... And here I thought I was the one teaching you." Tenderly, he wrapped a strand of her hair about his finger and tugged. "For one so young, you're very wise."

Ariana smiled back. "Wise, perhaps, but not terribly worldly. I know enough about your brother to guess that he is rigidly principled in his business dealings. I can see why that would create conflict with Baxter. What I don't see is how Vanessa fits into—"

"Let's say that Trent's and Baxter's differing philosophies extended to women as well."

"Women? But Vanessa was our sister!"

"Prior to Vanessa. As far back as I can remember." Dustin released Ariana's lock of hair, holding her gaze with his. "As you are well aware, Trent is a handsome, titled, and extremely wealthy man. Needless to say, women flocked to him in droves."

An unexpected twist of jealousy gripped Ariana's heart.

"There were many women over the years," Dustin continued. "Some were coveted by others, but were drawn to Trenton nonetheless."

Comprehension dawned on Ariana's face. "What you're saying is that Baxter and Trenton traveled in the same circles, and that the desirable ladies pursued Trenton, rather than Baxter."

Dustin nodded. "Yes, that's what I'm saying." Abruptly, he averted his gaze. "Your brother didn't take kindly to the situation. He took his affections elsewhere ... and his investment funds as well. His resulting way of life diametrically opposed Trent's."

Ariana gave a resigned sigh. "In short, Baxter gambled excessively and had indiscriminate affairs with married women. ... Trenton did not."

Again, Dustin started. "So you did know!"

"About Trenton? No. About Baxter, of course I knew, I love my brother, but I have no misconceptions about his questionable values. I simply accept them as part of him." She chewed her lip thoughtfully. "If Baxter disliked Trenton all those years, why would he allow Vanessa to become involved with him?"

"It wasn't Baxter's choice."

"So that's why Baxter and Vanessa argued," Ariana murmured, remembering how surprised she'd been to overhear her brother's and sister's sudden, relentless shouting matches. Until then, Baxter had never raised his voice to Vanessa; to the contrary, he'd perpetually indulged her as his most beautiful and prized asset.

"On your brother's behalf, Trent had, by that time, acquired a rather extensive reputation with the *ton's* unattached young women," Dustin added, attempting to soften some of the day's upsetting revelations. "So I'm sure that added fuel to Baxter's fire."

"Was Trenton's reputation earned?" Ariana heard herself ask.

Dustin's brows rose. "I'm not sure I should answer that question." Seeing the unmistakable distress and confusion in Ariana's eyes, he enfolded her hand between his. "Sweetheart, Trenton is much older than you: It's only natural that he—"

"I'm well aware of that, Dustin," she interrupted, pushing her nagging jealousy to the far recesses of her mind. "I'm not questioning the reasons for Trenton's past relationships. But he's so formidable, so menacing. Weren't women afraid of him?"

"Ariana ..." Dustin stared down at the small hand clasped in his. "Trent is not the same man he was years ago. Oh, he's always been the intense sort, deeply passionate about what he believes in. But in his twenties he was more congenial, charming, sociable ... with none of the bitterness you see now. His natural magnetism and self-assurance, combined with that overwhelming sense of power he emanates ... No, Ariana, women weren't afraid of him. Quite the contrary, actually."

"What happened to change him?" Ariana persisted, fighting the jealousy that once again reared its ugly head.

A pained expression tightened Dustin's face. "Our father died."

Ariana leaned closer, feeling she was hovering at the brink of a crucial precipice. "You told me Trenton and your father were very close."

"Very. Trenton ran all the family businesses and estates during the last years of Father's life. He gave up much of his youth, his education, his dreams. He was the most bloody devoted son I've ever seen."

"Was your father's death sudden?"

Harsh memories slashed across Dustin's face, drawing his mouth into a grim line of sorrow. "He had been weak for some time. But yes, his death was sudden."

"Was it precipitated by the shock of what Trenton did to Vanessa?" Ariana blurted out.

Dustin flung her hand aside as if her touch burned. "What *Trenton* did to *Vanessa?* Hell. Ariana, Trenton did *nothing* to Vanessa. ... It was very much the other way around!" Raking Ariana with condemning eyes, Dustin demanded, "Don't you realize my brother could never have lived with himself if he'd actually caused Father's death? As it is, he's torn apart. I thought I knew you, Ariana, but it appears that I don't. Not if you really believe what you just said."

Dustin's biting accusation pushed her over the edge.

Shattering into raw fragments, Ariana burst into tears, burying her face in her hands and shaking uncontrollably. "I don't know what to believe," she sobbed. "I'm so confused. … Help me, Dustin, I don't know what to do. Please, help me."

Regretfully, Dustin gathered her against him, pressing her head beneath his chin and stroking her back in soothing circles. "Shhh," he murmured, feeling her tears drench his shirt. "Of course I'll help you. Poor sweetheart, you don't know truth from lies at this point, do you? I'm sorry … I didn't mean to explode like that. It's not your fault; you're too young to remember, too innocent to protect yourself. Don't cry, little one, I'll help you."

"If my wife needs assistance, I'll provide it."

Ariana froze at the sound of Trenton's frigid words, her heart hammering frantically in her chest. The aftermath of her husband's violent assault still lingered on her lips, in her mind, and instinctively she burrowed closer to Dustin, seeking protection and comfort. Simultaneously, she realized how compromising they must look, clasped in each other's arms on the stable floor, clinging together as if they were involved in some sordid tryst.

She had no time to react before Trenton's hand closed roughly on her arm, dragging her away from Dustin and to her feet. "Did you need something, *Wife?*"

Ariana blanched beneath his blazing stare, his jaw clenched so tightly she thought it might snap.

"Trent … don't!" Dustin rose swiftly, stunned by the raw fury he saw etched on his brother's face—at the same time fully aware of its true cause. "Stop now before you do something you'll regret!"

"Before *I* do something *I'll* regret?" Trenton hurled back, his throat working convulsively. "I find my wife rolling around on the stable floor … with my brother, no less … and you want *me* to control *myself!*" His fingers bit into Ariana's arm. "Did I come in at an inopportune moment?"

Ariana winced. "You're hurting me," she whispered.

"Am I?" He released her abruptly and, without thinking, she took a reflexive step toward Dustin.

Thunder erupted in Trenton's eyes. "Don't push me, Ariana. I'm warning you, don't push me."

She turned to Dustin, white-faced.

"Go back to the house, sweetheart," he told her, his disbelieving gaze on Trenton. "I want to have a talk with my brother."

"Dustin," she protested, "I …"

"Fear not, misty angel." Trenton's tone was caustic, savage. "I'll restrain myself. … I won't murder Dustin."

Ariana stared at him, taking in his rage, his jealousy, the full impact of his power. Then, sick at heart, she heeded Dustin's suggestion and left the stable.

"You really have lost your mind, haven't you?" Dustin exploded the moment they were alone.

"You've noticed?" Trenton countered, kicking a pile of hay from his path.

"I've noticed a lot of things. It's time you noticed them as well."

"Are you referring to your feelings for my wife?"

"No … I'm referring to *your* feelings for your wife."

Trenton's eyes narrowed menacingly. "At this particular moment I'd like to throttle her. And if I'm correct, she fully expects me to do just that. Or worse."

"I don't blame her. You're behaving like a ruthless maniac."

"And you're going to save her from me, is that it?"

Dustin snorted. "Enough of this idiotic drivel, Trent. We both know there's nothing between Ariana and me."

"Then what is this about?"

"It's about the fact that you're falling in love with your wife."

Shock, undiluted and profound, registered on Trenton's face, altering quickly back to rage. Had Dustin been less observant or less adept at reading his brother's reactions, he would have missed the fraction of an instant that bridged the two emotions; an instant in which absolute raw panic dominated Trenton's expression.

But Dustin was both observant and adept, so he just leaned casually against the wall, watching as Trenton slammed his fists against the stall door, shouting vehement denials, followed by a vivid stream of expletives.

"The idea is less than acceptable, I presume?" Dustin inquired cheerfully over the din of his brother's bluster.

Trenton kicked the stall door wide and advanced furiously on Dustin. "Acceptable? It's ludicrous! You know damned well why I married Ariana! She's a Caldwell. The *last* Caldwell. And if by wrenching her away from Winsham I caused her brother endless suffering, it was worth the sacrifice."

"Sacrifice?" Dustin cocked a brow in Trenton's direction, entirely unbothered by the dark inferno stalking him.

Trenton came to an abrupt halt. "All right, perhaps *sacrifice* is too strong a word."

"I should say so." Dustin's teeth gleamed in the semi-darkened stall. "Considering the amount of time you and your *sacrifice* spend in bed."

"I've never denied wanting Ariana. She's a beautiful woman. But what you're seeing is lust, not love."

"Is it?" Dustin grew serious. "I think not. Be honest with yourself, Trent. Aren't your feelings for Ariana surprisingly intense, considering the enmity that instigated your marriage?"

"All my reactions to the Caldwells are intense."

"I'm not discussing your animosity."

Trenton's anger hovered an instant longer, then ebbed into ambivalence. "She's so damned innocent," he muttered. "And she embraces life with such trusting faith. I suppose there's a part of me that wants to shield her … from the demons of the past. …" His voice became low, his gaze haunted by indiscernible ghosts. "And from me."

Regaining his composure, Trenton stared at his brother, his eyes glittering fiercely. "So what you're observing is protectiveness and perhaps a little pity."

"You're not ready to see it, are you?" Dustin noted quietly, shaking his head. "Baxter Caldwell obviously did even more damage to you than he realized."

"I'm not sure that's possible," Trenton replied bitterly. "Nor am I certain that I'm capable of the kind of love you're suggesting. But, even if I am, it could never be with the sister of—"

"I've said it before and I'll say it again, Trent: She's not Vanessa."

Trenton inhaled sharply. "I know that only too well."

"Ariana's not just different; she's very special. And you're too damned pigheaded to appreciate it."

"That's irrelevant. This war is not about Ariana."

"But you're using her as ammunition, which situates her right in the heart of the battle."

"Then what do you suggest?" Trenton demanded. "That I let go of the past? We've been through this time and again, Dustin. I simply cannot do that. Tell Ariana the truth? Half the time I'm not even sure what that truth is. Furthermore, she'd never believe me ... not after her enlightening afternoon at Winsham. So what option does that leave me?"

Dustin straightened. "Take Ariana away ... as far away from the root of your hatred as possible."

Some of the tension seemed to drain from Trenton's body. "Away? ... Where?"

"To Spraystone. You could put some distance between her and her fears, allow her to enjoy herself for a change. These past weeks haven't exactly been easy ones for her. ... First the Queen's edict, and now your turbulent marriage."

"Spraystone," Trenton repeated thoughtfully. "I never considered taking her there. ... It's hardly a grand estate, the type the average young woman dreams of residing in."

"There's nothing average about Ariana." Dustin's grin returned. "Spraystone is plush with greenery, alive with birds and animals. Your bride would adore it."

"You're forgetting something," Trenton interjected, scowling. "Ariana and I would be virtually alone. And at the moment, that thought would terrify her."

"The Isle is far from uninhabited," Dustin reminded him. "Introduce her to Princess Beatrice, let her meet the folks of Bembridge, teach her to sail. Bring along the croquet set, if it would make her feel more secure. Then she can throttle you with a mallet if you become too threatening."

"Do you really believe she'd be pleased?" Trenton asked gruffly, ignoring Dustin's jest.

"Try her."

A pensive silence. "It *would* keep here away from her brother's vicious claws."

"Definitely."

"And perhaps ease some of the burden she's been forced to bear," Trenton added, warming to the idea.

"Precisely."

A suspicious look flitted across Trenton's face. "Did you plan to join us?"

Dustin carefully schooled his features, desperately fighting the urge to laugh. "No, actually I'd best be getting back to Tyreham. My colt is being readied for the fall races at Newmarket. I'll be needed." He inclined his head. "That is, unless you'd *prefer* me to accompany you."

"No." The word erupted from Trenton's mouth with the speed and force of a bullet. "Actually, what I'd *prefer* is for you to stay the hell away from my wife."

Despite his best efforts, Dustin's lips twitched. "Ah … I see. I suppose that could be arranged. Although, as you yourself pointed out, Ariana is an incredibly beautiful woman. She's also intelligent and sensitive, and …"

"Dustin, I'm not finding you at all amusing." Trenton's voice exuded a clear warning.

"Jealous, Trent? Now that is surprising, considering the fact that emotions play no part in your marriage."

"Dustin ..."

Ignoring Trenton's furious admonition, Dustin chuckled, patting his brother's arm. "First thing in the morning, I'll leave for Tyreham ... and you and Ariana will leave for Spraystone. Now I would suggest you go tell your bride to pack."

Trenton gazed soberly toward the house where Ariana had fled in order to escape his wrath. Lord alone knew what she was thinking, feeling. Shock and bewilderment, at best. And no one could alleviate that but him.

CHAPTER 13

Ariana was still trembling when she curled up in the center of her bed. She wanted to bury herself in the thick quilt and block out the world, the day, her meeting with Baxter, everything.

Not to mention her husband's violent, erratic behavior.

If she'd been frightened before, she was petrified now.

Trenton's venom had been a tangible entity, powerful enough to—she forced herself to complete her thought—to kill.

Her mind drifted back to Vanessa's letter. Was that the jealousy Trenton had demonstrated six years ago? Had that irrational, overwhelming possessiveness made her fear for her life?

Pressing her face into the pillow, Ariana battled the relentless images that slashed through her mind. Twice she'd fallen victim to Trenton's out-of-control jealousy: first, yesterday when he'd stormed across Broddington's front lawn, accusation blazing in his eyes after her croquet lesson with Dustin. And then again, just now in the stables.

Did he actually believe she and Dustin would deceive him?

Ariana's hands balled into defensive fists, leaving deep impressions in the soft feather pillow.

She could understand, if not condone, Trenton's lack of faith in her. She was his wife, yes, but still a veritable stranger, intimate in bed, but not in fact. He'd had no occasion to discover that, unlike her brother, she possessed a fierce sense of loyalty and an unbreachable set of principles. In Trenton's mind, she was simply a Caldwell: devoid of value, unworthy of trust.

But Dustin? Did Trenton truly believe his brother would *ever* deceive him, let alone disgrace him in his own home? The very concept was untenable. Surely Trenton must know that.

A gnawing possibility emerged, rearing its ugly head in Ariana's mind. Could it be, just as Baxter had said, that Trenton was genuinely unable to retain any degree of reason when it came to what he considered his possessions—a category in which she now very much fell? Under certain circumstances, was he beyond rational thought even when the supposed indiscretion involved his own brother?

That question brought her thinking back to Dustin: Dustin who had been nothing but wonderful to her ... until she'd implied that Trenton could be guilty of killing Vanessa. Then, from a warm and sensitive friend, Dustin had been instantly transformed into an angry and scornful stranger.

Not only had he defended his brother vehemently, he'd also implied it was Vanessa who had been the true culprit. What on earth had he meant by that?

And Dustin's reaction disturbed Ariana for another reason. Despite his love for Trenton, Dustin's verbal onslaught and irrational partiality were totally inconsistent with his personality. She had spent enough time in his company to recognize his innate objectivity, even when it came to assessing the behavior of those he loved. And yet, in this case, he was adamant in his conviction that Trenton was innocent—in spite of all the tangible evidence he must know. Why?

The answer was simple. Dustin believed in his brother, not with a sense of blind sibling loyalty, but with an absolute certainty that struck Ariana with all the force of a boulder. Because deep inside her she knew that Dustin wouldn't be so sure if there weren't a solid basis for his belief.

Pushing herself to a sitting position, Ariana dashed the tears from her cheeks, wondering uneasily what undisclosed details of the past Baxter had neglected to relay to her—and how she could uncover them. She might have learned more from Dustin if Trenton hadn't broken into the stables like a jealous madman, interrupting their conversation.

One thing she had managed to learn was that the subject of Richard Kingsley evoked great emotion in both brothers and that neither of them seemed willing to discuss the details of his death.

Elbows on her knees, Ariana leaned forward speculatively, resting her chin on her hands. Richard Kingsley had died very shortly after Vanessa. That much she knew. If his death hadn't been caused by the shock of his elder son's crime, then what had precipitated his sudden passing? And why did both Trenton and Dustin seem so determined to shroud the circumstances surrounding the late duke's passing in mystery?

Ariana frowned. She had nowhere to turn for her answers. She'd never resort to questioning outsiders; that would both embarrass and scandalize her husband. So how could she gain more information about Richard Kingsley without alerting Dustin and Trenton to her intent and without resurrecting old wounds that could only hurt the Kingsley name?

Trenton's sitting room.

The idea sprang into her head, an answer and a challenge. What a perfect starting point! She would go to Trenton's sitting room, explore a bit ... and maybe learn something.

Filled with a sense of purpose, Ariana came to her feet with a thud. She hadn't the slightest notion of what she hoped to find in a room that was virtually bare, but any shred of Richard Kingsley's memory, no matter how small, would be well worth an investigation of those barren walls. She'd intended to visit the room anyway to begin planning its redecoration—a feat she was determined to accomplish.

Quickly, Ariana ran a comb through her disheveled hair, the vision of Trenton's anguished expression when he'd spoken of his aversion to the sitting room, to the pain and loss it elicited, materializing instantly in her mind. Why that picture caused her such pain, considering her own fears and misgivings—not to mention Trenton's bizarre, contradictory behavior toward her—she couldn't say. Perhaps it was Dustin's trust in Trenton, perhaps it was her own instinctual faith. She only knew that she desperately wanted to do this for her husband; that if she could give him nothing else, she would give him this small realm of peace, this place to call his own.

And maybe, in the process, unravel the tangled web of the past.

On silent, bare feet, Ariana slipped into the hallway, glancing furtively right and left. The hall was deserted. She padded down to the sitting room and opened the door.

The room was as she remembered it: stark and empty. She glanced at the neglected armchair, which bespoke long, contented hours of reading and sketching, then hurried past it to the desk. For a long moment she stood, hand hovering over the top drawer. Never in her life had she pried into someone else's things, and guilt fell heavily upon her, reminding her that what she was about to do was a gross invasion of privacy. Determination swiftly intervened, successfully arguing that her cause was a just one. Just and necessary.

Her decision made, Ariana yanked open the drawer.

A pile of sketches filled the drawer, sketches Ariana quickly recognized as various renovations to Broddington. The notes on each were initialed *R.K.*, so she had no doubt as to who had made them. Lifting the stack of papers, she peered beneath. Nothing.

Undaunted, Ariana replaced the documents and closed the drawer, pulling open the one directly beneath. The contents were few and carefully placed: three gold frames containing three old photographs; a woman and two young boys. Her lips curving upward, Ariana studied them, recognizing the late Duchess of Broddington from the portraits of her that hung in the gallery and the younger, midnight blue-eyed lad with the mischievous grin as Dustin.

Still smiling, Ariana turned her attention to the third photo, her tender sentiments vanishing in a rush as her gaze locked with the penetrating cobalt stare of her husband. Dustin had been right: Even as a boy, Trenton was magnificently compelling, handsome as sin, with only a hint of the devastating charm time had yet to enhance. His youthful face, free of the harsh lines he now bore, together with his dazzling smile, equally as infectious as Ariana had noted in the maze where they'd met, made him almost irresistible in his appeal. And yet, even in boyhood, he seemed almost frighteningly intense, holding Ariana prisoner with his piercing stare. A prickle of fear shot up her spine, and she tore her gaze away, her breath coming in shallow pants.

Abruptly, she dropped the photos back in place and slammed the drawer shut.

The noise echoed through the vacant room and Ariana started, having forgotten the threat of discovery, having forgotten everything as she always did beneath Trenton's hypnotic stare. Anxiously, she squatted behind the desk, waiting to see if she had alerted the household to her whereabouts.

Long minutes ticked by, accompanied only by the violent pounding of her heart.

At last, she heaved a sigh of relief and rose to continue her search.

The bottom drawer yielded only two old volumes of literature: one Milton, the other Chaucer. Ariana looked through them carefully, hoping to find a note or a letter that had inadvertently been left between the pages. She found nothing.

Disappointed, she slid the books back into the drawer, only to find they no longer fit. With a puzzled frown she removed them and tried again, this time at a different angle, but to no avail. The drawer simply refused to accept both volumes.

Groaning softly, Ariana dropped to her knees, placing both books on the floor beside her. This was a complication she hadn't expected and intended to correct immediately. While she had thus far managed to disturb nothing of consequence in the room, she harbored not the slightest doubt that Trenton would notice if one of the tomes that was originally within the desk was now atop it. She peered into the drawer and at first saw nothing. She was about to arise when a slight-variation in color caught her eye from the rear of the drawer. It was a subtly lighter hue of brown than the walnut desk, nearly invisible unless one was looking.

And Ariana was looking.

Eagerly, she reached inside, her fingers closing around a slim ledger or pad—one she had apparently upset when she'd removed the books. Pulling it out, she saw that she held a worn, unmarked notebook that housed perhaps thirty pages. Curious, she sat cross-legged on the floor, draping her skirts about her, and folded back the faded cover.

The scent of roses immediately accosted her. Roses: Vanessa's unmistakable fragrance.

With a terrified cry, Ariana dropped the notebook to the floor, her entire body going rigid with shock. The book she held was Vanessa's journal.

Trembling, Ariana inhaled sharply, fervently wishing she had never thought of exploring the sitting room. But she had, and now her choices were nil.

Still shaking violently, she reached out a tentative hand and picked up her sister's journal, staring at the flowing, familiar hand.

She'd wanted the truth. Now she would have it.

Page one was dated April 28, 1869: the spring before Vanessa's death. Wetting her parched lips, Ariana began to read.

I've finally met him. The man I've awaited forever. Trenton Kingsley. What a magnificent name. What a magnificent man. He says we have the entire Season to dance in each other's arms. He makes me dizzy even when we aren't dancing. I want him—and I intend to get him, just as I've gotten everything else I've ever wanted.

Ariana swallowed and turned the page.

May 15, 1869

I'm the envy of every woman in London. Trenton is shameless in his intentions and his pursuit. When I'm not beside him, his eyes are always upon me. It's only a matter of time before our feelings take over and all discretion is cast aside. Then, all I crave will be mine.

A ponderous weight descended on Ariana's heart, oppressive and aching. She fought it, silently chastising herself for the idiocy of her reaction. The fact that Trenton and Vanessa had been lovers was no new revelation, but one she'd known for years. So why on earth did it agonize her to see a confirmation of the truth?

It's just the shock of finding Vanessa's journal, she assured herself, *together with the jolt of reliving the past through her eyes.*

Ariana's shoulders sagged. She'd never lied to herself before, and she wouldn't begin now. The true cause of her immediate distress had nothing to do with Vanessa's death and everything to do with her life. Quite simply, the thought of Vanessa in Trenton's arms, the image of her in his bed, made Ariana ill.

Because, unthinkable as it was, she was still in love with her husband.

A sharp sting made Ariana wince. She hadn't realized she was gripping the journal so tightly. Slowly, she uncurled her fingers, watching a rivulet of blood redden her thumb where the paper had pierced it. Instinctively, she raised the injured finger to her lips, soothing the cut with the tip of her tongue—but not before a tiny bit of blood had trickled onto the open journal.

Uneasily, Ariana stared at the smudge of red that slowly stained the next page of Vanessa's words, feeling a disturbing sense of foreboding seep inside her as she returned to her reading.

June 17, 1869

I belong to you, Trenton, as we both knew I would. Nothing can undo what we have forged between us. And yet, you're restless, angry. When you should feel assurance, you feel only doubt. Your inner demons frighten me. Don't you believe you're all I want? You say you do, yet you strike out, again and again. Everyone fears you. I fear you. Your intensity burns me, inside and out. You're so volatile, so savagely intense, so possessive. It's as if you want something more than I have to give. Oh, Trenton, I can't lose you. But I can't hold you. You thrill me. You scare me. And I know there's no escape.

Ariana raised her head and struggled for control. There was truth to Vanessa's words: enough truth to terrify her. Trenton *was* every one of those things: volatile, intense, possessive. Frightening.

Dear God, what had he done?

Her head spinning, Ariana skipped ahead to the last few journal entries.

July 2, 1869

Why do you refuse to believe me, Trenton? I've never betrayed you. Yet you keep lashing out at me, hurting me again and again. I'm no match for your strength, your physical domination. When we love it's as if you want to punish me, to destroy me and absorb me all at once. There's madness in your eyes. I see it, and I want to run. But there's nowhere I can hide where you won't find me. You've made me realize that. So I must endure whatever pain you choose to inflict.

Pain? Ariana fought back a wave of nausea, focusing on the journal's final page.

July 25, 1869

It's over. Us, life—I can sense the finality, the futility, as I prepare to meet you. The wind outside is wild and relentless, but it pales beside the storm that rages within you, a storm that cannot be silenced. Within me lies only emptiness. There's nothing left, Trenton, not even pain. You've killed it all, and now only a shell remains. Do with me what you will. It no longer matters. Nothing matters. I'll join you where you await me. And at the water's edge, we'll say our good-byes.

With a strangled cry, Ariana slammed the journal shut, the words she'd just read forever engraved in her mind. She jammed her fist into her mouth, trying desperately to suppress the choked sobs that refused to be silenced. At the same time, the conversation she'd had with Trenton yesterday—in this very spot—replayed itself in her mind.

"Let's say I have no affinity for this room. I associate it with pain and loss."

"I understand."

"I wonder if you do."

At the time, Ariana had assumed Trenton referred to the painful loss of his father. Dear God, had he meant Vanessa? Was it *her* loss he'd alluded to?

Tears streamed down Ariana's face, unchecked and unnoticed. Was this the sanctuary Trenton sought to think about Vanessa, to write to her, to plot how to keep her?

Ariana squeezed her eyes shut, unable to suppress the ugly speculations besieging her.

Had Trenton forced Vanessa to make love to him in this very sitting room? Was that why he loathed spending time within these walls? Had he buried Vanessa's memory here alongside her journal? And was it her loss or the part he'd played in inciting it that tormented him?

"So … have you found what you were looking for?"

The journal hit the floor with a thud and Ariana leapt to her feet, terror knotting her stomach at the sight of Trenton looming in the open doorway.

"From the horrified look on your face, I'll assume the answer to my question is yes." Trenton closed the door, leaning back against it. "How much did you read?"

She could scarcely get out the words. "All of it," she whispered.

Menacing shadows descended on Trenton's face, and condemnation blazed in his eyes. "I hope to God you know what you've done."

Ariana had a sudden, overwhelming urge to flee: from her husband, from Broddington, and from the hideous past that continued to unravel before her like some horrid, inescapable nightmare.

"Don't even consider it."

"Consider… what?" Ariana fought the dizziness that threatened to envelop her.

"Bolting. You won't get far. And even if you do, I'll find you."

Ariana blinked, staring at Trenton as if he were a stranger; and indeed, at that moment, he was. "And what would you do then? Drag me back to Broddington? Beat me? Terrorize me?"

"Murder you?" Trenton suggested, his tone low, ominous.

All the color drained from Ariana's face. "What kind of a man are you?" she asked in aching disbelief.

"A vengeful, heartless one." Without warning, Trenton moved toward her, his stride swift, purposeful. His arm swung outward, and, Ariana flinched reflexively, awaiting the oncoming assault.

It never came.

With a mocking simile, Trenton leaned past her and scooped up the journal, snapping it shut with a violent flourish. "You should have heeded my advice. I did warn you not to dredge up the past."

"What are you going to do with me?" she forced herself to ask.

"Do?" Trenton slid the journal back into the desk drawer. "For the time being, I'm taking you to Spraystone."

"Spraystone?" Ariana started. "Why?"

"Because I'll be staying there and, as my wife, so will you."

"No." The word was out before she could recall it.

"No?" Trenton repeated, as if the sound were foreign to him.

"I—I really don't wish to leave Broddington," Ariana stammered, feeling as if she were drowning. "I'm just becoming accustomed to it."

"You'll accustom yourself to Spraystone as well. We leave first thing in the morning." Trenton raised her chin with his forefinger. "Anything else?"

Ariana kept her gaze averted, studying the hard lines of her husband's mouth. "Will Dustin be joining us?" she tried.

"No. Dustin is returning to Tyreham at dawn."

"I see." Ariana's heart sank in resignation. "Very well, then. I'll advise Theresa. We'll be ready to depart after breakfast."

"Theresa will be staying at Broddington."

Now Ariana's head shot up. "What?"

"You heard me. Spraystone is not designed to accommodate servants. It is modest in size and design. Theresa will remain here."

"Why are you doing this?" Ariana breathed, searching his face for her answer.

Something brief flashed behind Trenton's iron mask, then dissipated. "Broddington is my property. Spraystone is my home. I plan to go home. I intend for you to accompany me. I believe that is reasonably clear."

"Are you punishing me for reading the journal?"

His lips twisted bitterly. "Ariana, if I were punishing you, you'd know it."

"But you're forcing me to go with you."

"Think of it as a wedding trip." Trenton released her chin, turning to go. "Now I'd suggest you begin packing. Oh, and Ariana?" He paused in the doorway, his voice emanating icy condemnation. "Don't invade my privacy again."

Flinching as the door slammed shut, Ariana wrapped her arms about herself to still the trembling that began deep inside. What in heaven's name had she done? She'd unearthed Vanessa's journal, yes; but instead of resolving the past it had only succeeded in further complicating the present.

Ariana pressed her lips tightly together, lambasting herself for her stupidity and her helplessness. Intuition told her that this final act had pushed Trenton to the jagged edges of his control. Lord only knew what he intended—or what brutality he was capable of inflicting.

For her to accompany him to his isolated retreat would be insane. Yet what choice did she have, with escape a virtual impossibility?

No, like it or not, tomorrow morning she was departing for the secluded isle of Wight. Alone … with Trenton.

"Why are you receiving this news so calmly?" Ariana demanded, flinging two of her gowns to the bed.

Theresa chewed her lip thoughtfully. "I wouldn't suggest taking those, pet. They're far too warm for this time of year."

"What?" Ariana glanced impatiently at the gowns. "I don't care which bloody gowns I pack, Theresa! Do you understand the ramifications of what I'm telling you?"

Theresa nodded calmly, unsurprised by her mistress's rare show of temper. "I heard everything you said, Your Grace. And I can well understand your distress."

Ariana shot Theresa an incredulous look. "My *distress?* I'm being dragged to an isolated estate by the man who, in all likelihood, killed my sister, and you call that reason for *distress?*"

"Ah, I see." Theresa tucked a wiry sprig of hair back into her drooping bun. "You're doubting your instincts again."

"My instincts are intangible. Vanessa's journal is concrete."

"'There is nothing makes a man suspect much, more than to know little,'" Theresa quoted Bacon, at the same time continuing to pack. "The journal's existence is indeed a fact, but its words are open to interpretation."

"But if you'd read it—"

"It would verify what I already know. That Lady Vanessa was plagued and puzzled by your husband, and that the duke is a volatile, intense, and possessive man."

Ariana gripped Theresa's arm. "Those were Vanessa's exact words to describe Trenton."

"Yes, I know." Theresa frowned, smoothing her apron. "Where is that lovely peach summer gown? I could have sworn I laundered it."

"You *do* know," Ariana repeated, realization striking her with the force of a thunderbolt. "You've seen the journal, haven't you, Theresa? You've read it."

Theresa inclined her head, regarding Ariana with her keen, birdlike eyes. "I've seen it, yes, but I haven't held it in my hands."

"What does that mean?"

"It means I've seen the journal, numerous times, but only in my visions. So have I seen it? Yes … I have. Others, however, would argue that I have not." She smiled, patting Ariana's cheek. "Such is the case with Vanessa's words … and with the duke's guilt. As I've pointed out, appearance is a fascinating thing: changing in accordance with one's perspective, and often not as believed to be."

"I'm afraid to go to Spraystone with him," Ariana confessed, her fingers tightening on Theresa's arm.

"Had the duke any desire to harm you, his access is equally good at Broddington," Theresa submitted. "Has he made an attempt to do so?"

Ariana bowed her head, unbidden memories of long, exhilarating hours in Trenton's arms assailing her. "No," she admitted. "But why is he so adamant that no one accompany us to Spraystone?"

"Is it so unusual for a newly married man to want time alone with his bride?"

Ariana flushed. "No … of course not."

"In the words of Sir Francis, 'A man must make his opportunity, as oft as find it.' Why not use this trip as a chance to seek the truth, to learn your husband as openly in heart as you have in body?"

Ariana was too intrigued by that possibility to be embarrassed by Theresa's open reference to the marriage bed. "Do you think Trenton might actually offer me the truth?"

Theresa smoothed Ariana's copper tresses. "Truth cannot be forced upon us. One can lead us to it, but the choice whether or not to accept it as fact is ultimately ours. The duke is perpetually offering you the truth, pet. It is up to you when to accept it."

"He's told me nothing!"

"Hasn't he?"

Ariana shook her head, totally baffled. "Why is it that you and Dustin can so clearly see things I cannot?"

"That is the easiest question of all to answer. It is because, unlike the marquis and I, you are in love with your husband."

Sighing, Ariana asked, "Is it so obvious, then?"

"Only if one is looking"

The clock downstairs chimed midnight, and Ariana glanced toward the door, torn between eagerness and apprehension. "I wonder ..."

"He won't come to you tonight," Theresa supplied.

Disappointment thudded heavily in Ariana's chest.

"You have much to resolve, pet," Theresa said quietly, squeezing Ariana's hand. "You need to clear your head, to free yourself of distractions, to permit nature's allure to work its magic."

"To go to Spraystone?" Ariana voiced aloud, fear momentarily held at bay by Theresa's compelling description. "Is Wight really as beautiful as they say?"

"I hear tell it is a veritable paradise, a picturesque haven with a life all its own."

"Do you?" A faraway look came into Ariana's eyes. "It must be a miracle. ... An island where the animals run free and the trees climb as tall as the heavens permit."

"A perfect place to resolve one's doubts," Theresa agreed.

Ariana jolted back to reality, her gaze meeting Theresa's. "I *do* need to find the truth."

"Yes ... you do."

A current of communication ran between the two women without a word being spoken. At last, Ariana crossed the room to her wardrobe. "It's late, Theresa. We'd best finish packing my things."

Theresa nodded briskly. "Yes ... Your Grace. Tomorrow is nearly upon us."

CHAPTER 14

"How beautiful!"

Ariana stared, transfixed, as the yacht sailed toward Ryde Pier, the Isle of Wight's main port. All the anxiety that had accompanied her for the duration of the tense, silent journey from Broddington vanished in a rush, lost in the wake of the Solent's deepening blue waters and the island's beckoning greenery.

"What is that building?" Ariana questioned, completely forgetting that she and her husband had not spoken a word since yesterday.

"Trinity Church," Trenton supplied, following her line of vision. "It's Ryde's most graceful structure, enhanced by exquisite gardens and surrounding villas."

"And that?" Ariana asked eagerly.

"That's the Club House of the Royal Victoria Yacht Club. The Prince Consort laid the first brick there himself, almost thirty years ago. The architectural design is magnificent. ..."

"Do the yachts race?" Ariana interrupted.

"Yes, of course."

"Can we watch?"

Trenton's lips twitched. "It can be arranged."

"Oh, Trenton, what is that impressive structure over there?" Her eyes widened, and she answered her own question before Trenton could open his mouth. "Is that the Queen's Osborne House?"

"It is. If we were closer, you could see the bustle of activity that accompanies all of Victoria's visits to Wight. By summer's end, she will depart for Balmoral, and Osborne will grow quiet until Her Majesty returns in the fall."

Ariana inhaled sharply. "Honeysuckle," she breathed reverently. "And jasmine and poppies." She raised her face to the skies, studying the heavens and listening intently. "A pair of white-throats," she said, breaking into a smile. "Not very pleased with one another, judging from their argumentative tone. And a group of swallows, probably searching for food. I expect they shan't be disappointed." She cast a quizzical look at Trenton. "Are there many song thrush at Spraystone? Their tune … as well as that of the robin … are the most wonderful melodies to awaken to."

"I suppose so … I couldn't say." Trenton squinted into the sunshine, locating the squawking white-throats. "Are there actually recognizable differences between birds, besides, of course, their sizes and hues?"

Ariana blinked. "Of course! That's like wondering if all people are alike, other than their height and hair color!"

Amusement flickered in Trenton's eyes, and, unconsciously, his mouth curved into the devastating smile that made Ariana's heart lurch. "Forgive my ignorance. … I admit that birds are not my area of expertise. However, I've been awakened often enough by their twittering to assure you that a multitude of them are available at Spraystone for your exploration. Not to mention a bevy of other creatures."

"You have animals?"

"Enough to satisfy even you," he confirmed. "If you'd like, we can go directly to the barn so you can see for yourself."

"Is Spraystone far from here?"

Trenton shook his head, coming to stand beside her and pointing down the island's eastern coast. "Spraystone adjoins Bembridge, just several miles from Ryde Pier. A ferry will take us directly there."

"The island has ferries?" Ariana looked surprised.

"Yes, Ariana," he returned wryly. "Ferries … and coaches, as well. Contrary to your perception of a vast, deserted wilderness, thousands of people make their home on Wight."

"I see." Ariana digested that information carefully.

"Feeling more secure?" he taunted, his breath ruffling her hair. "Don't be. Spraystone itself is every bit as isolated as you fear."

Ariana's eyes slid shut, a shiver going up her spine as she absorbed the implication of Trenton's veiled threat. Their journey was ending; in a matter of hours she would be totally at her husband's mercy.

The scandalous truth, Ariana admitted to herself, was that her trembling reaction to Trenton's mocking reminder was not caused by fear alone. Equally as powerful as the dread that constricted her chest and made her knees quake was the staggering surge of desire that accompanied it.

She licked her dry lips, heady with the impact of her warring emotions. *What's happening to me?* she wondered, nearly giddy from the sensation of the hot sun against her face, her closed lids. *We haven't even docked yet. Can the island's magic truly be as potent as Theresa suggested?*

Trenton's fingers brushed the tingling skin of her forearm. "Welcome to Wight, misty angel," he murmured. "Ryde Pier is just ahead."

Ariana's eyes flew open and she shook her head in an effort to clear it. Still somewhat dazed, she gazed about, taking in her new surroundings. The yacht was gracefully gliding toward a dock, away from which led a broad street, dotted with people and an occasional traveling coach, and lined with buildings of various sizes and stature. Off to the west, the shore curved gracefully, thick with trees at times, divided here and there by an isolated creek or cove, culminating in the regal walls of Osborne House.

To the east, the land pitched more sharply, ascending to a commanding cluster of Elizabethan turrets, followed by dramatic cliffs and green banks that stretched endlessly as far as the eye could see.

"Spraystone is beyond those cliffs," Trenton informed Ariana, helping her disembark. His hands lingered on her waist. "Are you all right?"

Ariana felt Trenton's fingers scorch her skin, searing through the layers of her gown and petticoats. "Yes," she managed, forcing herself to focus on the impressive buildings housed within the manicured gardens and trees that defined the hillside of Ryde. "But I had no idea Ryde was so ... big," she finished lamely.

Trenton stroked his thumbs idly over her waist. "Union Street has schools, a post office, two banks, and a wonderful theatre," he told her in a husky voice. "Sections of the Isle are quite sophisticated, although the pace is slower, the air fresher, more vibrant. Other sections are very rural, with isolated estates that have nothing surrounding them for miles and miles." He paused. "Estates like Spraystone."

"I see." For the life of her, Ariana could think of nothing else to say. The lush forbiddance of her husband's description melded with the heady scent of honeysuckle ... and the devastating pull of Trenton's presence. Wight's enchantment wrapped itself around her, lured her, and Ariana surrendered, drowning in the Isle's splendor and her own dizzy anticipation.

The ferry ride to Bembridge was brief, as silent as the trip from the mainland, but fraught with a different kind of tension. By the time the towering Chalk Cliffs appeared, just beyond the walls of a charming, tucked-away estate, Ariana wanted to scream with the unfamiliar frustration building inside her.

"We'll travel the final part of our journey by foot," Trenton murmured, taking Ariana's elbow.

Even that casual contact made her tense. She nodded, following Trenton from the ferry and through the deserted acres of greenery for what seemed to be hours.

"We're home," he said at last, pointing.

Ariana's head came up and she searched the cloak of trees until she found what she quickly recognized as the graceful manor she'd spotted earlier from the ferry.

"Well?" she heard Trenton ask, his tone drawn as tight as a bowstring.

"It's lovely." She could barely speak past the pounding in her chest.

"The barn is off to the side. Would you like to visit there first?"

Ariana stopped dead in her tracks, turning to look up at him, meeting his gaze for the first time since they'd arrived. "Later," she whispered, pretense and pride cast aside.

Trenton stared down at her, his eyes darkening to near black. "Damn," he swore softly, capturing her shoulders and dragging her to him. He tangled his fingers in her hair, growling her name in a primitive sound of undeniable need, taking her mouth with a ferocity that echoed the wildness she felt pounding in her head.

Swinging Ariana into his arms, Trenton took the remaining distance to the house in broad, purposeful strides. He slammed the door behind him, mounted the steps two at a time, and carried her into the bedroom, dropping with her to the bed. They kissed, hungry, open-mouthed, again and again, simultaneously tugging off their clothes, as desperate to be one as if months, rather than days, had passed since they'd been together. When Trenton rose to shed his trousers, Ariana reached for him, uninhibited and urgent.

"My naked goddess," he rasped, coming down over her. "If I don't have you I'll die."

"Love me," she demanded, opening herself to him. "Please, Trenton, I need ..." Her plea ended in a moan of pleasure as his first fiery thrust stroked deep within her.

"Is this what you need?" he asked huskily, rolling over to seat her astride him, deepening his presence in her body until he had buried himself to the hilt in her warm wetness. "Is it, misty angel? Because it's what *I* need ... more than I need my next breath." He withdrew, plunged deeper still. "Tell me, Ariana ... I know you fear me, doubt me. But do you need me?"

Unable to speak, Ariana only nodded, the escalating pleasure too acute to bear. With a helpless whimper, she answered with her body, tightening her legs about Trenton's flanks and beginning the rhythmic, deliberate undulations of her hips he had taught her.

Trenton threw back his head and groaned, valiantly battling the blazing climax that ignited his loins the moment he felt Ariana's softness close around him. Determinedly, he fought, intent that this time, unlike the last, his wife would peak in his arms, be completely fulfilled long before he exploded inside her.

It was a war not destined to be won.

With a growl of unwilling capitulation, Trenton rolled Ariana to her back, pouring himself into her in a bottomless, wrenching release, utterly astonished by his total loss of control.

Equally astonished by his wife's.

Ariana responded instantly, burying her face in Trenton's damp shoulder and crying out his name, dissolving into shivering spasms that convulsed tightly around him, drawing him into her very core. Then, with a great, gulping sigh, she relaxed, lying quietly beneath him as the final tremors jolted his powerful frame.

"God, what you do to me ..." Trenton got out between clenched teeth, blanketing her body with the weight of his.

"You do the same to me," Ariana murmured, her voice shy.

Trenton inhaled sharply, raising up on his elbows and regarding her soberly, an odd expression on his face. "Strange, isn't it? For your mind and body to be at war?"

"My heart and body are in agreement," Ariana whispered, candor glowing in her eyes. "Only my mind is uncertain."

"Not in bed, it isn't."

"No ... not in bed."

Trenton covered Ariana's mouth with his, rocking slowly, sensuously, within her until he felt her heated response. "Then let's relieve your mind of its burden," he murmured against her parted lips. He slid his hands down the length of her legs, gliding them high around his waist. "Make love with me," he urged softly, lowering his mouth to the curve of her breast. "All night." He wet her hardening nipple with his tongue, waiting until she begged before he drew the achingly sensitive tip into his mouth, tugging and releasing until he felt Ariana's nails score his back. "Until dawn … until day … until night," he breathed, raising his hips only to plunge back inside her with a tantalizing force that made her cry out. "Again and again …" He bent to her other breast, arousing her to the point of insanity. "Until there's nothing but this …" He withdrew and re-entered, deeper this time, her every aching pore open to his penetration, his rhythmic stroking. "And this …" He kissed her throat, her shoulders, her lips … taking her mouth with hot, lusty motions of his tongue; doubling his presence in her body with the sharp, probing lunges of his hips. "Are you still uncertain?" he whispered, cupping her soft bottom and lifting her into each deliberate thrust.

"No …" she gasped, winding her arms around his neck. "Oh, Trenton, no."

Long hours later, Trenton rolled them gently to their sides, hauling a blanket over their joined naked bodies. "Can you wait until morning to see the barn and tour Spraystone?" he murmured into Ariana's tangled hair.

"Ummm," she returned, already half asleep.

Had her eyes been open, she would have seen the uncustomary tenderness on her husband's face. As it was, she nestled against him, wondering sleepily how she could feel so safe with a madman … and how she could want him … love him … so very much.

"Sleep well, misty angel," Trenton said softly, sifting his fingers through her thick auburn tresses. For long moments he just stared down at her, lost in thought. Then, cradling her in his arms, he closed his eyes.

Consciousness returned to Ariana in gradual stages of awareness. With a contented sigh, she sank into the downy pillows, snuggling instinctively against the solid column of warmth behind her.

"Are you awake?"

The question, accompanied by a possessive lightening of the strong arms wrapped around her waist, greatly accelerated Ariana's waking process.

Instantly, reality returned.

"Yes." Her voice was small, a trifle flustered. Arising with Trenton, so appealing in the gray light of dawn, seemed terribly awkward in the bright light of day—especially after her wanton behavior last night.

And it most definitely *was* the bright light of day. The sun streamed into the room, bathing it in lemon splendor; the hands of the clock announced that it was nearly noon.

Ariana started. "I've slept half the day away!"

Trenton nodded against her hair. "True."

Something about his tone made Ariana suspicious. "How long have you been up?"

"An hour. Perhaps longer."

"And you haven't left the bed?"

"You prefer us to arise together," he reminded her. "Besides"—he kissed her shoulder—"I was afraid you'd get lost if you wandered about by yourself."

Ariana turned to face him. "You never did show me around last night," she reminded him.

"As I recall, I was busy doing other things last night."

She blushed. "We both were."

"Yes." He grinned. "I know." His appreciative gaze fell to her naked breasts, the harsh lines about his eyes temporarily softening. "And I remember every one of them ... in detail."

Her blush deepening, Ariana followed his stare and had to deliberately check the urge to cover herself. Seeing the knowing lift of Trenton's brows, she gave a self-conscious sigh, aware of how childish her reaction must seem, given her wild abandon a few hours earlier. "Forgive my naïveté."

"There's nothing to forgive." He nuzzled her neck. "Nor is there anything to hide. ... Your body is exquisite."

Ariana plucked at the sheet, feeling the need to explain her unwarranted shyness. "Lying naked ... even just *being* naked ... before a man is a new experience for me."

"I know."

"It makes me feel ... awkward."

"I know that too." Trenton cleared his throat roughly, alerting Ariana to the gravity of his next words. "If I haven't already said the words, let me say them now. It means a great deal for me to know I'm the only man you've ever permitted such liberties ... the only man you've ever been with."

Ariana blinked. "What a curious thing to say!" she blurted out without thinking. "You're my husband! Who else would I have been with?" Instantly, she wanted to kick herself, recognizing both the foolishness of her question and the dangerous avenue this conversation was taking.

As she feared, Trenton's features hardened, the predatory lines reappearing about his eyes and mouth. "Who indeed? Your question, Ariana, demonstrates a trusting sentimentality that is shared by few."

This time Ariana answered cautiously, knowing she was entering the realm of the forbidden. "Do most women lie with men other than their husbands?"

A shadow crossed Trenton's face: Whether sorrow or cynicism, she wasn't certain. Then he shrugged. "Some do."

Silently, Ariana considered her husband's reply. "Did you expect I was one of them?" she asked at last.

Trenton's expression instantly softened, and he shook his head, caressing Ariana's smooth cheek with his knuckles. "No, my refreshing misty angel, I knew you were very much a virgin." His penetrating cobalt gaze dropped to her lips. "An incredibly passionate virgin," he added huskily. "So extraordinarily responsive that, had I not worn you out until dawn, I would most assuredly keep you in bed through nightfall." Slowly, he brought their mouths together, fusing their lips with a fierce intensity that burned through Ariana like wildfire.

Abruptly, Trenton released her, his hot, restless stare and unsteady breathing clearly revealing the cost of his self-restraint. "With that in mind," he managed, rolling to his feet, "we'd best get up and eat something before we starve."

In a heartbeat, the enchantment vanished.

Reflexively, Ariana drew her knees up and wrapped the blanket around her, assailed by the same inner chill that repeatedly accompanied her physical separation from her husband. She knew his emotional withdrawal was directly related to his comment on faithless women. He'd been referring, of course, to Vanessa and his belief that she'd deceived him.

Had she?

The familiar combination of confusion and dread welled up inside Ariana, ghosts of the past hovering like a dark mist over her happiness.

"Would you care to tour Spraystone now?"

Ariana sat up, brushing strands of hair from her face, noting that Trenton was already fully dressed. "Yes, but I'd like to have a bath first," she replied uncertainly, trying to interpret her husband's mood. He seemed brooding, removed—yet devoid of the harsh fury he normally manifested after their long hours of lovemaking. "Would that be possible?"

"Of course." Trenton hadn't budged, his intimate scrutiny lingering on Ariana's bare throat and shoulders. Then with a deep swallow, he gestured sharply toward the bathroom. "I'll wait for you in the sitting room. It's down the stairs, the first room on your right."

Ariana nodded again, lowering her eyes. *Now* what should she do? Wait for Trenton to take his leave? Or arise, stark naked, while he stood before her?

"You'll find your clothing in the wardrobe," Trenton prompted. "I sent our bags on ahead and Clara unpacked before we arrived."

Clara. Ariana recalled the name at once. Trenton had mentioned that she was the wife of his manservant, Gilbert.

That recollection prompted a thought. "You said Theresa couldn't join me because Spraystone had no provisions—"

"Clara and Gilbert work here," Trenton answered her unfinished question. "They do not live here. Their home is in Bembridge. I've given them a few days off," he added.

"I see."

Trenton's eyes continued to bore into her, she could feel them. Nervously, she contemplated her knees.

"I trust you don't require servants to bathe?" he addressed her lowered head.

Ariana's fists gripped the sheets. "I am quite skilled at bathing myself."

"Ah." Trenton sighed heavily. "A pity. I was about to offer my assistance."

Ariana's chin came up, her startled gaze darting to his.

"Ah, so you *can* look at me," he drawled.

Seeing the glint of humor in her husband's eyes, Ariana realized with a rush of joyful surprise that he'd actually been *teasing* her. "Thank you … perhaps another time," she returned, eagerly embracing his uncustomary banter. "But in this case I fear your assistance would result in another delayed tour of Spraystone."

To Ariana's utter amazement, Trenton threw back his head and laughed. "I fear you're right, misty angel. So I'll take my leave and await your arrival to dine."

Ariana watched him go, blinking dazedly at the closed door. The sound of Trenton's laughter was exhilarating—as was the fact that she was its cause.

Happiness exploded inside her.

Bounding from the bed, Ariana hugged herself, giddy with a joyous anticipation that was long ago relinquished, but never truly forgotten. It was her childhood Christmas all over again, filled with that same tingling excitement, that wondrous promise of treasures soon to be possessed.

It was being loved.

Eyes aglow, Ariana walked naked to the window, savoring the wonderful gift she'd been given. It didn't matter that Trenton's feelings sprang from passion, for his tenderness told her that those feelings had now grown far beyond passion's limited bounds. Nor, at this moment, could the menacing shadows of his past extinguish the joy in her heart, for it was her heart that had remained steadfast in its faith.

Leaning against the window frame, Ariana drank in her first resplendent view of Spraystone, knowing full well that at that moment hell itself would be paradise.

But Spraystone was truly glorious, showered in sunshine, blanketed by trees, sheltered amid spellbinding cliffs. A veritable Eden waiting to be explored.

Ariana bathed in record time. Standing before her wardrobe, she frowned. The thought of wearing layers of inhibiting clothing while touring this lush Utopia seemed not merely unappealing, but downright unacceptable. Perhaps it was her elation making her bold, but before she could change her mind, Ariana donned a simple fitted beige and check morning dress, beneath which she wore only her chemise and drawers and one thin petticoat.

Studying her reflection in the glass, Ariana grinned. She looked scandalously undressed, but hadn't Trenton said Spraystone was deserted? She tied her hair back with a beige ribbon and, humming to herself, went in search of her husband.

He was, as promised, in the sitting room, an inviting haven of warm browns and greens that seemed to summon one into its cozy midst.

"How perfect!" Ariana exclaimed, running her fingers over the fine wooden walls. Immediately she noted that, in contrast to Broddington, these walls were lovingly lined with paintings, the whole room a study of authority and detail, Trenton's touch evident in every magnificent inch. "There's no doubt who designed Spraystone," she murmured aloud. "You reveal yourself in every glorious dimension."

"As do you."

At Trenton's pointed comment, Ariana blushed, glancing down at herself self-consciously. "I thought since we were going exploring—"

"A practical decision." Surprising her yet again, Trenton unbuttoned his waistcoat and collar, tossing the waistcoat onto the settee and rolling up his sleeves. Hands on hips, he faced Ariana in only his white linen shirt and dark trousers. "Better?"

She blinked. "Why, yes ..." Fascinated, she found herself staring at the dark, curling hair exposed on Trenton's chest, wondering why she had never considered the fact that a man might be as restricted by his attire as a woman was.

"Keep looking at me like that and you may never see Spraystone," Trenton warned huskily.

Ariana wet her lips. "I'll take that chance," she murmured.

He crossed over and cupped her flushed cheeks between his palms. "Let me show you at least the grounds, the barn, the animals." He bent over, rubbing his lips softly to hers. "That will please you greatly ... and deplete every ounce of my self-control. After which, neither heaven nor earth will prevent me from making love to you."

Ariana gave a shaky laugh. "My excitement at exploring Spraystone grows dimmer by the minute," she whispered.

His cobalt eyes caressed her, inside and out. "Then I'll have to ensure that our explorations rekindle your excitement until it burns hotter than ever before," he replied, his voice hushed with sensual promise.

"Let's begin our tour immediately."

"No breakfast?" Trenton's eyes twinkled as he glanced at his timepiece. "Or, in this case, lunch?"

"I'm not hungry ... for food." Were those scandalous words really coming from *her*?

Trenton pressed an open-mouthed kiss to her palm. "We'll dine later." His lips quirked. "Which brings me to another subject: Can you cook?"

"As a matter of fact ... yes."

"Good. Then Clara can extend her vacation ... indefinitely."

Ariana's insides melted. "As can Gilbert."

Trenton's gaze smoldered. "Let's begin our tour before I change my mind."

Spraystone was as exquisite as Broddington—and yet utterly different in its allure. Where Broddington was a wealth of manicured lawns and flourishing gardens, Spraystone was a secluded haven, lush with trees, scented with honeysuckle and yellow gorse, tucked away just before the steep drop of the Chalk Cliffs plunged into the Solent.

Ariana drank it all in with an innocent abandon that enchanted Trenton, tugged insistently at some unknown place in his soul. The grounds, the birds, the flowers: All of this she opened her arms to, embraced, as one would a cherished friend.

"Trenton, this isn't a barn, it's an estate for animals!" Amazed, Ariana stared at the enormous structure that housed Trenton's livestock. "Why, you have enough room here for hundreds of sheep, six dozen pigs, scores of chickens, and an army of dogs and cats."

"And several dozen cows," Trenton contributed.

"Why? What do you *do* with all of them?"

"Feed them well. And hopefully, as a result, obtain good-quality milk, dairy, wool ..."

"I *know* what livestock provide," she interrupted. "But you live here alone. Do you offer all these products for trade?"

"In a manner of speaking, yes."

"Is that one of your family businesses?"

"No."

"Then …"

"The sheared wool is sent to England, where it is woven into cloth. Then it is delivered, along with milk and eggs, to the farmers that live on Wight."

It took Ariana a minute to understand. "You mean you *give* these things to them?"

Trenton's brows arched. "Is that so astonishing? I have a great deal of money. Most of the farm laborers here are quite poor, their homes old and neglected. I can provide them with the assistance they need."

Pride swelled in Ariana's chest. "You never told me this."

"You never asked."

"And I presume you restructure their homes as well?"

"I do what I can."

She touched his arm. "What a wonderful man you are."

He stared down at her caressing fingers, his mouth thinning into a grim line. "I'm not a wonderful man, Ariana. I'm bitter and cold and unfeeling. As I've continually warned you, don't envision me as some romantic hero."

"I don't." She stepped closer, conviction striking sudden and swift, born with all the impact of her earlier fear. "I see you as you are: a man with a great deal of pain locked up inside him … and a great deal of anger. I feel your rage, and I'm afraid. But I sense your goodness, and I'm renewed, for somehow I know it will triumph in the battle that tears you apart."

"I could be a murderer," he reminded her harshly.

The naked anguish in his tone obliterated her last vestige of doubt, "You could be." She lay her hand against his jaw. "But you're not."

Roughly, he pulled her to him. "Damn you, Ariana," he muttered into the scented cloud of her hair. "Why do you make me want to be the man you believe I am?"

She didn't answer, only pressed her lips to the open expanse of his shirt.

He shuddered, his arms tightening reflexively around her. Pinpoints of feeling, long ago numbed, sprang to life, leaving him raw, exposed ... terrified.

"Damn," he hissed again, control evaporating in a heartbeat. He raised Ariana's beautiful, flushed face to his, searching the trusting light in her eyes. "Misty angel ... my exquisite, ethereal dreamer... why do you make me feel hope where none exists?"

Her answer crystallized with a life of its own. "I love you," she whispered.

Trenton groaned, seizing her mouth with all the force of a drowning man. "My shelter from the storm," he said gruffly against her lips. "Erase the darkness, if only for now. Surround me with your goodness, your faith. Love me, misty angel... love me."

He crushed her in his arms, taking her tongue, her breath, devouring her with a passion that sprang more from the soul than the body. He kissed her cheeks, her eyes, her neck, her throat, his body leaping painfully as Ariana pressed hungrily against him, eager and unafraid.

"I've dreamed of making love to you here," he breathed into her parted lips.

"At Spraystone?" she managed, barely able to speak.

"In the barn." He was already unbuttoning her gown, his fingers shaking violently. "With nothing surrounding us but the animals and flowers you adore. With nothing under you but hay. With nothing under me but you." He lowered his head, opening his mouth over the hardened outline of her nipples, tugging at them through the confines of her chemise.

Ariana cried out, her legs buckling beneath her. She clutched Trenton's strong forearms for support, feeling the world tilt askew as he lowered her to their rough-soft mattress. Her nostrils filled with the powerful aroma of hay, and she lay mesmerized by the fires banking in her husband's eyes, by the erotic images of what he intended.

Trenton unfastened the final button of her chemise, baring her to the waist, arching her into his mouth. The pleasure of his demanding lips and tongue was so acute Ariana thought she might faint. She cried out, again and again, twisting frantically in his arms.

When he released her, she was beyond modesty or thought. For the first time the aggressor, she dragged open his shirt, then stroked his flat male nipples with her thumbs. The already taut muscles of Trenton's abdomen went rigid, a wordless hiss erupting from his chest.

Ariana didn't pause. Shocking herself, she boldly reached down to press her palm to the hard ridge of flesh that pulsed beneath her husband's trousers.

He caught her wrist. "I won't get my clothes off in time," he rasped.

"I'll get them off for you." She unfastened his trousers, pulling them down his hips.

Trenton shoved her inexperienced hands away long enough to shrug his shirt from his shoulders and drag his trousers down his legs. Kneeling over her, magnificently naked, he hauled her gown and undergarments off, following their path with his lips. He paused where her stockings began, nuzzling the bare skin of her thighs for an instant before he savagely tore all the impeding garments away. He lifted her feet to discard the crumpled material, wedging himself into the cradle of her thighs. Raising her legs over his shoulders, he sank his tongue into her sweetness, taking her with relentless, heated strokes, reveling in her cries of ecstasy. This time he didn't pause at the height of sensation but took her over its shattering brink, holding her captive as she dissolved in his arms.

Ariana felt the world disintegrate, then rematerialize, her body still quivering with unbearable aftershocks. Her lids lifted as Trenton came down beside her, his eyes blazing with unsated passion, unspoken emotion. He moved urgently, reaching forward to drag her into his arms.

But Ariana acted more quickly.

Scrambling to her knees, she leaned over him, her hair a wild tumble of copper fire against his skin. Every bit the seductress, she was shameless this time, raking her nails lightly through the dark hair curling on his chest, bending to tease his nipples as he had hers. She thrilled to the way they tightened beneath her touch, exhilarated in her husband's groan of pleasure. Avidly, she explored every muscled plane of his body, the coiled force and rough textures. She ran her hands over his powerful thighs, then settled between them, lovingly caressing his painfully rigid erection with soft sweeps of her fingertips.

Trenton went deadly still, his breathing suspended, as he endured the unendurable ecstasy of her touch. Grappling with his voracious hunger, he knew there could be no more exquisite a sensation than Ariana's innocent hands learning him, touching him, feather-light and gentle.

He learned he was wrong.

When she took him in her mouth, needing to give him the same blinding sensations he'd given her, Trenton nearly exploded. Certain he'd never last, he commanded her to stop, even as his fingers tangled in her hair, urged her closer.

His climax was already upon him when he dragged her to her back, shoved her legs apart, and thrust wildly within her hot, clinging wetness. Like a man possessed, he poured blindly into her, the hard floor of the barn anchoring her to receive the endless flow of his seed.

Fervently, Ariana arched, taking all of her husband's scorching release, pulling him as deep as her body would allow. She absorbed the tremor that shook his powerful frame, the hot, revealing declarations that were wrenched from his soul and wrapped herself around him, melding their passion, their hunger, their tenderness.

Her own climax shattered through her, unraveling in a series of shimmering convulsions that stole her breath, her heart—and made them even more completely his.

"I love you."

She whispered the words again, not at the frenzied peak, but in the lulling aftermath, when Trenton would recognize their significance.

He did.

Inhaling shakily, he raised up on his elbows, confronting his wife's declaration head-on. "Our bodies make magic together," he admitted, stunned to hear even that revelation from his own lips. "But love? What is love, misty angel? Perhaps you can tell me." He pressed his loins to hers, his flesh still fully imbedded in hers. "Is this love? This explosion of pleasure you bring me, this insatiable need to make you mine ... is that love? Or is love something more? ... A fierce commitment that renders you vulnerable, that only results in pain? I don't know, Ariana. What is love?"

Ariana responded to the anguish in his eyes. "Love is wanting to be with someone, to share his life. It's wanting to heal his suffering, to understand his past, to join herself to him ... and not only with her body," she returned, her gaze soft and candid.

"I'm not sure I'm capable of an emotion that vast."

"I *am* sure."

For a long moment he was silent, studying her flushed face from beneath hooded lids. "And trust, misty angel?" he asked hoarsely. "Is not trust part of love as well?"

Ariana drew a slow, trembling breath, aware of the crucial nature of this never-before-broached question. "Yes, trust is most definitely part of love."

"Is it? Well then, do you trust me?" Cynicism darkened his expression.

"Most times ... yes."

"Most times." Trenton fought the jolt of disappointment that claimed him. Well, what the hell had he expected?

"Trenton, please, don't pull away." Ariana tightened her arms about his back. "I *want* to trust you completely, but I don't know how. You insist on closing me off ... from your life, your past and all your grim secrets ... even though those secrets involve my sister's death. What am I to think?"

"But you love me, remember? If trust is an integral part of love, shouldn't one automatically imply the other?"

"That's not fair," Ariana whispered.

"Life's not fair, misty angel." Trenton pressed his forehead to hers, another layer of his implacable, self-protective wall crumbling. "Give me time."

Ariana knew how much that request cost him, and her heart swelled with joy and compassion. "All that you need." She breathed the words against his skin, feeling more a wife than she had in all their hours of lovemaking combined. "And Trenton?"

"What?"

"I can't promise I'll never fear you, or even occasionally doubt you. But I can promise I won't stop loving you."

Trenton raised his head. "You have no reason to trust me, Ariana, nor to believe in my innocence. You've been a Caldwell for eighteen years, and a wife for three days. I don't expect a forced marriage to a virtual stranger to hold up against a lifetime of your brother's teachings."

A tiny smile touched Ariana's lips. "Give me time."

Tenderness softened the anguished lines about Trenton's eyes.

"All that you need."

CHAPTER 15

The following day Ariana lost her heart again—this time to the Isle of Wight.

Strolling through the village of Bembridge, climbing the cliffs overlooking the Solent, and running along the crystalline waters nearing Osborne Bay—this time having abandoned not only all her petticoats, but her stockings and slippers as well—Ariana's passion for Wight was immediate and overwhelming.

"Is the whole island like this?" She wriggled her toes in the sand.

Trenton felt as if he were discovering his home all over again. "No, actually, the southern half of the Isle is completely different, though just as beautiful. Rather than being quaint and picturesque, the south is much more dramatic, filled with deep ravines and sharp, jutting rocks. I'll take you there later this week and you can see which you prefer."

"Can we walk farther along this stretch of beach?"

"A bit, yes." He shielded his eyes, peering into the distance. "Osborne House is just a mile or so from here."

"Oh." Ariana looked crestfallen. "Then we'd best head back."

"Why?"

"Trenton, even I know that the Queen's grounds are not open to the public."

This, at least, he knew he could give her. "Would you feel better if I were to tell you that Victoria would have no objections to our strolling the grounds of Osborne?"

Ariana's eyes opened like saucers. "Truly?"

"Truly. The Queen and my family have been friends for many years."

"That's right; how could I forget? Her Majesty issued the edict for our marriage."

Trenton looked quickly at Ariana, searching her face for bitterness or regret. He found none. "Yes, she did. But not merely as a gesture of friendship." He wasn't certain why, but suddenly he needed to give Ariana some portion of truth. "The day following the Covington ball, Princess Beatrice suffered a boating mishap in Osborne Bay. I happened to hear her calls for help."

"You rescued her?"

"It was nothing dramatic. Nevertheless, Victoria was exceeding grateful. She insisted on granting my most fervent wish. I sought but one thing: vengeance against your family for ruining my life. Thus, the edict." He waited.

"Then I owe the Queen my thanks, for without her unwanted interference you and I would never have wed." Ariana gave him a brief, dazzling smile.

A knot of emotion coiled in Trenton's chest. He opened his mouth to reply but never got the chance.

"Trenton, listen!" Ariana pressed her finger to her lips, cocking her head intently to one side.

"To what? All I hear is a—"

"It's a cuckoo! Come!" She seized his arm, urging him to follow her. "Quickly!" Raising her skirts, she sprinted up the beach, away from the bird's noisy call, until she finally collapsed onto the sand about a quarter of a mile farther north.

"What was all that about?" Trenton easily reached his wife's side and dropped down beside her.

"Didn't you hear the cuckoo?"

"Of course I did. How could anyone miss that persistent screech?"

"He was repeating himself for a reason: That's his way of offering us good fortune."

"Now I am truly at sea." Trenton absently smoothed the layers of wet sand from Ariana's gown.

"Has no one ever told you that legend?" She sounded amazed, her tone sympathetic, as if Trenton had been denied something incredibly significant. "Whenever you hear the cuckoo's call, you begin to run, counting each call that follows, until you can no longer hear him. Whatever number you've reached will be the number of years added to your life." Ariana stared up the sky. "The summer is nearly gone. ... I very seldom see a cuckoo about. This one obviously visited for the sole purpose of bringing us additional time to enjoy all this splendor!"

Trenton stretched his legs in front of him. "A true miracle," he commented dryly. "So tell me, misty angel, how many total years have been added to your life, given that this is probably the fiftieth cuckoo you've discovered?"

"You don't believe me."

He turned, caught by the disappointment in her voice. "It isn't you, Ariana. I believe in very little."

"I know," she said sadly. "What I don't understand is why your cynicism is so ingrained. Your life is rich with blessings. Surely you haven't always been consumed with anger?"

"No ... not always." Shadows cloaked his face, resounded in his voice.

"Dustin is a wonderful brother," Ariana persisted, ignoring the warning tremor that shivered up her spine. "Surely he must bring you some measure of joy?"

"Dustin has been my lifeline these past years. He's not only the finest of brothers, but the very best of friends."

"You're fortunate. Most people would give anything for such a loving relationship."

The wistfulness in her tone obliterated Trenton's customary reticence, replacing it with the unexpected need to comfort. "Theresa seems as devoted to you as if she were your mother."

A fond smile touched Ariana's lips at the mention of Theresa's name. "She is. I'm terribly grateful for her. ... She gives me not only love, but a sense of balance." Ariana tossed Trenton an impish look. "You probably haven't noticed, but I have a tendency to lose touch with reality."

"Really? How surprising," Trenton returned her teasing. "And when is that? When you are pursuing birds?"

"Or pursuing whatever fantasy calls out to me." She wrapped her arms about her knees. "Sometimes dreams are infinitely preferable to reality."

Instantly, he sobered. "Has your life been so very difficult?"

"Oh, no. Never difficult. I was permitted to live as I pleased, with little or no demands placed on me." Ariana scooped up a handful of sand, sifting it slowly as she spoke, remembering a childhood as fleeting as the grains that passed between her fingers. "I suppose I always wanted something that was distinctly mine, something that gave me a sense of identity. Once Mama and Papa died, it was as if I were floating. Baxter and Vanessa were already grown, their paths in life clear. Baxter was the brilliant businessman, destined to manage the Caldwell assets. Vanessa was an unequivocal beauty, the epitome of social grace and charm. And I? I was neither, not brilliant nor beautiful. Even as a child I possessed no outstanding quality to set me above or apart. In short, I was average. It was up to me to find my own niche. So when I got older, I did. I discovered nature. I've never been sorry."

Shrugging philosophically, she turned to Trenton and was stunned to see the restrained fury on his face. With a sudden jolt of comprehension, she realized what she'd just said.

"I'm sorry, Trenton. I didn't mean to bring up Vanessa."

"How could you think that?" Trenton interrupted angrily.

"Think what?"

"That you are average, that your brother and sister were superior, enviable. Good Lord, Ariana, don't you know the truth?" Trenton pushed on before he could reconsider. "Your *brilliant* brother has done nothing but squander away your family's money."

"He didn't mean to. It's only that—"

"And as for Vanessa ..." The words poured out of Trenton's mouth on their own accord. "Yes, your sister was a dazzling, blindingly beautiful woman, but that's where it ended. Your beauty is far more vivid, richer. Don't you see yourself?" He shook his head in wonder. "You really don't, do you? You don't see how incredibly beautiful you are, how intelligent, how special? Damn it, Ariana, there is *nothing* average about you!"

"Trenton, don't." Ariana abruptly rose, turning her back to him. "Don't lie to me. I can learn to endure your secrets, but I cannot bear your lies. I know just who I am, and that is neither Baxter nor Vanessa. I'm not practical enough to be considered overly intelligent. ... My head is always in the clouds. And although I'm hardly unpleasant to look at, I will never approach my sister in beauty. So let's not pretend otherwise."

Trenton came to his feet, then turned Ariana to face him and cupped her chin. "Your head *is* in the clouds, misty angel. You're such a warm-hearted, oblivious little fool." He stared at her, an odd, faraway light dawning in his eyes. "Someday you'll realize the truth. Perhaps someday I'll be able to tell you."

Ariana caught his wrist, slowly shaking her head. "No." She was stunned to hear herself refuse. "I don't want to hear the truth ... at least not this part of it. I don't think I can bear hearing about your feelings for Vanessa. I suppose I'm a coward, but I can't help it. Forgive me."

"Forgive you?" He laughed harshly. "I assure you, misty angel, there's nothing to forgive. I only hope that one day you'll be able to forgive me."

Soberly, she stared up at him. "Let's not discuss my life ... or forgiveness ... any more. I want to learn about you ... not the Trenton of these past six years, but the Trenton who lived before."

He was silent, his expression guarded. "There isn't much I can add," he answered at last. "I've already told you about my schooling, my sketching. ..."

"Did you and Dustin quarrel a lot?"

"I suppose we did on occasion." The abrupt change in subject mystified him. "Why?"

"Did you share confidences? Protect each other from outsiders? Stand up for each other with your parents?"

"Yes, yes, and yes." Trenton laughed. "Why does my relationship with Dustin interest you so?"

Ariana's eyes glowed as she pictured the two boys she'd seen in the photographs. "I told you, I've never had a true sibling. Vanessa and Baxter were more like parents to me, especially since my real parents died when I was a child."

"Do you remember your father and mother?" Idly, Trenton rumpled her auburn tresses, watching the sunlight catch the bright strands and ignite them into copper fire.

"A bit. Mostly what I remember are our Christmases."

"Why your Christmases?"

"Because they were magic. When Mama and Papa were alive, Christmas at Winsham was a fairy tale come true. I remember everything: decorating the tree, hanging the mistletoe from the ceiling while I sat on Papa's shoulders, sneaking batter from the cookies Mama baked. Most of all, I remember that wondrous feeling: excitement, anticipation, and joy all rolled into one, an emotion so vast it made you want to hug yourself even while it caused butterflies to form in your stomach that kept you awake all night. But morning would finally come and all of us would topple down the stairs to the sitting room, gathered around the fireplace where we belonged … a real family. …" Startled, Ariana realized she was crying. "I'm sorry," she said shakily, wiping her cheeks. "We're supposed to be talking about you. I didn't mean to go on like that, nor did I expect to become so emotional. It's just that I haven't had Christmas since …"

"Don't explain." Trenton cut her off hoarsely, tucking her head beneath his chin. "Don't even try."

Slowly, Ariana's arms slid around him as she gratefully accepted the comfort she had long craved but never received. "Maybe we could spend this Christmas at Spraystone," she whispered hopefully against his chest. "We could gather evergreen sprigs and perhaps some chrysanthemums and camellias and black ivy berries. Then, if it snows, we could watch the world turn white, and the wrens would sing and the sparrows—"

"Yes," Trenton agreed huskily, his arms tightening around her. "We can do all that, misty angel. I promise."

She raised her head. "Broddington holds nothing for you, does it?"

"To the contrary, Ariana, it's hold is powerful … and terribly painful."

"Because you lost your father there?" Seeing Trenton's expression, she knew instantly he intended to shut her out. With a gentle, beseeching look, she reached up to touch his cheek. "Please tell me. I'll do my best to understand."

Trenton's lips twisted bitterly. "It was a long time ago, Ariana. Too much has happened that can never be undone."

"Dustin told me that your father's death was sudden, despite his depleted health. Is that true?"

Silence.

"Trenton?"

"Yes, dammit, it's true!" He jerked away, turning his back to the reminders her questions brought.

"He died just after Vanessa," Ariana persisted. "Are the two events related?" She saw her husband's shoulders stiffen and softly added, "I've told you I don't believe you killed Vanessa. Why won't you talk to me?"

"Because you wouldn't believe what I'd tell you, Ariana. Leave it alone."

"I can't. I love you."

"Bloody hell." He snatched up a rock and flung it into the water with all his might.

"Tell me."

"Fine." Trenton spun about, his eyes ablaze. "You want to know how my father died? I'll tell you. He was tortured ... slowly, cruelly; not physically, but emotionally; using that which he cherished most ... his family."

Baffled, Ariana struggled to understand the blinding rage emanating from Trenton. "But how—"

"Not *how*, Ariana. *Who*. That's the operative word here. *Who*. I'll tell you who: your brilliant, altruistic, contemptible bastard of a brother, that's who!"

"Baxter?" Ariana recoiled sharply, having expected anything but this. She had been certain Vanessa's suicide was somehow linked to the late duke's demise—but Baxter? What did he have to do with Richard Kingsley's death?

"Yes ... Baxter, that vile blackguard who raised you!"

"Why? What did he do?"

"Odd, I thought Caldwell filled you in on our history when you visited Winsham the other day." Enmity underscored Trenton's every word. "Or did he selectively forget to mention one or two realities? Like the fact that it was he who brandished your sister's heartbreaking suicide note to the world ... painted me as a seducer of innocents, a sinister madman ... or worse. Did he tell you that I came to him, begged him to stop, not for my sake or even for Dustin's—Lord knows, neither of us gave a damn what lies Caldwell spread—but for my father? Can you possibly imagine what it did to me to have to crawl to your despicable brother on my knees? To plead with him that my father had nothing left but his legacy: the Kingsley name and his sons? And that he was too old and weak to withstand such vicious slander? That the more people who doubted my innocence, the more deteriorated his condition became?"

Trenton faltered, swallowing convulsively. "But beg I did. I begged with the hope that Caldwell would summon up one shred of compassion—not for me, but for an old man who had done nothing to hurt anyone. I should have known I was wasting my breath. Caldwell just laughed in my face and threw me out, continuing to impugn me and my family, until the whole world ostracized us. My father was too frail ... his heart just couldn't take it. He died within weeks. And all because of your detestable brother."

Breaking off, Trenton drew in harsh breaths, striving to bring himself under control. He stared down at his hands, realized they were shaking, and raised his head to meet Ariana's horrified gaze. "Still glad you asked, misty angel?"

An eerie chill crept inside Ariana's heart. "I can't believe Baxter would intentionally—"

"Of course he wouldn't! I must be lying." Trenton's biting sarcasm cut through her like a knife.

"I didn't mean you were lying. Only that you might have mis-understood ..."Her voice trailed off, for even she was unconvinced by her words.

"Misunderstood? Hardly. Actually, I've only just scratched the surface of your brother's brutality." Brusquely, Trenton turned on his heel. "Your reaction was predictable. Now I know why I didn't want to tell you any of this." Rigidly, he walked away. "I'm going back to Spraystone."

"I believe you."

Her declaration was barely audible, a whisper of sound in the afternoon sky. But Trenton heard it.

Abruptly, he halted.

Ariana didn't pause but walked up behind him, wrapping her arms about his waist, pressing her cheek against his taut back. "I'm so sorry for your pain. I wish I'd been old enough to comprehend it, and mature enough to ease it."

At first Trenton did nothing; he merely stood, unmoving, in his wife's consoling embrace. Then he placed his hand over hers, enfolding her fingers, placing their joined hands over his heart.

The gesture conveyed more than any words he could utter.

The Isle had surrendered to twilight, its beaches bathed in the moon's silver luminescence, by the time Trenton and Ariana headed back to Spraystone. Neither of them spoke, for the feeling hovering between them was too new, too precious to give voice to.

The manor was practically upon them when a flash of white caught Ariana's eye, taking her by surprise. "Trenton?" She seized his arm.

"What is it?"

"I don't know." She peered through the semidarkness, toward the tall grasses surrounding the barn. Intuition impelled her forward.

"Where are you going?" Trenton followed quickly, frowning at the concerned knit of Ariana's brows.

"Oh … Trenton." She rushed forward, dropping to her knees in the grass, bending over a huddled white form.

Trenton peered over her shoulder. "It's an owl."

"Not just an owl," she whispered, turning damp eyes up to his. "My white owl. The one who brought you to me. Trenton … he's hurt."

"Be careful." Trenton stayed her with his hand. "Owls are wild, Ariana. He'll claw you mercilessly if you try to touch him."

"He can't hurt me … he's unconscious. Please, we've got to help him."

Cautiously, Trenton squatted beside her, looking from the unmoving creature to the solid barn wall beside him. "Apparently your owl flew directly into the barn … hard enough to knock him senseless."

Ariana nodded vigorously. "He probably wanted to perch inside the barn and struck the window trying to enter. Owls see glass as open space and often hurt themselves because of it."

"Well, I'd be surprised if he didn't have quite a concussion. However, he is breathing, and damned lucky about where he fell. The grasses here are very thick and, judging from the natural angle of his wings, I would suspect that nothing is broken."

"We have to take care of him, Trenton. I'll never ask another thing of you … but please help me save him."

Wordlessly, Trenton gathered the injured bird, then rose and moved toward the barn entrance. "We'd better hurry … before he awakens and scratches my eyes out."

"Thank you," Ariana said simply, rising to follow.

While Trenton held the owl, Ariana hurried inside and located a small crate. "Put him in the far corner of the barn, where it's warm," she instructed, carrying the makeshift cage with her. She waited while Trenton placed the owl on the ground, then lowered the crate over his inert form. "Now he'll be confined until he's strong enough to fly."

"I'm impressed," Trenton acknowledged. "Though I don't know why I should be. You've obviously cared for sick birds before."

"Yes … but this one's special." She knelt beside the crate. "He's free to soar the skies … yet he finds me whenever I need him: my own precious symbol of hope. He's like you, Trenton: offering so much, yet always searching, uncertain where he really belongs, seeking to find out." Her gaze softened as she stared at the owl. "My extraordinary wanderer … my Odysseus." She sighed. "Perhaps we're all really alike in the end: All of us wanderers, all of us searching, venturing into the world in the hopes of discovering our true purpose."

"So profound. And still you doubt your value, misty angel." Trenton leaned over, gathering her silken masses of auburn hair and pressing his lips to her nape. "I fear that your vision is far worse than that of your beloved Odysseus. He is blind only to glass. You, on the other hand, are blind to your own worth." Gently, Trenton drew her to her feet, silencing whatever she was about to say by laying a finger across her lips. "Your patient needs his sleep. As do you, if you want to be strong enough to properly nurse him back to health. Let's go to bed."

Ariana glanced over her shoulder, chewing her lip hesitantly. "I don't want to leave him. What if he awakens? He'll be frightened." She turned back to Trenton. "You go to bed. I'll join you later."

Trenton didn't answer. Soberly, he regarded his wife, then silently left the barn.

Feeling the evening chill set in, Ariana curled up beside the crate, wrapping her arms about herself for warmth. She wondered if she'd angered her husband by refusing to accompany him. If so, she couldn't blame him. After all, such devotion to an owl probably struck him as bizarre.

The barn door creaked, and a moment later Trenton sank down beside her, wrapping a blanket around them both. "Now at least we won't catch pneumonia," he muttered.

Ariana looked up, surprise, then gratitude, and finally tenderness registering on her face. "No," she whispered. "We won't."

The tawny eyes opened, blinked dazedly, slid shut, then opened again. Slowly, the owl lifted his head, peering unsteadily through the slats of the crate, meeting the sensitive scrutiny of his rescuer.

"Don't be frightened, Odysseus," Ariana soothed, her heart aching at the disorientation clouding his magnificent topaz stare. "You're all right now. No one is going to hurt you."

In response, Odysseus's head drooped back into the hay, and his eyes closed.

"Trenton ..." Instinctively, Ariana gripped her husband's arm beneath the blanket.

"He's only sleeping, misty angel." Trenton was as awake as she. "Listlessness and confusion are perfectly normal following a concussion."

"What can we do for him?"

"For now, nothing. He did awaken, and that's a good sign. He'll probably sleep a great deal over the next few days. We're keeping him warm and confined. Now we'll have to be patient."

"He *must* get well," she breathed, half to herself, thinking of all the times Odysseus had appeared when she'd needed him most, praying she could remedy his suffering in return.

"He will." Trenton framed her anxious face between his palms. "I give you my word."

"How can you be so certain?"

Trenton brushed her cold lips with his thumb. "Because faith as unwavering as yours has the power to heal far more than a mere concussion."

Ariana's tightly drawn expression relaxed, a warm glint lighting her eyes. "I thought you didn't believe in healing."

"I thought I didn't believe at all."

Tenderly, Ariana raised up and kissed her husband's mouth. Easing back on her haunches, she yawned. "I'm suddenly very sleepy. And now that I no longer doubt Odysseus will recover, I'd like to get some rest." She snuggled into the blanket. "I was right, you know." Her eyes drifted shut. "You really are a wonderful man."

Trenton stared soberly down at his slumbering wife, her affirmation echoing in his mind. A wonderful man. The fact that Ariana believed that of him was, in itself, an unexpected wonder.

But the true miracle was that, for the first time in eons, Trenton began to believe it himself.

The woman watched the French shoreline grow more and more indistinct, until it disappeared altogether, leaving nothing behind but miles of ocean and years of agony.

She lifted the hood of her mantle higher over her head, gripping it against her cheeks to block out the sharp winds and icy sprays. In truth, she hardly felt them. Long ago she had learned to block out physical discomfort by retreating into a secret place inside herself. It had become her means of survival.

Slowly, she averted her head, looking, for the first time in six years, toward England. And for the first time in six years, a ripple of anticipation stirred within her, growing quickly into a steady pulse, spreading like a long-craved narcotic through her greedy bloodstream.

"Ma'am? May I get you something?" The straight-backed crewman stood politely beside her, crisply accommodating and, perhaps, a bit curious.

The woman didn't turn. "No. Thank you."

She listened to his steps fade away until she was, once again, alone. No, he could get her nothing. As always, what she wanted, she would have to take herself.

And take it she would.

CHAPTER 16

"Now I understand why you abruptly lost your appetite at dinner," Trenton commented dryly, lounging against the barn wall. "That beef was supposedly your meal."

Ariana jumped up as if she'd been caught stealing something. "I really wasn't hungry."

"But Odysseus was?" Trenton strolled past her, over to the crate, where the owl was finishing off the slice of lean meat. "He certainly has improved these past few days—not surprising, given meals like roasted sirloin. Still, I thought you said something about restricting him to plain, lean beef?"

"I scraped off every bit of horse radish and pepper," Ariana defended instantly. "Besides, he's hardly eaten anything all week. The first three days all he did was sleep. Yesterday he ate bits of veal, but this is the first decent meal he's had."

"Meals," Trenton corrected.

"Pardon me?"

"Meals ... not one, but two."

"It's only a slice of meat—"

"His second in the past hour."

Ariana inclined her head. "I don't understand."

With apparent concentration, Trenton studied the wooden beam beside him. "I gave him a portion of my dinner while you were in the kitchen."

"I see." Ariana managed to keep her face straight. "Well then, I suppose he has had enough for now." She cast a loving glance at Odysseus, who stared back at her, unblinking and alert. "In another day or two you'll be fit enough to fly, dear friend. But not if you're laden with pounds of beef."

"Ariana ... I need to speak with you."

The seriousness of Trenton's tone startled her. "What is it?"

Trenton held out a note. "This message just arrived from my solicitor. Evidently, my permission, and my presence, are required in London in order to transfer a large sum of money to my bank account here in Wight. I need to complete that transfer so I can begin the renovations I designed for an entire section of farmhouses in Bembridge."

"You're leaving for Broddington?"

He nodded. "Not tonight. But soon." The vulnerable whisper of emotion Ariana had come to recognize flickered in his eyes, then vanished. "You don't have to accompany me. I know how happy you've been at Spraystone, and how attached you are to your white owl. I'll take care of my business—"

"I want to go with you," she interrupted. Oblivious to the look of unguarded surprise and pleasure that flashed across her husband's face, she studied Odysseus, assessing his condition. "If you can wait a few more days, I'm certain Odysseus will be eager and ready for his freedom. Then I can join you in Sussex." She hesitated. "Unless you'd rather go alone."

"No, of course not." Trenton cleared his throat roughly. "You're welcome to come."

"Good. Then it's settled." She inclined her head quizzically. "We will be returning to Wight, won't we?"

Trenton smiled. "Could I keep you away?"

"Probably not." She strolled out of the barn, wrapping her arms about herself and gazing at the plush green hills and brilliant flowers surrounding them. "I never expected to feel such a sense of belonging as I do at Spraystone."

"I know." Trenton came up behind her. "The Isle has a way of stealing your heart."

"You never did teach me to sail," she reminded him.

"You never left your owl's side."

"Never?" She turned, giving him a look that was an irresistible combination of innocence and seduction.

Desire, relentless and staggering, exploded in Trenton's loins, an inevitability he no longer questioned, only marveled at. Pulling Ariana to him, he threaded his fingers through the thick masses of her auburn hair. "I can't get enough of you, misty angel."

"Nor I of you," she whispered, reaching up to unfasten the buttons of his shirt. "We really should begin packing."

"Later." He tugged her head back, pressing his lips to the pulse at her throat

"How much later?" She drew open the sides of his shirt, running her palms up his powerful, hair-roughened chest.

Trenton's cobalt eyes darkened to near black. "I'm glad your owl needs more of your tender ministrations," he growled, sweeping her into his arms and heading toward the house, "because so do I."

"Trenton? Are you sure he's strong enough to fly? Perhaps he—"

"Look at him," Trenton answered gently, gesturing toward the crate. "His eyes are bright and clear. Tonight marks the fourth full day he's eaten well. He's been restless since morning. He needs his freedom."

"You're right." Ariana raised her chin determinedly. "It would be cruel to keep him captive any longer. Odysseus needs to soar."

"Perhaps he'll follow us to Sussex, as he did to Wight," Trenton suggested with a hint of a smile. "He has, it seems, appointed himself your protector."

"Oh, I have no doubt we'll be seeing him again."

"Additional faith, misty angel?"

"Perpetual faith, husband." She squatted beside the crate. "You're well now, Odysseus," she said solemnly. "Take the freedom that is yours by right." Without hesitation, she lifted the crate and backed away. "Until we meet again, my friend."

Odysseus pivoted his head, ostensibly noting that his confinement had been removed. For an instant, he leveled his penetrating topaz stare at Ariana, blinking once, twice.

Then, with an expressive screech, he spread his wings and sailed out the open barn door into the welcoming dusk.

Ariana snatched her lantern and hastened out after him.

"Where are you going?" Trenton called after her.

"I want to watch him. He's magnificent when he flies." She paused. "Come with me."

"I must be insane," Trenton muttered, following. "I run from cuckoos, I follow white owls; next you'll have me designing structures where your bloody birds can meet for social events."

Ariana laughed. "I rather like that idea. Hurry!" She tugged at his hand, and the two of them sped off across the ground and away from Spraystone. Odysseus's flight was graceful and easy to follow: He was the one stark streak in the darkening sky. Twice he landed on the branches of tall trees, briefly surveyed the land below, then took flight again, evidently testing his wings, reveling in his reacquired freedom and health.

"He's heading out over the Solent," Trenton noted, pausing as they reached the beach beside Brading Harbor.

"Maybe he's preceding us to Broddington!" Ariana ran on ahead, ignoring the wet sand that weighed down her gown and stained her shoes, stopping only when she'd reached the water's edge. Holding her lantern high, she silently bid her friend farewell, peering intently into the night sky until he'd disappeared from view.

"He's truly free," she acknowledged softly. Turning, she smiled at Trenton. "Some things are meant to be, and we have no control over them. This moment was one."

Trenton didn't answer. The incandescent glow of the lantern filtered out around her, turning the radiant copper of her hair to a fiery red. The water lapped at her feet, first catching the edge of her gown, then receding into the darkening waters.

Sudden, unbidden images gripped Trenton, seized his gut, wrenching like a knife. Slashes of memory sprang to life, uncontrolled, unforgettable.

"Some things are meant to be, Trenton. ... This moment is one of them." A shimmer of crimson hair, a golden haze of light.

"Yes, Vanessa. You're right. This moment was meant to be. But not for the reasons you think." He could feel the rage pump through his veins, the blind fury recurring as if it were happening right now. *"This is not the beginning, you vicious slut. ... It's the end. I intend to ensure that fact ... tonight. "*

"Trenton?" The lapping of the waves, the hush of the night.

The finality.

"Trenton?" Ariana went to him, her eyes wide with concern. "What is it? You're white as a sheet."

Trenton stared at her, unseeing, numb.

"You're frightening me. ... What's the matter?" Ariana clutched at his arms.

A chilling light dawned in Trenton's eyes, and he thrust Ariana away from him. "Not again, Vanessa. Never again."

Turning on his heel, he strode back to Spraystone.

The River Arun hadn't changed.

Illuminated by a single lantern, the dark, surging waters rushed through Sussex, emptying fiercely into the Channel, merging them into one.

The woman stared at the deserted bank, visualizing the man she wanted and the woman who was no more: an image that caused enmity to distort her still lovely features into a mask of hatred.

All that would soon be rectified.

"Miss?" The constable's footsteps were muffled by the sand. She hadn't heard him approach.

"Yes?" Swiftly, she pulled up the hood of her mantle, shielding her face from view.

"Are you all right?"

His weathered face was unfamiliar, she discerned at once, relief surging through her. "Of course, Constable. I'm fine. ... Just enjoying an evening stroll."

He frowned. "I saw the glow of your lantern. A young lady like you shouldn't be walking alone by the river at night."

She almost laughed aloud at the absurdity of his remark. Youth had long since passed her by, and she, better than anyone, knew that fear arose not from solitude, but from helplessness. "You're right, of course, Constable. It's time I returned home."

"Do you live nearby?" His shaggy brows knit in concern.

"Just beyond those trees," she answered quickly. "Thank you for your interest, Constable. Good night."

"Good night, miss."

She felt his eyes upon her as she glided purposefully toward the area she'd designated as home. In the future, she'd have to be more careful.

The wind picked up, cool against her flushed cheeks. She was half tempted to lower her hood and let the air rush through her hair, making her feel alive again.

But the risk was too great.

Her fingers tightened about the mantle, holding it firmly over her head.

One stubborn strand broke free, whipping defiantly about her face.

Only the moon witnessed its crimson glow.

"We have to discuss it."

Ariana's face was pale, her eyes red from a long, sleepless night. How many times had she confronted Trenton, pleaded with him to talk to her? But to no avail.

The yacht sails whipped in the stiff breeze, the Isle of Wight fading as they neared the English shore. "Trenton ... please."

He hadn't spoken since their encounter on the beach, nor had he moved since their ship had left Wight this morning. He stood at the yacht's railing, his gaze fixed on some distant point.

Ariana took a deep breath, attempting a more direct approach. "Did I resemble Vanessa more than usual last night, or was she just on your mind?"

Slowly, Trenton turned. "You don't resemble Vanessa ... not in any way."

Grateful that her husband was finally responding, Ariana rose, going to stand beside him. "Then why did you call me by her name?"

"I can't explain it. For a split second, I saw her."

"Why? Was it something I did? Said?"

"Stop it, Ariana." He averted his head, staring broodingly over the Solent. "I'm not ready to discuss this. ... *I* don't even understand it." His mouth thinned into a grim line. "I find myself in the untenable position of actually wondering what's real and what's fabricated."

"Were you in love with my sister?" Ariana blurted out the unrelated question without thinking. Astonished by her own brazenness, she wished she could retract her words. In this case, it wasn't Trenton's anger she feared, but his honesty.

"No." His response was instant and absolute. "Not then. Not ever."

Ariana's relief was so acute it hurt. "I'm glad," she whispered. She leaned against the railing, gazing out over the water. "I wonder where Odysseus is by now."

Trenton's head snapped around, amazement registering in his eyes. "That's it? You're not worried about my possible insanity or my propensity to violence? You only want to know my feelings for Vanessa?"

"For the time being, yes. I know you didn't kill her. Now I know you didn't love her. The rest you'll tell me when you're ready. The only reason I hope it will be soon is that it hurts me to see you suffer so."

A muscle worked convulsively in Trenton's jaw, and he drew Ariana roughly into his arms. "You humble me."

"I love you."

"Then I pity you, misty angel." He buried his lips in her hair. "But, Lord help me, I need you. And I'm too selfish to convince you not to care."

"You couldn't convince me if you tried. Besides"—she tilted her head back and smiled—"did you or did you not ask me for time?"

"Time cannot cure all things. Have you ever considered that I might be beyond cure?"

"I've considered it. I've also dismissed it."

He stared soberly down at her. "There is a great deal I need to resolve."

"Then I suggest you begin at Broddington. We'll be there in an hour."

"An hour." He repeated the words hollowly.

"Trenton," Ariana said softly, "the ghosts of your past have waited six years. They can wait a bit longer … until you're ready to confront them."

"It's time I *made* myself ready, don't you think?" Trenton's expression hardened. "I hope to God you know what you're letting yourself in for, Ariana."

She touched his cheek. "The pain is yours. Let the risk be mine."

CHAPTER 17

Trenton leaned against the closed door, surveying the barren sitting room. It was the same room he'd designed with his father all those years ago, the same haven in which they'd worked, sketched, talked. Here, more than anywhere else at Broddington, Trenton could submerge himself in memories, meet the past head-on.

He'd procrastinated long enough: It was a full week since they'd left Spraystone. And not once had Ariana pressed him for answers; in fact, she'd left him virtually alone with his thoughts, spending her days in the garden furiously scribbling, presumably making notes on her newest discoveries of nature.

But Trenton himself was ready. Despite his internal anguish, he recognized that, for the first time in years, he was actually feeling a glimmer of hope, a possibility that life might hold more for him than mere existence.

Not, however, until he'd resolved the past.

He strolled over to the desk, running his hands over its polished surface.

For six years, he'd avoided this room like the fires of hell. There had been no reason to confront the pain evoked by his father's passing; the Trenton he'd been then was dead and gone, in his place, a shell of a stranger. But if marriage to Ariana had taught him one thing it was that some fragments of the old Trenton still did exist, no matter how few or flimsy. He owed it to himself—and to her—to try to delve out those fragments and meld them into one.

For the first time since Richard's death, he'd allowed himself to remember this room as it had looked before: lined with paintings, piled high with sketches, a tribute to the man who had created it. He could visualize his father sitting amid the chaos, oblivious to the world as he contemplated a particularly intricate drawing, his brows knit in concentration.

Surprisingly, the vivid recollection elicited no pain, only a warm glow of tender nostalgia. Evidently, without realizing it, Trenton had, at some point over the years, come to grips with his father's death.

But never with its cause.

And never with the fact that Trenton could have—*should* have—prevented it.

Richard Kingsley had provided his sons with love, a strong set of principles, and every advantage money could buy. In return, he'd asked for only one thing: respect for that which he prided above all else: the Kingsley name. Vanessa had robbed him of that—and Trenton had been unable to stop her.

The familiar rage coiled in Trenton's chest. Automatically, his gaze traveled to the desk, and without giving himself time to reconsider, he stalked over and yanked open the bottom drawer.

The journal was just where he'd placed it, just where Ariana had found it weeks ago.

He'd never forget the look in his wife's eyes that day; the agony, the confusion.

How could he blame her?

Sinking into a chair, Trenton opened the journal.

The precise handwriting, the faint scent of roses: It all accosted him at once.

Six years evaporated as if they had never been.

Trenton clenched the journal savagely, images hurtling back in hard, stunning blows to his head.

Vanessa.

His first glimpse of her had been in March of 1867, at the onset of the London Season. She'd been waltzing at Devonshire House, moving breathlessly from one partner to the next, her green velvet dress swirling about her satin shoes, her cheeks provocatively flushed. He'd been unable to tear his eyes off her all evening, though it had taken some doing for him to intercede for a dance. But once the introductions had been made, her emerald gaze had claimed him, melted over him, offered him anything … anything.

Far from a novice at romantic liaisons, Trenton had read her invitation with perfect clarity. Anticipation had coursed through his blood, igniting his primitive male need to physically possess an eager, beautiful woman. It had been some time since he'd wanted one as much as he did Vanessa. Even if she were Baxter Caldwell's sister.

Indolent and self-centered, rumor had it that Baxter truly cared for only one person other than himself—and that was his resplendent sister Vanessa.

On that March night, as Trenton twirled about the floor, drinking in her provocative beauty and openly carnal gaze, he had understood why.

Lord, what a mesmerized fool he'd been. He'd actually believed that her coy smiles and suggestive glances were rooted purely in passion, and granted only to him. That her professions of longing were sincere.

That she was everything she appeared to be.

Richard Kingsley had seen through Vanessa immediately and warned his son of her questionable ethics. Arrogant and stubborn, Trenton had refused to listen.

How mortally wrong he'd been.

Heaven alone knew how many men had been the recipients of that perfect smile. How many she had been willing to whore herself for in exchange for the promise of wealth and a prominent title.

Trenton had both.

Had he been older and more experienced, he would have recognized and dealt with the signs: a beautiful, flirtatious woman, a wastrel brother, unscrupulous morals, failing family businesses—the fundamental elements were all there. Indeed, he'd fed right into them: young, rich, and available, heir to a dukedom.

Oh, she'd played him for the worst kind of fool. But he'd found out just in time—in time to give her a taste of the pain and degradation she'd caused him.

Yes, he'd thwarted Vanessa's cold blooded manipulations.

But the victory was ultimately hers.

For, ironically, she'd devastated him more thoroughly in death than she ever could in life.

Were you in love with my sister?

Ariana's question intervened in his reflections, causing a bitter smile to twist his lips. He'd experienced a gamut of emotion when it came to Vanessa: attraction, lust, disgust, repulsion, hatred. But love? Never.

He reread the final pages of the journal, then slammed it shut.

Was she delusional or was he?

He rubbed his temples, trying to recall any minor detail he might have overlooked, any hint he'd provided that would give rise to her groundless fantasies. He could think of none. To the contrary, by mid-Season any enchantment he'd felt had been thoroughly extinguished—ironically, by Vanessa herself.

Discovering her calculated trysts had been pure chance on Trenton's part.

One April night, he arrived unexpectedly at a ball held in Bath House. As had become his habit that Season, he scanned the room for

Vanessa. He spotted her instantly, for her flaming hair commanded attention.

So, this time, did her actions. She was leading the ecstatic, prominent old Earl of Shelford into the moonlight, turning her adoring emerald eyes up to him in silent invitation.

Slipping out before he could be seen, Trenton grappled with the probability that the woman he was fascinated with was a blatant, scheming wanton. It was unthinkable. He must have been mistaken.

He'd almost managed to convince himself when, a week later, the second episode occurred.

Trenton was descending the steps of the Covington bank when, across the street, he spied Vanessa. She was hastening along, looking furtively to the right and to the left, finally halting beside a waiting carriage. Swiftly, she climbed inside—into the ravenous arms of Henri Lenard, a disreputable, womanizing French nobleman, who, rumor had it, was on the verge of inheriting a scandalously large family fortune.

Instantly, denial ceased to be a possibility.

From that moment on, Trenton made it his business to watch Vanessa—covertly. He had to see with his own eyes that his father had been right. And what he saw was a scheming fortune hunter performing her art of seduction on several carefully selected, eligible, *rich* men.

Barely able to hide his contempt, Trenton's actions toward Vanessa changed drastically. He became cold and aloof, showing her in all ways but words that he intended to sever whatever tentative ties they had initiated.

His rejection had the opposite effect. Rather than being dissuaded, Vanessa seemed utterly intrigued by Trenton's spurning. She redoubled her efforts to win him over, gluing herself to his side, making it unquestionably clear that he was her possession: the man she'd ultimately chosen for wedlock.

Quickly, caustically, Trenton set her straight, making no attempt to spare her feelings. He accused her of being promiscuous, told her he never wanted to see her again, and turned his back on her, presumably forever.

But Vanessa Caldwell was a woman who was accustomed to getting what she wanted at any cost. And what she wanted was Trenton. So, ignoring his brutal dismissal, she deliberately went about convincing the world—and herself—that she and Trenton were on the heated verge of matrimony.

Snapping back to the present, Trenton stared broodingly at the closed journal, plagued, as he had been for six years, by the change in Vanessa's tone from the journal's onset to its conclusion. The early entries were definitely Vanessa: spoiled, arrogant, selfish. But the last ones, the ones filled with agonized delusions and fear, were totally inconsistent with her character, not to mention radically distorted versions of reality.

Most perplexing of all was her desolation in that final entry.

She hadn't been desolate that night; at least not when she'd arrived. To the contrary, she'd been the epitome of conciliatory enticement. Until the end.

Trenton could still envision her as she approached him, ever the consummate actress. Her emerald eyes were imploring, damp with tears, her carefully selected silk gown molded to her every curve. Oh, how she'd sworn that she loved him and only him, that there had never been anyone else.

Weeks before, he'd been disgusted.

That night, he was livid.

As of two hours earlier, he had finally learned the extent of her treachery, and he wanted to choke her with his bare hands. It wasn't enough that she'd played her little game—was still playing it—with him. When that pressure alone hadn't worked she'd evidently spread rumors throughout the *ton* that Trenton had ruined her, stolen her innocence, promised to marry her. That too was unsuccessful. So she'd embellished further, feeding the gossip-hungry *ton* with the horrid secret that Trenton was mad; he was insanely jealous and possessive; he was unstable. He was a man to be feared, in business and in friendship.

Slowly, the rumors found their mark, and the whispers began. The whispers soon became doubts, the doubts, rebuffs—not only by friends, but by colleagues.

And Richard Kingsley's health began to plummet as his worst fears were realized.

It was Queen Victoria herself who brought the situation to a head. Having enjoyed a long-standing friendship with Richard Kingsley, she'd taken it upon herself to tell Trenton the reason for his father's deteriorating health and his family's growing ostracism. Despite her own dubious opinion of Vanessa's accusations, she strongly advised Trenton to handle this "unpleasant matter" at once, lest his respected family name be permanently marred.

Her words struck home. Trenton was livid, furiously unwilling to allow one conniving trollop to hurt the people he loved, the reputation they'd built. He had to stop her.

He'd sent an urgent note commanding Vanessa to meet him by the River Arun. Pacing up and down its grassy bank, he waited, drinking himself into oblivion.

By the time Vanessa arrived, Trenton was fuming and soused. Rather than a beautiful woman intent on seduction, he saw only the spiteful bitch who was ruining his life and destroying his father. Vehemently, he plunged into a verbal tirade, enumerating all she had done, from her sexual escapades to her destructive gossip to her vicious lies.

Vanessa's response was feigned innocence. And Trenton went wild.

Seizing her shoulders, he shook her fiercely, half tempted to beat the truth out of her and then physically expel her from their lives.

Seeing no alternative, Vanessa begged, swearing that she never meant to hurt or deceive him, that she only wanted him to understand how much she loved him.

Trenton was unmoved.

Pleading cast aside, Vanessa flew into a rage, swearing that if she couldn't have him, she'd malign the Kingsley name so severely that no other woman would want him.

The roar in Trenton's head became deafening. Beyond thought or reason, he crushed her arms in a punishing grip, bellowing out that she was slowly killing his father.

Vanessa laughed.

And something inside Trenton snapped.

Fiercely, he flung her to the sand, thundering out his vow of vengeance.

She rose, flying at him hysterically, and his fingers closed around her throat, burning to choke the very life from her. Instead, he threw her harder into the slapping waves along the shore, watching as the waters rushed up to her legs.

He threatened to kill her.

But, God help him, he hadn't.

So how had she died?

Instinct told him that an unfeeling bitch like Vanessa, a woman who loved only herself, would never resort to suicide. Unless she truly was delusional, and she actually believed her own lies. Had she gone over the edge of insanity?

Trenton laced his fingers together, resting his forehead upon them. For himself, it no longer mattered, not about her passing or its cause. The ultimate damage had been done.

But now there was Ariana.

What could he tell her? That he despised her sister, that he hadn't killed her, but often wished he had? That the Vanessa he knew was either totally unscrupulous or completely mad?

And when his warm-hearted wife was still reeling from the impact, would he then have to tell her the truth about Baxter? About the journal and exactly how it had passed from Baxter's hands to his?

Would she even believe him? And if she did, would she prefer the ugly knowledge to blissful ignorance?

I love you, Trenton.... You really are a wonderful man. ... I believe you.

Trenton's head came up abruptly.

Ariana trusted him. Despite everything he was putting her through, she trusted him. His answer was as simple as that.

Snatching up the journal, Trenton stalked out of the room and down the hall, rapping purposefully on his wife's door.

"Yes?"

He found Ariana brushing her hair at the dressing table. Seeing the spontaneous joy that flashed across her face, he felt a stab of guilt. This was the first time he'd sought her out since their return to Broddington—except each night, when he fused their bodies in an urgent attempt to bury his pain along with his seed, to lose himself inside this miraculous woman who loved him.

Shoving the door shut, Trenton tossed the journal onto her bed. "Vanessa and I were never lovers."

Slowly, Ariana placed her brush down. "I see." She stood, walking over to him. "I'm glad."

"You believe me?"

"If you tell me you and Vanessa weren't lovers, then, yes, I believe you."

"Despite what you read in the journal?"

Ariana tipped her head back to look up at him. "Vanessa's words can't alter what I've learned about you this past month. You're an ethical, principled man. Seduction is not something you would treat lightly."

"I've told you I'm not a hero, Ariana," he warned quietly. "Nor was I so terribly noble when it came to women. I've had my share.... Your sister just didn't happen to be one of them."

A spark of amusement flickered in Ariana's eyes. "So I gathered from Dustin. Plus, don't forget I've experienced your ... proficiency first hand. So I assure you I'm not surprised to learn I wasn't the first woman in your bed."

Trenton stared down at her, unsmiling. "There was a time when I was greatly drawn to Vanessa. If I hadn't happened upon the truth when I did, things might have been different."

"What truth?"

He inhaled sharply. "I have a lot to tell you. None of it is very pretty."

"I'm listening."

Without giving himself time to reconsider, Trenton related the whole story. He spoke of his first meeting with Vanessa, her faithlessness, her obsession to wed him, her ultimate treachery. Last, he recounted the night she'd died.

"I did threaten to kill her," he admitted harshly. "I wanted to kill her."

"But you didn't kill her." Ariana's face was white, her eyes wide and stunned by all she was ingesting.

"Nor did she kill herself." Trenton shook his head adamantly. "Not unless she'd gone totally mad. You didn't know her, Ariana. Not really. I did. In her right mind, Vanessa would never have taken her own life."

"She was my sister, Trenton!"

"But you were a child. You didn't know what she was capable of ... what they were both capable of."

"Both?" Ariana looked ill. "This involves my brother, doesn't it?"

"If you don't want to hear it, stop me now." Trenton cupped her chin. "I detest hurting you any more than I already have, misty angel."

"Tell me," she whispered.

"Baxter apprised you of the fact that I had Vanessa's journal. Did he mention how I got it?"

"He said you threatened him and our family; that he had no choice but to give it to you." Her voice trailed off. "He was lying, wasn't he?"

"Yes." Trenton wanted to brutalize Baxter at that moment; not for what he'd done to the Kingsleys, but for what he was doing to Ariana. "Your brother sent for me immediately after Vanessa's death. He accused me of killing her. I denied it. He produced the journal, read me portions of it. I was shocked and sickened by Vanessa's warped interpretation of our relationship. But Caldwell wanted more than my reaction, even more man my humiliation. He wanted my money."

Ariana clutched at Trenton's forearms. "He blackmailed you?"

"Repulsive as it sounds, yes. He showed me Vanessa's suicide note, said the choice was mine. His precious sister was gone and nothing could bring her back. He wanted compensation ... and he wanted it now. In short, he was either going to quietly mourn Vanessa and go on with his life, or furnish the journal, and implicate me as a murder suspect. It was as simple as that."

"But the journal wasn't proof—"

"The authorities require proof. The *ton* doesn't."

"What did you do?" Ariana asked woodenly.

"The only thing I could to protect my family. My father was dying.... The Kingsley name was his life. So I paid Baxter ... fifty thousand pounds, to be exact ... in exchange for the journal." Trenton's throat worked convulsively, and he shook his head in furious self-disgust. "I should have realized that wouldn't be the end of it. Once the money was in his possession, he flourished the suicide note for the world to see. He couldn't accuse me of murder, not without that journal, so instead he accused me of driving his sister to suicide. The effect was almost as severe."

"Is that when you went to Baxter and begged?"

"Yes ... for all the good it did me."

"Your father died anyway." Ariana dashed the anguished tears from her cheeks and took Trenton's hands. "Oh, Trenton, I'm so terribly, terribly sorry."

Trenton's deep-rooted cynicism wavered beneath his wife's unconditional faith. "Are you? Even though I uprooted your life, using Victoria's edict as my ultimate retribution?"

"Yes. I can only imagine the pain you must have endured."

Incredulously, Trenton shook his head. "Surely you must have doubts, questions?"

"I have many doubts ... and I will address them very soon ... with the person responsible for them. As for questions, I have only one."

"Which is?" He steeled himself.

"Why have you punished yourself all these years? By hating my family, hating what they'd done, you've isolated yourself from the world, and from the wonderful man that you are. Neither Baxter nor Vanessa are worth that, Trenton. And from what I've heard of your father, I think he'd agree." Ariana raised up on tiptoes to kiss the hard line of his jaw. "You didn't kill your father, Trenton; you loved him. Love is a wondrous thing, enabling you to be strong when nothing else will.

"Let my love in," she urged softly. "Don't fight me. I'm not asking for your love in return ... not yet. But don't close yourself off from me, or from the man you are when we're together. He's really quite splendid."

Trenton's arms closed around her. "Keep loving me," he demanded. "Help me, misty angel."

Ariana buried her face against his chest, thanking the heavens for this first bittersweet victory.

Bracing herself for the battle that lay ahead.

CHAPTER 18

Baxter tossed off his brandy, contemplating his surprising dilemma. His plan to avail himself of the Kingsley fortune was proving even more difficult than he'd imagined. Allowing Ariana to wed the bastard had seemed the quickest way to get his hands on the duke's extensive funds. Oh, Baxter had known what his main obstacle would be: Ariana's bloody ethics. What he hadn't counted on was his baby sister developing feelings for the contemptible blackguard.

Slamming his glass to the table, Baxter began pacing the length of the library. Everything he wanted seemed to dangle tauntingly before him, only to be perpetually snatched out of reach. And always by the same man: Trenton Kingsley.

Damn him to hell. First, he'd robbed Baxter of Vanessa, now of Ariana. Surely there had to be *some* equity in this world, enough to compensate Baxter for his perpetual losses.

Losses that were total now, leaving him not only alone, but utterly destitute.

The only compensation left was money.

Which brought him back to his original quandary: How could he gain Ariana's cooperation?

He'd intended to ask her during her last visit, but they'd been sidetracked by that blasted note and journal. Plus, now that he realized she actually cared for the scoundrel, he'd have to try another approach.

But what? Ariana didn't have a dishonest bone in her body. She'd never agree to steal from her own husband. Even though, Lord knew, she was entitled to every penny. After all, she'd been forced to sacrifice her youth, her innocence, her entire future to the formidable Duke of Broddington.

What was it that women saw in him? Baxter wondered, coming to a halt. First Vanessa, now Ariana. The man's luck with ladies was as staggering as his luck with money.

While Baxter had nothing.

Leaning his head wearily against the walnut bookshelves, Baxter sought a miracle.

"Hello, Baxter."

The quiet, slightly husky voice was as familiar to him as his own name. Startled, he swerved about and gaped.

"I was waiting for Coolidge to go on holiday," the apparition continued. "I couldn't take any chances of being recognized." She loosened the hood of her mantle, dropping it to her shoulders. Reveling in the freedom from confinement, she shook out her luxurious red hair. "I never realized how difficult it was to be dead."

"Vanessa." He crossed the room in three strides and enveloped her in his arms. "Lord, I'm glad to see you! What the hell are you doing here?"

Vanessa gave a rich, throaty laugh and embraced her brother. "A mixed welcome, to say the least. Did you honestly think I'd stay away once I received your telegram? I left France the moment I could. I've been staying at an inn outside London."

Baxter blinked, still shocked by the reality that Vanessa was actually here. "The telegram. Yes. Thank heavens I saved that address you sent me. Given the circumstances, I thought you had a right to know what had happened. I never expected you'd actually return to England—" He interrupted himself. "An inn? Why didn't you come here? How long have you been in Sussex?"

"A little over a week. And, as I said, I couldn't risk coming to Winsham, not until you were alone. Besides"—she caressed his cheek absently—"I wanted to do a little snooping on my own. Being dead has its advantages."

"What are you talking about?" Baxter caught Vanessa's hands in his.

"I've missed England," she murmured, an odd light coming into her eyes. "I should have returned long ago."

"You couldn't. The consequences would have been dire."

With a hollow laugh, Vanessa pulled away, strolling idly about the room. "The consequences could not have been more dire than what I've endured."

Baxter squinted, looking—really *looking*—at Vanessa for the first time. "You look peaked, Ness."

"Peaked?" She spun about, tugging open her mantle and spreading her arms wide. "Look at me, Baxter. I'm old. My face is pale, I'm gaunt, my eyes are lifeless."

"You're a young woman, for heaven's sake!"

"In years, perhaps. In fact," she said, smiling wearily, "I'm a very old woman. The fates have seen to that. I'm here because this could be the last chance I have."

"What did your husband do to you?" Baxter demanded.

"Henri? Exactly what he promised he'd do when I ran off with him … except that he did it alone: lived hard and fast, spent money recklessly, traveled all over the world. What he also neglected to mention was that it was *my* money he would be gambling with, traveling with, frittering away … since he had not a penny to his name."

"What about the great wealth he boasted?"

"The joke was on me, Baxter. I married Henri, went with him to France, for all he could offer me: a title, money, prominence. What I soon discovered was that those were the very things he planned to take from me."

"He had nothing?"

"Oh, he had a title, for whatever good that did me. But he was penniless and powerless. And soon, so was I."

"Your letters said nothing of this."

"My letters were written under my husband's watchful eye. I didn't dare tell you the truth, or ..." She shuddered, that hollow look coming back into her eyes.

"What has he done to you, Ness?" Baxter whispered, frightened by the change in his vivacious sister.

Wordlessly, Vanessa unbuttoned the top of her gown, yanking down a sleeve to bare one severely bruised, scarred shoulder to her brother's horrified eyes. "This is just a sample of what the past six years have held for me." She rebuttoned the gown. "Trust me, you don't want to see the rest."

"Dear God." All the color drained from Baxter's face. "Why did you stay?"

"He told me he would kill me if I left; that even if I managed to escape him, he would find me, and torture me."

"Then how did you get away?"

"I stopped caring. Even death would be preferable to the hell that was my life. Your telegram was the motivation I needed. And here I am."

"Ness ..." He held out his arms.

"I didn't come for your pity, Baxter. I came for your help."

"I'd move heaven and earth for you, and you know it," he declared fervently.

She walked into his embrace, laying her head on his shoulder. "You would, wouldn't you? My wonderful, protective older brother. I'd forgotten how good it felt to be loved."

"I want to break that bastard's filthy neck. Where is he now?"

Vanessa shrugged. "With one of his mistresses, no doubt. I really don't care." Her chin set grimly. "All I know is that I'm not going back. Even if my plan fails ... even if he comes after me ... I'll never go back."

"I'll kill him before I let him touch you," Baxter bit out. Gently, he stroked her hair. "Your plan?" His sister's words suddenly sank in. "What plan?"

"I'll tell you in a moment." She stepped back. "First you tell me about our sister and her advantageous marriage."

Baxter frowned, shoving his hands in his pockets. "I told you everything in the telegram. Kingsley showed up here with an edict from the Queen. He and Ariana were married almost a month ago."

"So she is now the Duchess of Broddington."

"Precisely."

Vanessa threw back her head and laughed. "Ironic, isn't it? That after all my carefully laid plans, it is my timid little mouse of a sister who acquires it all. My, how she must have changed."

"Actually, Ariana is much the same; only older and lovelier." He smiled. "She looks a lot like you, Ness."

"Except that *she's* the one married to Trenton Kingsley!"

"After all that's happened, you still want him?"

"I don't want any man, Baxter." Vanessa turned away. "All I want is the vengeance that's owed me." She laced her fingers together. "When did you last speak to Ariana?"

"A fortnight ago. She's with Kingsley on the Isle of Wight."

Vanessa spun around. "They returned a week ago."

"How do you know that?"

"I told you. I've done some discreet checking." She smiled, a hard, cold smile. "Which leads me to my plan. A plan that I need your help with … and one that involves money; a lot of money … and a very discreet seamstress. Have I piqued your interest?"

Baxter's eyes gleamed. "I'm all ears."

"Baxter? Baxter, where are you?"

The angry voice and vibrating door echoed through the house and interrupted whatever Vanessa had been about to say.

"It's Ariana." Baxter lurched forward, seizing Vanessa's elbows.

"She can't find me at Winsham." Vanessa paled, whirling about, seeking somewhere to hide.

"She can't find you anywhere—she thinks you're dead," Baxter hissed back, already heading for the hallway. "You stay here. I'll handle it." He was out of the room in three strides, slamming the door shut behind him. "Sprite? Is that you?" He put as much distance between himself and the library as he could, before colliding with Ariana at the foot of the stairs.

"Where were you?" she demanded.

"What do you mean? I was in my study."

"Why didn't Coolidge answer the door?"

"He's on holiday. Ariana, what is the matter with you?"

"We need to talk, Baxter. Her turquoise eyes were ablaze with the kind of anger Baxter had never seen her display.

"Of course. Come with me." He led her down the hall, past the library, to the comfortable morning room. "I tried to reach you. Theresa said you and your"—Baxter swallowed hard—"husband ... were in Wight."

"We were. We've been back for a week."

"I see." Still reeling with the impact of Vanessa's appearance, Baxter was having a difficult time comprehending the reason for Ariana's rage.

But not for long.

"We're going to talk about Trenton," Ariana stated flatly, arms folded across her chest. "And about you. And about Vanessa."

Baxter visibly started at the mention of Vanessa's name. Ariana couldn't know anything, could she? "What about us?" he managed.

"After I left Winsham two weeks ago, I read Vanessa's journal."

Relief, potent as brandy, surged through him. "Did you? And how did you talk your husband into showing it to you?"

"That's not the issue, Baxter. The issue is that I now know everything our sister claimed happened between her and Trenton."

"Claimed?"

"I've also spoken with my husband." Baxter didn't miss the emphatic possessiveness in her reference to Kingsley. "He told me everything."

"Everything." Baxter was "beginning to feel like a parrot. But for the life of him he couldn't think of what to say.

"Yes. And now I'm here to *try* to understand how you could do such a thing. I know you're greedy and self-centered, but for God's sake, Baxter—"

"Wait just a bloody minute!" Baxter's stupor vanished instantly. "Greedy? Self-centered? Whose words are those, Ariana: yours or *Trenton's?*"

"Mine. Do you think I don't know what you are just because you're my brother?"

"You never maligned my character before!"

"I never had reason to. Your weaknesses never affected me … until now."

"I raised you from the time Mother and Father died—"

"I raised myself, Baxter. With Theresa's help. You gave me the roof over my head and spent whatever money Mama and Papa left for me. So let's say that I've more than paid you back for what you've given me and dispense with the theatrics, all right?"

Baxter's mouth opened and closed a few times before he spoke. "He's certainly turned you against me, hasn't he?"

"I'm not against you. I only want to know the truth."

"What truth?"

"Did you blackmail Trenton into paying you fifty thousand pounds for that journal? And did Richard Kingsley die as a result of vicious slander that you spread throughout the *ton?*"

Baxter inhaled sharply, then sat. "And here I thought you were discovering new species of birds on the Isle."

"Answer me: yes or no."

"It isn't as simple as that, sprite. Yes, Kingsley paid me … I believe it was fifty thousand pounds. But it wasn't blackmail. It was a debt he owed me."

"For what?"

"For what he did to our sister."

"That's blackmail," Ariana retorted, shaking her head in disbelief. "I was half hoping you would deny it, or at least explain it. But you can't, can you?"

"I'm trying to, Ariana. If you would just listen."

"You really believe you were justified, don't you? That's the most frightening part." Ariana dropped her arms dejectedly to her sides. "That's always been your problem, Baxter. You do what you want, then explain it away by blaming others. Ever the victim, never the culprit." Her eyes filled with tears. "I don't need to ask about Richard Kingsley. I know the answer. I suppose I knew it before I asked. Oh, Baxter, I pity you." She turned to leave.

"Ariana!" He stormed up behind her and whirled her around. "You've only been married to the man for a month. How can you believe his word over mine?"

"Because he is telling the truth."

"And what about Vanessa?"

"What about Vanessa? I don't think we'll ever really know the truth about her death. The only thing I do know is that my husband didn't kill her. Nor did he drive her to suicide." Ariana gave a hollow laugh. "The ironic thing is that he never even touched her."

"That's a lie!" Baxter bellowed, a vein throbbing in his temple. "If you'd seen her agony each night when she came home from him, when she left his bloody bed …"

"I'm not listening to another word." Ariana turned on her heel. "I may forgive you someday, Baxter. But only because you're my brother. What you did was despicable."

The door slammed behind her.

"Ariana!" He recovered slowly, then took off after her. He reached the front door in time to see the Kingsley carriage disappear around the drive.

The echo of a solitary round of applause rang out behind him.

"That was quite a performance. Worthy of the stage. I *am* impressed: Our baby sister has indeed become a creature of great passion."

Baxter swung around. "You heard?"

"How could I help but hear?" Vanessa asked, her brows raised in a sarcastic question. "Evidently, she and Trenton have become exceedingly close since wedlock." She wet her lips with the tip of her tongue. "Did you say Ariana is pretty? I've only caught glimpses of her from a distance."

"Yes, but what the hell has that got to do with anything?"

"I was only wondering if *His Grace* has seen fit to take her to his bed."

"You can stop wondering: He has."

"How can you be sure?" Vanessa snapped.

"I asked. Ariana told me." Baxter peered out the window to make certain there were no more surprise visitors, thus missing the look of twisted rage on his sister's face. "Ness, you shouldn't be out in the open like this."

"Stop being so jumpy, Baxter. No one will see me." Deliberately, Vanessa composed her features. "Ariana actually *told* you that Trenton had bedded her?"

Baxter nodded. "Yes. At first I was livid, thinking he had forced her ... the way he did you. I haven't forgotten the stories you told me, Ness, or the way you looked some nights when you'd arrive home. I knew the man could be brutal. It sickened me to think he'd be that way again, this time with Ariana."

"And was he?"

"No. That's the strange part. She seems ... well, happy, when she speaks of him. She cares for the scoundrel: It's written all over her face."

"I cared for him too." Venomous hatred filled Vanessa's eyes. "He used me. Discarded me like a pile of rubbish, destroyed my reputation. Or have you forgotten? He took my innocence, just as he took Ariana's. Only *mine* he stole *before* we wed, with the promise that I'd soon be his wife, a promise he had no intention of fulfilling. The whole world expected me to become Mrs. Trenton Kingsley. I could have been with child … *his* child—but did he care? Not a whit! He threw me into the wet sand and walked away, not giving a damn if I was alive or dead." She turned away, trembling with rage. "I'd forgotten how much I hate him. It's because of Trenton Kingsley that I was forced to marry Henri, flee to France, and live six years of hell."

"All that's behind you now." Baxter came to stand in back of her, placing his hands on her shoulders.

"It will never be behind me," she hissed. "Trenton Kingsley destroyed our lives. I thought we'd destroyed his in return. But apparently the price we extracted was far too low. He has enormous wealth, the highest of titles, great success, newly acquired acceptance, and now our sister. While we have nothing."

Baxter's jaw clenched. "I was pondering that very thing when you surprised me with your appearance. Somehow, some way, I intend to make that bastard pay."

"If my plan works, we'll bring Trenton Kingsley to his knees. We'll emerge victorious … and very, very rich." She averted her head to glance at Baxter. "Doesn't that sound intriguing?"

"Fill me in on this plan of yours."

"If Trenton were proved to be mad, completely insane, he would be committed and Ariana would have total access to his money, right?"

Baxter frowned. "Right, but you and I know he's not mad. Just as we know he's not guilty of murder."

"But *he* doesn't."

"You've lost me, Ness."

Vanessa laughed, spinning around to grip Baxter's hands. "Don't you think that after six years of bearing the onus of suspicion, there's a whisper of doubt in Trenton's mind as to what *really* happened that night?"

"I don't know; I never thought about it."

"Well, think about it now. A woman dies suddenly. Trenton Kingsley was the last person to see her alive. He had both motive and opportunity to kill her. The world deems him guilty. The cause of the woman's death is never determined, as her body is lost forever in the River Arun. Maybe, just maybe, as the years wear on, Trenton Kingsley occasionally awakens, bathed in sweat, wondering if he actually *did* kill her."

"That's an interesting possibility. I rather like the idea of Kingsley being tortured by doubt." On the heels of his taunting remark, Baxter sobered. "Let's suppose you're right. A shred of doubt is hardly enough to drive the man insane, especially if it hasn't done so already. Plus you're forgetting something else: Ariana believes Kingsley. You heard her. She thinks he's completely innocent. So if anything, she'll help to eliminate any doubts he might have."

"Unless we create new ones ... doubts so powerful that neither Ariana nor Trenton can ignore them."

"*We* can't do anything. You're dead, remember?"

"Yes, I am, aren't I?" Vanessa smiled triumphantly. "Only you and I know otherwise. So what do you think it would do to Trenton's mind if a dead woman suddenly returned from the grave? If she mysteriously reappeared—for his eyes only, of course—during sporadic moments and in specific places? How long do you think he'd remain sane?"

A victorious light shone in Baxter's eyes. "I always said you were brilliant, Ness."

"And I always agreed with you, Baxter."

"I presume you've worked out all the details?"

"Of course. Mysterious appearances are just the beginning of our little scheme. Can I count on your help?"

Baxter's lips curved into a vindictive smile. "When do we begin?"

Vanessa tapped her chin thoughtfully, her gaze automatically veering in the direction of Broddington. "Oh, we've already begun, dear brother."

CHAPTER 19

Trenton was as restless as a caged tiger.

Prowling from one room to the next, he could concentrate on nothing save what was transpiring at Winsham right now. It seemed days, rather than hours, since Ariana had marched from Broddington into the waiting Kingsley carriage, set on confronting her brother. She'd made no attempt to conceal her destination, nor to camouflage the fact that she intended to go alone.

Despite his anxiety, Trenton had to smile. He hadn't seen this side of Ariana before, this fiercely determined woman hell-bent on discovering the truth and avenging the apparent wrongs she felt her husband had endured. Evidently, his beautiful, ethereal bird-watcher could be as passionate in her principles as she was in her bed: a fact that Trenton found thoroughly exhilarating.

Sinking down onto the drawing-room sofa, Trenton leaned his head against the cushions, staring at the ceiling. His own emotions were extremely complex and raw at the moment: a combination of shock and pleasure that Ariana believed in him, tentative hope and wonder that she loved him still, unsettled agitation that the past had once again been resurrected—and a strange premonition of dread, the most troubling emotion of all.

Vaulting to his feet, Trenton began to pace, attempting to analyze the reason for his feeling of foreboding, simultaneously wondering how Baxter was responding to Ariana's onslaught. Was he denying all her accusations? Was he upsetting her? Frightening her?

The ironic thing, Trenton realized, halting abruptly, was that the only worry he never entertained was that Baxter might be swaying Ariana's opinion. Her faith was, quite simply, too strong. Lord alone knew what Trenton had done to deserve it, but he was as sure of its existence as he was that the sun would rise each day.

As sure as he was that he, in turn, trusted his wife.

Trust: That elusive feeling that had evaded him for so long, that same intrinsic belief Ariana felt for him, unfolded inside Trenton now. A miracle, perhaps, but real nonetheless. He trusted his wife.

Jennings cleared his throat from the doorway. "P-p-pardon me, Your Grace ..." He blinked rapidly from beneath his cap of red hair.

"Yes, Jennings, what is it?"

"There's a gentleman here, sir. He has a package for you."

"Fine. Accept it."

"But he demanded that you—"

"Just accept the package, Jennings," Trenton snapped impatiently. "I don't need to meet with the delivery boy."

"N-n-no, sir." Jennings swallowed convulsively. "But you don't understand. The gentleman is a merchant.... He is insistent that he deliver the package to you himself."

"Oh, bloody hell, all right. Send him in," Trenton boomed back.

Jennings leaped a foot off the ground. "Yes, sir. Right away, Your Grace. Yes, sir." He mopped his brow with his sleeve.

Belatedly, Trenton remembered Ariana gently chastising him about his brusqueness toward Broddington's new butler. "Thank you, Jennings," he added curtly.

The butler blinked in surprise. "You're welcome. My pleasure, Your Grace."

Trenton cleared his throat. "In case I haven't mentioned it, I'm very pleased with your performance at Broddington. You're doing a fine job."

"Oh, thank you, Your Grace." Jennings nearly swooned with joy. "Thank you, sir. ... thank you ..." He was still bowing and spouting effusive thanks as he left the room.

Seconds later, an elderly man with white hair, dangling spectacles, and a small, flat box was ushered into the room. "Your Grace?"

"Yes. What can I do for you?"

"My name is Wiltshire. I own a small bookshop in London. This package"—he extended it to Trenton—"is a gift. I'm sorry I was so persistent about seeing you, but I did promise your wife I would deliver it myself. Personally."

"My wife?" That got Trenton's attention. Striding forward, he took the box from Wiltshire's hands.

"Yes, Your Grace." Wiltshire shoved his spectacles back onto his nose. "The duchess was very specific ... and very earnest. The book was to be a special gift from her to you. She wanted to be certain you got it."

Trenton smiled fondly. "I see. Well, you have my thanks, Wiltshire. It was very kind of you."

"Your Grace." The man bowed. "Good day."

Carrying the flat parcel over to the sofa, Trenton sat and proceeded to open it, strangely touched that Ariana had purchased a present for him. Probably an anthology of birds, he thought with a grin.

It was a book of Shakespearean plays.

Trenton removed the volume from its wrapping, his eyes narrowed quizzically. Shakespeare? He didn't remember mentioning a fondness for Shakespeare to Ariana.

Looking more closely, he saw that something was wedged in between the pages, clearly designating a specific section for him to read. He complied, opening the volume accordingly.

A blood-red flower toppled out, somewhat crushed, its petals emitting a strong, sweet aroma that accosted him instantly.

A rose.

Trenton's stomach lurched, his eyes automatically focusing on what he had opened to: a portion of *Othello*, clearly marked with ink.

Yet she must die, else she'll betray more men.
When I have pluck 'd the rose,
I cannot give it vital growth again,
It needs must wither. …

Stunned disbelief gripped Trenton's gut, lodging his breath in his throat. Regaining his composure, he leapt to his feet, dropping the volume to the ground. He sprinted out the door, through the hallway, and into the drive.

Wiltshire was just climbing into a cab.

"Wait!"

The old man paused and turned at Trenton's command. "Are you summoning me, Your Grace?"

"Yes." Trenton stalked up to him. "You said my wife purchased this book?"

"She did, sir."

"What did she look like?"

"Pardon me, sir?"

"My wife: What did she look like?"

"Well, Your Grace, my eyes are not what they used to be." Wiltshire appeared distinctly uncomfortable and utterly bewildered by the question. "But your wife is not an easy woman to forget. A real beauty, the duchess is. All that glorious red hair and those splendid green eyes." He smiled fondly. "And so eager to please you, she was. Yes, Your Grace, if you don't mind my saying so, you are a lucky man."

Trenton nodded woodenly, an eerie, sick sensation forming in the pit of his stomach. Wordlessly, he returned to the manor, leaving Wiltshire to his cab. In the drawing room, he scooped the book off the floor and reread the marked passage.

She must die ... betray more men ... The rose, it needs must wither...

Die ... betray ... die...

With a hard shudder, he slammed the book shut.

Violently, he crushed the rose beneath his heel. Either Ariana had an unknown affinity for roses and *Othello,* or this was someone's very sick idea of a joke.

"Thank you, Jennings." Ariana smiled absently, handing her wrap to the butler. The outcome of her meeting with Baxter, although unsurprising, had drained her emotionally.

"Is that my wife, Jennings?" Trenton bellowed from the drawing room.

Ariana looked questioningly at Jennings, who had paled at the sound of Trenton's booming voice.

"Yes, Your Grace, it is," the butler called back. "The duke wanted to see you the moment you arrived home," he advised Ariana in a swift whisper.

"Very well ..." Ariana began. She had no time to finish her sentence before Trenton stalked down the hall, seized her hand, and dragged her into the drawing room and out of earshot.

"Trenton?" She gazed up at him, her eyes wide and startled.

"When was the last time you went shopping?" he demanded.

"Shopping?"

"Yes: Shopping. Specifically, to a bookstore in London. To buy me a gift ... a volume of Shakespearean plays."

"Trenton, I don't know what on earth you're talking about. If I'd been in London I would have told you. As far as Shakespeare, you never mentioned being a great fan of his. Were I going to buy you a gift—"

Trenton snatched the volume from the sofa and held it out to her. "You didn't purchase this book?"

Ariana gave the volume a cursory glance. "No, of course not. I just told you—"

"Are you certain?"

"My head is not *that* far in the clouds. I don't forget the purchases I make." She planted her hands on her hips. "Why are you interrogating me about this?"

Trenton cursed under his breath. "A merchant delivered this book today. He said my wife had bought it as a present for me and asked him to deliver it personally."

"Are you sure he said your 'wife'?"

"Positive."

"Then evidently he misunderstood whoever purchased it. Is there a note?"

"None."

"That's odd." Ariana's brow furrowed.

"Or intentional."

"Trenton, why would someone pretend to be your wife in order to send you a volume of Shakespearean plays?"

"You tell me." Trenton opened the book, pointing to the underlined section. "Read that passage." He waited while Ariana read. "The page was marked with that." He gestured toward the crushed rose.

The color drained slowly from Ariana's face. "A rose ... That was Vanessa's favorite flower, the scent she always wore. And the section from *Othello* ..."

"Is about death ... or, to be more specific, murder. Not merely a rose's, but a woman's."

"This has to be a mistake ... a horrible coincidence," Ariana whispered.

"Oh, it's no mistake, misty angel." Trenton's penetrating cobalt stare bore into Ariana. "The merchant described my wife as an incredibly beautiful woman with masses of red hair and splendid green eyes."

"Oh my God." Ariana sank down onto the sofa, feeling light-headed.

"My sentiments exactly. If *you* didn't buy this for me, who did? And why?"

"Red hair and splendid green eyes ..." Ariana swallowed past the lump in her throat. "Trenton, that's not really a description of me. My hair and eye color are not nearly so vivid. That sounds more like ..."

"Vanessa," he finished for her.

"Was the merchant reliable?"

"He was nervous as hell. He said something about his vision not being what it used to be."

"Could his description be wrong?"

"What do you think?"

Ariana laced her fingers tightly together. "The question is, what do *you* think?"

"Honestly? That this was someone's attempt to torture me."

"Baxter."

"You said it, not I."

"I find it hard to believe my brother would be so cruel," Ariana reasoned aloud. Seeing Trenton's jaw tighten, she amended, "I didn't say he wasn't selfish and greedy. But despite whatever else he may be, Baxter is not a sadistic man."

"Obviously you've been in his company this afternoon," Trenton said bitterly.

"What you're implying is unfair and untrue. Meeting with Baxter altered nothing, Trenton. I'm not as easily influenced as you evidently think."

"What did the bastard tell you?"

"Nothing I didn't already know."

"He admitted blackmailing me?"

"He had another term for it, but yes."

Thunderclouds erupted on Trenton's face. "I can just imagine how he presented his case."

"That makes absolutely no difference." Ariana rose, going to stand beside her husband. "Did you think I'd take Baxter's word over yours, especially after I've offered you my love and my trust?"

Trenton turned to face her. "No," he denied instantly. "But if Baxter didn't send me the book, who did?"

"I don't know. Another enemy, perhaps?"

"An enemy with very precise timing, wouldn't you say?"

Ariana assessed the torment on her husband's face and ached for his anguish. "Everyone knows you've been away from Broddington for years," she reasoned gently. "Baxter's rumors riled many people after Vanessa's death. ... You said so yourself. Perhaps your emergence re-ignited someone's ill feelings. ... Why, just think of poor James Covington, whose daughter Suzanne is probably still wailing over the betrothal to Baxter you forcibly severed." Ariana attempted a smile, determined to ease Trenton's ominous thoughts. "As you can see, you are not the most beloved man in England. In fact, you are quite a bear. Fortunately for you, I see beneath that brutal exterior."

Trenton stared into her eyes, desperate to believe her, incapable of doing so. "What about the bookseller's description?"

"Whoever is responsible for this obviously went to a great deal of trouble to upset you." She stroked his cheek. "I won't let them succeed."

Trenton drank in Ariana's tenderness, a balm to his raw nerves. Sifting his fingers through her hair, he murmured, "Who would ever have believed that a slip of a girl would be giving me her strength? ... Or that I would be needing it?"

Relief flooded through Ariana as she sensed the tension ebbing from her husband. She stood on tiptoe and kissed his chin. "*Girl?* And here I thought I had graduated from *girl* to *woman* weeks ago."

Fervently, Trenton clasped her to him. "You did. You have." Waves of emotion clogged his chest, and Trenton expressed them in the only way he knew how. "Come to bed with me."

Smiling, Ariana nodded against his throat. "The perfect place for me to exhibit my great strength and stamina."

"Ariana ..."

His wife leaned back in his arms. "I love you too, Trenton," she said softly.

Slipping her hand in his, she led him to the door.

Ariana slept peacefully, her hair a bright copper waterfall across Trenton's chest.

Smiling tenderly, Trenton gathered his wife closer, feeling her warm, even breaths against his skin.

In response, Ariana murmured something unintelligible and snuggled against him, deeply asleep in the aftermath of their soul-shattering passion, secure in the shelter of her husband's embrace.

Rubbing his chin absently over her satiny tresses, Trenton wondered who he truly sought to comfort by holding his wife so tightly in his arms: Ariana, or himself. Candidly, he acknowledged the blessed relief of feeling her warm, soft body pressed against his. It was almost as euphoric as the exaltation he experienced when he exploded inside her, poured his entire being into hers.

Lord, he loved this woman.

The realization, instant but absolute, elicited only wonder and joy, rather than doubt or reservation. The feeling was not a new one, regardless of Trenton's cowardice at assigning it its proper name. He'd loved Ariana for weeks: perhaps from that first moment he'd made his way through the mist of the Covington maze, only to lose himself all over again in the melting beauty of her eyes; certainly since their wedding night, when he'd joined his body to hers, made her his wife in every way.

Pressing his lips to Ariana's forehead, Trenton felt a wave of gratitude that God had seen fit to bring her into his life. In a mere month this extraordinary young woman, with her fundamental love of nature and her unconditional faith in a man that had long since ceased to exist, had broken through Trenton's rigid walls of isolation, surrounded him with her goodness and her love, and penetrated deep into his heart.

A heart he had thought would never thaw again.

Thanks to Ariana, Trenton could actually visualize himself as the man she believed him to be; and he wanted to be that man, desperately, for her.

Vengeance suddenly seemed a poor substitute.

Trenton frowned. At a time when he could actually consider burying the past, looking ahead rather than back, someone was making certain that the past remained very much in the present.

Who?

Staring at the ceiling, he contemplated the possibilities. The most likely, of course, was Baxter. Unlike Ariana, Trenton regarded Baxter not only as a greedy, selfish man, but as a heartless one, as well. He'd never forgotten the bastard's odious pleasure at refusing Trenton's request to spare Richard further grief, and the perverse satisfaction Baxter had taken in evicting Trenton from Winsham.

The man was indeed capable of cruelty.

But not without cause.

That was the part that nagged at Trenton's mind, made him doubt Baxter's guilt. Vindication alone was not enough to drive Baxter Caldwell; no, not unless he had something tangible to gain from it.

Money.

In this case, money was not an issue. Mentally torturing Trenton would bring nothing of monetary worth to Baxter. Which drastically reduced Caldwell's plausibility as a suspect.

So who had sent that book? Whoever was guilty had to be motivated by blatant viciousness, enough to pay someone to impersonate Vanessa in order to torment Trenton.

Masses of red hair and splendid green eyes.

Trenton squeezed his own eyes shut to block out the image that conjured up: Vanessa. Damn her even in death.

Rearranging the pillows, Trenton settled himself for sleep, determined to stop agonizing over that bloody book. Purposefully, he ran his hand over Ariana's soft curves, reaffirming what was real, what was important. Then, cradling her to him, he slept.

The lantern heralded her arrival, piercing the dark of night and illuminating her hair to a fiery crimson blaze. Her lime silk gown was snug, and she wore nothing underneath, clearly defining every tantalizing curve of her body.

He was unmoved.

He could hear her voice, sense the urgency that drove her. He could feel the silk of her gown as his fingers dug into her shoulders, the fragility of her bones as he shook her.... Dear Lord, the venom inside him was such that he could kill her. ...

Kill her... kill her... kill her ...

Trenton, don't ... don't ... don't ...

Bolting upright, Trenton felt sweat drip down his back, trickle along his forehead. It was a dream, only a dream. And yet, so very real.

Wild-eyed, Trenton looked down at Ariana, who had rolled onto her other side and was curled away from him, still sleeping soundly. He wanted to wake her, to crush her against him, to bury himself inside her, to forget.

He couldn't run forever.

Easing out of bed, Trenton dressed and left the room. Broddington was dark, the grandfather clock in the hall telling him that it was nearly midnight. Quietly, he slipped out into the night, inhaling long and hard.

He realized he was still shaking. That damned dream had unnerved him even more than he thought.

Strolling about the grounds, Trenton wished he were at Spraystone. His head was so much clearer there, his thoughts better able to crystallize. And heaven only knew he needed that, needed to achieve some semblance of peace.

He walked endlessly, staring vacantly ahead. Moving automatically, he let his feet take him where they would.

They took him to the River Arun.

Gazing at the deserted shore, Trenton felt that familiar chill encase his heart. Six years. It had been six years since he'd paced along this shoreline, waited for Vanessa to arrive.

His life had never been the same.

Hands balling into fists, Trenton muttered a savage oath and turned away.

It was then that he saw it.

Laying on its side, candles extinguished, the brass lantern was half buried in the sand, only its upper portion visible. Like a man possessed, Trenton walked toward it, squatting to take a closer look.

A groan escaped his throat.

The lantern was unique: a gazebo cage exterior with space for three candles within, ornate, intricate, unchanged.

It was the lantern Vanessa had carried the night she died.

With trembling hands, Trenton lifted it from its sandy bed. Had it been here all these years? Impossible. The police had searched every inch of this beach when they'd scoured the waters for a trace of Vanessa's body—and discovered only her bloodied gown.

Then where the hell had it come from?

The wind whistled through the trees, and Trenton lifted his head slowly, with the sudden, eerie feeling he was not alone.

From fifty feet away, a woman beckoned him. She wore a tight-fitting lime silk gown with a low, square-cut bodice reminiscent of the 1860s. Her hair, a lush mane of flaming red, billowed out around her, catching the moonlight and reflecting it back.

Suddenly she extended both arms in his direction and uttered a single word. *"Trenton ..."*

"No!" Trenton shook his head violently, staggering to his feet, unsure whether he was running toward the apparition or away.

It didn't matter.

For when he looked again, she was gone.

CHAPTER 20

Trenton wasn't sure how many hours he blindly walked the beach; but the sky's harsh cloak of black was softening to a muted gray, signifying the oncoming dawn, when he found his way back to Broddington.

He had traversed shock and denial and moved into self-censure by this time, contemplating the possibility that he was indeed losing his mind.

"Trenton?" Ariana appeared at the foot of the stairs, wearing only a nightgown and robe, her auburn hair tumbling about her shoulders. "Are you all right?" She followed him into the drawing room, where he proceeded to pour himself a healthy portion of brandy. "Trenton!" She seized his arm, frightened by his disoriented, disheveled state. "What's happened?"

Trenton stared blankly at her over the rim of his brandy glass. "Hello, misty angel. I've returned from hell only to find it again."

Ariana snatched the glass from him and slammed it onto the table. "I've been worried sick about you—you've been gone all night! And while I was agonizing, you were out drinking, of all things?"

"I assure you, I am completely sober. That brandy you just wrenched from me is the first drink I've had. However," and he picked up the bottle with a hand that shook violently, "I intend to finish every last drop until I am so soused I can hardly move, let alone think."

"Why? Where did you go? What happened to reduce you to such a state?"

"Vanessa happened." He lifted the brandy bottle to his lips, taking a long swallow.

"Vanessa? Oh, Trenton, is this about that book again? I thought I'd helped you understand—"

"It's not about the book." He dragged his hand across his forehead. "At least not the book alone." He stared broodingly at the bottle he held, emotions racing across his face. "Dammit!" he exploded suddenly, hurling the brandy bottle against the marble column with all his might, sending a spray of shattered glass and brandy throughout the room.

"Dear Lord …" Ariana was truly frightened. "What is wrong with you? Why are you acting like this?"

Trenton's head snapped around. "Because I, apparently, am insane. Did you know that, misty angel?" He raked long, unsteady fingers through his hair. "I've lost whatever little portion of my mind I had left. So if your brother told you I was crazy, he didn't lie."

"You are *not* crazy." She frowned. "Is that where you were? With Baxter?"

"Hardly. No, I was walking."

"Why?"

"I couldn't sleep. I went out to clear my head."

"Where did you walk?"

A pause. "To the River Arun."

"Oh, Trenton." Ariana touched his wrist tentatively, afraid to send him into another rage. "Why do you insist on torturing yourself?"

"I didn't. *She* did."

"She? Who?"

"I told you: Vanessa."

Slowly, Ariana clasped his fingers in hers. "Vanessa is dead."

"Yes, *I* know that. But apparently her ghost doesn't."

"Her ghost?" Ariana paled.

"Ah, I see your confidence in my sanity is ebbing."

"What is it you think you saw?"

"I don't *think*, Ariana ... I *know*." He slapped his palm on the table. "I found the lantern she used that night; it was buried in the sand."

"The lantern? But the authorities checked thoroughly—"

"I'm sure they did. It wasn't there before, but it is now. I was examining it when I sensed someone watching me. I looked up. That's when I saw her."

"Her?" Ariana's heart lurched. "You don't mean Vanessa?"

"The very same. Looking exactly as she had that last night, right down to the gown she wore." He laughed hollowly. "So you see, misty angel, I am indeed insane. Because no matter how hard I try to convince myself that there is some logical explanation for all this, that I didn't *really* see a dead woman ... hear her call my name ... I cannot. Because I did. And so did she."

Ariana clutched the lapels of his coat. "Trenton, anyone could have placed a lantern on the beach, and we already suspected that someone was impersonating Vanessa."

Trenton shook his head vehemently. "No. Impossible. The lantern was the exact one she carried that night; I've never seen another like it. And the woman I saw was no impostor, Ariana; it was Vanessa."

"Stop saying that." Ariana shivered. "You're frightening me."

"I'm terrifying myself."

"Trenton." She raised her chin and looked him straight in the eye. "I refuse to believe that you're insane."

"Then how do you explain it?"

Frantically, Ariana's mind raced. "Remember that last night at Spraystone? The way you reacted when we set Odysseus free?"

"At the water's edge," he said slowly.

"Yes. You were looking at me but seeing Vanessa instead. Something triggered that: my resemblance to her, my proximity to the water, my lantern ... perhaps all of these. The point is, you were visualizing Vanessa, right?"

"Right, but—"

"You didn't actually *see* her, you saw a memory of her." Ariana paused to catch her breath. "When was the last time you visited the River Arun?"

Trenton was silent.

"You haven't been there since the night Vanessa died, have you?"

"No."

"Then of course you were shaken. That, combined with the mysterious delivery of that book and your raw nerves, would be enough to prompt your brain to play tricks on you. You didn't really see Vanessa. Maybe you saw someone, but it wasn't Vanessa. My guess is that it was the same person who bought you that book and who obviously went to the trouble of duplicating Vanessa's lantern."

"Do you really believe that's possible?" The agonized hope on Trenton's face tore at Ariana's heart.

"Of course." She slipped her arms about his waist, resting her head against his chest. "I won't allow you to think you've lost your mind."

"He thinks he's lost his mind." Vanessa bit into her warm scone and gave Baxter a triumphant smile.

"I'm sure he does. But I don't like the risks you're taking." Baxter paced back and forth across the small room in Winsham's rear wing, the one-time servants' quarters.

"I'm not taking any risks, Baxter." Finishing the last flaky crumb, Vanessa dabbed at her mouth with a napkin and leaned back in her chair. "I stay cooped up in Winsham all day, crammed into these tiny quarters like a damned insect. No one in England knows I'm alive, except you."

"And that bloody merchant at the bookstore," Baxter reminded her grimly.

"Wiltshire?" Vanessa threw back her head and laughed. "The man is old and near-sighted; that's why I chose him. The hat I wore concealed most of my face, and my mantle was so loose-fitting, it completely concealed my body. All Wiltshire saw was what I wanted him to see: my hair, which I intentionally wore down, and my eyes, which are vivid enough to make an impression on any man." She inclined her head. "So what are you worrying about?"

"Aren't you forgetting one minor detail?"

"Which is?"

"Trenton Kingsley."

Vanessa poured herself another cup of tea. "I assure you, my dear brother, Trenton Kingsley is one detail I *never* forget."

"He saw you last night, at the river."

"Correction: I displayed myself for him last night at the river. The whole scene was carefully planned and brilliantly executed, if I must say so myself. As far as Trenton is concerned, he saw a ghost."

"How can you be so sure, Ness?" Baxter's brow furrowed. "Kingsley is a very clever man. Don't underestimate his cunning."

"Don't *you* underestimate mine." Vanessa lowered her cup to its saucer. "I'm sure because I saw Trenton's face, his eyes. He was horrified, white with shock. There's not a doubt in the world that he believed me to be some apparition created by his slowly deteriorating mind." A triumphant smile touched Vanessa's lips, then froze in place, an odd, faraway light dawning in her eyes. "Time has only improved Trenton Kingsley's incredible magnetism. Not only has he gone from marquis to duke, but from handsome to magnificent. Our sister must be receiving quite an education in her bedroom."

"Stop it!" Baxter ordered. "It sickens me enough to think of Ariana with that bastard. I don't need you to remind me of it—especially after what he did to you!"

Vanessa's features hardened and she raised her chin defiantly. "Don't worry, Baxter. Trenton will pay. I guarantee you, Trenton will pay."

Ariana scribbled a change at the bottom of the page, then held it away to assess it critically. Her face fell. It was no use. Her sketching ability was beyond redemption.

Tearing out the offending page, she tossed it to the floor, disgusted with her pathetic attempts. Evidently, Theresa had been doing her a favor by hiding her childhood sketchpads. Her self-image would only have suffered irreparable damage had she continued her futile efforts.

Ariana rose from the chair, squinting at the bare walls and meager furnishings. Instantly, her imagination broke free of the sitting room's barren limitations. In their stead, a vision erupted in her mind, vivid in detail, rich in dimension; a vision not of the sitting room as it was, but as it would be when she'd completed it.

When she'd made it Trenton's.

She could envision it all, right down to the needlepoint on the wall. The problem was, she couldn't draw worth a fig.

But she *could* write.

A detailed journal-keeper, Ariana had long ago learned to capture her every thought, her most minute concept, on paper. That way she could recreate in words what she was unable to do in pictures.

She opened her notebook again, ignoring her feeble struggles to capture the room visually, skipping right to the written section of notes in the back. There. With a satisfied smile, she read through her intricately outlined pages, certain that she had described the room precisely as it was meant to look.

Now all she needed was the right architect to implement her plans. And Ariana knew just the man for the job.

Tyreham was nestled in the hills of Surrey, just a few hours' drive from Broddington and, not surprisingly, close to Epsom Downs, where Dustin could race his Thoroughbreds to his heart's content. Ariana arrived there just after noon, having left careful instructions with Jennings that His Grace was to know only that she had gone into London to shop.

"Ariana? What a wonderful surprise!" Dustin came out to greet her himself, arms open wide. After giving her a huge hug, he stepped back to survey her carefully. "You look radiant," he declared with smug satisfaction. "Evidently, my brother has mended his ways."

"Somewhat," Ariana returned impishly. "Never completely."

He chuckled. "Touché." Curiously, he glanced at the Kingsley carriage. "You've come alone?"

"Yes. Trenton has no idea that I'm here. But fear not," she hurried on, seeing the worried scowl on Dustin's face, "my reasons are sound, my motives are sincere. ... And my husband trusts me," she added softly, a tender glow in her eyes.

Dustin's expression gentled. "A major accomplishment indeed." He gestured toward the door. "Come. You've succeeded in arousing my curiosity. I'll arrange for some tea and we can talk."

"So you see," Ariana concluded, leaning excitedly toward Dustin, "I *know* the room would suit Trenton perfectly; it would keep your father close in mind and heart and be the final link in Trenton's metamorphosis. He'll become the man he once was ... the man he always has been ... and Broddington will be a home." She paused to catch her breath. "It's just the balm Trenton needs to soothe the jagged edges of his life and ..." Seeing the twinkle in Dustin's eyes, Ariana broke off. "I'm babbling again, aren't I? I seem to do that a great deal around you."

"You're nervous."

"Is it *that* obvious?"

Struggling to keep a straight face, Dustin gestured toward the tea table. "You've put six lumps of sugar in your tea and eaten four scones in five minutes."

Ariana looked mortified.

Dustin chuckled, leaning forward to squeeze her hand. "You're charming when you're nervous," he assured her. "But I wouldn't like to think that *I'm* the perpetual cause."

"You're not. It's only that I seem always to be turning to you for help."

"I'm flattered … and delighted that you feel comfortable enough to come to me. Now, what can I do to assist in your plans?"

"I want *you* to design the sitting room for me. Trenton would want it that way."

For long moments Dustin did not answer, staring silently at Ariana until she feared he meant to refuse. Then, with a tender expression, he brought her fingers to his lips. "Remind me to tell my brother how lucky he is." Releasing her hand, he extended his own open palm. "Let me see your drawings."

Ariana's joy rapidly faded. "Well, you see, that's the problem."

"What is?"

"I'm not a very good sketcher. You might not be able to picture my ideas too well." Ariana inhaled sharply. "The truth, Dustin, is that I am perhaps the worst artist in England. Were I to display my sketches, babies would cry and hunting dogs would howl as far as twenty miles away."

Dustin threw back his head and laughed. "I see. Then what do you propose? Would you like to describe what you have in mind and I'll sketch while you talk?"

"That won't be necessary. I've written detailed descriptions of every portion of the remodeling," she supplied, eagerly handing him the notebook. "I think you'll be able to create wonderful sketches based on these."

Quickly skimming a few pages, Dustin nodded. "These are excellent, Ariana. What you lack in artistic ability you make up for in imagination and writing skill. I'll do some samples right away … especially since I have the feeling you want this project completed yesterday." He grinned, pointing to something in the notebook that caught his eye. "One question: Do I need to pick these specific flowers myself?"

"No, of course not." Ariana gave him a sheepish smile. "I'll take care of that part."

"Good. Because I have absolutely no idea what hawthorn looks like."

"I'm sure you don't. You probably don't run from cuckoos either."

"Pardon me?"

"Never mind." Ariana rose. "I won't take up any more of your time. I'm sure you need to get back to your horses."

"Would you like to see them before you go?"

Her eyes lit up. "Oh, I'd love to!" A shadow crossed her face. "On second thought, perhaps next time. I'd best get back to Broddington in case Trenton needs me."

"Ariana." Dustin stayed her with his hand. "What aren't you telling me?"

She hesitated, not because she had any reservations about Dustin's trustworthiness, but because she knew Trenton would wring her neck if she upset Dustin by telling him about this bizarre situation.

"Ariana …" Dustin's tone was more emphatic this time. "Is something wrong with Trent?"

Her instincts and her heart won. "Not physically. But some peculiar things have been happening, and he's terribly upset."

She proceeded to pour out the whole story, from Trenton's vision on Wight, to the mysterious book delivery, to the inexplicable appearance of the lantern. Last, she told him about the apparition of Vanessa that Trenton was convinced he'd seen.

Dustin listened silently, the clenching of his jaw the only indication of his distress.

"Trenton believes Baxter is behind this," Ariana concluded.

"That doesn't surprise me. … And it is the logical assumption." Dustin paused. "The question is, what do *you* think?"

Ariana shook her head. "I know my brother. Groundless cruelty has never been his forte, nor is he devious by nature. He is, however, greedy and shallow … neither of which would precipitate so complex a plan. He'd cajole a robin out of her nest if the eggs were worth a large enough sum, but not for the sole purpose of torturing the bird.

I know he detests Trenton. But what could he gain from intentionally tormenting him?"

"That's true," Dustin agreed pensively. "It does seem to leave a piece of the puzzle still missing. Not to mention that Baxter's guilt wouldn't explain the identity of the woman posing as Vanessa."

"No ... but someone *is* intentionally masquerading as my sister," Ariana rushed on to defend. "Trenton didn't imagine what he saw at the river. ... I'm as sure of his sanity as I am of my own."

"You'll get no argument from me." Dustin gave her shoulder a reassuring squeeze. "I'm on your side, sweetheart."

Ariana bowed her head, her long lashes sweeping her cheeks. "I know you are. ... And I'm sorry if I snapped at you. It just hurts me so to see him suffer like this." Her hands balled into fists at her sides. "I intend to unravel this mystery."

"Where is Trent now?"

"Asleep ... finally. He was out walking, all night and agonizing all morning. I left word with Jennings that I was in London shopping." A faint smile touched her lips. "I want the sitting room to be a surprise."

"My lips are sealed." Dustin cupped her chin, raising it so he could meet her troubled gaze. "Let me help you solve this dilemma. We both love Trent. But we also both know he is a stubborn, difficult, and unyielding man."

"Who'd be more apt to accept help from his brother than from his wife," Ariana finished defeatedly.

"No. Who is profoundly in love with his wife and determined to protect her."

"You mean in case Baxter *is* involved?"

"To some degree, yes. Also remember that whoever is actually committing these bizarre acts could be unstable, possibly even dangerous."

Ariana wet her lips with the tip of her tongue, her mind focusing on something Dustin had said. "Dustin, do you really think Trenton is in love with me?"

"I don't *think*… I *know*."

"He's never said so."

"Hasn't he?"

Understanding dawned, coupled, with hope. "In his way … I suppose he has."

"Words are very difficult for Trent. Have patience with him, Ariana. Someday the words will come."

Ariana nodded, swallowing past the lump in her throat. "Thank you, Dustin," she whispered.

He gathered her against him for a brief, comforting hug. "Go," he instructed into her bright hair. "You have a husband who needs you and I have some sketches to design for a very demanding patron."

"Were you in London all this time?"

Hollow-eyed and pale, Trenton rose from behind his heavy library desk, looking questioningly at Ariana over the pile of papers that were strewn everywhere.

"I just got home," she answered evasively, taking in his haunted expression with great concern. "I thought you'd still be in bed."

"I couldn't sleep." He came around to face her. "What did you need in London?"

"Nothing special. I just wanted to do some shopping."

"And did you?"

"Did I what?"

"Do some shopping?"

"Yes … no … well, actually, I did browse, but nothing caught my fancy."

"Really." He sounded odd, but Ariana didn't dare meet his gaze for fear of betraying herself. Instead, she kept her gaze level with his waistcoat.

"Was the road repaired?"

"Pardon me?" Ariana tensed.

"The road to London. It was in sad need of repair. Did the carriage driver have any trouble?"

"I don't think so… I'm not certain… I don't recall…"

"Were you at Winsham?"

Ariana's head fell back with the impact of Trenton's harsh accusation, his words lashing through her with the force of a whip. "What?"

"You heard me: Were you with your brother? Did you tell him everything that's been happening?"

"Of course not!" Twin spots of red appeared on Ariana's cheeks. "Do you honestly believe I would deceive you like that?"

"Not deceive me, misty angel … protect me." Trenton's jaw was clenched, as rigid as his tone, but his eyes were filled with tenderness. "I was afraid you'd had some misplaced notion of confronting Baxter and finding out if he was behind the bizarre events of the last few days."

"No. I didn't."

"Good." Trenton cupped her face. "I don't want you involved. Whoever … whatever … is going on could be dangerous. I'll deal with it myself."

"Don't shut me out." She gripped his forearms. "Please, Trenton, I—"

"I know," he answered gently, drawing her against him, enfolding her tightly in his arms. "Lord knows what I've done to deserve it, but I know."

Laying her head against her husband's chest, Ariana closed her eyes, forcing herself to focus on the strong, steady thud of Trenton's heart.

Panic seized her, overwhelming, incomprehensible.

She loved this man, and her every instinct proclaimed that he loved her too.

Yet Ariana had the sudden, terrifying fear that a force more powerful than either of them could imagine lurked just out of reach, waiting to tear them apart.

CHAPTER 21

"The Viscount Winsham is here to see you, Your Grace."

Ariana dropped the fern she had been trimming and rose to her feet. "My brother? Here?"

"Yes, ma'am." Jennings bobbed his bright head. "He's waiting in the drawing room. Shall I show him to the conservatory?"

"No, Jennings. I'll go to him." She glanced anxiously beyond the doorway. "The duke has left for London, hasn't he?"

"Nearly an hour ago, Your Grace."

"Good." Nearly weak with relief, Ariana smoothed" her gown and headed down the hall. She had no idea why on earth Baxter had come to Broddington. But, thankfully, Trenton was meeting with his solicitor today to discuss the transference of Kingsley funds from London to Wight. So there was no chance that he and Baxter would run into each other.

"Baxter." Ariana entered the drawing room, closing the door behind her. "What do you want?"

"Hello, sprite." He came to his feet, all charm and smiles. "I'm so pleased to find you at home."

"You knew I was at home, Baxter. Just as you obviously knew that Trenton was not. So you can amend your tactics and stop patronizing me." She lowered herself to a cushioned armchair, folding her hands primly in her lap. "I've said all I intend to say. So why are you here?"

Baxter stared, the smile frozen on his face. "You astonish me, Ariana. Truly you do."

"Why? Because I see through your facade?"

"Perhaps. Perhaps because I'm unused to viewing you as a very intelligent, very grown woman and not a child."

"That's the first honest thing you've said." She gestured toward the sofa. "Can I offer you some refreshment?"

"No." He reseated himself. "I didn't come here to receive anything from you. I came to give something *to* you."

"Which is?"

"A heartfelt apology. Not only for hurting you, but for my unethical deeds of the past. You were right: I should never have accepted money … *demanded* money," he corrected, "from Kingsley."

"No. You shouldn't have." Ariana inclined her head, skepticism written all over her face. "Why have you suddenly decided to repent?"

"Because I love you. Because you're my sister and I obviously hurt you deeply. Because you made me look objectively at my actions and myself. And what I saw didn't make me very happy." He leaned forward, gripping his knees tightly. "I'm not an evil man, Ariana. I never intended for Richard Kingsley to die. I was hurting … badly. Vanessa was gone, and I knew I'd never see her again. I wanted to kill the man who had taken her from me."

"Trenton didn't kill Vanessa."

"Sprite." Baxter held up his hand. "I didn't come here to argue. I came to ask your forgiveness … and to make amends."

"How do you propose to do that?"

"I can't bring the late duke back to life, any more than I can alter any other events of the past. But I can return the fifty thousand pounds I took from your husband six years ago."

"What?" Ariana started.

Baxter's pale eyes beseeched her. "I'm not saying I don't hate Kingsley. I'd be lying if I did. But for your sake, for the sake of our relationship, I'll do it. You're all I have left, sprite." He seized her hand. "I don't want to lose you. So I'll do it."

"Where in heaven's name are you going to get fifty thousand pounds?"

"I've come into some unexpected money. No, not gambling," he assured her, seeing the suspicious lift of her brows. "Mother and Father left me two paintings that I'd always thought to be practically worthless. Last week I had occasion to meet with a man who, as luck would have it, is an expert in assessing valuable paintings. When he heard the description of mine, he asked to see them. Evidently, they are worth a great deal of money."

"You're selling them?"

He nodded. "I'll be receiving my first payment tomorrow: thirty thousand pounds. I'd like to turn it over to you."

"*I'm* not the one to whom you owe the debt... Trenton is."

Baxter's lips drew into a tight, grim line. "There's just so much humiliation I'm willing to endure ... even for you. I have no intention of seeing Kingsley's despicable face. You'll have to give the money to him yourself."

"Trenton will be home from London tonight."

"I see." Baxter scowled. "Then you and I obviously can't make the exchange at Broddington." He raised his head. "You come to Winsham. Tomorrow afternoon. At four o'clock."

"I don't know, Baxter." Ariana hesitated.

"Why not? For God's sake, Ariana, it was your home for eighteen years. All I'm asking is for an hour's visit in order to hand you my check. Is that asking too much? Or have you disowned me completely?"

"No, Baxter, I haven't disowned you." Seeing the genuine plea in his eyes, she felt herself relent. "All right. I'll be there."

"Good." He rose, making no attempt to disguise his relief. "Oh, I forgot something." From around the side of the sofa, he extracted a large, flat box. "I brought you a gift."

"That wasn't necessary."

"It was something I wanted to do." He extended his arms. "Open it."

Beneath the lid and filmy pink tissue was the loveliest peach silk morning dress Ariana had ever seen. "It's beautiful," she said, stroking the soft material. "Thank you, Baxter."

"You like it?"

"Of course I like it."

"Then wear it tomorrow."

"Tomorrow?"

"Yes. When you come to Winsham. It would make me very happy. And it would prove to me that you're willing to accept my apology. Please, sprite." He tugged at a lock of her hair.

"Fine." Ariana gave him a guarded smile. "I'll wear the gown. And I'll be at Winsham as you've asked."

"Wonderful!" He hugged her enthusiastically. "Then I'll be on my way." Dropping a quick kiss on her cheek, he headed for the door. "Until four o'clock tomorrow."

Ariana watched him go, glancing down at the delicate fabric she held in her hands. First an apology, then a gift: What a drastic transformation Baxter had undergone. And in so short a period of time too. Perhaps too short and too drastic.

Returning the gown to its box, Ariana wondered uneasily if her initial reasoning had been sound. Could Baxter be involved in the horrifying events of the past few days? Lord, she hoped not. Not only for his sake, but for her own. She wanted so badly to trust her brother.

But she knew she couldn't.

In Broddington's drive, Baxter paused. Quickly he scanned the grounds, the gardens, the walls of the manor. Then with a decisive gesture to his driver, he climbed into the Caldwell carriage and was off.

"I don't want you alone with that bastard. I don't trust him."

Trenton paced the length of Ariana's room, his features taut with anger.

"Nor does he trust you." Ariana slid a pin into her hair and turned to face her husband. "But I do. So please have faith in me."

"I *do* have faith in you, misty angel. It's your judgment I question. Why must you go to Winsham? Why couldn't he merely have the check delivered to Broddington? In fact, why is he doing this at all? I don't even *want* his bloody money!"

Ariana inclined her head thoughtfully. "I think he feels that the check is a symbolic gesture, as is presenting it to me personally. The same applies to my wearing the gown he bought me."

"I still don't like the idea of your going there."

"Trenton, he's my brother," she said gently, laying her palm against her husband's shirt front. "If he'd wanted to hurt me, he could have done so numerous times in the past. There's nothing to fear. But," she added, "if it will ease your mind, I'll take Theresa with me."

"You're determined to see him?"

"Unless you forbid me to go, yes." She gazed up at him, waiting.

Trenton clasped her waist. "I won't forbid you. You are his sister. But, Ariana ..." His eyes blazed cobalt fire. "You are also my wife."

"I don't intend to forget that." She stood on tiptoe to kiss his chin. "Theresa and I will be home in a few hours."

"Home?"

Ariana smiled softly. "Yes: Home. To Broddington. And you."

"How do I look?"

Vanessa whirled about, her eyes gleaming with triumph.

"Amazing." Baxter shook his head. "The resemblance is staggering."

"Between the gowns? Or the women?"

Baxter shot her an impatient look. "The gowns go without saying, Ness. They're not only similar, they're identical. I insisted that the dressmaker ensure that. No, I was referring to the resemblance between my sisters."

"Then I succeeded?"

"Did you doubt that you would?"

"I had only your description to go by, Baxter. If you recall, I haven't seen Ariana face-to-face since she was twelve. Apparently"—Vanessa smoothed her gown's peach bodice with a dark smile—"she's changed a bit in six years."

"In all ways but her innocence," Baxter concurred, with more than a trace of guilt. "Our baby sister is still the naïve dreamer she was as a child. Life has spared her much of its ugliness and disenchantment." He frowned. "I only wish I could have sheltered you from the same."

Vanessa's features hardened. "Well, you couldn't. But that's all behind us. Now is the time for retribution. And have it, we shall." She tucked a loose crimson strand behind her ear. "I'm not used to wearing my hair in so simple and unadorned a style. Are you certain Ariana prefers it this way?" Waiting only for Baxter's nod, she continued: "Tell me again the best entry to Broddington."

"Definitely through the chapel. It's secluded and surrounded by trees. No one will see you approach."

"Where is Trenton's room located?"

Baxter started. "Ness, are you crazy?"

"Not in the least. For what I have in mind I need access to his bedroom. Do you know where it is?"

"I couldn't very well ask Ariana if I might explore the second level of her husband's home. It was hard enough scrutinizing the main floor and the grounds without being found out. Besides"—he shook his head—"I don't want you in that madman's bedchamber."

"If I can slip through the main hall and up the stairs, I should be able to find the right room without too much trouble," Vanessa mused aloud, totally ignoring Baxter's protests. "From what you've told me, there are few servants living there. It's afternoon: too late for the maids to be straightening up and too early for the cook to be preparing dinner. My only problem should be the butler. And, based upon your description of the pathetic, nervous fellow," she said with a dismissive shrug, "he should be easy to outwit. The rest is up to me."

The grandfather clock chimed three.

"It's time," Vanessa announced.

"I'm worried, Ness." Baxter rubbed his palms together nervously. "What if someone should see you? Or worse, what if Kingsley discovers your pretense?"

"No one will see me, Baxter. Nor will Trenton figure out who I am. In fact ..." Vanessa scooped up a waiting parcel and headed for the door. "By the time I've left Broddington, the Duke of Broddington won't recognize truth from lies, reality from fantasy." She paused at the threshold. "Or sanity from madness."

"Trenton is not mad, Theresa."

"Mad?" Theresa sniffed. "What an absurd notion. The duke is deeply troubled and confused ... but never mad."

Ariana leaned back in the jostling carriage, frustrated and despondent. "Yet he is questioning his own sanity." She rubbed her eyes. "Oh, he has ceased discussing it, but I feel the anguish that relentlessly gnaws at him. He lies awake half the night, staring at the ceiling and trying to make sense of the bizarre events that have occurred. I don't know how to help him."

"Have faith, love." Theresa patted her arm soothingly. "I know it seems that your husband is walking through a dark tunnel from which there is no return. But he is strong. He will prevail. Remember what Sir Francis said about adversity."

Ariana had to smile. "What brilliant words did Sir Francis have on the subject?"

"'Certainly virtue is like precious odors, most fragrant when they are incensed or crushed: for prosperity doth best discover vice, but adversity doth best discover virtue.'"

"The latter most definitely applies to Trenton." Ariana tilted her head questioningly at Theresa. "One of my main worries is that the former applies to Baxter."

"Your brother is indeed a greedy man. If wealth has been placed in or near his hands, he may cast scruples aside."

"Do you think he is behind the delivery of the book and the eerie incident at the beach?"

Theresa studied her folded hands. "He has both the motivation and the hatred. But he lacks the cunning and the fortitude."

"My thoughts exactly. Still"—Ariana shook her head, baffled—"I have the nagging suspicion that Baxter's desire to make amends is just a little too timely to be mere coincidence."

"Your instincts again, pet. Heed them well."

"But Baxter's potential involvement still doesn't address one important question: Who is impersonating Vanessa?"

"Ah. Now we need to return to my view of appearance."

"Your view of appearance?" Ariana was completely at sea. "How does that apply here?"

"Because as I've said, appearance varies depending upon one's perspective and is often not as one believes it to be."

"Meaning that Vanessa's impostor is not what she seems?"

"Indeed." Theresa turned to look out the window, a clear indication that the subject had been exhausted. "Think about it, love," she advised. "Think hard; think well."

"Do you know who the woman is?"

"I only know that she is a threat to your husband's sanity, and that she represents danger," Theresa replied. "The rest is still in shadows … shadows you must unveil."

Broddington was silent.

Staring moodily out the window, Trenton wondered why he had sought out the sitting room in which to think. Aside from his visit here the other day, he never ventured into his father's domain.

The answer was simple: He felt closer to the truth here.

Hands clasped behind his back, Trenton gazed into the late-afternoon sky, wishing the hours would speed by and bring Ariana safely home. Rational or not, he felt terribly uneasy about her meeting with Baxter. True, she had lived with the man for eighteen years, during which time no real harm had befallen her. But that was before she'd become Trenton's wife, before she'd come to care for the man who was her brother's enemy.

Before Trenton had fallen in love with her in return.

Warily, Trenton pondered Baxter's intent. Was he engineering some sinister plot to drive Trenton to his knees? Did he plan to use Ariana as an unsuspecting accomplice? If so, would Ariana be able to recognize his ploy? She was so damned trusting and innocent.

So unlike Vanessa.

Trenton began to prowl the room fitfully, the concept of Vanessa crowding his mind, consuming his thoughts. The one thing he couldn't accuse Baxter of was conjuring up Vanessa's image the other night at the river. Had Baxter paid someone to play the part? Was that possible? Could *anyone* so closely resemble the vivid bitch who had destroyed Trenton's life?

And the most frightening question of all: Had anyone actually been present that night, or was Trenton truly losing his mind?

Sweat breaking out on his brow, Trenton stalked out of the sitting room, the ghosts of the past too powerful to withstand. He stood in the hallway, his breathing shallow, grateful that no one was about to witness his uncharacteristic loss of control. Grimly, he battled the emotional weakness, reminding himself that his reserves were depleted, for he'd had little more than two hours' sleep the past few nights.

Sleep. The very solution.

Trenton made his way to his chambers, determined to rest, if not doze, until Ariana's return. Perhaps then his mind would be fresh and he'd be able to view the entire situation more objectively.

The room was warm with late-afternoon sunlight. Trenton leaned back against the closed door and inhaled deeply.

Roses.

Instantly, the scent accosted him, icy fear encasing his soul, bile churning through his gut. In a rigid, trancelike state, Trenton crossed the room, each step bringing him closer to some inescapable, unknown atrocity. He sensed it with every fiber of his being, steeling himself for its discovery.

No amount of fortification prepared him for what awaited.

With a low groan, Trenton clutched his nightstand, staring at the scene before him. His bed was carefully turned down, a tattered lime silk gown crumpled on the floor at its foot. The stark linen was barren, but for a single rose that lay upon the pillow amid a bright crimson stain.

Blood.

With shaking hands, Trenton bent to lift the gown from the floor, already knowing what he would find. More blood was streaked across the delicate fabric, the bodice ragged, but still discernible.

It was the gown Vanessa had worn on the night she died.

Flinging the garment to the bed, Trenton backed away, shaking his head in denial. It couldn't be. Dear Lord, it couldn't be.

And yet it was.

He took the stairs two at a time, unsure exactly where it was he was running—and from whom. A lone maid glanced curiously in his direction, but she was far too timid to approach the duke in his obviously agitated state.

The conservatory door was open, the flowers bright and beckoning. Mindlessly, Trenton stumbled inside, unconsciously seeking whatever haven Ariana seemed always to find here, desperately craving peace.

It was unattainable.

"*Trenton ...*"

The chanting sound of his name accosted him, struck a chilling chord of recognition. It was *her* voice: not only the one he'd heard two nights ago at the river, but the one he'd heard six years ago.

It was Vanessa.

"*Trenton ...*"

Feeling as though he were living some heinous nightmare, Trenton forced himself to turn his head, following the sound with his eyes.

She stood directly outside the conservatory door leading from the manor. As he stared, ashen-faced, she raised her arms, beckoning him toward her.

"*Please, Trenton ... don't hurt me ... don't leave me ... not again.*" She raised her chin, gazing at him with brilliant emerald eyes. "*Come to me, Trenton. Stay with me.*"

A hoarse cry rose in Trenton's throat, and something inside him seemed to snap. Violently, he erupted, knocking flowers and plants out of his way, racing toward the loathsome apparition, wild fury and terror converging.

She was gone.

He shaded his eyes with his hand, dragging air into his lungs in hard, shallow rasps. Each breath was accompanied by the lingering scent of roses, a taunting reminder of Vanessa's presence. Trenton raked the grounds with his savage cobalt stare, refusing to concede defeat by allowing the apparition to escape. Whoever ... whatever ... she was, he would find her.

A snatch of color caught his eye and he took off in pursuit. Rounding the corner of the house, he stopped dead in his tracks.

She was leaning against the trunk of a sweeping oak tree, gazing intently at the sky and jotting idly in some kind of notebook.

Trenton closed the gap between them in ten long strides, seizing her elbows and slapping the notebook from her hands.

"Damn you! You won't get away from me this time!"

She blinked up at him, her green eyes wide and startled. "Trenton? What is it? Why are you so upset?"

Of their own volition, his fingers wrapped around her throat, digging into the soft skin. "Who are you? Why are you doing this to me?"

She began to struggle, looking totally bewildered and utterly terrified. "Trenton … it's me: Ariana. Don't you recognize me?"

All the color drained from his face. "Ariana?"

"Yes … your wife." She shoved at his forearms, trying to ease his biting grip. "I'm not doing anything to you; I saw a robin feathering her nest and was noting it in my journal. Why are you so angry at me?"

Trenton's hold grew lax, and he swallowed the sickness that rose in his throat, staring at the woman as if seeing her for the first time. Ariana? This wasn't Ariana. It couldn't be. Where was the gentle turquoise of her eyes, the copper softness of her hair, the delicate innocence of her fine features?

"No!" he denied vehemently, shaking her shoulders until she whimpered aloud. "No!"

"Trenton … you're hurting me." She began to struggle, the loose waves of her hair spilling over her shoulders. "Please … let me go."

He stared at the soft tendrils, thinking of all the times Ariana's unbound tresses had cascaded around them, a bright, unrestricted waterfall. Could it be?

Dragging the woman closer, Trenton's granite features hardened to stone as he studied her face, her coloring.

No. This wasn't his misty angel. This was her detestable older sister. Hard. Vicious. Bitter. Vanessa. It had to be.

Didn't it?

"Trenton?" The woman reached up to touch his cheek.

"You're frightening me ... Why are you looking at me like that?"

Vanessa was dead; this couldn't be Vanessa.

"Would you like to walk with me? It's a glorious day, and the robin I mentioned is on that thick branch just over our heads." She pointed. "If I were dressed differently, I'd be tempted to climb this old oak myself so that I might see the nest firsthand."

Dressed differently.

The words triggered a thought in Trenton's dazed mind and, automatically, his gaze dropped to the woman's morning dress: the same dress Ariana was wearing when she'd left Broddington hours before.

A harsh groan escaped his lips. "Your gown ..."

She glanced down at herself and sighed. "Do you really dislike it? Or is it only because Baxter gave it to me? He means well, Trenton, truly he does." She inclined her head. "Still, if it troubles you so, I'll return it."

"Dear God, what's happening to me?" Trenton flung her from him, grabbing his head and stumbling backward in a haze of disorientation.

The apparition opened her mouth to speak, but her words were lost amid the deafening buzz inside Trenton's head.

"What's happening to me?" he repeated in a horrified whisper, cold sweat drenching his entire body.

He didn't wait for an answer.

Propelled by the fires of hell, he staggered back toward the manor.

CHAPTER 22

"Trenton? I'm home!" Ariana scanned the deserted hallway, then looked questioningly at Theresa. "I wonder where he is."

"He wonders the same."

"Pardon me?"

"Your husband needs you, pet. Find him." Theresa's probing black eyes conveyed a definitive message to her mistress. "Quickly, Your Grace." She patted the volume in her apron pocket. "And bear in mind that 'the virtue of adversity is fortitude.'"

A knot of apprehension formed in Ariana's stomach. Theresa's quotes of Sir Francis, her sage advice, were never without purpose. Hardship evidently loomed ahead: hardship that would take its toll, require all of Ariana's inner strength.

Suddenly, locating her husband seemed imperative.

"Trenton!" She raced through the house, first upstairs, then down, colliding with Jennings outside the music room. "Jennings ... where is the duke?"

"Why, I'm not sure, Your Grace. I haven't seen him all afternoon. Perhaps he ..."

But Ariana wasn't listening. She'd already sprinted past the butler, her anxiety increasing by the second. Where could he be?

"Trenton ..." The word lodged in her throat as she stood in the open chapel doorway. The back of Trenton's dark head and broad shoulders were visible from where he sat, slumped in the first-row bench. "Trenton?" Ariana hastened up the aisle, touching him gently on the arm.

Slowly, Trenton turned his head, gazing up at her with dark, tormented eyes.

Her heart hammering, Ariana dropped to her knees beside him. "What is it?"

His expression never changed. "Why are you still torturing me? Haven't you taken enough from me already?"

Ariana turned white. "Torturing you? What are you talking about?"

"About you. Whoever you are. Why have you followed me here?"

"Trenton ... it's me ... Ariana." She swallowed, battling the sheer panic threatening to envelop her. "I've just arrived home from Winsham. Baxter gave me the check. I'm fine. Everything is all right."

Trenton drank in her earnest features, reaching out to caress her throat and shoulders, stroking down to her arms. "I hurt you," he muttered, staring at her smooth skin. "Forgive me, misty angel. I vowed that night in the maze never to harm you. And I never intended to. Forgive me."

"You haven't harmed me ... you've *never* harmed me. Trenton!" She seized the lapels of his coat. "What's happened since I left Broddington? Why are you acting this way?"

"Did I bruise you?" he asked, massaging the gentle curve of her neck, frowning as he inspected the unblemished area. "No, thank heavens I didn't. I can barely live with myself as it is. I don't know how I could have withstood it if I'd marred that flawless skin." Soberly, he kissed the curve of her shoulder. "I never should have forced you to marry me, misty angel. Never should have touched you. You're far too fine and untainted for a destructive madman like me."

"Stop it!" She seized his hands, her own fingers cold and trembling. "Why are you saying these things? What happened while I was away?"

"Ah, but you weren't away. You were right here at Broddington. In the gardens. Directly in front of me. In my sight ... in my mind. It was you. I didn't know it, but it was. Once again I thought you were Vanessa, just as I did the night you freed your white owl. Only this time I hurt you. I nearly choked you. Who knows what I might do next time? What I've done in the past but can't recall? What I'm *capable* of doing if provoked?"

"Listen to me." Ariana was losing control—fast. "I've been at Winsham with Theresa. We just arrived home a few minutes ago. I don't know who you saw, but it wasn't me."

"You're so bloody beautiful," he murmured, rubbing his thumb across her collarbone. "How could I confuse you with Vanessa?"

"Trenton ... I love you," Ariana replied desperately.

He went rigid. "Don't say that again. Ever."

"But—"

"Dammit, Ariana!" For the first time he reacted, coming to his feet in one savage motion. "I'm unstable, deranged, insane—the last person on earth to be worthy of your love!" He saw Ariana cringe, and his guts twisted in response to her obvious terror. Instinctively, he looked toward the altar, knowing that even prayer could no longer save him. "You're frightened," he told his wife bleakly. "You should be. I don't know who I am or what I've done. Nor can I be certain of what I might do in the future. You can't stay with me. ... You have to go."

"Go?" Ariana's voice sounded wooden to her own ears.

"Yes. For your own safety."

"No." Tears filled her eyes. "I won't ... I *can't* leave you."

Trenton clenched his fists, summoning up all his strength. "Fine. Then I'll leave you."

"You'll ... what?" Ariana clutched the bench for support.

"I'll pack immediately and be gone from Broddington by night-fall." The pain in his wife's eyes was nearly Trenton's undoing, but he forced himself to stand firm—for Ariana's sake. "You'll lack for nothing; I'll see to that. All of Broddington will be at your disposal, the servants advised to jump to your command."

"I don't care about Broddington!" Ariana burst out, tears sliding down her cheeks. "I care about you."

For a split second Trenton's features twisted with anguish. Then his expression changed to one of brittle resolve. "Don't, misty angel. I'm not worth it."

He turned and headed for the door, wincing at the sound of his wife's quiet weeping.

Walking away was the hardest thing he'd ever done.

Dustin alighted from his carriage, grateful to have finally arrived at Broddington. The short drive had seemed endless, his mind filled with unanswered questions and uneasy doubts.

Ariana's brief message had said only that Trenton was away for several days and, therefore, could Dustin possibly use this time to implement his plans for the sitting room?

It was what she hadn't said that worried him.

Why was Trenton away? What was his current state of mind? Had there been any further unnerving occurrences?

Armed with the sitting-room sketches, Dustin came to find out for himself.

"Dustin! I'm so glad you could come." Ariana greeted him in the hallway, a warm smile lighting her face.

Dustin saw beyond the smile, troubled by the dark circles beneath her eyes, the hollows in her cheeks that hadn't been there last week. "I'm delighted to have been invited," he said aloud, kissing her hand. "Am I to assume that the sitting room is to be totally transformed by the time Trent returns?"

A shadow crossed Ariana's face.

This time Dustin didn't pretend not to notice. "When is Trent coming home?"

"I don't know."

Dustin studied her pale face. "I'm aware that your marriage is none of my business. I apologize in advance for making it my business." He caught her chin gently in his hand. "Did you have an argument?"

"No." Ariana turned away.

"Sweetheart." Dustin placed his hands on her shoulders. "I had hoped you thought of me as your friend."

"I do."

"Then let me help you."

Ariana's shoulders began to jerk convulsively. "I don't even know where Trenton is." She wept. "He's been gone for three days; I don't know what to do."

"Tell me what happened."

"Baxter came to see me, supposedly to make amends. He asked that I come to Winsham the following day. Evidently, he planned to repay a portion of the money he'd extorted from Trenton six years ago."

Dustin started. "Trent told you about that?"

A shaky nod.

"I see." Stifling his surprise, Dustin asked, "And did Baxter repay you?"

"Yes. I accepted the check, then came straight home. But apparently …" Her voice broke. "Something happened while I was away." She managed to keep herself in check long enough to tell Dustin of Trenton's bizarre behavior: his belief that he was mad and dangerous, his conviction that Vanessa had appeared before him, and his incoherent ramblings that suggested he'd confused Vanessa with Ariana.

"I don't know what to do," Ariana concluded in a shattered tone. "I've done nothing but think for three days, desperately tried to make sense of all this. Someone is tormenting Trenton's mind. But who … and how? I want to help him; I'd do anything for him, with or without his permission. But how can I fight something I can't even see and don't understand?" She placed her hand over Dustin's. "I'm sorry I summoned you. It was the coward's way out. But I didn't know where else to turn."

Dustin's heart wrenched, not only for Trenton, but for the beautiful, innocent girl who was his wife. "I'm glad you sent for me. Together we'll solve this insanity, once and for all." He squeezed her fingers. "As for Trent, we can both venture a good guess as to where he is."

"Spraystone."

"Exactly. That's where he always goes when he's in pain."

Ariana turned. "I love him, Dustin. I want my love to bring him joy, not grief."

"You've brought more joy back into my brother's life than I ever dreamed possible. You've given him a reason to live again, to see beyond the pain and guilt of the past. Just the fact that he'd place your well-being above his own should tell you something about the way he feels about you."

"I suppose it does," she whispered.

"Come." Dustin gestured decisively toward the staircase. "I think much better when I'm working. Let's continue this conversation in the sitting room. I'm eager to see your reaction to my designs."

"The sitting room is aired out and ready, and I've had tea and scones sent up so you can eat while you work," Theresa announced, descending the stairs. "I've also left samples of the fresh flowers the duchess specified in her notes, so you can visualize them in the finished room." She disappeared toward the kitchen.

Dustin nodded approvingly at Ariana. "That was a clever idea, asking Theresa to gather those flowers."

"I didn't. In fact, I never even mentioned them or showed her my notes."

"Then how ..." Dustin broke off, grinning. "Never mind. I must admit, baffling as she is, I like your Theresa more each time I see her."

"When all is done, the help of good counsel is that which setteth business straight." Theresa issued the proclamation from far down the hall.

"Sir Francis again?" Dustin asked Ariana, his eyes twinkling.

"None other." Ariana smiled through her tears. "I believe Theresa returns your affections. That says a great deal about your character."

"Now if only my drawings live up to my charm and my appetite."

Carefully, Ariana dried her eyes. "I don't doubt for a moment that they will."

"Shall we go up and see?"

"They're perfect!" Ariana knelt on the sitting-room floor, sketches spread out all around her. "Oh, Dustin, they're exactly what I had in mind."

"Good. Because I've taken the liberty of purchasing the furniture you described. It will be delivered this week."

"I don't know how to thank you." Ariana's eyes glowed with gratitude. Clearing her throat, she broached what she hoped would be the greatest surprise of all for her husband. "There's just one more thing."

"Which is?"

"You mentioned that your father's personal things are stored at Tyreham. How would you feel about having them sent to Broddington to be displayed in the sitting room?"

Dustin smoothed his mustache, his expression clouded by ambivalence. "Truthfully, I don't know how Trent will react to any of this, Ariana, least of all to so blatant a testimonial to our father. There are some reminders that still tear him apart, some memories he may never be ready to face. I just can't predict what his response will be."

"I'll take the responsibility ... and the risk." She stood, went to perch on the edge of the desk. "It would mean a great deal to me."

"Then we'll give it a try." He attempted a smile. "The worst Trent can do is fume and shout."

Ariana lowered her gaze.

"It *is* the worst he can do, Ariana," Dustin pressed gently.

"I know. I never believed otherwise. But, obviously, someone else does."

Dustin leaned back in the chair, folding his arms behind his head. "Let's explore this, beginning with all Trent's overt enemies, their motivations and what they would gain by mentally torturing him."

"I gather quite a few people hated him after Vanessa died."

"They wouldn't if they knew the truth," Dustin returned without thinking. Abruptly, he fell silent.

"Dustin," Ariana said with quiet understanding, "I know what happened between Vanessa and Trenton. As well as what didn't happen. I also know that her actions, her death ... and Baxter's thoughtless greed ... were responsible for your father's sudden passing. You don't have to shield me any longer."

"Trent told you all that?"

"Yes."

Dustin whistled softly. "You clearly mean more to my brother than even *I* realized. He's never opened up and shared that information with anyone other than me. His pain ... his guilt ... were too deeply embedded."

"I understand his pain. But his guilt is so unfounded! He tried everything to protect your father!"

"Yes, but Trent blamed himself for having instigated the scandal." Seeing Ariana's perplexed look, Dustin sighed. "You already know what happened. What you may not know is this: My father disliked and distrusted your sister from the first. He'd evidently had ample opportunity to observe her over several London Seasons and was convinced that she was a faithless fortune hunter. He adamantly advised Trent to stay away from her ... for his own sake, and for the sake of the family. Trent didn't take kindly to the invasion of his personal life, nor did he agree with Father's assessment ... at least not until he'd seen firsthand what Vanessa was capable of. By then it was too late. Trent's never forgiven himself for not heeding our father's warning. He's convinced that if he had, Father would still be alive today."

"I see." Ariana swallowed. "I never thought I could feel such contempt for my own family. It seems I'm learning otherwise."

Dustin's deep blue eyes softened with compassion. "I'm sorry, sweetheart."

"So am I. Sorry that Baxter and Vanessa ruined Trenton's life. Sorry that I wasn't old enough to restore it. But I'm old enough now, Dustin." She folded her hands tightly in her lap, raising her chin with solemn determination. "I can't rectify the past, but I can remedy the present *and* ensure the future. I intend to do just that; for Trenton's sake. Which brings me to a grim reality: I don't think we can dismiss Baxter as a suspect in the unsettling events of the past few days."

"No, we can't," Dustin agreed. "Despite the number of people who scorned Trenton after Vanessa's death, I can't think of anyone else who would still harbor such rage, feel such malice six years later."

"The timing certainly suggests Baxter's guilt. And there's another thing: Who but Baxter knew Vanessa well enough to train someone to impersonate her? If Trenton were physically close enough to this impostor to actually grab her arms, she must not only resemble Vanessa but behave like her as well." A further realization dawned in Ariana's eyes. "For that matter, Trenton rambled something about confusing her with me. So whoever arranged this facade must know my mannerisms too."

"Consequently, assuming Trent was lucid when he told you that, we're right back to Baxter again."

"Dustin, something else is troubling me." Ariana took a deep breath and plunged on with a nagging inconsistency that had plagued her for days. "Do you think Baxter could have tampered with Vanessa's journal?"

"What?" Dustin started, taken aback, both by the abrupt change in topic and by the question itself. "What on earth makes you ask that?"

"It's just that her written perceptions, unless she was delusional, are so different from what I now know to be the truth. How can that be?"

"You've *read* Vanessa's journal?"

"Haven't you?"

"No. Trent never showed it to me."

Ariana leaned over the desk and slid open the bottom drawer, reaching in to extract the hidden book. "Trenton never showed it to me either. I found it myself. But he knows I've read it." She handed the journal to Dustin. "I'd like your opinion."

Dustin stared at the book for a moment before he reached out and took it. Wordlessly, he scanned the pages, one after the other, until, twenty minutes later, he raised his head. "I'd kill her myself if she weren't already dead," he bit out, tossing the journal to the desk. "Either the woman was totally deranged or so corrupt that she was lying to herself as well as the world." He turned blazing eyes on Ariana. "I hope you don't believe a word of this. Vanessa and Trent were never involved … physically or emotionally … much less betrothed. Why, to read that trash one would almost think—"

"That Vanessa's words were written specifically to implicate Trenton," Ariana finished.

Dustin stopped in midsentence. "What?"

"I've thought about it again and again since I read the journal. I remember my sister, and she was *not* insane. I can't imagine that she would totally fabricate a nonexistent relationship, at least not in her own mind. She might manipulate the *ton* into believing she and Trenton were to be wed and even go so far as to spread vicious lies about him when he didn't concede to her will. But why would she lie in her private writings? After all, no one reads a journal but the one who keeps it, right?"

"Unless someone intends for that journal to be read by others," Dustin continued slowly, completing Ariana's thought.

"Exactly."

"You believe that, once Vanessa died, Baxter altered the pages of the journal in order to blackmail Trent?"

"It is something my brother would do. After all, his antipathy for Trenton was no secret." Ariana's shoulders sagged. "But that's where my theory falls short. I studied that journal carefully, and I'm absolutely certain that the handwriting is Vanessa's, not Baxter's."

"Could Baxter have coerced Vanessa to write specific things prior to her death?"

Ariana shook her head adamantly. "No one could force Vanessa to do anything. Least of all Baxter. He's not a strong-willed man by nature, and he was especially malleable when it came to Vanessa. Besides, what would have been the point? Vanessa was alive, so the journal couldn't serve as blackmail. And Baxter had no way of knowing that Vanessa was going to be the victim of a tragic drowning. If he had, he would have moved heaven and earth to save her."

"So we've reached an impasse." Dustin frowned. "Unless Vanessa penned the incriminating entries herself, then left the journal in a conspicuous place so it could be used against Trent."

"That would make sense … *if my* sister premeditatedly planned her own death. But Trenton believes Vanessa was too self-centered to intentionally plot her own suicide. And, quite frankly, I agree."

"Then how did she die?"

Ariana wagged her head slowly from side to side. "I don't know. Perhaps it was an accident. If it was suicide, it had to be totally on impulse. It's the only way Vanessa would kill herself."

Dustin stared thoughtfully at the discarded journal. "Do you mind if I keep this for a few days?" he asked at length. "Rereading it might spark something."

"By all means." Ariana gestured for him to take the journal. "You have more right to it than I. You're Trenton's brother."

"And you're Trenton's wife ... very much his wife," Dustin returned emphatically. Seeing Ariana's flush, he shook his head. "I wasn't referring to a physical union, Ariana. I was referring to a spiritual one. A month ago you were wed. Now you're married. Think about it." He stood, stretching. "I believe I'll take the journal and retire to my room. After all, I have days of renovation ahead of me." He ruffled Ariana's hair. "Stop worrying. You're going to provide me with an army of nieces and nephews to spoil. And just think of all the stories we'll be able to share with them."

Automatically, Ariana lay her palm against her abdomen, struck by the wondrous possibility Dustin had evoked with his affectionate comment. She *could* be carrying a child. Trenton's child.

Myriad emotions welled up inside her at the thought—overwhelming tenderness, protectiveness, yearning. A baby—someone who needed her, who turned to her for love; someone on whom she could lavish all the attention and nurturing she had been denied in her own childhood.

And Trenton—Would having a child make him happy? Would he gaze at his son or daughter with that intense emotion he tried so hard to repress and only Ariana could see?

Yes, somehow she knew he would. Together, they would raise their child, provide him with all the precious things life had to offer: sisters and brothers to play with and parents to envelop him in their ever-growing love.

And, year after joyous year, Christmas would come.

Tears welled up in Ariana's eyes as she recalled the afternoon she and Trenton had walked along Osborne beach, the magical moment when he'd promised her Christmas at Spraystone, a private Eden filled with snow and laughter and love.

With their entire world in turmoil, would that dream ever be realized?

"He'll be back, Ariana," Dustin said gently. "I promise you, Trent will be back."

Ariana blinked away her tears. "Of course he will." She stood, squeezing Dustin's arm. "Go rest. We have a great deal of work to do before the sitting room is absolutely perfect. And who knows? Trenton could arrive home any moment."

Even as she spoke the words, she prayed they were true.

CHAPTER 23

The sitting-room renovations were a blessing in disguise. For only when she and Dustin were immersed in the restorations did Ariana find peace. And, with the number of details to complete, the refurbishing took several long days.

Her nights were hell: lonely and empty; filled with doubts and fears. Trenton's whereabouts were no longer a worry, for although he himself had made no attempt to contact her, his solicitor had, advising Ariana that Trenton was living at Spraystone. Lawrence Crofton had arrived at Broddington five days after Trenton's disappearance to check on Ariana and to ensure her that His Grace had wired him from Wight and arranged for huge sums of money to be made available to his duchess.

Ariana didn't give a damn about her newly acquired affluence. What she wanted was her husband.

She knew Trenton well enough to realize that neither coercion nor begging would bring him home. Nor did she foolishly believe he was staying away because he no longer cared for her. To the contrary, it was *because* he cared that he had banished himself from her life, returned to exile out of some misbegotten conviction that he was protecting her from himself.

No, the only way to bring Trenton back was to unravel the mystery and resolve the past. But how?

"He's been at Spraystone a week now, Ness." Baxter folded his hands behind his head and regarded his sister quizzically from the room's single armchair. "Shouldn't we be doing something?"

Vanessa smiled, reclining on the pillows. "What makes you think we haven't been doing something?"

"What do you mean?"

"Trenton hasn't been spared surprises during his stay on Wight. Ferries and yachts travel back and forth to the Isle quite frequently, you know."

Baxter blinked, startled. "You've been to Spraystone?"

"Why of course! Twice, in fact. Both times under cloak of darkness. Once I merely left a handwritten, rose-scented note in the barn."

"Saying what?"

A throaty chuckle. "Only that I loved him, that I couldn't understand why he'd destroyed me, that I'd never leave him ... not even in death."

"Are you insane, Ness? What if Kingsley shows that note to someone? Someone who recognizes your handwriting?"

"What explanation would Trenton provide? That he received a letter from a dead woman? Who would believe him? Plus I didn't date the note, Baxter. It could have been written any time, such as six years ago." She arched one delicate brow. "May I continue?"

Baxter nodded.

"During my other visit to Spraystone, I called out to Trenton from beneath his bedroom window. It was the middle of the night. As soon as he appeared, I vanished into the trees. His estate is so isolated, it makes coming and going without being seen extremely easy."

"I still don't like the idea of your taking so many risks. ... Why don't you let me handle some of this?"

Vanessa shot Baxter an impatient look. "I hardly think you'd do an effective job of impersonating me. No, this is one aspect of the plan I have to handle myself. But don't worry, darling. Your chance will come ... very soon."

"Theresa, I can no longer remain idle," Ariana announced.

Leaning past her mistress, Theresa placed the vase of fresh wild-flowers on Ariana's dressing table. "No, I'm sure you can't."

"I love Trenton very much. There must be something I can do to help him."

Theresa dropped her hands squarely onto Ariana's shoulders, meeting her mistress's gaze in the looking glass. "Your confusion has lifted like the morning mist. Your faith in your husband has become absolute. You no longer doubt his integrity or question his innocence. Fear has ceased to play even a small part in your marriage. The veil of uncertainty no longer obscures your vision; not when you view the duke, nor when you view your brother. It is now only a question of discovering that which remains hidden to the eye and not to the heart." Tenderly, Theresa patted Ariana's cheek. "Yes, pet, I would say there is definitely something you can do."

"Help me, Theresa," Ariana pleaded softly. "Tell me where to look."

"Questions are always best answered at the source of their origin."

"I have no questions of Trenton. I believe everything he's told me, except for the absurd idea that he is mad. The only person I question is Baxter."

"Then perhaps your answers lie at Winsham."

Ariana twisted around in her chair and looked up at Theresa. "Is Baxter responsible for Trenton's suffering?"

"You know the details as well as I."

"I don't mean what occurred six years ago. I'm referring to what happened last week."

"As am I."

"So you too believe Baxter is involved?"

"I believe the answers lie within your reach, and that, at last, you have the courage to face them."

Ariana didn't reply, she merely searched Theresa's lined face with a steady gaze. "I'll visit Winsham in the morning," she said at last.

"Would you like me to accompany you?"

Earnestly, Ariana clasped Theresa's hands. "That would give me great comfort, dear friend. But this time, I must go alone."

"Ah, but you won't be alone. You go armed with your instincts, which, as I've said in the past, have never failed you. You also go with my teachings … and my love."

Ariana reached up and hugged her lifelong friend and mentor. "With riches such as those, I can't help but succeed."

Dustin sipped the last of his brandy, staring idly out his bedroom window to the moonlit grounds of Broddington. The combination of his worry over Trenton and the strain of keeping up an optimistic facade for Ariana was beginning to take its toll. The sitting room was nearly complete, thus removing his last plausible excuse for remaining at Broddington.

And still there was no sign of Trent.

Draining his glass, Dustin opened Vanessa's journal for the umpteenth time. Ariana was right: Something about the abrupt change in Vanessa's tone seemed unnatural, contrived; altering from her typically self-centered, demanding tenor to that of a desperate, frightened, and deranged woman.

Like Trenton, Dustin remembered Vanessa only too well, and mad was the one thing she was not. In fact, every one of her actions was as carefully and meticulously arranged as her hair and wardrobe. So what had prompted the transformation? Was it genuine or intentionally devised?

And how did it factor into the bizarre events of the past few days?

Rubbing his eyes wearily, Dustin's thoughts returned to Trenton and the impact all this was having on him. What was his current state of mind? Why the hell was he staying away for so long? The bloody fool: Didn't he realize that by cutting himself off from Ariana he was eliminating his only salvation?

The answer to that was no. Trenton was too muddled to recognize his own needs. Evidently, someone would have to do that for him. Someone like his brother.

Trenton didn't know where he was. Nor did he care.

He'd spent most of the past five days in a drunken stupor, alternately drinking and passing out, coming to only to lose himself in his liquor again. He hadn't left Spraystone, nor did he intend to. He also hadn't seen anyone.

Except Vanessa.

Damn the spiteful bitch: Even in death she taunted him. He'd read the suggestive note he'd found in the barn three times before his fuzzy mind absorbed it, and then he wished he hadn't.

Where had the letter come from? When had Vanessa written it?

The one night he'd tried to sleep, he'd been awakened by *her* voice. Staggering to the window, he'd been confronted with the heinous nightmare that plagued him relentlessly, refused to be extinguished: Vanessa, calling to him, begging him to come to her, pleading with him not to hurt her.

Maybe he *had* hurt her ... even killed her.

Perhaps the vision before him was no impostor, but Vanessa herself, returned from the grave to torment him for murdering her.

Reality ceased to exist, melding with conjecture into a dim, muted memory, dulled further by the effects of his brandy. Vanessa was dead ... Vanessa was back ... he must have killed her... why else would her ghost be haunting him?

Obviously, he was utterly, entirely insane. And madmen were capable of anything, even murder.

He'd come close to brutalizing his own wife.

Ariana. The only beautiful, precious sanity left in his frenzied world. She loved him, believed in him, trusted him. And what had he done? He'd hurt her, nearly choked her ... actually confused her with a dead woman.

Dear Lord, he'd lost his mind.

He was sprawled on the sofa, one arm flung over his face to shield him from the offensive sunlight, when he heard the hammering noise.

Groaning, he turned his head away. No. Not again.

The pounding continued, louder this time. "Trent!" A voice accompanied the clamor.

Trenton squeezed his eyes shut, determined to block out the sound.

"Dammit, Trenton, let me in!"

Dustin.

The reality penetrated at last, and Trenton raised his head, opening his eyes a crack. What was his brother doing at Spraystone?

"Trent, I'm not going away. So I suggest you unlock this door."

Staggering to his feet, Trenton steadied himself, then weaved his way down the hallway. After three attempts, he jerked open the door. "Dustin?" He leaned against the wall for support, focusing, with great difficulty, on his brother's anxious face.

It took Dustin a full minute to size up the extent of Trenton's deterioration, and ten seconds to plan his own strategy. Then he acted, cursing under his breath and stomping into the house. "You're a stupid, bloody fool, do you know that?" he demanded. Without waiting for an answer, he seized Trenton's arm, propelling him down the hall and into the sitting room. "Wait here." He maneuvered his swaying brother into an armchair, then disappeared into the kitchen.

Trenton wasn't certain how much time passed before Dustin returned, shoving a steaming cup of coffee into his hands. "Drink this," he ordered.

Blindly, Trenton took a swallow, then began to cough violently. "What the hell is this?"

"*Strong* black coffee. Just the right medicine for a reckless idiot who's drunk himself into oblivion."

"I have reason to."

"You have better reason *not* to. And that reason is waiting for you at Broddington, worried sick over your state of mind."

Trenton stared bitterly into the dark brew. "Ariana deserves better. And I *have* no mind. I lost it years ago … if I ever had it at all."

"Your mind is intact. It's your judgment that's lacking."

"You don't know what you're talking—"

"I know precisely what I'm talking about. And I have every intention of discussing it with you … *when* you're sober. So hurry up and down that coffee. There's a whole potful in the kitchen. And you're going to consume every last drop."

Trenton narrowed bloodshot eyes on his brother. "Dustin …"

"Drink. Before I pour it down your throat."

In no condition for an argument, Trenton complied, gulping down the intolerably strong coffee until his stomach lurched, his eyes watered—and his head cleared.

"Good. Now we can talk." Satisfied with the results of his labor, Dustin stretched his arms across the back of the sofa. "Why are you doing this to yourself?"

"Because I'm crazy. But if you've seen Ariana, I presume you already know that."

"You're no more crazy than I. And yes, I've seen Ariana. I don't know what you've ever done to deserve that exceptional young woman's love. But you have it. So why are you hurting her like this?"

Trenton rubbed the back of his neck. "Did Ariana tell you everything?"

"Yes. We've done nothing but wrack our brains trying to figure out who's behind this monstrous plan."

"Perhaps no one is behind it… no one, but Vanessa."

"Vanessa's dead, Trent."

"True. But she haunts me nonetheless."

"I don't believe in ghosts. Neither do you."

"You haven't seen one."

"Nor have you."

"Then what the hell have I seen?" Trenton rose, clasping his head in his hands. "She's appeared to me again and again ... I've lost count of how many times. She begs me not to hurt her, her journal entries do the same. And I *did* hurt her that last night ... I *wanted to* hurt her. I shook her and flung her to the sand, not once, but twice. The second time she fell into the water. ... I remember the river dousing the hem of her gown. I was blinded by rage and hatred. She shouted my name ... again and again ... but at some point I recall only silence. I walked away and never looked back. Maybe I *did* kill her! Has *that* possibility ever occurred to you?"

"No ... it hasn't." Dustin rose and went to his brother. "She was alive when you left her, Trent. You told me so yourself. The only reason you're feeling these doubts is because someone is compelling you to feel them. Don't let that bastard win. Fight back, Trent. You of all people know how. You also have someone to fight for."

Trenton met his brother's gaze. "How is she?" he asked hoarsely.

"Ariana, like you, is a fighter. She's determined to find a way to uncover the truth ... for your sake."

"Did she ask you to come to Spraystone?"

"No. She has no idea that I'm here, nor does she intend to beg or demand that you return to Broddington. What she wants is to eliminate the cause of your suffering so you'll come back on your own. She's an incredibly loyal, selfless young woman." Dustin's voice grew soft. "That doesn't mean you aren't in her thoughts. You are. Every minute."

"I never stop thinking of her," Trenton returned in a strangled tone. "Every bloody bird, every flower reminds me of her. I hear her laughter in every corner of Spraystone, feel her softness in my arms at night. Dammit, Dustin, I need her so badly." He gave a mirthless laugh. "I'd finally stopped fighting the inevitable, steeled myself to relinquish the cursed autonomy I'd held on to all these years. But now everything's changed, my world is in chaos … and I won't destroy Ariana's life along with my own."

"You're destroying both your lives by staying away."

"What can I offer her? My torment? My insanity?"

"Your love." Dustin clamped his hands firmly on Trenton's shoulders. "Let's stop speaking in euphemisms, Trent. You're in love with your wife. You know it. I know it. Isn't it about time Ariana knew it too?"

"What good would it do to tell her?"

"None, unless you intend to behave like a real husband. Go home. Be strong for your wife; the way she's strong for you."

"To what end?" Trenton's eyes were dulled more with pain than with the effects of alcohol. "Answer me that, Dustin. If I go to Ariana, tell her of my love, accept hers in return, what can that do but hurt her? I can't change the events of the past, nor can I promise her a future. Not if I'm a madman, a murderer … or both. So what could be gained from speaking my heart?"

"It would give you the strength you need to get through this nightmare. It would give Ariana the joy she deserves to awaken to each new day. That in itself is reason enough, despite what the future may hold."

"She deserves more."

"She loves *you*."

"I love her too." Trenton spoke the words aloud for the first time, stunned at how easily they emerged. "I want to give her everything … all the lost years of childhood she never had, all the luxuries her scoundrel brother robbed her of, all the indulgences she was never permitted." Trenton shook his head in disbelief. "Do you know she actually feels inferior to Vanessa? That she's convinced that her beauty, her vibrancy, all that she is, are secondary to the attributes of her despicable sister? And what's worse, my tenderhearted wife merely accepts all this as given, harboring no resentment, no jealousy, only kindness and compassion for that slut of a sister and parasite of a brother."

"Not any more," Dustin interjected.

Trenton swung around, a questioning look on his face.

"You haven't spent the past few days with Ariana, Trent. I have. Whatever pieces were still missing I filled in for her. And while I don't disagree that she is grossly unaware of her own radiance and self-worth, I can vouch for the fact that she no longer views her family through subjective eyes. Not Baxter, and not Vanessa."

A muscle worked in Trenton's jaw. "That shouldn't surprise me. When I recounted the past to Ariana, she listened to every detail ... and believed me. She took my word ... that of the unknown blackguard who forced her to the altar ... over her family's, and never doubted me. Not once. Faith such as that is humbling."

"I agree. It comes along once in a lifetime—if you're lucky. You happen to be lucky. So don't be a stubborn fool and let it get away." Dustin gripped Trenton's shoulders. "You can give her all those things you described. But all she really wants is you."

"And Christmas," Trenton added in a voice thick with emotion. "I promised her Christmas."

"What?"

"Ariana hasn't had a real Christmas since her parents died. She misses it terribly. A holiday celebration with all the elaborate trimmings is her greatest wish. It's all she's ever asked of me."

Dustin nodded his understanding. "I remember she mentioned something about her long-ago Christmases when I showed her around Broddington. She spoke of Winsham's Christmas trees, the drawing room's transformation to a winter garden."

"I'm determined to give that to her. All she should have had but didn't."

"She wants to give you the same: happiness, peace of mind, love."
A pause. "Children."

Trenton's features went taut, and he was suddenly completely
sober. "Are you saying …"

"No. Or rather, I have no way of knowing. If Ariana were expecting your child, I'm hardly the one she'd be confiding in." A corner of
Dustin's mouth lifted into a half-smile. "But surely you recall how
babies are created, Trent. And even I can attest to the fact that you've
done your damnedest to increase the probability of your becoming
a father."

Unsmiling, Trenton stared at his brother. "I've been so steeped in
memories … I never even considered … Lord, Dustin, what if Ariana
really is pregnant? How will the events of my past… and present…
affect my child?"

"A better question is, how will your desertion affect him? You just
cited all the deprivations Ariana endured growing up alone, without
her parents' nurturing. Is that what you want for your child? To come
into this world without the foundation of his father's love? Is it?"

Trenton's jaw set. "You've become bloody unconscionable, you
know that?"

A grin. "I learned from the best—my older brother." Dustin
released Trenton's arms, heading for the stairs. "I'll help you pack.
We can catch the next ferry back to Sussex and be at Broddington in
time for lunch."

Broddington—in time for lunch. The words sank in, bringing
with them an inordinate sense of relief and the first pleasure Trenton
had known in days. God help him if he was being unfair, but he
could no longer squelch the need that gnawed at his gut—a need only
Ariana's love could fill.

The possibility that his child was growing inside her made
Trenton's soul swell with pride, and an emotion so vast it hurt. But the

truth was, whether there was a child or not, whether he was totally mad or entirely sane, he had to be with his wife.

"All right, Dustin," Trenton agreed, his voice choked. "Let's go home."

The brothers' gazes met, both men simultaneously struck by the enormity of Trenton's transformation. Not only had he fallen totally in love with his wife, but something equally profound had occurred, something Trenton's own pronouncement had just revealed.

Over the past month Ariana's love had changed not only her husband's life, but his home as well. Broddington, Richard Kingsley's great architectural achievement, was no longer a magnificent mausoleum.

Ariana was there.

And now it was home.

CHAPTER 24

Even Theresa was still asleep when Ariana left Broddington that morning.

It was rare for Ariana to arise before her lady's maid, but today it was remarkably easy, considering the fact that she'd never been to bed. Instead, she'd spent the long hours of night assimilating all the information she had acquired. By dawn's first light, she was more convinced than ever that the only solution was for her to go to Winsham. Immediately. If Baxter were guilty, she would discover it herself—today. If not, she would eliminate that possibility once and for all and proceed with her investigation.

Scribbling a quick note for Dustin, Ariana left the manor. There was no point in awakening him; for, as she had told Theresa yesterday, this was something she had to take care of herself.

During the carriage ride, Ariana thought about Trenton, praying that he was coming to grips with his pain. She wondered how a man who was capable of being so very gentle and caring could condemn himself as a coldblooded murderer. As to the rest of the world's denunciation, surely someone besides her could see the real Trenton; the compassionate man he kept buried beneath layers of self-protection and bitterness.

Soberly, she reflected back over their tumultuous marriage and its hurtling emotions: tenderness to passion, passion to anger, and yes, sometimes to fear. But through it all, some innate sense of trust had always reassured Ariana that her husband would never hurt her.

How could a man who initiated his bride so gently, with such worry and candor about causing her pain, be violent or devious? How could a man who nursed a sick owl back to health be cruel? How could a man who gave freely to the poor, helping them with no expected compensation, be brutal?

He couldn't.

Ariana knew it. Dustin knew it. Theresa knew it.

Some of Theresa's sage comments about Trenton's history came to mind.

I don't believe love was ever the issue.... You recall your sister, he doesn't want you because of Vanessa ... he wants you in spite of her. Fear had as little to do with the events of the past as did love.

Finally, Ariana could clearly discern what her friend had been subtly conveying to her. With her astute observations, Theresa had been clarifying Trenton's character—and Vanessa's.

The wise lady's maid had also intimated that Ariana had to find her own answers—if she was strong enough to seek them. Well, she had become strong enough.

Leaning her head back against the carriage seat, Ariana vowed to learn the truth, at whatever cost. But regardless of what her trip to Winsham revealed, her belief in her husband would remain steadfast.

In short, someone was guilty.

Trenton was not.

The sun was rising over Winsham when Ariana alit from her carriage. She didn't pause but climbed the steps and knocked.

"Your Grace?" Coolidge looked stunned—and sleepy.

"I want to see my brother. Now."

"I returned from my holiday late last night and saw the viscount only briefly. I believe he is still abed."

"Then awaken him." Ariana folded her arms across her chest, her chin raised determinedly.

"But—"

"Fine. I'll awaken him myself." She headed for the stairway.

"Ariana?" Baxter descended from the second level, tying the belt of his robe, looking thoroughly perplexed. "What on earth are you doing here at dawn? Is everything all right?"

"No. We need to talk."

A flash of emotion—was it concern or fear?—crossed Baxter's face, then disappeared. "All right. Come into the morning room. Coolidge can serve tea. Would you like breakfast? He can—"

"I'm not hungry. I'm impatient. No refreshments are necessary, Coolidge," she assured the flustered butler. "I apologize for disrupting you so soon after your return from holiday. Go back to bed."

"Yes, Your Grace." Still half-asleep, Coolidge stumbled back to his quarters.

"Ariana, what's wrong?" Baxter hurried after her as she headed purposefully down to the morning room.

Ariana closed the door firmly behind them. "We are going to have a frank conversation. I'll begin by telling you the following: I'm in love with my husband. I don't believe he killed Vanessa, nor do I believe he was responsible for her suicide." Ariana held up her hand to ward off Baxter's protest. "That's not all. Someone has been tormenting Trenton the past week. I have reason to suspect it is you. Is it, Baxter?"

Baxter opened and closed his mouth a few times. Then he shook his head in exasperation. "I don't know what the hell you're talking about. Where would I get the opportunity to torment your husband?"

"I notice you questioned only your opportunity, and not your motive," Ariana returned coldly. "In answer to your question, you wouldn't need the opportunity. You'd do it indirectly, hire others to take care of it for you."

"Take care of what? What's being done to Kingsley?"

"The atrocities of the past are being brandished in his face, either as a cruel reminder or a sick joke."

"Atrocities?" Baxter appeared to be struggling to understand.

"Vanessa's death. Vanessa herself. Someone is recapturing her death and replaying it for Trenton."

"Are you sure of this?"

"Quite sure. First, Trenton received a volume of Shakespeare, marked with a rose." Ariana paused while the significance of the sender having chosen Vanessa's favorite flower as a page designator sank in. Then she continued. "The rose marked that section of Othello where he contemplates murdering Desdemona."

"What does that have to do with—"

"According to the merchant who sold the book, the woman who purchased it for Trenton referred to herself as his wife. The shopkeeper described her as being a vibrant red-haired, green-eyed woman. That was only the first incident. There have been many others since. Shall I recount them to you?"

Ariana didn't wait for a reply. "Late that same night Trenton found a discarded lantern in the sand along the River Arun ... a lantern that was identical to the one Vanessa carried on the night she died. As Trenton was examining the lantern, a woman appeared in the trees—a woman who looked astonishingly like Vanessa. She vanished before Trenton could question her.

"But she's reappeared several times since. Ironically, one of those occasions was on the exact day—at the identical hour that I visited Winsham to accept your check—at *your* request. Quite a coincidence, wouldn't you say?"

"What are you accusing me of?" Baxter sputtered.

"Someone is impersonating Vanessa. Are you behind it?"

"No one could impersonate Vanessa. She was unique, incomparable. Tell me, Ariana, who has seen this supposed impostor? Other than your husband, that is. And some elderly merchant who probably wouldn't know his own wife, let alone someone else's."

Silence.

"I thought as much. So all you're really confirming is that Trenton Kingsley is every bit the madman I've always claimed him to be."

"That's a matter of perspective. You see Trenton as crazy. I see someone else as vindictive." Ariana's eyes sparked fire. "You despise him, Baxter. You'd do anything to destroy him. The question is, how far are you willing *and* capable of carrying that hatred? Only you can answer that. And I want an answer. Now."

"I'd choke him with my bare hands if it were legal!" Baxter burst out. "But it isn't. And I'm not stupid enough to torment a man who would only take his rage out on my baby sister. So, no, I'm not behind this fictitious plot your husband has conjured up. Nor do I believe it exists."

"Then who bought that book?"

"How the hell should I know?"

"And who has Trenton been seeing?"

"His bloody imagination, that's who! Deranged people are capable of fabricating anything!"

"I don't believe that."

"Well, apparently you stand alone. Because if Kingsley were so certain of his own sanity and his own innocence, why did he flee, yet again, to the Isle of Wight? Why isn't he here with you, accusing me of this grand plot against him?"

For a long moment Ariana said nothing, merely stared mutely at her brother's angry face. Then she drew a slow breath. "I never thought of it that way," she said shakily. "I can't argue the point; Trenton should be here to plead his own case."

Baxter's smile was immediate and triumphant. "Of course he should. *If* he's innocent." Crossing over, Baxter smoothed Ariana's hair with a soothing caress. "I'm not suggesting that you're entirely wrong, sprite. Maybe Kingsley isn't lying; maybe he's just too damned unbalanced to know what he's seeing. If that's the case, he could be dangerous. Not just to himself, but to you."

Ariana gulped, her face buried against Baxter's shirt. "I hope you're wrong."

"I hope so too. But think about it. A man who sees a dead woman, not once but several times? A man who has a history of violence, of brutal jealousy, of mental cruelty—is that the kind of man you want to entrust your life to?" He shook his head sadly. "I never thought he would deteriorate to this degree, or, edict or not, I'd have refused to allow you to marry him. But it's too late now." Soberly, he held Ariana away from him. "Sprite, if the situation becomes unbearable, if he ever threatens you in any way, promise me you'll come to Winsham, turn to me for help. Promise me."

"I'll look to you at once," Ariana vowed solemnly.

"Good." Baxter kissed her forehead gently. "I'm glad you brought this problem to me, even if you did believe I was some kind of culprit. Do you feel better?"

"Yes ... everything is much clearer now." Ariana sighed. "I'm exhausted, Baxter. This whole predicament has taken its toll on me. Do you mind if I go home to bed?"

Baxter gave her arms a reassuring squeeze. "Of course, sprite. Get some rest. And remember, if you ever need me, I'm here."

"I won't forget that ... or anything else you've said." She yawned. "Don't trouble Coolidge; he's probably gone back to sleep. I'll see myself out." She patted her brother's hand. "Thank you for putting everything in perspective."

Baxter's compassionate gaze followed her from the room.

Leaning back against the closed morning-room door, Ariana let out her breath in a rush, battling to bring herself under control. Shuddering, she wiped her hand across her forehead, hopefully obliterating Baxter's kiss along with it.

Her despicable brother had been lying.

She'd known it from the moment they'd spoken of the Shake-spearean volume Trenton had received. Ariana had never supplied a description of the merchant. How then had Baxter known he was old and doddering?

And if that weren't enough, how had Baxter known Trenton was at Spraystone? She hadn't mentioned it; in fact, no one other than she, Dustin, and Lawrence Crofton knew Trenton's whereabouts.

Except whoever was tormenting him.

As far as Ariana was concerned, she had her answer. Baxter was involved—somehow, some way—with the past week's happenings. Her every instinct confirmed it.

But this was one instance when her instincts alone were not enough. What she needed was proof.

She intended to get it.

Glancing furtively about the empty hallway, Ariana acted quickly, before Baxter could emerge from the morning room. Hurrying to the front door, she slipped outside and spoke rapidly to her waiting carriage driver.

"My stay here will be far longer than I originally intended," she said in a terse whisper. "Go back to Broddington. I'll send for you when I'm ready to return."

"Very good, Your Grace," the driver replied.

Ariana stayed him with her hand. "Wait until I've reentered the house and closed the door. Then, count to ten. At that point, you may leave."

The driver looked flabbergasted. "Pardon me?"

"Please ... just do as I say!"

"Yes, Your Grace." Brows knit in bewilderment, the driver nodded.

"Thank you." Ariana flashed him a swift, grateful smile. Word-lessly, she hastened back into Winsham, praying that Baxter hadn't followed her out immediately.

The hallway was deserted.

With a sigh of relief, Ariana closed the door—loudly—behind her. Then, without pause, she sped into the sitting room, ducking down behind the massive sofa.

She had just tucked her skirts tightly around her when she heard the unmistakable sound of horses' hooves. Her carriage was departing, precisely as she intended.

An instant later Baxter emerged, making his way to the front door and peering out. Evidently relieved by what he saw, he turned on his heel and strode off.

Thank goodness, Ariana told herself silently. *Now he'll go back to bed and I can begin my search.*

Her breath caught in her throat when, instead of mounting the stairs to return to his room, Baxter stalked past the sitting room and disappeared into the rear of the house.

Where is he going? Ariana wondered. *It's barely dawn.*

Frowning, she reevaluated her strategy. She had planned to search Baxter's study first, then make her way through the lower level of Winsham while Baxter was asleep and before Coolidge arose to begin his chores. But obviously that was not to be. So she'd just reverse the order she'd intended, beginning with the second level and eventually exploring the first.

When the silence extended into long minutes, Ariana took her chance. Scooting out from behind the sofa, she peeked into the hall, then sprinted across to the stairway and hastily ascended, praying all the while that the upper level was unoccupied.

Again, the fates were with her.

She slipped into Baxter's room, closing the door carefully behind her. Without hesitating, she made her way to his desk.

Over the next half-hour, Ariana cautiously searched every square inch of her brother's quarters. She had no idea exactly what she was looking for a receipt, a note, a name. What she discovered was nothing.

Wearily, she sagged against the wall. Apparently Baxter kept none of his records in his room. She'd have to find a way to get into his study.

Heart pounding, Ariana inched her way downstairs, pausing after each step to listen. Where was Baxter? Hopefully not in his study.

Fortunately, the study door was ajar, the room vacant.

It took Ariana twenty nerve-wracking minutes to thoroughly scan the desk drawers. Again, nothing.

Surely evidence had to exist somewhere.

Impatience making her bold, Ariana crept down the hall, curious now as to where her brother had gone. Had her confrontation unnerved him? If so, had he retreated to wherever his papers were kept?

She *had* to find out.

Inching her way, she glanced into each of Winsham's rooms, hoping for a clue as to Baxter's whereabouts. He appeared to have vanished into thin air.

Ariana stopped when she reached the servants' quarters. Surely he wasn't with Coolidge.

A drone of voices interrupted her thoughts, and quickly Ariana dashed into a coat closet, burying herself beneath the mounds of outerwear. The voices grew louder, and Ariana pressed her ear to the door, making out only snatches of conversation.

"Convinced her... Kingsley ... deranged ... proceeding ... perfectly..."

The voices disappeared from earshot.

Yes, Baxter, Ariana thought, sitting back on her haunches. *You've certainly convinced me. But not of Trenton's insanity; of your own maliciousness.*

Muted or not, the voice she'd just heard belonged to Baxter. The question remaining was, who was with him? The only thing Ariana had ascertained from the second person's monosyllabic replies was that it was a woman.

But who?

Ariana's head came up. Could it be the woman who was impersonating Vanessa? Was Baxter keeping her here, at Winsham?

It made sense. Now Ariana had to prove it.

The instant she felt it was safe to do so, Ariana crept from the closet and into the servants' quarters, down the corridor from which the voices had emerged. Coolidge's room was way at the end of the wing with a dozen unoccupied rooms in between. She would search every one, if need be.

The first room was dingy and musty-smelling; definitely uninhabited. So was the second.

The third room was dark, the drapes drawn tightly, allowing only a dim light to filter in. Ariana entered.

The powerful scent of roses accosted her at once, pervading her senses and telling her all she needed to know.

Someone was living here. And that someone was dousing herself in Vanessa's scent.

Ariana's stomach knotted with dread.

Silently closing the door, Ariana tugged open the drapes, suffusing the room with light.

A cry rose in her throat.

Clothing was strewn about: various gowns, all dark in color.

Except one peach gown that caught Ariana's eye at once. Trembling, she picked it up. Recognition was instantaneous. It was the identical gown Baxter had bought for her.

Ariana sank down to her knees. So that's why he had given her that gift. He'd wanted his hired impostor to own the same gown, to wear it in order to confuse and bewilder Trenton.

Yet another piece of the heinous puzzle fell into place.

"This dress is proof enough," Ariana muttered to herself. "Not to mention the roses, and the dark clothing meant to obscure its wearer from view. I'll bring this to Trenton. ... Then he'll believe me." She shuddered. "Where did Baxter find someone convincing enough to portray Vanessa?"

"Nothing is as effective as the real thing, darling." The taunting voice hit Ariana like a bucket of ice water. "Anything less would have been unacceptable."

All the color drained from Ariana's face, and for a moment she couldn't breathe. Then, as if in a trance, she rose, gaping at the crimson-haired beauty in the open doorway. "Vanessa?" she whispered.

"You really have become quite enchanting, little sister." Vanessa entered the room, sweeping Ariana's trembling form with cold, assessing eyes. "Not to mention resourceful. A bit too virtuous for my tastes, but lovely nonetheless."

"Oh my God." Ariana clutched the bedpost for support, her mind desperately trying to absorb the reality that had evaded her for six years. "You're alive."

"Disappointed?"

"I ..." Ariana's mouth opened and closed a few times. "Why did you ... where have you ..."

"Because of Trenton Kingsley and in France."

"Ness, have you taken to talking to yourself?" Baxter stepped into the room—and stopped in his tracks. His face turned chalk-white, and a muscle began throbbing at his temple. "Ariana ..." he managed.

"Dear God ..." Ariana breathed again, staring from her shaken brother to her still-alive sister. "So the two of you ..."

"Evidently, Baxter, you didn't do nearly as convincing a job as you'd believed," Vanessa commented. "Judging from Ariana's appearance in my room, I'd say she wasn't at all convinced of her husband's"—she spat out the word "guilt."

"I don't understand," Baxter said dazedly, still staring at Ariana. "You accepted my reasoning. Your carriage left Winsham. ... I heard it depart."

"Apparently, it departed without its occupant," Vanessa concluded, a glimmer of respect in her eyes. "It seems, Baxter, that our baby sister is far more ingenious than we gave her credit for. Something you said must have given her reason to suspect you were lying. So she staged her exit, then hid and searched the house. Isn't that right, Ariana?"

Ariana's head was still reeling with the discovery that her supposedly dead sister was very much alive.

Vanessa walked forward and lifted Ariana's chin, evaluating her as one would inspect a fine jewel prior to its purchase. "Are you in shock or merely unwilling to acknowledge your scheme?"

"*My* scheme!" Ariana jerked her face away, jolting out of her reverie at the impact of Vanessa's words. "You have the audacity to interrogate me about *my* intentions? *You* who have feigned death for six years and returned only to further torment a man you've already cruelly and unnecessarily stripped of six years of his life! Dear God, Vanessa ..." Ariana's expression was a mixture of disbelief and revulsion. "You really are a vicious monster, aren't you?"

"That's enough, Ariana!" Baxter intervened in a warning tone.

"And you ..." Ariana's biting gaze swept over her brother. "You can defend her? After all she's done, reappearing after all these years?" Seeing the guilt flash across Baxter's face, comprehension struck Ariana full force. "You knew," she breathed. "All this time, you knew she was alive. You let me go on thinking my sister was dead, that she'd been driven to suicide ... or worse ... when from the first you knew it was a lie! Why, Baxter, why?"

"You know the answer to that as well as I," he returned bitterly and without regret. "Trenton Kingsley. He destroyed Vanessa's life. It gave me great pleasure to destroy his."

"*She* was the one who destroyed *his* life!" Ariana shot back. "How can you condone that? Good Lord, Baxter, was I *so* wrong about you? I thought you had some humanity! Have you none?" She stared at her brother as if seeing him for the first time. "Even after brutally accusing Trenton of murder, forcing him to live with the possibility that a woman took her own life because of him, still you weren't satisfied. You had to blackmail him, didn't you? Get every damned cent you could out of the situation. Never let it be said that my money-driven brother allowed a lucrative opportunity to escape him." Abrupt realization dawned in Ariana's eyes. "Or was blackmail not an afterthought? Was it all part of the original plan? Is *that* why you both tampered with Vanessa's journal? To make it as incriminating as possible? Tell me, Baxter, when did you alter the journal? Just prior to Vanessa's *suicide?* Did the two of you sit up nights writing her implicating entries … so you could just *happen* to find the journal a mere day after her tragic and untimely death and twist the knife still deeper in Trenton's heart? Is that how it worked?"

"What the hell are you talking about?" Baxter exploded. "I altered nothing! Everything in that journal was the truth!" He strode forward, seizing Ariana by the shoulders. "I already admitted to you that I took money from Kingsley. And I've never tried to hide the fact that I detest the man. Dammit, Ariana, I haven't lied to you about anything! I've only tried to protect you." He winced at the glaring accusation on her face. "All right, I lied to you about Vanessa. It's true I knew she was alive. But I had to keep her whereabouts a secret … for her own sake. What if Kingsley had gone after her? Tried to hurt her again? I couldn't risk it. Everyone had to believe her dead … including you. Besides …" and his tone turned icy, "thanks to Kingsley, she was gone forever. She could never return to England; not after the circumstances that drove her away! If she returned, she'd be ridiculed, shunned, possibly even jailed! While Kingsley would be suddenly hailed a hero, rather than the demented madman that he is! So why should I torture you by telling you the truth? Your sister was lost to you forever. It was best you believed her dead."

"You're still doing it," Ariana said in amazement. "Justifying your malicious, selfish actions with absurd, fabricated motives and blatant lies. You actually believe what you just said, don't you, Baxter? You tampered with a man's life, indirectly killed his father and stripped his family of their honor, and you feel vindicated?"

"What about what he did to Vanessa?" Baxter demanded, shaking Ariana in frustration. "Don't you give a damn that he robbed your sister of her youth, her life?"

"Trenton never even touched Vanessa!" Ariana burst out. "Everything she sacrificed … her youth, her reputation … she brought on herself. And you know it!" Focusing on Baxter's oblivious expression, Ariana blinked. "You *don't* know, do you?" she whispered, the final pieces falling into place. "You really don't."

"Know what?"

"That the journal entries were indeed devised … brilliantly and creatively, I might add," Vanessa said calmly. She closed the door behind her, leaning against it to block off any attempt at escape. "But not by Baxter, darling. You should know by now that the formulation of devious plans is not his forté. He executes them splendidly and with great enthusiasm, but the actual planning requires a level of cunning that is mine and mine alone."

Baxter released Ariana and snapped around to face Vanessa. "What are you talking about?" He looked so stupefied that Ariana almost pitied him in that moment. "Are you telling me you *invented* the contents of your journal?"

"Embellished, darling. Only embellished."

"Fabricated," Ariana corrected. "Every word. Other than the fact that you wanted Trenton desperately and would do anything to get him. Including spreading false rumors designed to coerce him into your arms and eventually to the altar. And when that was unsuccessful, feigning desperation, pretending to be despondent enough to take your own life. *That's* how irrationally you wanted him.

"But you didn't count on one thing." Ariana raised her chin proudly, meeting Vanessa's mocking gaze head-on. "Trenton didn't want you."

338 ANDREA KANE

Hatred twisted Vanessa's fine features. "He was a fool ... a stupid, stubborn fool. I would have been the perfect wife for him. But he wanted a sweet little virgin. Well, he got one, didn't he?"

"Ness ... what about all the things you told me?" Baxter asked weakly. "His jealousy, his violence, his rage?"

"It was all lies, Baxter," Ariana supplied. "Every last word. Trenton and Vanessa were never intimate—he never even laid a hand on her." Ariana's gaze locked with Vanessa's. "What I still can't figure out is, why did you come back? Merely to resume your torture? Why now, after six years? ... Surely you must have made a life for yourself in France?"

A bitter laugh. "A life? No, Ariana, not a life. A living hell... one you could never in your wildest dreams fathom. I'm married, darling. To a respected French nobleman ... a spiteful, savage parasite. You, on the other hand, are married to the eminent Duke of Broddington, affluent and powerful, seductive as sin itself."

"You still want him," Ariana murmured, incredulous.

"I don't want any man!" Vanessa snarled back. "But I'll be damned if one of them will spurn me and go unpunished! I vowed that Trenton Kingsley would pay for his rejection and pay he did ... with years of exile and humiliation. Now, after six years, you come along and suddenly all his agony is erased as if it had never been?"

"Trenton's agony will never be erased, Vanessa." Ariana felt tears of outrage sting her eyes. He hasn't known a day of peace since that horrible night."

"*He* hasn't known a day of peace?" Savagely, Vanessa seized the front of her gown, rending it from throat to bodice to expose ugly portions of scarred skin surrounded by a dozen recently inflicted angry red welts. Ignoring Ariana's shocked gasp, she bit out, "*This* is agony, Ariana. Not what your husband has endured. This. I've lived with torture every day of my life, relinquished more than anyone can ever restore." She dragged the sides of her gown together. "But I intend to seek vengeance in any way I can. I've earned it and, dammit, I'm going to have it!"

Ariana swallowed convulsively, sickened by the physical abuse Vanessa had suffered. Recognizing the horrifying outcome of her sister's deceit, Ariana could almost forgive her—almost. "How will driving Trenton mad ease all you've endured?" she asked, pity and anger warring inside her.

"It will ease nothing. What it will do is ensure that I never have to bear it again." Vanessa inclined her head toward Baxter. "Would you like to fill her in, darling?"

"Vanessa … you let me believe … all these years … that Trenton Kingsley terrorized you … why?" Baxter's eyes were damp. *"Why?"*

"To ease your conscience, darling." The pathetic Vanessa of moments ago had disappeared, replaced by the vindictive, regal queen who preceded her. "It was far easier for you to blackmail and ostracize a madman who threatened your sister's life than a mere suitor who rejected her."

"I've always hated Kingsley and you knew it!" Baxter protested. "All you had to do was tell me the truth. Dear Lord, Ness …" His voice trailed off. "Why didn't you just tell me the truth?"

"What difference does it make now?" she snapped impatiently. "The important thing is, now our plan will be that much easier to accomplish. Because now"—she flashed a malevolent smile at Ariana—"we have Ariana to help us."

"Help you!" Ariana's eyes widened. "You're the one who must be mad, Vanessa. I have no intention of helping you hurt my husband."

"I rather think you will." Vanessa tapped her chin thoughtfully. "Unless you want your husband, rather than a murder suspect, to be a murder victim."

Ariana and Baxter gasped simultaneously. "Vanessa, what the hell are you talking about?" Baxter asked shakily. "We never spoke of murder. Our plan was to drive Kingsley insane and have Ariana leave him on those grounds, taking his money with her."

"Yes ... that is what we discussed, isn't it? The only problem is, we grossly underestimated Ariana's touching loyalty to her husband. Obviously, she will never desert him of her own accord, will you, darling?" Vanessa raised derisive brows in Ariana's direction. "Therefore, a bit of coercion is in order."

"Coercion?" Baxter sounded ill.

"Yes. You see, Baxter, in order for us to permanently enjoy Trenton's outrageous fortune, we would have to force Ariana to leave him, and then, once the money was in our hands, ensure her silence by having her vanish... for good." Vanessa sighed. "I, better than anyone, know how difficult and tedious that sort of disappearance can be—unless one truly is dead, of course. The easiest thing, under the circumstances, would be if Ariana really were dead. Then Trenton would be framed and convicted of the murder and you, dear brother, would receive a large portion of his vast fortune as compensation for the loss of your only remaining sister.

"But just to demonstrate to you both that I still do have a heart," Vanessa continued, ignoring the horrified looks on both Ariana's and Baxter's faces, "I will assure you that I have no intention of killing my own sister. Therefore, that course of action, no matter how effective, is rendered totally unacceptable. See?" she announced, her tone laced with scorn, "I do have a conscience."

Neither Baxter nor Ariana replied.

"In my opinion," Vanessa concluded, "the best alternative is to have Trenton committed to a lunatic asylum. Then Ariana can freely indulge in his wealth ... as can we. *That* is our best choice." She turned cold green eyes on Baxter. "You offered to assist me. Now is your opportunity to do so. Convince our sister to write a letter to her husband, stating her fear of his violent instability and begging him to seek help; tearfully advising him that she will otherwise have no alternative but to leave him forever, assuring him that if he agrees to commit himself, she will stand by him until he recovers ... and have her add whatever other romantic drivel you deem necessary. Actually, have her write two letters, one to be delivered to Broddington, the other to Spraystone. That way Trenton will be sure to receive it, regardless of his whereabouts. If things go as I hope, Trenton will be committed to an asylum and we will be quite wealthy." Her jaw tightened. "And with enough money I can make certain Henri never hurts me again."

"And if I won't write the letter?" Ariana demanded. "If instead I go directly to the authorities and tell them of your sick scheme?"

"Then I'll kill your precious husband, Ariana." Vanessa smoothed back her hair. "Remember, a corpse cannot be convicted of murder. And even if I am discovered alive and sentenced for my crime, it would be preferable to going back to Henri. So you see, baby sister, I have nothing to lose."

A coldhearted smile touched Vanessa's lips. "Unfortunately, darling, you do."

CHAPTER 25

Broddington seemed unusually somber, almost as if, during the duke's absence, a heavy cloud had settled upon its sculptured walls.

Trenton frowned as he mounted the steps, wondering if the unsettling sensation were only his imagination playing peculiar tricks on him. Lord only knew, it was quite adept at doing that. Still …

"Quiet, isn't it?" Dustin verbalized Trenton's thoughts aloud, scanning the grounds before following his brother through the front door. "At this time of day, Ariana is normally trailing about the gardens, taking notes on various flying creatures. Unless she's …" He glanced toward the main staircase, silencing the remainder of his thought. If Ariana were nowhere to be found, she was probably in Trenton's new sitting room, putting final touches on the wall hangings.

"Unless she's where?" Trenton jumped on Dustin's hesitation.

"Your Grace! I wasn't expecting you!" Jennings hurried toward them, blinking his beady eyes in distress. "I didn't receive word you'd be returning today."

"I sent no word," Trenton returned. "On impulse, I decided to return from Wight with the marquis. So you can calm yourself, Jennings. You had no way of knowing I'd be arriving at Broddington this morning."

Jennings visibly relaxed.

"Is the duchess already dining?" Trenton asked, handing Jennings his coat.

"Why, no, Your Grace. The duchess has been away from Broddington since daybreak."

Every muscle in Trenton's body went taut. "Where did she go?"

Nervously licking his lips, Jennings sprinted over to the calling-card table in the hallway and snatched up a note. "She left a message for the marquis."

"I'll take it, Jennings." Quickly, Dustin unfolded the note so both he and Trenton could read it.

> Dustin:
>
> I've thought of little else but our talk and all it revealed. The answers lie at Winsham, and I've gone to seek them. This is something I must do alone. With any luck, a solution awaits us. Don't worry about me.
>
> Ariana

"She's with that unscrupulous brother of hers." Trenton jerked his coat from Jennings's hands and slammed back into it. "I'm going after her."

"Don't, Trent." Dustin grabbed hold of his brother's arm. "It would solve nothing. Baxter's not going to hurt her and perhaps she really will learn something. Have a little faith in your wife."

After a lengthy silence, Trenton nodded. "All right," he conceded reluctantly. "But if she's not back by midafternoon, I'm going to Winsham and bringing her home myself. I don't trust Caldwell, or his motives."

"But you trust Ariana."

"Yes."

"Then wait."

Another terse nod. "Until three o'clock. Not a moment longer."

As it turned out, they had only to wait until noon before the message arrived.

"A letter for you, Your Grace," Jennings announced in the drawing room entranceway. "From the duchess."

"For me?" Trenton scowled even as he strode forward to take the message. "How did Ariana know I'd returned?"

He didn't wait for an answer, just tore open the letter and began to read. With every word, his expression stiffened, his eyes registering first shock, then pain, and finally anger and bleak resignation.

At last, with a vicious oath, he crumpled the note into a ball and flung it to the floor, stalking over to gaze out of the window, his back turned to the other men.

Dustin rose, dismissing Jennings with a swift inclination of his head. The butler hastened from the room, closing the doors discreetly behind him.

"What is it, Trent?"

"Read it yourself." Trenton's tone was strangled.

Dustin scooped up the crumpled page and read:

Dear Trenton:

I'm sending you this letter both at Broddington and at Spraystone to be certain that it reaches you. What I have to say is far too important to take the risk of its not finding its way into your hands.

My love for you is absolute, and will never vacillate or desist. Never forget that.

These past few days of solitude have given me the opportunity to objectively ponder your behavior and how it affects our life together. You know I'm afraid of you. I've told you so more times than I can recount. At first I had only your irrational anger and vengeance to contend with, and perhaps, by themselves, I could have withstood them. But now you've become delusional, seeing people who no longer exist, striking out at me as if I were a dreaded enemy—one you mean to destroy.

I have wracked my brain for a solution to this agony, one that would help you and, at the same time, make our marriage a viable one. What I have decided may sound cold and unfeeling, but I assure you, I do believe it is our only hope; not just yours alone, but ours as well.

I ask that you commit yourself to an appropriate facility—for a short time only—where you can be among people who are able to help you understand the reasons for your disturbing visions and the mental confusion that has overtaken your life.

I know that, with the proper guidance, you will resolve your internal turmoil and soon be restored to the fine man you truly are.

Until you have acted upon my plea, I've decided to stay at Winsham with Baxter, for my own protection. I know the fact that I am safe and secure will comfort you greatly. I cannot, in all honesty, claim that I will miss my weeks at Broddington, nor am I eager to return. Without you there, the estate is a shell of a dwelling, reflecting no part of my soul amid its empty walk. Perhaps with your recovery, that will change and we can begin to build a life together, making Broddington a home and breathing vitality into its sterile rooms.

Please, Trenton, for my sake as well as your own, please heed my plea. Take the necessary steps. It's the only way.

All my love, Ariana

Dustin reread the letter three times before he looked up, confused and uneasy. He was about to express his worry, when he noted his brother's taut shoulders and rigid stance. A wave of compassion swept through him as he realized what Trenton had inferred from the note, obviously having read the lines but not between them. And now, beneath his proud exterior, Dustin's invincible older brother was emotionally crumbling.

There was no way Dustin would permit that.

"Trent ..." He went over to lay a hand on his brother's shoulder. "You don't understand. ... It's not what it seems."

"I understand perfectly, Dustin." Trenton didn't turn around, but his voice was hoarse, laden with emotion. "Ariana's right. I was a fool to believe otherwise. I *am* insane. ... It's the only possible explanation for all this. I don't blame her for being afraid. I'm twice her size. ... I'd be able to crush her with my bare hands. How can she continue to live with me, share my life, my bed?" He swallowed audibly. "Perhaps an asylum of some kind is the only way."

"Listen to me, you blind, stubborn fool!" Dustin exploded. "Ariana doesn't believe one wretched word in this letter. ... She's trying to tell you something!"

Abruptly, Trenton turned. "What the hell are you talking about? She's making her feelings perfectly clear!"

The anguish on his brother's face was nearly Dustin's undoing. "The handwriting is Ariana's, Trent. But the sentiments are not." He waved the letter under Trenton's nose. "Read it again; only this time *really* read it." Arms folded across his chest, he waited patiently while Trenton reread the note.

"She wants me to seek help." Trenton's eyes were red-rimmed and grim. "If I don't heed her plea—"

"Precisely: her plea. She's asking for your help, Trent. What worries me is, I don't know why." Ignoring Trenton's skeptical look, Dustin pointed to the flowing hand. "See? She's hoping you'll believe in her love enough to realize she'd never leave you like this. She reinforces that with every line. Would you *really* feel soothed knowing she's with Baxter? She knows damned well you wouldn't! Is she *truly* afraid of you? Think about that, Trent. Is she? Has she ever been?"

A sliver of an image flashed through Trenton's mind: the Covington maze; the night he and Ariana had met.

"What's the matter, misty angel? Are you afraid of me?"

"No ... I'm not afraid ... I'm still not afraid. ..."

Their forced wedding ceremony ... their wedding night ... time after countless time when she could have been—*should* have been—terrified of him, she wasn't.

"No," Trenton admitted aloud. "Ariana is not afraid of me."

"That's right. Nor does she believe you're delusional or unstable. *I* was with her last evening. I should know."

"If you only knew how badly I want to believe you're right." A flicker of hope glinted in Trenton's eyes.

That did it. Dustin scanned the rest of the letter—and made a decision, one he felt confident Ariana intended that he make. It was the strongest hint she was providing; and the least likely one for Trenton to understand. But Dustin knew something Trenton did not.

"Let your wife convince you herself." Dustin gestured toward the door. "Follow me."

"What?"

"Just do as I say." Dustin didn't wait but flung open the drawing-room doors and made his way down the hall and up the stairway to the second level. Several times he glanced behind him to make certain Trenton was following. He was, treading with automatic, wooden footsteps.

Until he saw where they were heading.

"Why are we going into that room?" he demanded, halting in his tracks.

"You'll see." Dustin swung open the door and waited. "If you don't enter on your own, I'll drag you in. The choice is yours."

Trenton's eyes narrowed on his brother's face. Then he complied. "All right, Dustin. I'll go into Father's sitting room. But if this is your idea of comfort or your attempt at making a point ..." He stopped, his voice catching in his throat.

"It's not Father's sitting room any longer, Trent," Dustin said softly. "It's yours."

"What have you done?" Trenton choked, his legs carrying him forward of their own volition.

"It's not what *I've* done. It's what Ariana has done. That's how I knew her letter was a lie. She left the greatest part of her soul amid these walls. ... She left you her heart. Broddington's walls are empty no longer, Trent. Ariana has seen to that. All because she loves you ... deeply. As for what I did, my part was easy. I had only to assist her. The concept, the designs, the personal touches ... they're all your wife's."

Slowly, reverently, Trenton surveyed the room: the sweeping mahogany desk at the window, the thick oriental rug on the floor, the enlarged marble fireplace on the eastern wall. And the walls themselves: lined with drawings and sketches Trenton recognized immediately from a joyous lifetime ago—his father's creations.

But even more moving were the loving accents that cried out Ariana's name: the fragrant arrangement of flowers—blossoms he wouldn't have recognized by name a month ago but now knew were marigolds, hawthorn, and violets—sprouting from a tall crystal vase on the side table; the architectural tomes that carefully lined the mahogany bookshelves; and, most of all, the meticulously stitched needlepoint that proudly graced the wall beside the window—a magnificent depiction of a great, wild bird in flight.

It was their white owl.

Emotion clogged Trenton's throat, constricted his chest so tightly he couldn't speak.

"Now you tell me," Dustin asked quietly. "Is this the act of a woman who intends to abandon you, who has left no part of herself in your home, who doubts the longevity of your marriage? Is it, Trent?"

"When did she do all this?" Trenton managed.

"She came to see me some time ago. ... In fact, it was the day Jennings told you she was in London shopping. We planned the sketches then. But the reason Ariana summoned me to Broddington this week, during your absence, was to help her complete the room prior to your return. She stood here beside me every day, organizing and arranging. ... Praying that you'd come home soon—to Broddington ... to her. I've said it before, Trent: You're a lucky man. Ariana's love is something rare and precious and, as she tells you herself in that otherwise fabricated letter, her love is absolute and will never vacillate or desist." Dustin laid a hand on his brother's shoulder. "To echo your wife's words, never forget that. Never."

"I won't," Trenton vowed, his expression humble, his eyes damp. He walked over to the needlepoint, traced its intricate rim, and smiled at the perfect replica of Odysseus his wife had created. The owl was, just as Ariana wished, unhindered by man, winging his way through the skies, able to soar wild and free.

Free.

Instantly, Trenton stiffened, and he spun about to face Dustin, his expression lethal. "If Ariana needed to disguise the truth in her letter, it means her bastard of a brother forced her to write it. And *that* means he's keeping her at Winsham against her will." Trenton inhaled sharply, realization striking with the force of a tidal wave. "I'll kill him."

Dustin's brow furrowed as he once again tried to make the pieces fit. "That's what I don't understand: Why would Baxter force Ariana to write that letter?"

"Now *you're* the one who's being obtuse, Dustin. Think about it: If Ariana stays at Winsham, if she convinces me that I am, indeed, mad and unfit to live with, what would happen?"

"You'd probably do as she begs you to do."

"Exactly. I'd commit myself to an asylum. Leaving my poor, abused bride alone, at Winsham ... with my money." Trenton's eyes blazed cobalt fire.

"With your money *and* her greedy brother …" Dustin clarified, comprehension dawning. "So Baxter *is* the one behind your eerie visual escapades these past weeks!"

"That filthy son of a bitch!" Trenton was already out the door and halfway to the stairs.

"Wait! I'll go with you!" Dustin raced after him.

"No." Trenton stopped in his tracks, venom glittering in his eyes. "This is between Caldwell and me. That bastard robbed me of my father, my life, my self-worth, and now, nearly my sanity. At long last the past has come full circle." Trenton took the stairs two at a time, pausing only when he'd reached the bottom. "I don't give a damn what that blackguard's done to me, but God help him if he's laid a hand on Ariana. Because if he has, everything he accused me of six years ago will come to pass.… "And I really will be guilty of murder."

"Ariana, you really should eat something, darling." Vanessa finished her last mouthful of roast duck and dabbed lightly at her mouth with a linen napkin. "I realize the atmosphere isn't all it could be, but as you know I'm restricted to these quarters for most of the day. Detection would be highly ill-advised, I'm afraid." She sipped at her coffee. "But that doesn't mean I should starve."

"Why am *I* being confined?" Ariana demanded, ignoring her lunch and pacing the room.

"Because, baby sister, we have to await your beloved husband's reaction. If he concedes to your demands like a good, docile little boy, you are free to move about Winsham as you wish. If, however, he attempts to burst in here in some cavalier attempt to win you back, it wouldn't do to have you speak with him. Sadly, you are a very poor liar. So, for your own protection … as well as your husband's"—the unspoken threat hung heavily between them—"Baxter will handle the duke and tell him you don't wish to see him. Once Trenton departs, you can leave the servants' quarters and return to your old bedroom.

Actually, you are far more fortunate than I, who must remain in hiding until the Kingsley money is safely in our hands. So count your blessings, darling."

Ariana didn't reply but went over to gaze expectantly out the narrow window, searching for what, she wasn't sure. A miracle perhaps. Lord knew, she needed one—desperately.

Squeezing her eyes shut, Ariana prayed that Trenton's innate cynicism and fragile faith would not prevent him from reading the truth she'd carefully hidden beneath the lies. And even if her meaning was lost to his embittered eyes, she prayed that Dustin, due to his brother's absence, would read the copy of her letter Baxter had forwarded to Broddington. Dustin would understand. And with fate's assistance, he could convince Trenton, before it was too late.

"What are you looking at?" Vanessa asked idly, nibbling at a spoonful of lemon custard.

"The heavens. The birds. The trees." Ariana gave her sister a caustic look. "Life's true blessings, Vanessa ... the things money can't buy."

Vanessa raised her delicate brows. "Testy, aren't we?" She wagged her head pityingly. "I never understood you as a child, and I still don't understand you. What pleasure can be gained from observing a flying feathered creature or an inanimate green-leafed stalk of wood?"

"You're right. You don't understand me." Ariana turned back to her observations.

"Speaking of pleasure, there is one I am most curious about. Is Trenton really the incredible lover he was always reputed to be?"

Ariana felt tears sting her eyes, not of embarrassment, but of a loss so vast it hurt.

"Ah, I see. Evidently, he takes his attentions elsewhere. Well, don't be too hard on yourself, darling, you are a mere child, after all. Besides, no man is satisfied with just one woman, regardless of her prowess. It's too bad, really. I would have enjoyed passing the time hearing about some of your duke's favorite diversions."

"Shut up, Vanessa."

Vanessa blinked. "Now *this* is a side of you I've never seen." She rose, stretching gracefully. "I'm going to take a hot bath. Then we can resume our delightful sisterly chat."

Ariana winced as the door closed behind Vanessa. Once again, she turned her attention to the skies, seeking the peace nature brought her. *Please,* she begged silently. *Please let him come. Please.*

The flash of white was so subtle that at first she almost missed it. But the second time her eye sought it out, zeroing in on the great, soaring creature that descended slowly, than alit on the branch just outside her window.

Odysseus blinked his penetrating topaz eyes.

"Odysseus ..." Ariana whispered his name, her heart racing.

As if he had heard, the owl met her gaze, staring solemnly at her pale face.

"Oh ... Odysseus, you're here." Instinctively, Ariana pressed her palm against the pane, feeling closer, somehow, to the precious bird who always appeared when she needed him. "I wish you could bring Trenton to me," she murmured. Her hand fell away. "But, even if you could, what good would it do? As soon as Baxter heard the carriage arrive, he'd lock me in this room. I'd never see my husband and he'd leave, believing the worst of me. Oh, Odysseus, there must be a way."

The owl remained, still as a statue.

But something else moved.

Tearing her gaze from Odysseus, Ariana peered off into the distance, trying to discern the motion. It was a dark, moving object of some kind, making its way stealthily through the deserted woods at the rear of Winsham. A wolf?

It was a man.

Ariana's breath caught in her throat as she realized that the intruder was indeed human. Whoever he was, he was intent on avoiding detection.

Without knowing why, Ariana tensed, her nails biting into her palms as she watched, waiting, while the man came closer to the manor. Then suddenly she knew why.

It was Trenton.

Ariana bit her lip to keep from calling out his name. Vanessa was in the bathroom just down the hall: Any loud noise would alert her to the situation.

Desperate and frustrated, Ariana wracked her brain for a way to signal Trenton as to her whereabouts. In a minute he'd be at the manor, and Baxter would see him, confront him—and put an end to any opportunity she had to speak with her husband.

There had to be a way, to capture his attention. But how? How?

A rustle of feathers diverted her concentration back to her faithful owl, who was now peering downward in Trenton's direction.

"Odysseus," she whispered, wondering if he could make out her words, understand her urgency. "Please ... fly. Let Trenton see you ... call his attention to me. Please, dear friend. I need you now."

The owl raised his head, blinking soberly once, twice. Then, without preliminaries, he emitted a shrill cry, spread his majestic feathers, and soared.

Below, Trenton paused, startled by the unexpected sound, scanning the heavens for its cause. Ariana knew the moment he spotted Odysseus; she could see the look of amazement on his face.

Odysseus seemed to know too. The moment he captured Trenton's attention, he winged toward the window, sweeping past it, only to repeat the motion again.

Trenton's gaze found his wife's.

Tears glistening on her lashes, Ariana watched her husband's cobalt eyes darken with an overwhelming emotion that was a mirror reflection of her own.

"I love you ..." she mouthed.

Trenton nodded, a muscle working in his jaw. He averted his head long enough to give Odysseus a solemn salute, then veered purposefully toward the front of the house, all attempts at concealment forgotten.

He stopped just prior to disappearing from Ariana's line of vision, tilting his head back to stare directly into his wife's anxious eyes. "We're going home." Ariana read the words clearly from his lips, and she smiled through her tears.

Trenton didn't smile back. Thankfully, humbly, he drank in the poignant beauty that was his and his alone. "I love you, misty angel," he mouthed.

With that, he closed the distance to Winsham.

Ariana sagged weakly against the wall, joy and gratitude converging into a fathomless sense of euphoria. Trenton knew. He knew that she never meant to leave him. He knew that something at Winsham was amiss. He knew that she loved him—and he loved her in return. And he was here, ready to take her home.

Abruptly, Ariana straightened, her elation temporarily stilled. What he didn't know was that Vanessa was alive. And Lord only knew what would happen when he found out.

With swift resolve, Ariana went to the door, gingerly testing the handle. The fates were with her: Vanessa hadn't locked it when she'd left.

A minute later, Ariana was in the hallway, carefully assuring herself that it was deserted. It was.

She waited not a moment longer, sprinting through the servants' quarters and into the main wing of the house. Winsham's entranceway was in view and she planned to reach it.

Three things happened at once.

Deafening pounding erupted at the front door, Coolidge emerged from the drawing room, and Baxter collided with Ariana outside the library.

"What the—where are you racing to, sprite?" Baxter caught hold of her arm.

"Let me go, Baxter." She struggled valiantly to free herself. "For God's sake, show me that I wasn't completely wrong about you. Let me go."

Glancing curiously at the ruckus behind him, Coolidge opened the front door.

Trenton exploded into the house.

"Take your despicable hands off my wife, Caldwell!" Trenton was beside Ariana in a dozen strides.

Baxter looked totally bewildered, crumpling like a small, pathetic child watching his favorite toy being smashed to pieces. "Kingsley?" he tried inanely. "What are you doing here? Didn't you get Ariana's letter?"

"Baxter … don't," Ariana said quietly. "In the name of heaven, let the lies be over." She extricated herself from his now-lax grip and went directly into her husband's embrace. "Trenton," she whispered, burying her face against his shirt, weak with the relief of being where she belonged.

"Are you all right?" Trenton demanded gruffly, his arms tightening reflexively around her.

"Yes." She raised her face to his and smiled. "Now I am."

"Good." Trenton looked past her to Baxter's abashed expression. "Then I'll merely beat your brother senseless instead of killing him, as I'd originally planned."

"Trenton … don't." Ariana pressed her palms against his chest. "Baxter didn't hurt me. The blame is not entirely his. In many ways, he's as much a victim as we are. Please, listen to me."

Instinctively, Trenton made a move toward Baxter. "You greedy, immoral bastard … you kidnapped your own sister just to get your hands on my money?"

"Trenton!" Ariana made a final attempt. "Before you do something you'll regret, I must tell you—"

"I'll speak for myself, baby sister."

Hearing the hated, never-forgotten voice, Trenton reacted violently, his fingers digging into the soft skin of Ariana's arms. Blindly, he turned his head toward the sound, his heart thundering wildly in Ariana's ear. For a long moment he just stared, confronted with the ghost that had haunted him not only these past weeks, but for six long years. At last he spoke, his voice a strangled hiss. "Vanessa."

"A most attractive corpse, wouldn't you say?" Vanessa smoothed her gown and approached him, bitterness glittering in her emerald eyes. "No loving reception, darling? I would think you'd be thrilled! After all … I'm not dead, and you're not crazy. Who could ask for anything more?"

"Trenton …" Ariana reached up to touch her husband's taut jaw. "You're not seeing things. Vanessa really is alive. She's the one who's been—"

Brusquely, Trenton shoved Ariana behind him, as if to protect her from some heinous creature whose evil she underestimated. He towered over Vanessa, assessing every breathing inch of her, abhorrence, shock, and rage emanating from his powerful form. "You *are* alive," he pronounced at last. Fists clenched at his sides, he battled the urge to choke her.

"Indeed I am."

"Why?" he demanded.

"Which question am I answering: Why did I feign my own death, why did I implicate you, or why did I return to England? You'll have to be more specific, Trenton."

"All of it!" He raised his hand as if to strike her, then drove his fingers forcefully through his hair. "All of it, damn you!"

Vanessa's spine straightened. "Go ahead and hit me. I'm used to it: It's the only way men have of asserting their power."

"I never struck you, you lying bitch; although Lord alone knows I should have."

"Then why didn't you? The physical scars would have been far easier to bear than the agony of your rejection!" Her voice shook. "*No one* rejects me … least of all an arrogant hypocrite who discarded me like an old shoe simply because he wasn't the only man in my life." Vanessa raised her chin, raking Trenton with icy disdain. "Is virtue the only condition your wife must fulfill, Trenton? Evidently so, although I wonder if you still find it as attractive a quality as you did prior to taking your virgin bride to bed!"

A vein pulsed in Trenton's neck, and only Ariana's gentle hand on his back kept him from losing all control. "Your lack of innocence was the least of my objections to you, Vanessa. Your duplicity, your deceit, your manipulations, your cruelty, your self-indulgence, your greed …" Trenton drew in a furious breath. "*Those* are the reasons I wanted nothing to do with you."

"You wanted me. I *know* you wanted me."

"At one time, yes, I wanted you. Until I discovered just how high your price was. Frankly"—Trenton gave her a thoroughly deprecating look—"you didn't come close to being worth it."

"You bastard!" She drew back her hand and slapped him across the face. "I've lived through hell because of you!"

"No, Vanessa. You've lived through hell because *of you.*" A spasm of agony flashed across Trenton's face as the full impact of Vanessa's existence began to sink in. "And so did I." His hands shook. "My God, all these years … my father … my sanity …"

"Trenton … don't," Ariana whispered, coming around to stand beside him, wrapping her small fingers around his strong, trembling hand.

"And now my wife," Trenton continued, venom reappearing in his gaze. "You heartless bitch, *you* were behind this sick scheme, weren't you? This attempt to drive me insane and get your hands on my fortune by using Ariana, keeping her here against her will? It wasn't Baxter's plan, it was yours!"

"Yes … yes … it was mine!" Vanessa shrieked. "And why shouldn't it be? I've spent six years with a sadistic parasite, relinquishing my youth, my dreams, my last dollars, and my last shred of pride! I've been beaten, isolated, abused until I didn't care if I lived! And all because of you!" Hard, wrenching tears wracked her body, contorting her beautiful face into a mask of anguished loathing. "My only consolation was that your life was over too! You were banished to Wight, forced to live as a recluse, with no hope for your future and no joy in your present. And then …" She dashed the tears from her cheeks, her body shuddering with sobs. "My baby sister blundered her way into your life. I hoped she'd make it hell for you. … But instead, the stupid chit became infatuated with you. Not only that, but you were *good* to her. She had your money, your title, your bed … all the things *I* should have had! And damn you to hell, I was going to have them … no matter what the cost!"

"I want you locked up," Trenton ground out. "And I want the warden to throw away the key."

A sudden, eerie calm settled over Vanessa. "Then do it. No prison could be more horrible than the one I've endured."

"Trenton … wait." Ariana stepped forward, studying Vanessa with pity and sorrow. "I despise you for what you've done … to my husband, to all of us. You're a very unstable woman, Vanessa, and a very cruel one as well. But despite the fact that you yourself incited all your own grief, no one should have to suffer the life you've been forced to withstand." Ariana half-turned to Trenton. "If my husband is amenable, I'd like to give you a portion of the money you so worship, in exchange for the promise that you'll never set foot in England again. Go wherever you wish, as far from your sick husband as you choose. But equally as far away from us."

Ignoring Vanessa's stunned expression, Ariana's eyes met Trenton's. Then, before he could respond, she turned to Baxter, who was leaning listlessly against the wall, limp and depleted of whatever emotional reserves he had left after listening to Vanessa's shocking revelations earlier today.

"As I've always said," Ariana murmured, "you're a weak man, Baxter. Not evil, but weak. And a very poor judge of character, it seems." She shook her head with dismal finality. "You've been punished enough. You've destroyed whatever small amount of family allegiance existed between us. Now you truly have nothing."

With that, Ariana turned and walked back to her husband's arms. "While we, on the other hand, have the greatest blessing life has to offer." She lay her hand over his heart. "I love you, Trenton," she whispered, watching the rage fade from his eyes in the wake of something far more powerful. "Neither Baxter nor Vanessa is worth your hatred, only your pity. I know how much you've given up because of them. ... But the ultimate deprivation is theirs. Money is a meager substitute for what we have. Please, darling ..." She reached up to caress his jaw. "It's time to let it go."

Closing his eyes, Trenton turned his lips into Ariana's palm, nodding slowly against her smooth skin. "Give them whatever you want, misty angel." His warm breath caressed her hand. "Just get them out of our lives."

"Thank you," she breathed.

"No ... thank you." Wrapping his arm about her waist, Trenton drew Ariana toward the door, away from Winsham and all its ugly memories. Once he paused, turning back to where Vanessa stood, unmoving. "My solicitor will deliver a check to you tomorrow. After that, I expect you to be gone from England by nightfall, never to return again. Should you decide ever to show your face in this country, I won't hesitate to have you thrown in prison for the rest of your life. Is that clear enough for you?"

Stripped of her bravado, empty-eyed and dissipated, Vanessa nodded, an old woman destined to spend the rest of her life with only the shallow wealth she coveted as her companion.

"As for you," Trenton said to Baxter, "stay the hell out of our lives … mine and my wife's. Permanently."

Bleakly, Baxter murmured his acquiescence.

No other words were necessary, and none were exchanged.

With purposeful tenderness, Trenton guided Ariana back into the sunlight. "Come, misty angel," he said softly. "I know just the place where we can heal."

CHAPTER 26

Dustin's brow furrowed in confusion when he read the cryptic message that arrived at Broddington an hour later. Gratefully, he absorbed the fact that everything was resolved and Ariana was where she belonged: with Trent. It didn't matter that Trenton's message contained no details; those could wait until later. What baffled Dustin was the odd tenor of the message, which was perplexing, at best. Anxious to decipher Trenton's meaning, Dustin followed his brother's advice and sought out Theresa at once.

"I received a letter from Trenton," he announced.

"Yes." Theresa's answer was a statement, not a question. She continued to ready the duke's and duchess's bedroom for their return.

Dustin cleared his throat, skimming past the letter's preliminaries, focusing on the curious section that followed. "Trent writes, *'that which is past is gone and irrevocable.'*"

Theresa nodded sagely. "His Grace is quoting Sir Francis. A wise choice."

"Oh." Dustin stared at Theresa. "I see. Well, Trent assures us that he and Ariana are both well and will return home from Spraystone in several days."

"Four days, to be precise: a sensible decision." Theresa straightened, inclining her head quizzically in Dustin's direction. "What is your question, my lord?"

Shaking his head in perpetual amazement, Dustin returned to the note. "Trent goes on to say that Shakespeare knew of what he wrote when he said, '*At Christmas I no more desire a rose, than wish a snow in May's new-fangled mirth; but like of each thing that in season grows.*' He concludes by asking me to seek you out to say that your taste is superb and that 'a man must make his opportunity, as oft as find it.'"

"Sir Francis again." Theresa patted the bulging volume in her apron pocket.

"What does it mean, Theresa?" Dustin was at his wits' end.

The elderly lady's maid smiled. "It means, my lord, that you and I have our work cut out for us."

"Are you sure Dustin and Theresa know we're all right?" Ariana asked, propping her chin on her husband's chest.

"Positive. I sent them a message before we left port." Trenton gathered handfuls of his wife's glorious hair, tugging her face down to his. "Why? Are you so eager to leave Spraystone?"

"No." She breathed the word against his lips, knowing that anywhere Trenton was would be home for her.

"Have I thanked you for my sitting room?" he asked solemnly.

"Do you really like it?" Ariana disentangled herself from her husband's embrace, her eyes alight with pleasure.

"It's everything you willed it to be and more: a perfect combination of an apt tribute, a cherished sanctuary and a magnificent testimonial of my wife's rare and precious love." Trenton framed her face between his hands. "Thank you, misty angel."

Ariana's eyes grew damp. "I owe you thanks, as well. Never have I seen a more selfless gesture than the one you displayed at Winsham today. After all the anguish Vanessa has put you through ..." Ariana felt emotion well up inside her. "To not only allow her to go free, but to provide her with funds."

"The idea was yours, not mine," Trenton reminded her.

"Nevertheless, you agreed. In spite of everything."

Trenton traced Ariana's soft lower lip with his thumb. "From what you told me on our boat ride to Wight, your sister has paid bitterly for her ruthlessness. I'd be lying if I said I feel forgiveness. I'm not even certain I'm capable of compassion where Vanessa is concerned. However"—Trenton's expression softened—"she did inadvertently provide me with what I now recognize as my life's greatest treasure. You."

"I love you," Ariana whispered.

"I know. Thank God for that."

"Trenton?"

"Hmm?"

"About Baxter." Ariana took a deep breath. "I don't expect your opinion of him to change … and I respect your reasons; those stemming from the past as well as the present. But he's not a wicked man, Trenton, only a pitiful one. In my heart I know he cares for me, although his love is shallow and will always take second place to his less than reputable priorities."

"And he's your brother." Trenton had remained quiet throughout Ariana's hurried explanation. Now he silenced her by laying his forefinger across her lips. "Personally, I detest the man. But I happen to love his sister very much; so I can afford to be magnanimous. Give me some time, misty angel. Then, if you want to see him, I won't stand in your way. But never at Winsham and never alone."

"Agreed." Ariana's eyes shone. "You see? I told you you're a wonderful man."

"And I told you I'm no hero."

"You're wrong."

"You're beautiful." Words suddenly inadequate, Trenton rolled Ariana onto her back, gazing down into her fathomless turquoise eyes. "I love you," he told her reverently. "I still don't know what I did to deserve you, my extraordinary wife, but I don't ever intend to lose you."

"I don't ever intend to give you the opportunity." Ariana caressed the bare expanse of his broad shoulders, wound her arms around his neck. "Fate intended for us to be together. Theresa foresaw that from the start. I should have recognized it, too … from the moment you rescued me … and my ankle … from the Covington maze."

"Is that what happened?" Trenton opened his mouth over hers, urging her thighs apart and settling himself between them. "Odd, I see it differently. I rescued you, yes, but in the end it was I who was saved. Although I admit my loss that night was far more extensive than yours."

"*Your loss?*" Ariana's voice was breathless, her body opening to receive the intimate invasion of his. "I don't understand …"

Reverently, Trenton gazed down at his wife, burying himself, body and soul, in her welcoming warmth. "On that night, my love, you lost only your way. While I lost my heart."

"Sorry to leave Spraystone?" Trenton asked, resting his chin atop Ariana's bright head as the Kingsley carriage made its way to Broddington.

"Yes … and no," Ariana replied truthfully, warm and content in Trenton's arms. "The past few days have been heaven. But I miss Broddington and Theresa and Dustin. Poor Dustin …" she smiled ruefully, "he must be thoroughly confused and pacing the floors awaiting our return."

"I suspect Dustin has kept himself quite busy." The sparkle in Trenton's eyes was lost to his wife, whose face was buried in her husband's shoulder. "Besides, I more or less explained the outcome of things in my letter. Dustin won't be worried."

"Nor will Theresa. I'm sure she knew even without the letter."

"I'm sure she did."

Ariana tilted her head back to gaze out the window at the darkening sky. "I wonder where Odysseus is. I half-hoped he'd visit us on Wight."

Trenton smiled. "As did I. I owe him a huge debt of thanks. Your owl turned out to be quite a hero."

"As I said, he's much like you, Trenton: an unwilling champion and a solitary wanderer seeking his way."

Gratefully, Trenton tightened his hold about his wife. "My solitary days are over. I've found what I'm seeking."

Anticipation coursing through him, Trenton knew there was but one thing remaining to make his joy complete.

Twilight had given way to dusk when the carriage passed through Broddington's iron gates. The manor was quiet, devoid of activity.

Ariana frowned as Trenton helped her alight. "I wonder where Jennings is: It's not like him to ignore a message. You did tell them when we'd be returning, didn't you?"

"I did." Trenton looped an arm about Ariana's waist, guiding her away from the front door and toward the path that led to the side of the house.

"Where are we going?"

"You'll see."

"Trenton … what on earth is going on?" Ariana was totally bewildered. While the manor itself seemed deserted, a bright glow emanated from the direction in which they were headed.

"Come, misty angel, we don't want to be late."

"Late? Late for what? Where are you taking—" Her voice was abruptly silenced, transformed into a quiet gasp of stunned disbelief. "Oh my God …"

The conservatory rose before them, regal and majestic, its doors thrown open wide. In the center of the room was an enormous fir tree, illuminated by hundreds of tiny wax tapers, decorated with candy, fruit, and charms. The glow of the candles drenched the conservatory in golden light that spilled out onto Broddington's waiting grounds.

Draped around the room, from corner to corner, were ropes of evergreen sprigs; laurel leaves with rosettes of bright colored paper, punctuated with wreaths of ivy and berries. Delicate chrysanthemums and camellias were arranged in baskets, and a huge table, piled high with gifts, was tucked against the far wall, beckoning Ariana toward it.

Most of all, were the beloved, smiling faces: Dustin, Theresa, even Jennings, beaming at Ariana, sharing her joy, their eyes filled with love.

It was Christmas.

"Trenton ... I..." Tears flowing unchecked down her cheeks, Ariana couldn't speak.

"Come, love." He took her hand, guiding her into the fairy-tale-come-true. "Aren't you going to open your presents?"

"Wait!" Dustin called out, pointing to the ceiling. "You're standing underneath the mistletoe."

With a twinkle, Trenton drew Ariana into his arms and kissed her. "Merry Christmas, misty angel," he murmured.

"But it's September," she whispered inanely, unable to absorb the enormity of what he'd done for her. "It's too early ..."

"No, it's years too late." Trenton framed her face between his hands. "You haven't had a Christmas in nearly a lifetime. I think it's permissible for it to come twice this year. Besides ..." He kissed her again, softly. "Didn't you say you wanted to spend Christmas at Spraystone? This way we can enjoy the holiday at both our homes: the one I built, and the one you built for me."

"Trenton ..."

"I love you, misty angel," he finished for her. "I'd give you the world ... and your childhood back ... if I could."

"You've given me everything," she breathed fervently, love shining in her eyes. "There's nothing more I could want."

A shrill cry from the skies reminded Ariana that she was wrong.

Overhead, heralding their holiday and their miraculous love, came nature's own miracle: the messenger nature and fate had together devised to bring together the Duke and Duchess of Broddington.

And, like their love, the owl soared.

ACKNOWLEDGMENTS

I owe a wealth of thanks to the following people for their support and infinite patience:

Len Soucy of the Raptor Trust, a brilliant owl expert and the most patient educator. Without you I could never have brought Odysseus so vividly to life. I hope I did you proud. Odysseus remains, as he is destined to be, proud and free!

Pat, for books of edicts, hours of time and valuable friendship.

Michael, my quintessential source on Queen Victoria. Thanks for sharing your vast wealth of knowledge and your equally vast library with me.

Lisa, a special fan, a wonderful friend.

Jayne Ann Krentz, who took the time out of her own whirlwind schedule to read and endorse *Echoes in the Mist*. Jayne, I'm proud and grateful for your enthusiastic support.

And last, but never least, a few perpetual thank-yous.

To the incomparable other two thirds of my "dream team," Caroline Tolley and Alice Harron Orr—the finest, most caring editor and agent any author could hope to work with.

And to my critique partner, Karen Plunkett-Powell, whose abilities never fail to astound me and whose insights are indispensable. Welcome back, Plunk.

We hope you enjoyed this book from Bonnie Meadow Publishing.

Connect with us on BonnieMeadowPublishing.com for more information on our new releases!

Other ways to keep in touch with Andrea Kane:

📺 andreakane.com

🅕 facebook.com/AuthorAndreaKane/

🐦 @andrea_kane

🅖 goodreads.com/AKane